Andrew Hammond began his working life in a cheap suit, sitting in the bowels of York Magistrates' Court, interviewing repeat offenders who always said they 'didn't do it'. After three years in the legal profession, Andrew re-trained as an English teacher. CRYPT is Andrew's first fictional series but he has written over forty English textbooks for schools and he can spot the difference between an adjectival and adverbial phrase at fifty paces (if only someone would ask him to). Andrew lives in Suffolk with his wife Andie and their four angels – Henry, Eleanor, Edward and Katherine – none of whom are old enough yet to read 'Daddy's scary books'. But one day . . .

By Andrew Hammond

CRYPT: *The Gallows Curse*
CRYPT: *Traitor's Revenge*
CRYPT: *Mask of Death*
CRYPT: *Blood Eagle Tortures*
CRYPT: *Guardians' Reckoning*

CRYPT

GuarDians' Reckoning

ANDREW HAMMOND

headline

First published in 2014 by
HEADLINE PUBLISHING GROUP

1

Cataloguing in Publication Data is available from the British Library

ISBN 978 0 7553 7825 8

Typeset in Goudy Old Style by Avon DataSet Ltd,
Bidford-on-Avon, Warwickshire

Printed and bound in Great Britain by Clays Ltd, St Ives plc

Headline's policy is to use papers that are natural, renewable and recyclable
products and made from wood grown in sustainable forests. The logging and
manufacturing processes are expected to conform to the environmental
regulations of the country of origin.

HEADLINE PUBLISHING GROUP
An Hachette UK company
338 Euston Road
London NW1 3BH

www.headline.co.uk
www.hachette.co.uk

For Kitty

THE HISTORY OF THE CRYPT

In 2007, American billionaire and IT guru Jason Goode bought himself an English castle; it's what every rich man needs. He commissioned a new skyscraper too, to be built right in the heart of London. A futuristic cone-shaped building with thirty-eight floors and a revolving penthouse, it would be the new headquarters for his global enterprise, Goode Technology PLC.

He and his wife Tara were looking forward to their first Christmas at the castle with Jamie, their thirteen-year-old son, home from boarding school. It all seemed so perfect.

Six weeks later Goode returned home one night to find a horror scene: the castle lit up with blue flashing lights, police everywhere.

His wife was dead. His staff were out for the night; his son was the only suspect.

Jamie was taken into custody and eventually found guilty of killing his mother. They said he'd pushed her from the battlements during a heated argument. He was sent away to a young offenders' institution.

But throughout the trial his claims about what really happened never changed:

'The ghosts did it, Dad.'

His father had to believe him. From that day on, Jason Goode vowed to prove the existence of ghosts and clear his son's name.

They said Goode was mad – driven to obsession by the grief of losing his family. Plans for the new London headquarters were put on hold. He lost interest in work. People said he'd given up on life.

But one man stood by him – lifelong friend and eminent scientist Professor Giles Bonati. Friends since their student days at Cambridge, Bonati knew Goode hadn't lost his mind. They began researching the science of disembodied spirits.

Not only did they prove scientifically how ghosts can access our world, they uncovered a startling truth too: that some teenagers have stronger connections to ghosts than any other age group. They have high extrasensory perception (ESP), which means they can see ghosts where others can't.

So was Jamie telling the truth after all?

Goode and Bonati set up the Paranormal Investigation Team (PIT) based in the cellars of Goode's private castle. It was a small experimental project at first, but it grew. Requests came in for its teenage agents to visit hauntings across the region.

But fear of the paranormal was building thanks to the PIT. Hoax calls were coming in whenever people heard a creak in the attic. Amateur ghost hunters began to follow the teenagers and interfere with their work. Suddenly everyone was talking about ghosts.

To prevent the situation from escalating out of control, Goode was ordered to disband the PIT and stop frightening people. Reporters tried to expose the team as a fraud. People could rest easy in their beds – there was no such thing as ghosts. Goode had to face the awful truth that his son was a liar – and a murderer. The alternative was too frightening for the public to accept.

So that's what they were told.

But in private, things were quite different. Goode had been approached by MI5.

The British security services had been secretly investigating paranormal incidents for years. When crimes are reported without any rational human explanation, MI5 must explore all other possibilities, including the paranormal. But funding was tight and results were limited.

Maybe teenagers were the answer.

So they proposed a deal. Goode could continue his paranormal investigations, but to prevent more hoax calls and widespread panic, he had to do so under the cover and protection of MI5.

They suggested the perfect venue for this joint operation – Goode's London headquarters. The skyscraper was not yet finished. There was still time. A subterranean suite of hi-tech laboratories could be built in the foundations. A new, covert organisation could be established – bigger and better than before, a joint enterprise between Goode Technology and the British security services.

But before Jason Goode agreed to the plan, he made a special request of his own. He would finish the building, convert the underground car park into a suite of laboratories and living accommodation, allow MI5 to control operations, help them recruit the best teenage investigators they could find and finance any future plans they had for the CRYPT – all in return for one thing.

He wanted his son back.

After weeks of intense secret negotiations, the security services finally managed to broker the deal: provided he was monitored by the Covert Policing Command at Scotland Yard, and, for his own protection, was given a new identity, Jamie could be released. For now.

The deal was sealed. The Goode Tower was finished – a landmark piece of modern architecture, soaring above the Thames. And buried discreetly beneath its thirty-eight floors was the Covert Response Youth Paranormal Team.

The CRYPT.

Jamie Goode was released from custody and is now the CRYPT's most respected agent.

And his new identity?

Meet Jud Lester, paranormal investigator.

CRYPT

GUARDIANS' RECKONING

CHAPTER 1

WEDNESDAY, 8.10 P.M. (9.10 P.M. LOCAL TIME)

ALLÉE CHÊNE POINTU, CLICHY-SOUS-BOIS, PARIS

On the sixteenth floor of a high-rise block in a poor and neglected part of Clichy-sous-Bois, a man rested his head on a smoke-stained window and gazed over the sprawling mass of suburbs that stretched into the distance like a concrete carpet. The sky was darkening and the rush-hour traffic was dying. Night was enveloping the city's slums, and the few lights that worked were slowly blinking into life, casting an orange glow that barely stretched across the pavement and left shadows where danger lurked.

Behind him lay an apartment that resembled an indoor refuse site. The place was strewn with dirty clothes, sacks of rubbish, stale snacks and newspapers – thousands of them, read, reread, annotated with scribbles and then discarded onto the cluttered floor. The smells from the bin bags and the half-eaten takeaways would have made any visitor gag, but there were two reasons why this didn't matter: the man never received visitors, and he'd become so accustomed to the aroma that he'd stopped noticing it years ago.

It was his sanctuary. His home.

In many ways the man was a recluse; he rarely left the giant apartment block that rose up to the sky like a vertical village. Everything he needed he bought online. Food and supplies were delivered to his door. He never met anyone socially and he rarely spoke to anybody except the delivery drivers (who always dreaded dropping at his address because of the stench), to whom he said a muffled '*merci*' and then shut the door.

About a year and a half ago he'd ventured out into the city to purchase some new computer equipment. His trip had lasted no more than a morning, but it was enough to confirm his suspicion that everyone and everything in the world wasn't worth the trouble of seeing. He lived in two dimensions, through his computer screens. If he wanted adventure, he used Google Earth. He'd been doing it for so long now that his mind was able to fill in the third dimension when enjoying locations through the flat screen, even the sounds and smells too. He'd toured most of the world's cities, explored jungles and savannahs, traversed seas and scaled mountain ranges. He'd always had a vivid imagination. As a kid he would spend hours in his room, on imaginary adventures, locked inside his little brain. He had no brothers or sisters – in real life, that is.

Then, early in his teens, he'd realised that physical reality – the mass and energy around us – only appeared the way it did because of how we sense it. He'd concluded that his ability to see and hear and touch things didn't mean that was how things *really* were. It was only how they appeared to him. So why should the things he pictured in his mind be any less real? If he could gain pleasure by imagining adventures in his head, why should they be any less real than the boring events at school or at home? Who said the things he dreamed up weren't real? Who was the judge? If anyone disagreed he would simply say that maybe it was they who weren't real, and he had imagined them too. There could be no answer once he'd said that.

Surely nothing could be more real than the thoughts inside his head? They were the only things that *really* existed because they didn't need to be touched or seen by anyone, they just *were*. And in any case, the 'real life' that everyone saw and smelled and heard was far less interesting than the worlds he created inside his own mind. Behind his eyes, that's where the real fun was. So that's where he lived.

He watched the dirty pigeons and gulls squabbling for scraps on the balcony of a high-rise opposite and then he shuffled past his own rubbish, out of the room and into the narrow hallway that dissected his apartment. He entered the spare bedroom at the back of the flat. It resembled a scene from a science-fiction movie: technology everywhere. There were three large computer monitors on the metal shelf that ran the length of the opposite wall, each one perched on its own PC unit with a wireless keyboard and mouse. There were other black metal boxes that looked like PC units dotted about the place, with separate hard drives and various add-ons and a labyrinth of leads running from them to the monitors and to other TV screens that filled a second shelf on an adjacent wall.

On the other two walls in the room were rows and rows of improvised bookshelves – crooked metal struts that bowed under the weight of too many books, magazines and yet more newspapers. And in the furthest corner from the door stood two large, grey filing cabinets, each one heaving with documents. On top of each cabinet were half-empty, neglected coffee cups, in which a unique caffeine fungus grew: green with bluish spots and a brown crust around the edge.

He cleared a black leather chair of newspapers, revealing a couple of large rips in the seat, and sat down with a sigh.

As he waited for the screen in front of him to boot up, he saw his own reflection. For a man who took no exercise he was remarkably thin, but that was due to a combination of factors: he rarely ate (couldn't be bothered) and what little food he did consume was soon burnt off through nervous energy. His gaunt, aquiline face stared back at him through the screen. There were dark rings beneath his eyes and his jaw and cheek bones were covered in a thin wispy beard.

He'd thought of giving up on it all many times, but something always kept him going. It was the only thing that drove him on these days, the only thing that kept him alive. All the technology, the research, the reading and studying, the self-educating and the hours of endless monitoring had all been for one thing.

Revenge.

And it was getting closer.

A cough suddenly rose up inside his throat and the man exploded, spraying the screens and keyboards around him with yet another layer of green and brown phlegm. The coughing fit continued for a couple of minutes, as it usually did. It was hard to stop once he'd started. Years of living in such cramped conditions, surrounded by stale, germ-infested air, were taking their toll on his health. And he knew it. But soon, soon it would be over and he could do something else, go somewhere else. Maybe live in the Caribbean, or perhaps Thailand or Malaysia, where the air was warm and wet and the girls were beautiful. They wouldn't be figments of his imagination any more, they'd be real enough.

He wiped away the gunk from his gloopy mouth and let his bony fingers skip and dance across the keyboard once again.

CHAPTER 2

THURSDAY, 9.01 A.M.

UNDISCLOSED BANK,
CITY OF LONDON

The strip-lights in the large, minimalist office were piercing and clinical. The furniture was equally unwelcoming: a polished black-glass desk and dark leather chairs with shiny metal arms and legs. The floor was a pale, polished laminate pine effect. There was no clutter, no files or papers, no boxes or bins. Just two large computer screens and wireless keyboards. Across the room the white blinds rattled quietly against the tinted glass as a slight breeze blew in through the crack in the half-opened window. The traffic hummed down on the street several hundred feet below.

Will Sharpe felt uncomfortable. Everyone on the trading floor where he worked knew that if the boss, Hans Gärtner, called you into his office first thing in the morning, it was rarely to give you good news.

Hans said nothing, as he often did when you'd done something wrong and he wanted you to know about it. Like the most vindictive Victorian schoolmaster, he just sat staring at you until you broke and spoke first.

But Will wasn't going to break. It was Gärtner who'd called him so he could damn well speak first. Will knew he couldn't push it too far, of course; this was, after all, only his third month at the bank. He'd been through more interviews than he could ever have imagined were necessary to get the job. It wasn't his first year in the industry – he'd been in banking for six years now – but the bank's reputation for cautious risk management extended beyond its investment policies to its own recruitment policy too. Gärtner went to great lengths to minimise the risk of recruiting the wrong person onto his precious trading floor. But Will had passed through every hoop facing him and he felt he'd earned his place – a place he wasn't about to give up now by being petulant.

That's why Gärtner always got his way in the end. He knew none of his traders wanted to give up their chance of making serious bonuses. He was a tough captain, but everyone knew they were lucky to be on board his ship. He was physically overbearing – perhaps that was one of the reasons why he was so feared – with his six-foot-three, burly frame squeezed into an Armani suit, and his trademark slicked-back, greased blond hair and dark-rimmed glasses. Sometimes he wore stubble, but his hair was so fair you couldn't tell unless you got up close – which nobody dared to do, of course.

No one crossed Gärtner and survived to tell the tale.

Besides, just like most of his colleagues in the City, Will and his girlfriend had expensive tastes: a flat in a fashionable part of town, an extremely fast car and a couple of luxury holidays already booked for later in the year. Little wonder there was a sinking feeling growing in the pit of his stomach. The longer the silence from Gärtner, the worse the news was – that was what people said.

And he'd still not said anything.

'Is there something wrong, boss?' Will pierced the silence – he just couldn't wait any longer.

It was another couple of torturous minutes before his line manager spoke to him. He stared through his designer glasses and sucked the end of a Montblanc pen. Then, finally, 'What do *you* think, boy?'

Calling the younger guys 'boys' was another of Gärtner's habits that grated with Will.

'I don't know, boss. I've not caught up with the markets this morning. Was something wrong last night? I closed the deals off – everything was okay, wasn't it?'

Gärtner raised one eyebrow but said nothing.

Without warning, and with a sudden gesture that startled Will and fanned the flames of fear that were rising within him, Gärtner lifted the phone receiver, pressed a button and promptly said, 'Tim, get in here, will you. Bring us what you've found.'

Will shifted in his chair and looked furtively over his shoulder. This was one of those moments when you wished Gärtner's office wasn't made of glass. He could see some of his pals stealing anxious glances in his direction over the top of their computer monitors.

'Can you tell me what's wrong, Hans?' he said respectfully.

'All in good time, boy.'

A few more agonising moments of awkward silence and then the door opened and Tim Wellsey walked in. A fat, oafish sort of man with little glasses that bent and stretched across his pudgy, sullen face, he headed up Regulations and Compliance downstairs. He had a reputation for being literal – that is to say he showed no emotion, and only dealt in facts and figures. He wasn't interested in how people felt, only what they made on the markets. Will had only met him once, during the interview process, when Wellsey had asked some direct, almost rude questions with an expressionless face. What the hell was he doing here now?

'Right, I'll cut to the chase, Will,' said Gärtner. 'No point in wasting your time or mine. I can't imagine this'll take long.

Tim's been doing some routine checks, haven't you, Tim? You know we do these every now and again. Always keeps the boys at the FCA happy.' He didn't need to explain to Will how vigilant the Financial Conduct Authority could be, but the mention of those three letters brought a chill to his bones. Making sure the bank met the FCA's stringent regulatory requirements was a full-time job for Wellsey and his team.

So what the hell had gone wrong? Will was sweating now. He kept twitching his eyes and running his hands through his fashionably unkempt hair.

'Tim has found some positions you've yet to settle, Will. In Equities.'

'Oh yeah? What about them? Something wrong?'

Gärtner smiled wryly. 'You're damn right there's something wrong, boy. Go ahead, Tim.'

Wellsey spoke in his cool, unemotional monotone and explained the losses he had unearthed, caused by some un-authorised trades Will was alleged to have made in the Equities market over the last three weeks.

'Whoa! Wait a minute,' cried Will, acutely aware of how serious this was getting. 'I'm not responsible for any of those trades. I don't even know what you're talking about. I've not—'

'Oh, so it's Rumpelstiltskin, is it?' said Gärtner. 'I mean, someone else steals in here when you're away, is that it? Huh? Is that what you're saying to me? I expected something a little more elaborate than a total denial, Sharpe. You can do better than that. Tim and I knew you'd squirm, but we didn't expect *nothing* – not even an explanation, *huh*?'

Will glanced over at Wellsey who just smirked and stayed silent. He was enjoying this.

'But I don't know what you're—'

'*Don't bullshit me, boy!*' Gärtner thundered at him. 'Tim's not even finished yet. You've dug yourself into a giant hole here, Sharpe, and if we'd not found it, it could have been big enough

for all of us to fall into. Thank God we've found you out now.'
He turned to Wellsey. 'But keep goin', Tim. He's gotta hear everything.'

Wellsey allowed another wry smile to leak out of his flabby lips and continued with a list of the unauthorised deals he'd claimed to have found recorded against Will during the routine check. Every one of the trades had his name all over it: his pass code, his account, his computer. And the debts were mounting.

Will sat frozen still. He couldn't believe this was happening. Words failed him. He didn't recognise any of the trades – not one. Rogue trading was the severest and most well-publicised crime any trader could commit – God knows the whole world knew what damage could be done by unauthorised deals like this these days. Whole banks had been brought down because of the risks taken by a few greedy, ambitious traders.

Was he about to become infamous too?

Luckily Tim stopped before Will's imagination could run any further and the total could reach billions of dollars. But hundreds of thousands was still enough to make Gärtner mad. Seriously mad.

'You've made the wrong judgements, boy, and you've tried to cover each one up. This is how banks fall. You make the wrong call, then you gamble again and keep trading until you can recoup your losses. Telling no one. Lying. Cheating. I've met people like you, boy. I've been around the block. I was working the markets when you were picking your nose at the back of maths class. Did you think you'd get away with it, huh? I just thank God you've not been here long enough to do any lasting damage to the company. But if you'd been here a couple of years, I mean . . . I don't wanna think about it.'

'But—'

'So, tell me, did you think you could fool us? You think you're a clever boy, huh?'

'No, but—'

'You said it, boy. No buts. No defence. No excuses. Maybe it's cleaner this way. Or maybe you've already spoken to your damn lawyer. Told you to say nothing, did he? Deny everything, huh?'

Will fell silent. He could see there was no point in trying to defend himself. His brain, already one of the sharpest on the trading floor, was trying hard to keep up with this – processing the scenario in front of him and calculating the risk of saying the wrong thing, or saying nothing at all. Words, sentences and possible responses were running through his brain like a swarm of wasps. What should he say? What would a lawyer advise? It was all bullshit he was hearing, all lies. He had no idea what they were talking about. Had they got the wrong man? He'd done nothing wrong, but would they interpret his silence as guilt?

What the hell had been going on behind his back? Who was feeding them this stuff?

Gärtner watched Will for a moment and then exchanged a glance with Tim.

When he next spoke his voice was low and resolute. 'Go clear your desk,' he said. 'You're fired.'

CHAPTER 3

FRIDAY, 2.14 A.M.

MARBLE ARCH, LONDON

There was no moon. No stars. Just a misty gloom that merged with the glow of a lone streetlamp. From time to time the darkness was punctured by the jagged halogen rays of a passing car, and the silence was broken by a sweeping of tyres and an engine accelerating. Black tree trunks rose up into the dark sky, their leafless branches resembling giant gnarled hands that clutched and grasped at the blackness that enveloped them.

It was quiet. The freezing wind rose again, sending a shiver through Jud Lester's bones. Hailstones pelted the back of his head as he lay there, his face pressed against the cold, hard pavement, his body resembling a slab of meat on a butcher's block. He splayed his hands out on the concrete and pressed hard, intent on rising again.

It was not over yet.

He staggered to his feet but soon felt a sharp blow, like a sledgehammer, to the back of his knees. He toppled like a bowling pin on a slippery alley. Smash - his forehead hit the ground. He opened his eyes, rolled onto his back, lay still and blinked away the raindrops. He was tired, hungry and thirsty. His face was numb with cold. He opened his mouth and felt the freezing water falling on his tongue. He raised a hand to wipe his sodden face as the pain from the front of his skull seeped into his consciousness. He rubbed his head and saw that his fingertips were stained with blood.

He sat up and tried to focus his eyes quickly so he could anticipate the ghost's next move. Where would it strike now? In the shadows over by the bushes? Or back underneath the great arch, where he first saw it?

Jud had not lost his cool – he never did whenever he encountered a ghost, even a violent one – but the figure was stronger than anything he'd met before. And its face had been startling – misshapen, as though it had been pulverised in some way. Its skull looked concave on the right side of its face – a large indentation that stretched from the eyes down to the lips. It seemed like half its jaw and cheek bone were missing, but its nose was still intact, long and hooked like a beak. It had vanished as quickly as it had set upon him.

His heart beating fast in trepidation, Jud looked across the deserted park towards the great landmark, Marble Arch. No sign of the figure yet. But the arch itself looked different now. Almost translucent. The outline of the marble stones seemed to merge with the mist that swirled around it. A passing car illuminated the scene once again and Jud braced himself for another shocking glimpse of the hideous figure. The lights lit up the archway but the ghost was gone.

Any relief he felt was fleeting. As he turned to his left he saw the figure again, standing in the fading headlights.

It looked taller now. So tall it resembled one of the poplar trees that swayed on the park fringe. A trick of the light? Just an elongated shadow? It moved towards him again, walking on long, stilt-like legs that tottered and wobbled like some grotesque giant Pinocchio. It tilted its head to one side in a chilling mechanical way and kept edging closer. It was tall and thin and brittle.

What the hell was going on? Had he banged his head so hard that he was seeing things now? Was he delirious? He looked down at the pavement and saw a steady trickle of blood that came from his sleeve. It was running down his collar, onto his coat and down his arm.

No, this wasn't happening, he told himself. He was imagining it. He'd hit his head so hard he couldn't see straight. But as he glanced around the gloom, he realised the figure wasn't the only thing that was misshapen. The trees over by the bench had taken on a human-like form, bending and swaying like a row of hooded figures, their branches poking out of dark veils. They'd ceased swaying to a single breeze but were moving independently, lifelike, beckoning him to come closer.

He looked back at the place where he'd seen the giant figure hobbling towards him. It had vanished. He saw the great marble monument again, only this time he saw two arches at its centre, then one, then two. He was seeing double. The blow to the head was clearly far worse than he'd thought, and the pain was building steadily.

He staggered to his feet, dazed. He knew he had to get help, but from where? He saw no one. With a hand clutched to his head and the other stretched out in front of him like a blind man, he limped towards the road, his eyesight continuing to play tricks on him and sending his balance haywire. He shook his head, rubbed his eyes and soon felt relieved to be seeing one arch again. A quick flick towards the row of trees and he saw they were still.

His eyesight restored, at least for now, he limped on. The rain continued to fall, running down his collar and sending tributaries of blood-red trickles down his back and arm.

And then he stopped and caught his breath.

Far to his left, his peripheral vision had spied something, over by the dark bushes, to the left of the great arch. A tingling sensation ran up his spine; it wasn't fear – he'd long forgotten how that felt – it was surprise. Though the figure Jud had seen was less gruesome than the disfigured giant-like ghost, it was so *unexpected*. The shock made him feel sick.

There, in the bushes, framed by the dark, ominous clouds that gathered in the skies behind, was a child no more than four feet tall.

It was staring straight at him.

Dressed in a white christening robe, it was hard to make out if it was a girl or a boy. What little hair it possessed was sodden and matted and clung to its tiny head. Its pale robe was drenched, and through the thin cloth Jud could just make out a frail, bony ribcage.

Another car swept past the scene and Jud winced as he saw the child's face lit up for a brief second – it had no mouth, just pale skin that stretched across its whole jaw beneath its angular nose. And like the huge, hobbling figure, it kept tilting its head to one side in an awkward, bird-like manner while its body remained still.

And then it started moving towards Jud. The sight of it sent tremors through his whole body. Jud started to run but slipped on the wet paving stones and fell to the ground once more. The ghost child was approaching. Its eyes were jet black and seemed too large for the bony sockets that surrounded them. It walked unsteadily, tottering like a toddler, and put out a tiny hand towards him, its head still cocked to one side.

'No!' he yelled. 'Leave me!'

Jud shook his head vigorously and continued to yell. The little ghost's hands were moving towards his neck. Its blank, expressionless face looked ghoulish in the gloom that enveloped it.

'Get away! Leave me! No!'

A hand was at his shoulder, another at his forehead.

'It's okay. Wake up. Wake up, you're safe.'

Jud opened his eyes and blinked.

A man dressed in a policeman's uniform was staring down at him with a curious expression. Behind him stood a second police officer shaking his head pitifully.

Jud sat up on the park bench on which he'd passed out several hours before. 'What . . . ? Where . . . ?'

'You're in London, mate. On a bench in Marble Arch. You've been drinking, I take it?'

Jud said nothing but shook his head solemnly and rubbed his eyes.

'Good party was it?' the other officer jeered, rolling his eyes at his colleague. This wasn't the first drunkard they'd found that night and he probably wouldn't be the last.

Jud quickly put a hand to his head to check if there was any blood. It was clean and dry. There was no pain. And it wasn't even raining.

Realisation dawned, but it brought him as much comfort as the violent dream he'd just experienced. Reality was a bench in the middle of London, alone and hungry, when he should have been in bed.

'I gotta go,' said Jud.

'Yeah, you better, son. But where to, eh? Do you live in London?'

Jud nodded.

'Tell me your address then.'

'Er . . . well, I live in London, yeah. But I can't tell you where. I mean, well . . . Look, I'm okay. Just leave me, yeah? Don't . . . don't worry. Thanks. I'm sorry, I've really gotta go.' He stood up quickly. 'I must've stopped here for a rest and then fallen asleep. I'm alright, honest. Just tired. I gotta go. My family'll be worried.'

Jud began to run and after a few seconds glanced over his shoulder to see if the policemen had bothered to come after him. They hadn't. They'd obviously not seen the point in chasing a lone teenager and escorting him home. It was the ones in gangs they had to worry about. Like most nights in London these days.

Jud turned and disappeared into the darkness, bound for the CRYPT. With any luck, he could slip into the building and into the safety of his own room without anyone knowing, where he would sleep off yet another hangover and another night spent wandering the streets trying to find some solace. His own company was all he knew these days. He couldn't handle being with anyone else. Bonati would probably give him another lecture about looking after himself, like he always did, and no doubt Bex de Verre would have something to say about the state he was in. Why was it everyone had an opinion? Why couldn't they get on with their own lives and allow him to live the way he chose?

It was always the same. He'd been the topic of conversation for too long; the subject everyone liked to discuss and debate. It had become a fashionable bandwagon to jump on – to express a trendy concern for Jud Lester and his downward spiral. People would shake their head and tut and give some crappy fake expression to pretend they were really concerned for him. But he didn't need their sympathy or their pity.

Jud Lester – Jamie Goode – was a survivor, and he'd get through this in his own time and in his own way. If walking the streets at night was the only way he could get some peace and quiet, then he would. Life was cruel. Get used to it. He'd lost his mother, whose murder he was wrongfully charged with, his father rarely spoke to him, and he was a prisoner at the CRYPT. All that he had learned to deal with, but to lose his closest friend, the one guy with whom he could relax and have a laugh, that was the final thing that tipped him over the brink.

Jud was toughening up. He was hardening. The glimmer of warmth that had remained in him all these years, the flicker of love which Bex had found and had been trying with all her might to cultivate, was cooling quickly. He was becoming the hardened, unfeeling spirit which circumstances had made of him. He didn't need anyone now. Self-preservation had kicked in. It was time for him to truly accept what he was, who he was, and the hand which life had dealt him. He was a loner. Needing no one. He would be tougher than anyone, braver, reckless maybe. He'd take on anybody and anything. Ghosts held no fear for him. Not any more. What could they do? Was there anything he could experience that was worse than what he'd already been through, and survived?

But his routine was becoming all too familiar, and it was a path to self-destruction: go through the motions during the day, do what he was told, fight whatever ghost he was sent to fight, and then get the hell out of the place until everyone else was in bed, finding solace in walking the streets. Working was okay – he could handle that. But it was the evenings he hated most. The time spent with friends. He had nothing to say, nothing to offer a friendship any more.

His one true friend was dead, and why the hell should he bother to make any new ones? They'd probably just die, up sticks and leave, or turn on him like everyone else in this miserable, God-forsaken life. It was every man for himself now. The drawbridge on his emotions was well and truly up and no one would ever bring it down again. His body was a stone keep. Locked.

Chapter 4

FRIDAY, 12.31 P.M.

BLACKFRIARS BRIDGE, LONDON

It was lunchtime and the city's streets were packed with office workers wearing fancy suits and carrying trendy brown bags containing bagels and baguettes and all manner of salads tightly packed into plastic tubs, while in the other hand they clutched their precious coffees. Some balanced tightly folded newspapers under their arm. No one stopped, everyone was rushing, anxious to use every last minute of their precious half-hour escapes to freedom on whichever available bench they could find, while their coffee was still warm.

They swarmed over Blackfriars Bridge, dodging the cyclists and the cars and taxis that swept past. A few paused in the middle of the bridge to admire the views up and down the River Thames: the London Eye and the solid concrete block of the National Theatre to the west, and the giant, shiny sky-scrapers of London's banking district to the east. The weather had treated the lunchtime fraternity to a rare moment of sunshine, and on days like this it seemed London wasn't such a bad place to work after all. The grime, the noise, the litter and the frenetic pace were usually forgotten when the sun shone over the gleaming dome of St Paul's Cathedral.

High-flying financier Kit Berry took another drag from his electronic cigarette and blew the odourless vapour out over the river. He leant over the pink and white balustrades of the bridge and watched the dirty brown waves of the Thames wash beneath him.

He often liked to watch the water; he felt drawn to it, having grown up in a small coastal town on the southern edge of Devon. How far he'd come, a young lad from a rural school, now working in the centre of one of the world's most famous cities. Most of his friends from school had gone into jobs locally, but Kit was different. He'd strived for something new, something challenging. Maths had been a good subject for him at school, one of the few that captured his interest, truth be told, and so he'd chosen to study maths and economics at Exeter. Living in student digs in the centre of Exeter, he'd grown accustomed to city life and so had decided to make the move to London as soon as he'd graduated. It turned out that his skill for numbers was even better than either he or his maths teachers from school had thought. He earned himself a First and bagged a top graduate job with a central bank in London.

That was three and a half years ago and now he was flying. But he'd still not lost his love of being near water; its sound comforted him. And even here, surrounded by traffic and conversations and alarms and phone calls and horns beeping, he could still shut out the noise and connect with the waves beneath him, his imagination painting in the added sounds of sea gulls and children laughing on a beach.

The water was hardly blue, more a murky brown, but it was still water and it was enough to provide Kit with a few moments' peace every day, when he could reconnect with his childhood and the life he'd left behind in Devon. His life before Nisha.

He'd met her at a party at the bank almost a year ago. She was a marketing executive and had been invited to the party because of some work her company had been doing for the bank at the time. He remembered seeing her enter the room with her colleague. It was one of those thunderbolt moments, like he'd been struck down. Love at first sight. Up until then he'd thought the idea was bullshit, there was no such thing. There was lust, for sure. He'd seen plenty of girls since moving to London, plenty of sexy girls in sexy suits, out for a coffee at lunchtime. The city was full of them. But Nisha was different. He knew, instantly, that not only did he fancy her, he wanted to know everything about her, to protect her, to spend the rest of his life with her.

Luckily for him, the feeling was mutual, and six months later they were engaged to be married. She always insisted it was her who came to talk to him first. She'd caught sight of him before he'd seen her, so she said. It was she who chose him, not the other way around. Either way, a whirlwind romance had struck up and they were besotted.

These lunchtime rituals had become an essential part of their days. The rendezvous on the bridge was something they both looked forward to all morning, and it got them through the pressures of work.

He worked in the City, she worked over the river in Southwark, so it seemed the obvious place to meet, provided the weather was nice, that is. When it wasn't, Kit travelled to a bar near Nisha's office. He didn't like her having to get wet if he could avoid it. And he never minded the rain.

He turned to face the road on the bridge and looked up and down. No sign of her yet. He was early, again. Kit was usually in more of a hurry to get out of the office than Nisha was. She loved her work and was very good at it too. She'd earned herself quite a reputation in the field of marketing already and was destined for greatness. She was never going to earn the kind of money Kit would, as a banker, but she wouldn't be close behind if she played her cards right. The luxury apartment overlooking the Thames was not going to be far away if they could stick at it and keep saving for the deposit.

He was leaning on the usual statue, the place where they always waited: a large, solid block of neatly cut stone, its plinth painted in white and silver. Gaudy, you might say, though Kit liked it. The colours matched the red and white on the cross of St George, which was painted across the large shield clasped in the claws of the dragon that stood proudly on the plinth. The size of a lion, its face was that of a dog, its ugly snarl showing razor-like teeth, its great paws oversized, out of proportion to the rest of its body. But then, what did a dragon, or griffin, look like anyway? There wasn't exactly a blueprint you could follow. The animals were mythical creatures, after all, belonging in children's fantasy novels or the myths of ancient times. Though Kit had seen this, and other dragons, every day since arriving in London, he was still unclear as to whether it was indeed a dragon or a griffin or some other mythical animal, and why, more importantly, it was there at all. Why were these creatures, which seemed more at home in a Chinese fable, so common in London? He'd noticed many others of different shapes and sizes dotted across the city, some on bridges like this one, others on the sides of buildings, others perched menacingly over the tops of windows and doors. His favourite, of course, was the giant dragon of Temple Bar, though he seldom had reason to go there.

But despite passing them so regularly, he'd rarely studied them, noticed the grimace on their faces, or seen the sharpness of the teeth that protruded from the great snarl in which their faces were always fixed. Kit and Nisha had met at the same spot so often, yet he'd seldom noticed the gruesome features. In the days before Kit had switched to the electric cigs, he'd even stubbed out the real fag ends on the statue's face. It was just a stone figure, like so many others across the city, that went unnoticed by anyone except a few foreign tourists, who thought it odd that such ferocious animals should receive such little attention from anyone else.

Kit took another long drag and blew the vapour out in rings this time, proudly watching each 'O' rise gently and then disperse in the breeze that blew across the bridge. He glanced in the direction of Southwark again, leaning casually against the statue, with his back to the water. The traffic rattled past and the pedestrians walked by, some making a deliberate coughing sound as they inhaled the odourless, harmless vapour from his electric cigarette. A bus roared past, too close to the kerb, which caused splashes from puddles to reach the trouser legs and shoes of disgruntled commuters.

And then Kit felt something clutch his right shoulder.

He spun round. Nothing.

Was it a bird? It must have been a bloody big one, like some of the giant gulls he was used to in Devon. But here? In London? He turned back to face the road, keeping his cool, as the people continued to walk past. He was sure he'd felt something grip his shoulder. Or was it a nerve that had pulled? A spasm maybe? He'd certainly been pumping iron lately, having joined one of London's many gyms with Nisha. She preferred toning exercises on the mat, while Kit, like so many other guys, liked to rip his muscles pumping weights, in the hope the muscle tissue would rebuild itself even bigger each time. And it was working too. His shoulders and biceps were growing, as he often liked to show Nisha. He rubbed his shoulder. There was no pain, no scratch, but he'd not dreamt it. He looked up and down the bridge again. Passers-by went about their usual business. No one had stopped next to him. No one else could have touched his shoulder and then disappeared again that quickly, like some silly kid in school assembly. It must've either been a bird or a twitching nerve. Maybe he should give the gym a miss tonight.

He had his back to the statue once again, keeping an eye out for Nisha. Come on, he said to himself. His stomach was rumbling and he wanted to see her anyway. He loved to play the familiar game of seeing her face in the crowd of people passing by and imagining meeting her for the first time.

He was just about to take another puff on the e-cig when he felt the twinge again, in the same place as before, but this time it was stronger, sharper. It couldn't possibly be a muscle or nerve spasm, it was too penetrating, too physical for that. And then he felt something clutch the back of his neck. He grimaced and yelled, 'Ow! Jesus!'

The clutching stopped as quickly as it had started, and he tried to spin round to see what was behind him. As he did so he caught sight of the people either side of him who'd stopped now. He saw their expressions before he saw what had attacked him. The look of terror on their faces made him feel sick. They began to turn and run from where he was standing. Glancing over their shoulders at him, their pace quickened with each step.

When Kit saw what it was that had grabbed him it felt like he'd slipped into some kind of dream. A nightmare. Was this really happening?

'Jesus Christ. What the . . .'

Though people heard his cries, they'd already fled, running in both directions over the bridge. Kit went to run but it was too late.

Only one person was running in the opposite direction to everyone else, sprinting towards Kit, screaming his name as she approached. 'Kit! Oh my God!'

Nisha was horrified.

'Kit!' she cried again. 'Wait, I'm coming!'

But he didn't hear her. She was too late. He'd already slumped to the ground, semi-conscious.

She was just metres away when she stopped and placed her hands up to her face to hide her eyes from the horror that was unravelling in front of her. It was too gruesome to see. She fell to the floor, her knees slamming onto the cold, hard pavement, just yards from Kit.

She saw the stone dragon. It was alive.

The red and white shield was hurled off the bridge, tumbling into the water below as the creature flexed its claws, heaved itself up from its position on the plinth and flew again at Kit, now crumpled on the floor. It began tearing at his face with its giant talons, like a vulture claws at carrion. Blood was spurting across the pavement like spilled wine. Kit made no sound, but his body jerked and writhed. The dragon opened its giant mouth and sunk its fangs into his throat. His body twitched again momentarily, like a boxer on the ropes, and then it fell ominously still.

Through the cracks in her fingers, Nisha saw the white electronic cigarette roll through the blood and tumble into the gutter, disappearing into a grate.

Kit was dead.

CHAPTER 5

FRIDAY, 8.31 A.M.

CRYPT HEADQUARTERS, LONDON

'Jud's obsessed, Bex, you know he is. He's got issues.' Grace took another slurp from her cappuccino and glanced back at her magazine. 'Don't get involved, trust me.'

'Don't get involved?' said Bex, incredulously. 'Bit late for that, isn't it? Up to my neck already, I'd say.'

'Look, we all know how much you like him – and I'm not saying you can turn those feelings off automatically – I'm just saying give him some time, that's all. He'll come around in the end. He always does. He's deep that guy, but you know better than anyone how to humour him. At least you should by now.' She raised her eyebrows cheekily. Everyone knew Bex and Jud were an item these days. Or thought they were. And Grace Cavendish was Bex's closest friend in the CRYPT, so she knew better than anyone.

'He's not my boyfriend, Grace. It's not like that.'

'What do you mean?'

'He's just hard to get close to, that's all.' She felt like adding, 'But it's hardly surprising, given what he's been through,' but she decided it was best to keep silent. Jud's secrets – and there were enough of them – were safe with her.

'Oh, come on, Bex. It's common knowledge you've got the hots for each other. Don't try and deny it, girl. He likes you too, we all know he does. Do you mean to say you still haven't kissed him? Or . . . you know, anything else?'

'Oh, shut up!' Bex snapped, but still half smiling. 'I don't want to talk about him any more.'

'Fine by me,' said Grace, 'You brought him up.' She settled back to her magazine, mumbling 'as usual' under her breath.

Bex stared across the busy cafeteria, filled with the typical hustle bustle of a workday morning, as sleepy-faced agents lined up for breakfast. Some of the greedier ones piled extra hash browns and sausages onto large plates over at the hot buffet. Others lavished too much milk into heaving cereal bowls, spilling white droplets randomly as they shuffled to the nearest free table.

'Why can't Jud just be, you know . . . normal?' Bex said. 'Like everyone else here.'

'I thought you wanted to drop the subject?' said Grace, smugly. 'But I hardly think any of us in here are *normal*, Bex, otherwise we wouldn't be here, would we?'

'You know what I mean. Look, just forget it.'

'I already had.'

Grace saw there were tears in Bex's eyes. She was a tough girl – there was no one tougher at the CRYPT – but she knew Bex could be just as sensitive as the next person. She had a heart and it was as fragile as anyone's. She was clearly stressed. Grace had often wanted to go and tell Jud Lester just what she thought of him, of the way he was messing her friend around. Why did he have to be so weird, always leading Bex on and then shutting himself away again?

'Look, like I said, Jud's a complicated guy,' Grace said more gently now. 'He's deep, a real thinker. And that's why you like him. Why we all do. I just think—'

'But I never see him any more!' interrupted Bex. 'He's practically a recluse since Luc died. He never sees anyone, never talks. It's like he's a ghost himself.'

'But you do investigations with him!' said Grace, surprised. 'You were with him on the last case, I thought? At that stakeout over in . . . where was it?'

'Chiswick. Domestic haunting. Nothing much happened.'

'But you were with him. So how can you say you never see him?'

'That's different. I mean, I never see him when we're off duty. He just disappears in the evenings.'

'You should tell him he's not the only one missing Luc. He was my partner, you know. I went through more with Luc than anyone else did.'

'I know. I'm sorry. Have you still not been partnered with anyone else yet?'

Grace shook her head.

'I'm sure you will be. Any ideas who you want?'

'No. Not bothered. It's not going to be the same as it was with Luc, whoever the professor gives me. But I hope it's someone as fun as he was.'

They sat in silence for a moment, remembering Luc's playful side and his wicked sense of humour. He'd balanced Jud so well. Together, the four agents had made a fantastic team.

Things had been difficult for everyone since Luc's death. It was the first time they'd ever lost an agent – despite all the dangers they'd faced – and it had hit them hard. Bonati had been brave, as always, and tried to keep the team going. He'd often say how Luc would want them all to keep going for his sake, how he was probably looking down and wondering why they were moping about instead of getting on with hunting ghosts and protecting the public.

But the agents could all see how the death had affected Professor Bonati too. He was supposed to be in charge of them, after all. They were his responsibility, ultimately.

Since the tragic incident, security had been stepped up considerably. Bonati's gadgets expert and Head of Technical Support, Dr Kim Vorzek, ran regular workshops on personal protection. There was no way she was ever going to issue her agents with guns, so it was about being smart, noticing things before they got too dangerous. Guns would be pointless against ghosts, but, as everyone was all too aware, Luc had been killed by a human, not something paranormal. The agents were in the front line, not only against the supernatural, but against people who had something to hide, out to protect their images and their reputations. 'Stay alert,' Vorzek kept repeating in her workshops.

There was something about ghost hunting that exposed people for who they really were. So many of the ghosts they'd encountered were returning to right a wrong. Injustices in life lingered on after death, and no wonder some of the living had reason to be violent when the CRYPT agents came poking around, uncovering crimes that had been committed and would otherwise have gone undetected had the ghosts not come back to haunt the perpetrators. This was why the CRYPT's links to MI5 and Scotland Yard were so important. The agency operated under licence from MI5 after all, and the work often led to joint operations.

Bonati had even suggested, soon after Luc's death, that agents should be accompanied by armed police on certain hauntings, where there was evidence of fatal crimes having been committed and the chance that the criminals would do it again. It wasn't a game any more.

Briefings were different now. Everything had become serious. The agents had all known that their work at the CRYPT was not exactly a holiday. MI5 had agreed to support them from the very start because of the danger involved in their work. It was important, and most often it was dangerous and difficult and frightening. The threats the agents faced every day were of the kind that would terrify most ordinary people. But there was an excitement about the place that everyone found so exhilarating. Before Luc's death an agent would think themselves lucky to be given a case to investigate, instead of the constant research work in the labs, or the historical work delving into people's past lives. There was a thrill from the moment Bonati assigned an agent to a live haunting.

But everything had changed now. There was a cold, hard threat that hung over their heads.

This was real. Like soldiers, they faced the threat of harm every day, and it had taken Luc's death to make them realise it. But they had pulled together. Like brothers in arms they'd learned to support each other through the grief, finding distractions whenever they could. Throwing themselves into assignments, not so much for the thrill of it, but because it took their minds off Luc and the dangers of being a CRYPT agent.

'You both need another assignment, that's what you need,' said Grace, keen to break the silence before the familiar grief returned again. 'You really do. Something that'll take your mind off things and give you a proper challenge again.'

'Yeah, I know. But he's so difficult to talk to at the moment. And Bonati knows he's unpredictable right now. Maybe he doesn't trust him.'

'Didn't the professor insist on those therapy sessions for him? I thought he was seeing someone now?'

Bex shook her head. 'As far as I know, he only turned up for the first one and then never went again. When Bonati tried to insist and started talking about punishments if he didn't, the therapist said it wouldn't work unless Jud really wanted to be helped. She said it could make things even worse if Jud resisted seeing her; he'd become even more withdrawn. It's not like when it's your leg or your arm or something. You have to believe in it. You know, go with it. Or you become even more defensive, that what's she said. I reckon I've spent more time talking to Jud's therapist than he has. He has to *want* to talk about what's troubling him – and, God knows, I've tried that.'

'Makes sense, I suppose.' Grace shrugged her shoulders and gazed across the crowded room. 'So where is he now? Don't tell me, in the SPA again?'

Bex shrugged miserably. 'I tried his room earlier – no answer. I texted and called but he's turned his phone off. He's either hiding in bed or down in one of the SPAs, yeah. I'm tired of looking for him. It's all I ever do.'

'What does he do down there, Bex?'

'In the SPA?'

'Yeah.'

Bex could guess exactly why Jud spent so much time in the Simulated Paranormal Activity rooms and what he did down there, but she was never going to tell. 'Oh, you know, always the same kind of thing. Trying to make contact with the other side. Practising his skills. Getting better at what he does. He likes to test himself, you know that.'

Grace looked concerned. 'He's got to let it go, Bex. It'll send him mad. Grief does that. I had a cousin who lost her best friend and after a while I hardly recognised her. She lost weight, never went out and became so withdrawn. It was horrible to watch.'

'And now?' said Bex. 'Is she over it?'

'A little. She talks a little but she's a shadow of what she was. My aunt says she still spends hours in her room, just lying there, wrapped up in her own thoughts. It's what happens sometimes. Until you get lifted out of it. Distracted by something new.'

Bex wished she could tell Grace all the reasons why Jud struggled with grief. How he'd been obsessed with contacting the other side even before Luc died. How he spent every waking hour thinking about his mother's death. And now Luc's.

She stood up. 'I'm going to find him,' she said resolutely. 'I am. I'm going to fix this once and for all. I won't stand by and let him destroy himself. I want him back. I'll stand outside his bloody room and shout all day if I have to. He *will* let me in.'

CHAPTER 6

FRIDAY, 9.22 A.M.

CRYPT HEADQUARTERS, LONDON

'Look, I'm not going to leave here until you open this door,' Bex said in a loud whisper. Talking through a closed door was something she had become accustomed to these days. It was like being in a confessional, except she'd done nothing wrong. 'You can't stay in bed all day. We need you. *I need you.*'

'I've got a hangover,' came a muffled voice from inside. 'Just go away.'

'I'll make it better.'

'And my body aches.'

'I'll make that better too, if you're lucky.'

Silence from inside the room. Had she gone too far? Jud was probably in no mood for jokes, never mind anything else.

'Come on, J. Let me in. I . . . I . . . Well, I miss you.'

Still silence.

'Oh, come on, J! It's me. There's no one else here.'

'Don't tell me, let me guess – Bonati sent you,' Jud said miserably. 'Be a good girl and go tell him I'm fine.'

Bex didn't reply. When would this guy realise what he meant

to her? How could he accuse of her of being sent by the professor? No one needed to put her up to coming because no one else cared like she did.

'Hello?' he said eventually. Even Jud knew he shouldn't have said that. No one would have sent her. That was low, even for him. But why did she have to keep bothering him like this? When would she finally take the hint it was over – not that there was any 'it' in the first place. There was nothing to end, because nothing had started. It was all in her head. She needed to move on and find some other loser to fancy, if losers were what she liked. It certainly looked that way.

Of course Jud knew they'd been growing closer – how could he deny it? – and that there were things about him that she should never have known, but did. She knew about his life as Jamie Goode. She knew about the fateful night at the castle when his mother died. She knew about the court case and how he was wrongfully charged with her murder, and she knew about the conditions of his eventual release, that he should remain at the CRYPT and assume a new identity, for his own protection.

It seemed like she knew everything about him, maybe knew him better than he knew himself. But since Luc's death, self-preservation had kicked in and there was no way he was going to let anyone get close to him again, not a good mate, not a girlfriend. Not even Bex. So now their conversations were confined either to work-related matters whilst on assignment (he refused to talk about anything else when they were on investigations, and always hid behind the excuse 'not while we're working, Bex') or these snatched duologues on two sides of a closed door.

'Why won't you leave me alone?' he shouted again.

'Because you're not meant to be alone.'

'How can you say that? You're blind. All the evidence suggests that if any person on Earth was destined to be alone, it's me, Bex. It's just life. It's what I'm meant to be. A loner.'

'Yeah, sure,' said Bex. 'You've been watching too many movies, Jud Lester. The lone cop walks off into the shadows, off to another town, another case, with nothin' but a bottle of bourbon for company.' Her American accent wasn't the best but it served its purpose. She heard a faint chuckle from inside the room.

'You're mad, Bex.'

'Of course I am. Who else would spend so much time talking to a door, huh? Who else would hang around you like some kind of limpet? Of course I'm mad. Anyone's gotta be mad not to have given up on you by now.'

Jud lay back on his pillow and looked up at the ceiling.

'Come on,' she said again. 'Open up.'

He smiled. You had to hand it to the girl, she didn't give up. She was gutsy and brave and resilient. Or was she just stubborn? Whatever it was, she'd obviously made up her mind he was the guy for her and she just wasn't letting up. Jud liked to kid himself that he was in control, but he knew full well he wasn't. It was only a matter of time, and he knew it. He could resist, but her stubbornness was bigger than his resistance. She would win on the stubborn scale, hands down.

But then that was always the case with his mother and father, just like anybody's parents, he thought. Men always gave up first, on anything. Women's survival instinct was stronger. It was biological. And if she'd chosen him, as he guessed she had, he'd little choice now.

'Please?' came a shrinking voice again. 'I won't go away, you know.'

'No,' whispered Jud to himself, 'I know you won't.'

The door slid open, startling Bex for a moment but bringing a welcome smile to her lips, and disappeared inside the wall of the corridor to Bex's right. She entered the tiny, gadget-filled bedroom. Everyone referred to the dorms as iPods because of their compact size, their dark décor, and because they were usually filled with every application you could dream of: music stations, computer technology, and every electronic game on the market (and some that were not even available yet – from Goode Technology PLC, of course). But Jud had ceased playing his Xbox, or anything else for that matter, since his gaming buddy had been gunned down. He had lost his appetite for violent games. Luc was gone and there was no point any more. Jud found his kicks at the bottom of a vodka or whiskey bottle these days, or anything else he could lay his hands on. He was developing an addiction to drinking and, deep down, he was getting worried about it.

Bex could see the room was in a dreadful state. Jud was never tidy at the best of times, but now he'd sunk to an all-time low. The place reeked of cold pizza; no wonder, thought Bex – she could see the remains of a Meat Feast thin crust just below Jud's bed, and some other kind of fishy pizza lurking on his desk in the corner.

'Anchovies?' she said, pulling a face.

'Yup. Help yourself. It's only a week old, that one.'

Jud was still in bed. Only his face was visible; the rest of his body was safely cocooned inside a filthy-looking duvet that was strewn with old socks, a pair of wrinkled jeans and various T-shirts and tops. Shiny chocolate wrappers poked out from beneath old clothes and magazines on the floor, and in the corner was a precarious-looking stack of Coke cans. Jud's trademark black leather jacket was strewn over the back of a chair near the table. At least he'd managed to hang that up, or tried to.

'Is this some kind of art installation then?' said Bex. 'Like a Tracey Emin? What have you called it? "Teenage life" maybe?'

Jud said nothing, just buried his head back into the duvet. 'What do you want? You're not my mother. Oh yeah, I just remembered, I don't have a mother. Just like I don't have a best mate any more either. I have a father, but I have to pretend he's not my father. I have a home, but I have to go there in secret. Remember?'

'Ssh, keep your voice down,' said Bex, pressing the button next to the open door and waiting for it to slide shut before speaking again. 'What're you doing, J? Stop talking like that. Someone will hear you.'

'I don't give a shit if they do. I don't care any more. They can all know everything. There's no reason to keep any of my life secret now. Why should I? What's the point? Nothing matters now.'

Bex knew that she was out of her depth here. If Jud was about to lose it and start revealing his entire life history to everyone, she knew she should be calling for Bonati, or even his father, Jason Goode, or at least a medic, but she thought their presence in the tiny room would only worsen Jud's mood.

She was no stranger to his changing temperaments. She knew how to calm him down when he was feeling angry, knew how to build him up when he was depressed, and knew how to make him laugh. Though she was sure he'd deny it, they had become really close of late – able to share their deepest secrets and worries and hopes. Somehow the intensity of the investigations they'd endured together had made talking easier. Jud had confided in her. Perhaps it was just the adrenalin from being on missions together, but they had definitely started to talk recently – really talk. Until Luc died, that is. Since that fateful day when the news of his death had come, Bex, like everyone else at the CRYPT, had lost Jud to himself. He'd become even more withdrawn than usual – if that were possible. And impregnable, like a stone wall.

'Get up, I've had enough of this,' she suddenly snapped, and started tugging his duvet, but his grip was like iron.

'Get off, Bex. Pack it in! You're gonna get a mouldy pizza in the face in a minute. Just leave me alone, will you.'

'You let me in here,' she said.

'I know. And I wish I hadn't.'

She picked up a discarded slice of the mouldy, fishy pizza on the table and wafted it near to the small mound that was his head inside the duvet. After a few seconds the pungent aromas penetrated through the thin sheet and Jud groaned. But Bex heard the beginnings of a chuckle as the groans subsided and she knew she would win this time.

She turned to look at the other end of the bed and tried to feel her way to his feet. She started tickling them.

'Bugger off!' he chuckled.

She didn't say anything, but kept tickling and prodding and annoying him, trying to rattle him out of his dark mood. Then she stopped and just looked at the pathetic body shrouded in sheets. He was like a baby, hiding under the duvet, wanting the world to go away. She could hear him breathing but neither of them said anything. She sat down on the only available bit of bed beside his curled-up body.

'You're an addiction, Lester. I can't stop feeling the way I do. God knows, I've tried. I've tried hating you, or even just disliking you, but I can't.' Her voice was breaking now, though she hated herself for allowing her emotions to bubble to the surface in this way. She usually managed to keep them well hidden. But not this time. It had gone on too long and she was yearning for his company.

Jud pushed his head up out of the duvet. His eyes were screwed up, he had dark stubble on his chin, and his bed-hairstyle was wild.

'Are you hittin' on me, De Verre? Trying to take advantage of a sleepy, defenceless guy? Is that it?'

She smiled at him. And they looked at each other for a moment in silence.

God knows this girl had not given up on him, thought Jud. He had to admire her for that. Anyone else would have cleared off ages ago – and maybe asked for a different partner. All the things they'd been through together. All those investigations. All the scrapes and near misses. And she'd never given up on him. Never left him. Maybe she never would.

But how did he know that for sure? Could he really trust her?

She knew he was thinking it all through – she could see it in his eyes. Should he – could he – open up to her? Trust her?

But he already had! This was stupid. There was nothing about this guy that she didn't already know. He just needed to take the final plunge and let her in. And stop playing so hard to get.

'I won't leave you,' she said.

'Yeah, I know,' he muttered, half-heartedly.

'I mean it,' she said. 'Look at me.' She placed a hand on his sleepy face and forced him to look at her. 'Look at me, J. I said I won't leave you.'

'I know.'

'I won't leave you.'

'I heard you! Shuddup!'

She said it again, but Jud had gone silent now, his eyes staring at the floor.

She saw a lone tear fall from his dirty cheek onto the duvet. It was a rare glimpse into the dark and lonely world inside his head.

'I won't leave you, J.'

She knew something rotten was buried deep within him that just had to come out. But no more tears came. He sniffed hard, pursed his lips, biting away the grief.

'Please,' he said, looking straight at her. 'I get it. I can hear you.'

'So let me in.'

He stared at the floor for a while longer. Neither of them said anything. And then he raised an arm and the duvet lifted. For a second she saw his sinewy, muscular body and his dark trunks, and then she snuggled in close to him.

CHAPTER 7

FRIDAY, 2.00 P.M.

CRYPT HEADQUARTERS, LONDON

'Alright everybody, settle down. I said *settle down*, all of you! Listen to me.'

Bonati had heard the anxious chatter before he'd even entered the briefing room and he knew he had to stamp on it quickly. Briefings were difficult at the best of times, with so many agents in one room, all energised and ready for action, but today they seemed particularly rowdy.

'Settle down. We don't have long and I have a lot to get through.' Bonati was anxious and the agents at the front of the packed briefing room could see it in his face. Excitement grew further. Everyone knew to expect something big when Bonati looked rattled. His cheeks were flushed and his manner, usually so cool and measured, seemed agitated. Nothing got past the CRYPT agents; they were recruited for their extrasensory perception after all. They knew when someone was feeling unsettled. Even the professor.

Rumours and theories had already spread about what the next assignment might be, and the reason for this emergency briefing. All agents, whether new – known as zombies – or more experienced team members – known as skulls – were excited when unplanned meetings like this were called and the order went out for every free agent to assemble in the largest briefing room in Sector 2. And today was no exception. Whether they had been in their rooms, or elsewhere in the living quarters in Sector 1, or even down in the laboratories and SPA rooms in Sector 3, they stopped what they were doing and assembled quickly, anxious not to miss out on the next big thing.

Bex glanced across to Dr Vorzek to see if she too was showing signs of nerves. She was her usual calm self and just stared at Bonati, waiting for him to speak. Either she knew something the agents didn't and was hiding it well, or she was in the dark like they were.

The room was used for a variety of purposes – meetings, functions, even social events sometimes – but there was nothing like a briefing to bring everyone together and make them feel united. And Bonati's presence always brought a sense of anticipation. All the agents, even the newly recruited zombies, had interviews and regular 'catch ups' with the professor – he liked to monitor things closely and be there to support them when they needed help – but he still commanded huge respect from everyone. And when he said he wanted to see you, you knew to drop everything and come running. Keep the professor waiting and you'd soon know about it.

The chatter died down and Bonati cleared his throat to begin. His voice was low and laboured. His stare from behind the rimless specs was serious.

'Earlier today I received a visit from Detective Chief Inspector Khan.'

'Brace yourself,' Bex whispered to Jud who was sitting next to her. 'A visit from the DCI usually means something out of the ordinary. This could be fun, and I'm ready for a nice big assignment. I hope it's our turn.'

Jud looked at her and shrugged. 'Whatever.'

'Oh, come on, J,' she teased. 'You need to get your teeth into a new one, it'll do you good.'

Bex's new-found cheekiness wasn't lost on Jud, and he could hardly play it cool now and glare at her like he usually did, given how close they'd just been in his room. She had certainly managed to win him over and they both knew it. For a brief moment he had let his guard down and she felt closer to him for it.

'When you've finished,' Vorzek said quietly, staring in Bex's direction. Bex blushed slightly and those around her chuckled before the professor shot them a glance too.

'Thank you, Dr Vorzek. It seems our agents are in a childish mood today. Perhaps there are some of us who are not ready for a new assignment?'

The room quickly fell silent. All eyes on Bonati.

'Khan had some very important news to report, and it's vital that you listen carefully. It's one of the most unusual cases we've been given. I've now had the chance to speak to representatives from MI5 too, and I can confirm our instructions to act – and quickly. The situation is dangerous and there are developments all the time. Pressure is mounting.'

Come on, thought Jud, get on with it. He knew the professor liked his big build-ups.

'You will know of the city's dragons, I assume.'

The city's what?' someone shouted from the back.

'Dragons. You will have noticed, I am sure – because you are employed for your powers of observation, not to mention your knowledge of history – that there are many stone and bronze statues of dragons dotted around the capital, mainly in the old city.'

'Dragons?' whispered Bex. 'What's he talking about dragons for?'

'Ssh!' said Vorzek.

'Don't tell us they've come to life!' Nick shouted from the corner, causing a ripple of amusement.

'That's enough from you, Nick,' the professor replied. 'Or perhaps you'd prefer not to hear what the inspector said? Hmm? Now listen carefully, all of you. I will need to deploy many agents onto this.

'Whether you said it in jest or not, you are quite correct, Nick. There are indeed reports coming in that certain statues have taken on a life force. Reports are coming in that some of them have been seen to *move*.'

'Move?' said Bex. 'You mean they're coming to life. Seriously?'

'I've not assembled you in here for a joke, Rebecca,' snapped Bonati. 'And you know I would not say something unless it were true. I'm sorry to say it but that is exactly what is happening. MI5 have confirmed it. The reports from eyewitnesses are quite startling – especially those who have seen the fatalities.'

'Did you say *fatalities*, Professor?' said Jud. Even he was hooked now.

'Yes,' said Bonati, solemnly. 'There was a fatal attack on Blackfriars Bridge and another report has just come in of a similar killing on High Holborn.'

'What about the giant dragon outside the courts, sir?' said Grace. 'At Temple Bar? If that one comes to life, God help us all.'

Other agents raised their eyebrows with excitement. Some just couldn't hide their lust for another decent assignment.

The professor sensed the rising mood and said abruptly, 'Before anyone gets too excited, may I remind you that I just said there have been fatalities. This is not a game and your lack of respect for the victims saddens me.'

Sombre faces returned, for a while at least.

'The Temple Bar dragon has not attacked anyone yet, but it has been seen to move and twitch. Khan said his team have received several reports from pedestrians in the location. It is only a matter of time. That section of Fleet Street has been closed, I'm told, and DCI Khan and his men are already stationed at various other locations where dragon statues are situated. Historians have been recruited to identify every site where an incident may occur. I assure you there are many.'

'Any theories yet as to why the statues have absorbed energy, sir?' said Jud. 'And how?'

Bonati turned to Vorzek to answer this one.

'We know from past cases,' she began, 'that even inanimate, stone objects can absorb energy. The atoms that make them, just like anything, can change form. Nothing is set forever. And there is plenty of evidence to suggest that any object can absorb energy, whether living or not. We ourselves are composites of inanimate substances which, when combined, create energy. We don't know why. Take the elements that make us apart and they amount to nothing but basic matter. We are dealing with forces that none of us can quite predict, at a quantum level. As to the reason why, in this case, that is for you to find out.'

'So who's free right now?' said Bonati, wanting to move the meeting on before it descended into an elemental lesson in science. 'Who's not working on an assignment currently?'

A large number of hands shot into the air, some from agents who were already consumed with less enjoyable cases. Bex's hand went straight up and she nudged Jud who was sitting still next to her.

'Come on,' she whispered. 'You need this.'

'Thank you,' said Bonati. 'I will need plenty of agents on this. But it should be led by some experienced hands.' He glanced over at Jud and Bex. The professor knew that since the tragic death of Luc, Jud had become reclusive and desperately needed shaking out of it. This was the opportunity Bonati had been waiting for to snap him out of his depression and kick start him into action. The fact that Jud had not even raised his hand to volunteer was evidence that he needed to be pushed. He would normally have been the first to sign up for a new assignment.

'Jud and Bex, I'd like you to lead this one. Grace, you can go with them. And . . .' he paused for a moment, mindful that the agents in the room were half-expecting him to say Luc's name, like he always did when Grace was assigned to a case. He had been her partner, after all.

'And Raheed. You too. I'd like you to partner Grace on this one. It'll be good experience.'

Grace looked across at Bex and rolled her eyes. This was the last thing they needed – a new recruit on the team. Having to train him up and answer all those pointless questions you often got from the newbies – the zombies – Grace wasn't looking forward to that. But she'd known, of course, that soon she would be paired up again. She couldn't work alone forever, it wasn't CRYPT policy. But Raheed?

He'd practically only just arrived. Was unproven. In fact few agents really knew him; he had kept himself to himself since arriving at the CRYPT. Some said he was 'super bright' and that he'd come from some college up in Manchester, where he'd been specially recruited for his talent for all things technological. Dr Vorzek often mentioned Raheed and how he would bring a lot of knowledge to the table. Knowledge maybe, experience no, thought Grace. But anything was better than being stuck at headquarters, working on research assignments. And though quiet, there was nothing offensive or arrogant about this new guy. He'd seemed perfectly polite whenever she'd met him in the dining room or the living quarters. Tall, handsome and athletic, he spoke in a soft voice, on the rare occasions he spoke, that is.

Raheed was seated across the briefing room and he looked over eagerly to see if Grace was looking in his direction. She wasn't. This was the opportunity he'd been waiting for – the chance to prove himself, both to the powers that be and to the other agents too. He could do it. And working with Jud, too. He knew, just like all the other zombies, that there were some agents whose reputations preceded them. Despite being known for his unsociable manner and his temper, which you didn't ever want to provoke, Jud Lester was the bravest and toughest man on the team. Nothing fazed him, and his ability to solve cases was legendary. His ESP was more finely tuned than anyone's at the CRYPT, and he was able to feel and sense things long before they registered on anyone else's inner radar. Raheed felt thrilled at the prospect of working with him.

Grace rolled her eyes at Bex. So it was Raheed then. Another quiet guy, impossible to read. They both knew it would be them who'd be doing the talking, as usual.

CHAPTER 8

FRIDAY, 4.09 P.M.

CRYPT HEADQUARTERS, LONDON

Jason Goode swivelled his black leather chair around in Bonati's direction, still clutching the *Financial Times*.

'Have you read this, Prof? About the bankers?'

The professor nodded solemnly. 'I know. I tell you, it's weird. I thought we'd left the age of rogue traders and corrupt bankers behind us. I thought there was more regulation these days.'

'There is. Maybe that's why so many are being caught. But in such numbers, Giles. It says here that there have been seven cases of serious illegal trading discovered in the last week alone. Can you believe it? Seven! In each case the banker involved has been told to clear his desk and leave. Some of them have even been arrested. And it's not just one bank, it's happening across the City. What's going on, Giles?'

'It's all part of the cleanup operation which the Government keep promising, I guess. They've got to be seen to be cracking down on these bankers who everybody loves to hate. I've always wondered why the hell they get such a rough ride, Jay. After all, they can't operate alone. They need lenders or investors. The money has to come from somewhere. And their clients aren't stupid, they can think for themselves. It's about people like you and me, borrowing too much or investing too much or falling for these get-rich-quick deals. You can't blame a banker for trying to sell his wares. It's the consumer's fault for being too greedy too, isn't it?'

Goode was bored with this. As a global entrepreneur he'd spent more time with bankers than most people and he rarely trusted them. Just like lawyers. He had little time for any of them. He admired his friend's trust in such people, but it was in Giles's nature to believe most people had good intentions; Jason would always find it amusing when the professor then felt disappointment when someone turned out to have their own agenda.

'Don't fall for that one, Giles,' he said. 'And anyway, these cases here have nothing to do with the consumer. They're saying the rogue traders have been doing dodgy deals on the inside and have cost their banks – and their clients – millions of pounds. The quantities they're saying here are mind-boggling. They just don't seem to understand how much money they're playing around with. I hope they end up behind bars.

'You watch, it'll be no time before the BBC are headlining with "Banking Crisis" again,' he continued his rant. 'It'll be on the news tonight, and tomorrow, and every God damn day for the next three months. Mark my words. I tell you, Giles, I'm tempted to keep my money under the mattress from now on.'

'You'd need a pretty big mattress, Jay.'

Goode grinned. 'Yeah, I guess I would, wouldn't I. So what's happenin' in the paranormal world, huh? I've been in the States for too long. What have I missed, my friend? Anything exciting?'

'Well, there is a curious case that's just come in,' said Bonati. He filled Jason in on the news from DCI Khan.

'MI6 confirmed we're on the case, yeah?' said Goode. 'You've got the green light?'

Bonati nodded.

'Who've we got workin' on it?'

'The best.'

'J?'

'Yes, with Bex. And I've assigned Grace and that youngster, Raheed Sarin.'

'It sounds like a big case for a new recruit to be working on.'

'No, he's a good lad, don't worry. Very bright. Something tells me this is going to be a complex investigation and we need the best brains we've got, Jason.'

CHAPTER 9

FRIDAY, 7.48 P.M.

COUNTING HOUSE, CORNHILL, LONDON

'This ain't no ordinary Friday night, it's mad,' shouted Clint to his colleague, as he pushed his way back to the bar, bringing yet more empty glasses for washing. Every Friday night was busy at the Counting House, but the place was especially packed that evening. Clint had never seen so many bodies crammed into one place – the bar area resembled the tube trains which the same bodies pushed their way onto every morning. There was no need for music at the Counting House. No point. The room was a hub of excited conversation and laughter. Or it usually was. Though the pub was the busiest Clint had ever seen it, there was a different air that night. Gone was the usual boastful laughter and banter. Instead, the customers, in suits and rain-coats, were all huddled together in conspiratorial packs, talking nervously about who would be next to go. News of the sackings, and even arrests in some cases, of fellow bankers had shot right round the financial district. Drinks were being ordered at an unusual rate, and Clint and his two colleagues were struggling to keep pace with the orders. The queue at the bar itself was three rows deep with thirsty customers, all waving twenty-pound notes in the direction of the poor bar assistants.

'Forget the glasses, Clint!' shouted Jane. 'Just keep serving.'

'With what?' said Clint. 'If I don't collect the empties and wash 'em they'll be drinking from the taps. I've never seen it like this before.'

'I wouldn't mind if we were on commission,' said Jane. 'Pass me another two wine glasses, please. If you can find any.'

Across the crowded room, an older gent, dressed in the usual Savile Row suit and dark raincoat, had managed to procure a small round table to himself and was taking his time over his pint of dark stout. His face was obscured by the large broadsheet newspaper he was reading. Only his wispy grey hair was visible above the paper. Clearly he liked to keep himself to himself, which wasn't unusual.

Clint served a few more impatient customers, washed some glasses and then fought his way back through the bar again to collect more empties. He moved towards the man sitting behind the newspaper and his eyes flicked across the front page.

Odd, Clint thought. Must be a commemorative issue. He didn't read the *Financial Times*, though he'd seen enough copies of it lying around to know what its front page usually looked like. But this was different. It was darker, more brown than the usual pale pink. There were no pictures, no colour and no giant, attention-grabbing headlines. Just a large page of tiny articles with small headings, all squashed in together. Clint leant in closer and saw the date: February 11, 1876.

'Hey, where did you find that, mate? It's ancient!' Clint said to the man behind the paper.

No response.

'Please yourself, whatever,' Clint muttered under his breath as he shrugged and then moved on to collect three pint glasses and a tumbler from the neighbouring table, squeezing between the customers huddled around it.

He fought his way back to the bar, where Jane was still fending off too many impatient customers. 'Come on!' she said. 'Give me a hand here.'

Clint jumped behind the counter and began pouring a pint of ale for the first person he saw. 'See that guy in the corner?' he shouted across to Jane at the other end of the bar.

'What? Oh yeah. What about him?'

'Look at his newspaper.'

Jane stood on tiptoes and looked over the heads of the people waiting for drinks. 'What about it?'

'Don't you think it looks odd? It's dated 1876!'

'So? He's probably just some history buff who likes reading old issues. Lots of people do that. What did he say?'

'He didn't say anything when I asked him. Nothing.'

'Probably deaf.' Jane turned to a waiting customer. 'That'll be seven eighty, please. Thanks.'

Over in the corner, at the table Clint had just cleared of glasses, a group of young bankers were enjoying a welcome rest from the stresses and strains of the day, listening to another tale from Jonnie, the joker in the pack. He always managed to cheer others up with his sharp wit. He reached the punchline of his story and Karin, seated opposite him, rocked back in her chair with laughter. But as she did so her chair fell further than she was expecting. It landed on the lap of the old man just a few inches away. The old man with the newspaper.

As the paper crumpled behind her head, Karin raised her eyes to the man's face and was about to apologise when she screamed.

Her shrill cry pierced right through the conversations across the pub and brought a sudden silence. Everyone looked in her direction.

The figure whom Karin had so rudely disturbed was dead. And by the looks of the rotting flesh that hung from its face, dead for a long time. The man's eyes were lifeless but they seemed out of proportion to the thin, angular face that surrounded them. Remnants of skin clung to its jaw bones and cheeks, like an old carcass or a joint of meat at a carvery. Its mouth was open wide, revealing black and brown teeth and releasing a foul odour that made Karin gag.

The figure was dressed in a suit, not unlike the ones worn by the people around it, but its neck was so scrawny and bony the white collar seemed oversized around it. The grey wispy hair on its head was combed in a strict side parting, but through it you could see a scabby scalp covered in lesions.

'Agh!' Karin cried again. 'Get me off, get me off!'

The guys at her table shook themselves out of their silent shock and leapt to her aid. They pulled her off, but as they did so the figure's hands dropped the paper and fell like a guillotine onto Karin's neck. They locked into position and Karin couldn't move. She was choking, making pitiful squeaks and throat rasps as she tried valiantly to fight with the ghost's arms.

A bulky, athletic-looking young man in an immaculate blue suit launched himself at the ghost, raining down his large fists on the figure's bony body, breaking it up like brittle twigs. Quickly its arms and hands released Karin and she slipped to the floor, where she was comforted by her friends.

Up on the seat, others had joined the first guy and they too were smashing the ghost into pieces. It was brutal to watch – surreal – as the old man's body broke and fell apart like a piece of unwanted sculpture, wrecked by its sculptor. Some people were screaming and making for the doors, intent on getting the hell out of there, while others were watching in morbid fascination as the first ghost they'd ever seen was broken up.

What little energy this ghost had managed to harness had dried up within seconds and they were now battling with a corpse, but one as brittle as the dead branches of a fallen tree. It gave no resistance. Its head plopped onto its now limbless chest and its assailants pushed it further to the floor, where they continued to kick and stab at it like frenzied dogs.

Anyone passing the window might have thought they were watching the brutal, merciless killing of an old-age pensioner. Until they saw his skeletal face.

It took Clint another hour to calm everyone down, rid the place of the smell of rotting flesh, and wait for the police to arrive on the scene to restore confidence and order.

His prediction was right – this was no ordinary Friday night.

CHAPTER 10

FRIDAY, 10.21 P.M.
(11.21 P.M. LOCAL TIME)
ALLÉE CHÊNE POINTU, CLICHY-
SOUS-BOIS, PARIS

The man lay in his filthy bed, staring at an old, battered photo album and blowing smoke rings up at the ceiling, already brown with tobacco stains. He took another long drag, so deep it brought on another coughing fit that made his body convulse and heave. He stabbed out the cigarette in a crowded ashtray beside his bed, cursing under his breath. He knew his health was deteriorating fast, but he also knew how powerful a driving force his revenge had been all these years. There was no way he was going to quit yet. Not just when it was getting exciting. There was still life in him. The dregs, admittedly, but it was enough. He wiped the phlegm from the photo album – lucky the old photographs were covered with a cellophane layer or they'd have been ruined by now, so frequent was his coughing and spluttering. Everything around him seemed to be covered in a greasy layer.

He lay back on the pillow and held the album up to his tired eyes.

There he was, in the centre, looking cool, flanked by two friends. Those were the good old days. How times had changed. How their individual fortunes had differed. They were successful, rich and full of their own importance; he was poor, lonely and bitter with resentment.

But soon he would have the last laugh. Soon all his years of research and planning would bring the result he most desired. He didn't need wealth and all its trappings; his prize was simpler, purer.

Revenge.

The spires on the ornate buildings in the background of the photo rose to the sky with the same lofty arrogance that appeared on the faces beside him. Though he'd been happy at times, he'd always known he hadn't belonged there. With people like that.

He turned from the image of dreaming spires and neatly clipped lawns to the shabby apartment around him. How could he possibly have known back then what course his life would take?

For a brief moment he stepped outside his world and saw himself, his existence.

It was no life, not as ordinary people would have it, anyway – the kind of people in the photo, who needed to surround themselves with possessions and cars and homes and relationships and achievements in order to prove they were truly alive. His couldn't be described as a life by their standards. They would call him freak. Loser. While they surrounded themselves with 'things', he had nothing.

But he believed, deep down, that he had everything and it was their lives which were empty. There was no limit to his life, no boundaries, because he didn't live by the same rules as the scum in the photograph. He didn't live in the same world as they did, bound up by their own ambition and wealth and greed; their own weak, narrow-minded views of reality. They called themselves scientists! But they were no more enlightened than the grass they were standing on. They were as blind as everyone else. They were the ones who needed freeing, not him. Worshipping the usual demons of a material world, they needed to be shown the error of their ways. He despised what they stood for, the paths their own lives had taken, compared with his. How their pretend knowledge of science and the way the world worked had brought them riches. But he was pure; they were soiled. Though he was surrounded in garbage, it was them who were up to their necks in shit.

He closed the photo album and placed it carefully under his bed, hearing empty crisp bags and old cigarette packets crumple beneath it. He turned and dragged himself out of bed. The movement brought on another coughing fit and he held onto the bed frame to prevent himself from falling. He waited for the coughing to subside, took a careful, deep breath and stood upright again. There was a pounding in his temples – the result of staring at a computer screen whilst consuming copious quantities of vodka and precious little else for most of the day.

He moved to the window, pulled back the curtains and, like a caged animal, stared blankly at the world.

Patience. Soon things would change.

CHAPTER 11

FRIDAY, 11.45 P.M.

FARRINGDON, LONDON

Lack of sleep was catching up with Jud and he knew it. Out here, on the streets, he was disorientated and his body felt heavy. But there was no time to rest, not now. As soon as the agents had been given the assignment in the briefing room that afternoon, Bonati had ordered them to research the locations, compile a route map and get pounding the streets to take readings at the sites of the dragon statues. They'd carried so much equipment around the locations, and still hadn't taken a break. It was the same in each place: the EMF meters and Geiger counters had registered high levels of radiation. How the stone statues could absorb this kind of energy was still beyond them, but if the eyewitness accounts were to be believed, these dragons had developed the capacity to wreak havoc. And fear spreads quickly in London.

When the agents suggested to the police that they remove the statues and place them in storage at CRYPT HQ, the answer was always the same – there were orders from above that they should remain. Removing the statues completely would only make the fear and panic worse – it was like confirming that it wasn't safe to walk past a statue. And where would that end? Would all statues have to be removed? DCI Khan had already delivered an impassioned plea to the public at a press conference that afternoon, saying that there was no reason for alarm. The eye-witnesses had been encouraged to keep silent, in the usual way on these investigations, to prevent panic, but some had been greedy and had already called the *Evening Standard*. That night's edition was running with the story on its front page.

Now, here the agents were, instruments at the ready, with the rain lashing down, watching and waiting for a stone statue to move.

'It's like going to the zoo,' said Raheed.

'What?' Jud said, looking unimpressed.

'I mean, when you go to see the lions or tigers they hardly perform, do they? They usually just sleep. And you spend hours with your face pressed up at the glass or the cage, waiting for them to bat an eyelid or yawn.'

'There's a slight difference here,' said Bex. 'You'd be more surprised if this thing opened its mouth, wouldn't you?'

'Yeah, but it hasn't, has it,' said Raheed. 'That's just the point.'

'Patience, zombie,' said Grace. 'You haven't been on many assignments, have you? You don't realise how most of our work involves sitting and waiting, and staring at an EMF needle to see if it fluctuates. You think it's all action and fighting and zapping ghosts.'

'No I don't.'

'Yeah, sure you do,' said Bex. 'It's what we all think when we join the CRYPT. It's why we call you zombies, after all. You go around in a daze, thinking it's all so wonderful and exciting. And then you realise.'

Grace was nodding in agreement. 'You realise that it's about hard work and standing around waiting for something to happen. But when it does it'll happen so quickly, and you have to be ready, before it's all over again and you go back to waiting.'

'Alright,' said Jud. 'Knock it off, will you? You're beginning to sound like Bonati.'

They knew exactly what he meant. The professor was famous for his speeches to zombies and skulls alike. No one was spared his lectures when he was in the mood for some straight talking to toughen them up and make them realise they were there to work hard. His favourite analogy was to say it was like fighting in the trenches in the Great War. New recruits thought they were going off to fight for king and country, he'd often say. They thought it was going to be full-on attack, attack, lots of brave battles and coming home in a blaze of glory. But they didn't appreciate two truths. There were the long, agonising periods of silence, just waiting; minutes, hours, days would drag by with nothing, *nothing* to do but sit and wonder whether the next minute would be their last and a giant shell would hit their little stretch of trench. And then there was the fighting itself, as brutal as it was sudden, no time for thinking how brave they were being or how their country would be proud of them, or how they would tell their grandchildren of their experience. Just total, blind fear.

That, as the professor would say, was *real* bravery. Real sacrifice. And though no one really believed that life at the CRYPT could ever be as desperate as life in the trenches of Normandy, Bonati's speeches did their job. The agents knew then that they needed courage and they needed patience. They were there to place themselves between the public and the perils that haunted them. Even if they were stone dragons that harnessed a source of electromagnetic energy and came to life.

There was a cold breath of fear and panic sweeping through the streets of Central London and you didn't have to be an agent with extrasensory perception to sense it. The cones and police tape around the dragon statues on bridges, streets and buildings across the financial district had not exactly helped.

The journey to Farringdon, and to the other sites in the city,

59

had been eerie. Fewer people were on the streets tonight. There were the hardened, Friday-night drinkers, of course, high on the usual Dutch courage that came from too many beers, but the streets were emptying faster than usual. Most people had read the *Evening Standard* and hurried home after work instead of remaining for that usual drink or two.

Jud looked around the quiet street. 'Look, let's pack up. Nothing's going to happen here tonight, and we've still got another seven sites to visit before the morning.'

He gazed miserably at the silver-coloured dragon on the plinth in front of them. It was reaching up on its hind legs, its front right paw in the air and its left resting on the top of a large shield, across which was emblazoned the flag of St George, just like the one on Blackfriars Bridge. Its mouth was open and an unfeasibly large, red tongue licked its giant fang-like teeth.

'I hate to agree with a zombie, but maybe we should press on. We've taken the readings and I don't think we'll see any action from this guy tonight.'

'If it is like the zoo,' said Bex, 'he won't start dancing until we turn our backs anyway. Let's go.'

Grace was reluctant to move. 'There's something in the air. Can't you feel it?'

'Yeah, it's called rain,' said Jud. 'I can feel it alright. I've been feeling it for the last hour. Come on.' He started packing up the instruments and disconnecting them from the two laptops they had set up under the makeshift shelter they'd created in the middle of a large intersection along Farringdon Road. It was impossible to hide. Those people that were out seemed to have taken refuge in cars and taxis, which passed them in a steady stream.

'No, wait,' said Grace. 'Just stay still and feel it.'

The agents didn't move, although Raheed couldn't stop fidgeting and glancing around the street.

'Wait!' Grace repeated. 'Just sense it.'

The rain continued to lash down and the late-night taxis were spraying great arcs of water as they sped past roadside puddles, their drunken customers' faces pressed up against the rainy windows for a good stare as they went by. The police officer on the street kept moving everyone past. No one was allowed to loiter.

It was wet, it was noisy from car engines and the wind was beginning to pick up, but Grace was right. There was something in the air and the agents were beginning to sense it.

'There is something, isn't there?' said Bex. 'Like a . . . a threat. It feels ominous.'

'There's a storm coming. That's all,' said Raheed. 'It's that moment before the pressure explodes. Nothing else.'

'No, you're wrong,' said Jud. He'd detected something too. 'It's not the air pressure. This is on a different level.'

'This is going to sound stupid,' said Grace, 'but you remember at school when you're taught about life on the home front in the Blitz. How some people could sense when the planes were coming, even before the sirens went off and you could hear the engines.'

'Yeah, I know. That's it. It feels like there's an attack coming.'

The agents fell silent and stared up at the sky, expectantly. The rain had lessened now and there was an eerie calm in the air. None of them would have been surprised if they'd heard the low hum of bomber planes in the distance. But there was nothing. The police officer a few metres down the road continued his slow patrol, up and down, oblivious to any atmosphere.

'These dragons are protecting us,' said Grace.

'Protecting us?' said Raheed. 'You wouldn't say that if you were one of the victims, or one of the people who saw the attacks happen.'

'I know it sounds weird,' said Grace, 'but whatever is threatening us, I can't help thinking this dragon knows about it. Look at its eyes.'

They stared, closer than before. The expression on the dragon's face had altered, they were certain. It was like a dog when it senses trouble. It seemed more alert somehow. As if it was sniffing the air for danger.

Jud quickly set up the EMF meter and Geiger counter once again. The needles soared to even higher levels of radiation.

'There's something happening on the other side,' said Bex.

'You mean in the spiritual world?' said Raheed.

'Yes. There's activity, for sure. Grace, you stay here with Raheed and Jud and I'll take the other set of instruments on to the next location. Okay?'

'Great,' said Grace, sarcastically. She wanted to stay with Bex, rather than be stuck with the zombie, but she couldn't deny the statue was emitting serious radiation and there was a likelihood they'd miss something if they all left now.

She watched Jud and Bex pack up the instruments and head off in the direction of Holborn, where the next dragons stood waiting for them. Bex was glad of another opportunity to be alone with Jud, even if it was at the end of a very busy evening of traipsing around London. But there were more sites still to check out.

'So do we just sit here and wait again?' said Raheed, unimpressed.

'Guess so.'

They saw a police car pitch up and drop off a second police officer, who'd come to relieve the first. Lucky guy, thought Raheed, envious of the officer who'd now return home to his warm bed, no doubt.

Grace climbed onto the ledge of the plinth and stretched up for a closer look at the dragon statue, watching its eyes. She studied its sharp fangs and long, rolling red tongue that lashed around its teeth.

And then she saw something. There was a tiny, almost imperceptible trickle of steam emitting from the dragon's flared nostrils. Was it her own breath bouncing off the cold stone? She watched it closely. No, there was definitely some smoky substance coming *from* the dragon. Like it was exhaling.

She turned to Raheed, who was standing a few metres away, talking to the new police officer. 'Hey, come and look at this!'

She turned to face the dragon again and screamed, a deafening squeal that ricocheted off the solid concrete and steel buildings all around her.

The dragon moved its right claw and jabbed it straight into Grace's face. Its jaw bone cracked and moved, it emitted breath from its nostrils and mouth. Its red tongue sprang to life, licking its lips. Grace fell to the floor, holding her left eye.

'Ow! God, help me. It caught me in the face.'

Raheed rushed to her aid, only to watch the dragon become even more animated and thrust its metal shield to the floor, narrowly missing Grace who was still clutching her face. She couldn't open her eyes from the searing pain that ran right through her eyeball and down her cheek. Blood was starting to pour through her fingers.

The dragon went for Grace again. Raheed dived over her, covering her body with his. He winced in pain as he felt vicious scratches at his back. The dragon was piercing his flesh. The police officer stood a few feet away, mouth open, eyes wide. What the hell could he do? He stood frozen to the spot.

Raheed managed to break free and quickly picked up the metal tripod used for the video camera which they'd not yet set up. He smashed it into the dragon's body, waving it frantically at the beast. It was no match for the dragon's stone frame. It buckled and bent in Raheed's hand. He took cover again, arching his body over Grace. There was no point in trying to grab her and run; the dragon would be far quicker. He closed his eyes and braced himself for yet more puncture wounds to his back, or worse, but suddenly there was an almighty thud and shattering of glass. A passing driver had slammed his brakes on at the horrific sight unfolding in front of him and another car had piled straight into the back of his. Luckily the unexpected sound startled the dragon and it took off. The police officer and the passing drivers, who were staring out of their cars, windows firmly shut, watched it soar into the sky and then dip again, further down Farringdon Road.

Raheed rose to his feet just in time to see the dragon disappear in the distance. God knows where it was heading, but he pitied anyone who was in its path.

'Did that just happen?' said the police officer. 'For real?'

'I know. Man, that was seriously close,' said Raheed, and then he saw Grace, still on the floor, clutching her face.

'Oh, Christ. You okay, Grace?'

'Help me. Ow, my eye! Please. It must've been a claw. Oh, God. It's hurting.'

'Let me see,' said Raheed, trying to pull her hand away. He needed to examine the injury, and quickly. She wouldn't let him take her hand at first, but eventually he saw what the dragon had done to her. On seeing the state of her face, blood pouring from her left eye socket and from the giant gash in her left cheek, he opened his eyes wide and Grace caught his reaction, squinting through her other eye.

'Don't tell me,' she cried. 'Ow, God! It's hurting. Don't tell me what it looks like, just . . . just get me to hospital.' Her voice was choked. 'Now, Raheed!'

The police officer radioed for immediate help.

'It's okay,' said Raheed, sitting next to her on the pavement. 'Don't move. It'll be alright. Help is on its way. Don't try to open it.'

'I can't, Raheed. It's swollen so much, I can't.'

She was right. Raheed could see her left eye resembled that of a boxer after twelve rounds. He quickly grabbed a handkerchief from his coat pocket and gave it to Grace. She pushed it to her cheek to stop the blood pouring from the wound.

Moments later they heard a siren wailing and a police car sped to where they were standing. Raheed quickly packed up the instruments while Grace was helped into the back of the car.

Seconds later, with the bags of equipment hurled into the boot, Raheed, Grace and the officer sped through the traffic en route to St Bart's Hospital, the closest one to them. As Grace daubed her ripped face with the blood-soaked handkerchief and gritted her teeth, Raheed glanced back in the direction of the intersection on Farringdon Road and saw the stone plinth, now missing its dragon.

CHAPTER 12

SATURDAY, 7.08 A.M.

CRYPT HEADQUARTERS, LONDON

Professor Bonati glanced up at the electronic screen set into the wall of his spacious study. The familiar map of London was lit up with tiny red lights at various locations dotted across the city's financial district. Each one indicated where an incident had occurred in the latest investigation.

DCI Khan was sitting across the room from Bonati, slurping his coffee loudly. Jud, Bex and Raheed were sat in a row on one of two large, leather sofas in the room. They looked shattered, having been up for most of the night. Jud and Bex had gone off to check another two dragon sites after they'd left the others and were horrified when Raheed had called from the hospital to explain what had happened.

Grace was now in surgery, as doctors fought to save her left eye and patch up her cheek. Raheed had said they couldn't tell whether she would see out of it again or not, but what was certain was that she would be left with some pretty ugly scars as a result of the attack.

This changed the game and the agents could see the anxiety

in Bonati's face. He felt responsible whenever agents sustained an injury, as they sometimes did. It was he who had had to telephone Grace's parents in the night. And it was he who, once the meeting was over, would have to meet them at the hospital and do some explaining.

'I don't need to tell you how serious this is becoming,' he said, gravely. 'We have dragons on the loose in the city and fear is spreading like wildfire.'

'Tell me about it,' said Khan. 'You should see our switchboard. We've had dozens of calls overnight. They're running amok, Professor. What the hell are you doing about it?'

'Don't start,' Bonati said calmly. 'We need a clear head and we need to work together on this. Now is not the time to start pushing responsibilities around. We're all responsible, Khan. If you've got nothing to add, I suggest you leave us in peace.'

Khan looked unaffected by the professor's patronising tone. Years on the force had toughened his sensibilities – very little rattled him now, least of all Bonati. He was fed up with having to work with CRYPT, truth be told. It had been some time now since the Tyburn case – the moment when his judgement had lapsed somewhat and Bonati had found him to be involved with Lucien Zakis. It was a time in his career he'd like to forget, but his new-found association with CRYPT would prevent that from ever happening.

Lucien Zakis, owner of the famous Zakis Hotels chain, had persuaded Khan to turn a blind eye and bend the rules too many times, in order to get his hotel built right in the heart of London. It had backfired spectacularly when the very site he'd chosen to build on, near Marble Arch, had turned out to be the place where thousands of prisoners had lost their lives, hanged on the infamous Tyburn Tree that had once stood there. CRYPT had been called to save the public from the armies of highwaymen whose souls Zakis and Khan had disturbed. Then Khan had been given a choice: face a stretch in prison for his part in the plan, or work with CRYPT.

Ever since then he'd resented the fact that the professor could call on him at any time. But that was the deal, and he knew it: remain in your job and assist the CRYPT when called on, or join Zakis behind bars.

But once the professor discovered the exact reason for his visit that morning, Khan knew he'd start to pay him a little more respect. The message he was bringing had consequences for everyone in the building.

'I will leave you in peace, Professor, don't worry, once I've told you the reason for my being here.'

'What? I thought you were just coming to see what we'd done overnight? Your usual impatience, Inspector, wanting to know what was happening?'

The CRYPT agents suddenly felt uncomfortable, or at least Raheed and Bex did. Jud was grateful for his ringside seat if something was going to kick off. He liked Khan about as much as the inspector liked him, and if the professor was about to give the DCI both barrels then he wanted to see it happen.

DCI Khan paused for a moment, looking around the room at the agents. 'Can I have a word in private, Professor?'

Bonati was defiant. 'Anything you say to me you can say to the agents here. I trust them implicitly. What is the problem, Inspector?'

'I'm sorry, Professor, I'd prefer to speak to you without agents around. And with Mr Goode please. Is he available?'

Bonati couldn't hide his frustration. He knew he had to wrap this meeting up soon, so that he could get over to St Bart's Hospital and so his agents could get on with solving this investigation before anyone else was injured, or worse. The last thing he needed was DCI Khan holding things up.

But he'd got to know Khan well by now, and he knew that he wouldn't ask for such privacy if he didn't have something confidential, perhaps even damaging, to say. He trusted him that much.

Without answering, Bonati walked to his desk and picked up the phone. He whispered to Khan with his hand over the handset, 'He may not even be out of bed yet, you realise.'

Jud smiled wryly. He knew his father was as attached to his bed as Jud was to his. But at least his father had the excuse of jet lag whenever he was back in town. He had just flown in from the States the day before. Goode was rarely in one place long enough to acclimatise to its time zone.

'Hello, Jason?' said Bonati. 'It's Giles. Are you up?'

'Am I up?' snapped Jason. 'I didn't get to sleep until three a.m., God dammit. I'm still on US time – five hours behind you guys. What the hell do you want?'

Bonati decided not to start teasing him about being in bed with so many others listening in. He needn't have worried; Goode's words were heard by everyone as he shouted down the phone line.

'Er, well, DCI Khan is here and he'd like a word.'

'Well talk to him then, Giles. He doesn't need me there.'

Bonati looked across at Khan who was mouthing, 'I do.'

'I'm afraid he does need to see you. He's asking to see us both together, Jason. Says it's important.'

'Okay, okay. Come up in five. Give me chance to get my pants on. Sorry, you call 'em trousers, don't you. I'll make some coffee. Don't ask me to think until I've had an espresso.'

Bonati put the receiver down despondently; he hated being summoned up to Goode's penthouse. Not because he didn't enjoy seeing him – they'd been friends since student days – but because of his intolerable vertigo. Goode's penthouse was on the thirty-eighth floor of Goode Tower, and had giant glass walls that ran right the way round the apartment. It was the perfect nightmare for someone like Bonati, and he knew just how much Goode liked to tease him for it. Given the fact that Bonati had just woken him up too, doubtless Goode would be in vindictive mood.

He downed his coffee and took a deep breath, turned to the agents. 'I'm afraid I'm going to have to adjourn this meeting for a while. Raheed, contact Dr Vorzek please and go with her to see Grace at St Bart's. Jud, Bex, you can stay in here and use the screen and equipment or go down to the labs. Just work out why the hell the city is being plagued by dragons. I'd like an answer by the time I'm back. Meeting adjourned.'

He swept out of the room followed by DCI Khan.

Bex stood up and moved closer to the giant screen with the red lights flashing across it. 'You heard the prof. We're supposed to crack this.'

Jud wasn't listening. He was worried. It was unlike Khan to be so secretive these days. They'd worked hard to build a trust between them after the rocky start on the Tyburn case, and Jud knew something was seriously wrong for him to be left out of the conversation now. Why couldn't he say what he had to say in front of the agents?

And then it hit him like he'd been punched in the solar plexus. Of course. Why was he being so stupid? There was only one reason why Khan would request a private audience with Bonati and his father. It was about *him*. He was in trouble again.

For the first time in a while, Jud felt an acute reminder that he was living a lie. Was his past coming back to haunt him again?

CHAPTER 13

SATURDAY, 7.15 A.M.

PENTHOUSE SUITE, GOODE

TOWER, LONDON

Jason Goode scratched his head, causing his short, grey hair to be even more ruffled than it was before. He looked far too fashionable for a man his age, thought Bonati. But then he would. The professor had known Jason since they were at Cambridge together, and ever since those student days Jason had been the fashionable one, while Bonati had always resembled a lawyer or surgeon, albeit a handsome one. Where Bonati was well-kempt and elegant, with his perfectly fitting suits, expensive specs and silk shirts, Jason wore T-shirts, jeans and creased linen jackets. His fashionable bed-hair suited his style, and his closely cropped grey stubble looked better on him than it would have done on anyone else his age, including Bonati. On the rare occasions the professor had not shaved, he'd resembled a tramp.

But the relationship between the two had never faltered, despite all the things they'd been through, or perhaps because of them. The two men enjoyed a friendship stronger than most. The best.

But, boy, could Jason be frustrating. He was erratic,

unpredictable, prone to obsession and generally unreliable. But, as Bonati knew, that's what you got with a creative genius. You don't build an empire the size of Goode Technology PLC without being a little mercurial at times.

And today was clearly no exception. He was obviously disgruntled at being woken so early and was not about to engage in any polite conversation until he'd had his first espresso, at least. He shuffled around the open-plan kitchen, with its black granite work-tops and steel fittings, fishing for a clean cup. He found one, rinsed it under the tap and promptly dropped it. The hard marble floor did its job of shattering the Harrods china into a dozen pieces.

'May I assist?' Bonati said coolly from the other side of the giant room.

'No! I can manage,' said Jason. Then, after searching in cupboards for more clean cups and finding none, he changed his mind. 'Go on then. I can't find a damn thing in this place. You'd think I didn't employ cleaners.'

'You don't,' said Bonati, rolling his eyes at Khan. 'You said you didn't need them because you're never here.'

'Okay, whatever.'

Bonati found the cups without hesitation and turned to offer their guest a drink.

'Cappuccino, thanks,' said Khan.

A few minutes later the three men were seated around an unnecessarily large glass-topped dining table.

'What's on your mind, Inspector?' said Jason. 'Shoot.'

Khan took a few seconds to begin. He'd rehearsed this speech in the car on the way over, but had clean forgotten his opening line. How on earth was he going to broach this delicate subject?

'Mr Goode, you will have been following the banking situation these last few days, I assume?'

'Followed it? It's impossible to escape it, Khan. The newspapers and the TV are full of it. More greedy bankers out to make a secret dollar again, huh?' He gulped down his espresso. 'Sorry, I suppose I should say pound sterling.'

'We had assumed you were here to talk about the investigation, Inspector,' interrupted Bonati. He was already impatient to return to the CRYPT and did not want to spend any longer at the top of this skyscraper than was absolutely necessary.

'No. It's true I'd like to hear your thoughts on the case so far, Professor, but that's not the reason for this particular visit. Our friends at the FCA have—'

'Come again?' said Goode. 'The what?'

'The Financial Conduct Authority. It used to be called the FSA, Financial Services Authority.'

'Oh, the FSA. You mean the guys who keep tabs on the bankers in this place? The ones who stop the dodgy deals – or don't in this case. Like the Securities and Exchange Commission back home?'

'Yes, exactly,' said DCI Khan. 'Those "guys" as you put it. In fact Scotland Yard is talking to the SEC in the US too.'

'Okay, so how does this involve us?' said Bonati. 'How can we help, Inspector?'

'Well, it's a strange thing,' Khan continued. 'I mean, I don't really know how to say it.'

'Oh, get a move on will you, Inspector,' said Goode, with his usual impatience. 'Say what you've come to say and then we can all get on with our day. I'm starving.' He got up and moved towards the kitchen to begin exploring the possibility of there being any food left in the place since his last visit.

'I think you might want to sit down,' said Khan calmly.

Goode turned and looked at him, his usual carefree arrogance fading. He sat down at the table again and said, 'Go on, I'm listening.'

'Well, you see, we've been told that there have been a large number of bankers in several different banks across London who have been making illegal trades. They have risked huge sums of money and have cost their employers hundreds of thousands. And it doesn't end in London, I'm afraid. We are reliably informed that similar frauds are being unearthed in New York and Paris too.'

'Okay, well, that's very serious, Inspector. But again, I still don't understand what this could possibly have to do with CRYPT,' said Bonati.

'Oh, it's not CRYPT I've come about,' said Khan. 'It's Goode Technology PLC.'

Jason sat up in his chair and stared straight at Khan. Now the inspector had his full attention. 'My company? Talk to me.'

'Yes, sir.' Khan cleared his throat with another sip of coffee then began. 'You see, representatives from both the FCA and the SEC have confirmed that there is more to this banking crisis than they first thought. Every banker arrested so far has completely denied any knowledge of the dodgy deals discovered. And, as it turns out, they may have been telling the truth.'

'What? I don't understand. I thought the money was all gone. The deals have been made?' said Goode.

'Yes, they have. Senior figures in the banks that we've spoken to in the last couple of days have all confirmed that the illegal trades have gone through. But they have also told us they suspect that their computer systems have been hacked.'

'Hacked?' said Goode, unable to hide his surprise.

'Yes, sir.'

'And don't tell me,' Goode continued, beginning to realise the reason for Khan's visit, 'you need us to advise you on how this might have happened, yeah? You want Goode Technology to help you, is that it? I suppose we are the world's authority on IT right now, but that doesn't mean to say we can know what the hackers have been up to. I mean, there are some weird people out there, Inspector.'

'If I could just finish, Mr Goode. Our officers at the Police e-crime Unit have made a discovery which, I must say, even I was surprised to hear.'

'Go on,' said Bonati.

'Well, they believe they have already traced a number of the hackers involved. It seems this investigation has been going on longer than any of us thought, behind the scenes. There have been illegal trades and dodgy deals going on for several weeks now. And our men think they've traced the perpetrators.'

'And?' said Goode, now feeling uneasy.

'And they believe that they all have one interesting thing in common.'

'Which is?' said the professor.

'Which is they all work for Goode Technology PLC. Your company, Mr Goode.' Khan stared straight at Goode now, watching his reaction closely.

Silence fell on the room for a few seconds while Khan's audience took in the seriousness of what their guest had just said.

'My company? They work for *me*?' said Goode in disbelief.

'Yes, sir. And what's more, we'd like you to come to Scotland Yard with us to help us with our enquiries.'

'You'd *what*? Are you arresting me, Khan?' Goode shot up and walked quickly across the room, trying hard to take this all in.

'No, no, no,' said Khan. 'I mean, well . . . look, it's true there were those at my place who wanted me to march in here with several officers and march you off the premises, believe me. But I wasn't having any of it.'

'Gee, thanks,' said Goode.

'We've gone in heavy-handed in the past and it doesn't work. It's not necessary in this case anyway. I mean, we know each other, don't we.' Khan forced a smile, but it was lost on Goode and Bonati. They were looking at each other incredulously. Trying hard to understand how and why and when these allegations were first dreamt up, and by whom.

Khan misinterpreted their glances as something else. 'Is there something you want to tell me, Jason? If I can call you that? I think we've known each other long enough now for there to be no secrets between us, eh?'

'Now just a moment,' said Bonati, managing to keep his composure. 'I hope you are not suggesting that either I or Mr Goode – and I think he'd prefer that name, Inspector – are in some way involved in this scandal? And that we have something to confess to you?'

Goode raised his eyes to the ceiling. 'For God's sake,' he said, and walked off in the direction of the glass wall that overlooked the great city skyline beneath them.

'Well, do you?' said the inspector, unaffected by Bonati's steely, authoritative tone. He still hadn't received an answer to his question, after all. 'You'd be better off telling me now rather than waiting for some superior officer at the Yard to give you a good grilling in the interview room.'

Goode turned and walked back to the table, more composed. 'Detective Chief Inspector Khan, you can line up as many senior officers as you like to give me a "good grilling", as you call it. I know nothing about this. I am as in the dark as you are and I resent any suggestion whatsoever that either I or Giles here are wrapped up in this somehow. Come on then. Let's go.' He made for the door. 'Well?'

'Jason, wait a moment,' said Bonati. 'Let's just stay—'

'No! I'm damned if I'm gonna listen to this guy's threats to pull me in and interrogate me or whatever his sordid little friends at the Yard want to do. Bring it on, I say. I've nothin' to hide, Giles. And neither have you.'

'Your presence is not required at this time, Professor,' said Khan, rising to his feet to join Goode at the door.

'But . . . I mean, wait a minute,' said Bonati, finding it hard to remain cool. 'You're not going with him, are you, Jason? You're not being arrested for God's sake, you don't have to go anywhere. Stay here and help me find out what the hell's been going on. If Khan wants you he'll have to return with an arrest warrant, surely.'

'You can come with me now, Mr Goode, or you can indeed wait for me to return with—'

'Spare me the speeches, Khan,' said Goode. 'We're not on some crappy TV crime soap. Giles, I wanna know exactly what's been going on and I'm guessing the best way to find out is to ask these guys. They obviously know more than we do on the subject. Khan, let's go.' He opened the door that led out to the lobby. 'You stay here, Giles, and get on the phone to New York, then Paris, and then every goddam office we have from here to Sydney. I wanna know why Khan's friends at the Met seem to think we're involved. I want chapter and verse when I get back.' He left the room, but returned quickly. 'Oh, and yes, I *will* be back!' he said, and slammed the door before following Khan down the corridor to the elevator.

Giles was left alone in the giant penthouse suite. It was rare for him to be lost for words, or to be anything other than in full control, but the last conversation had been one of the strangest he'd ever had and something definitely didn't add up. He gazed out over the city skyline, quite oblivious to the vertigo that usually crippled him when up in the penthouse. He looked at the great skyscrapers of Canary Wharf and pictured the thousands of bankers usually sat in front of screens inside each tower block. What on earth was going on out there? Who was behind this? How was Goode Technology involved? Surely his oldest friend was telling the truth? Wasn't he?

He could sense a strange feeling growing inside his stomach and moving up to his chest, an emotion quite alien to him.

A fear of the unknown.

CHAPTER 14

SATURDAY, 10.40 A.M.

CRYPT HEADQUARTERS, LONDON

'So, let me get this straight,' said Jud, impatiently. 'The people behind this so-called banking crisis are computer hackers and they're all working for Goode Technology. Are you *serious*?'

'That's what is alleged, J. But that doesn't mean it's true. I can assure you it most certainly is not.'

'And what does my father say?'

Bonati quickly flicked an anxious look in Bex's direction. Should Jud be talking so freely about his father with another agent present? Shouldn't he be calling him Mr Goode, like everyone else?

Jud noticed his concern and said, 'Oh, please, Professor. Bex knows everything there is to know about me. You can trust her.'

The professor thought for a moment about this revelation and how reckless Jud had been in confiding in someone. Had he forgotten his history? Had he forgotten how the condition of his release from prison was that he must assume a new identity and become the property of CRYPT? What the hell was he playing at? But he knew there was enough to worry about without adding to his stress by having a stand-up row with Jud. Besides, if she did know everything, what would be the point of pretending any more?

'We shall revisit this matter at another time, Jud. I may need to remind you of the conditions of your early release. But for now I—'

'You don't need to remind me, for God's sake. Don't you think I already—'

'That's enough! Let me finish. I was going to say, but for now there are other matters more pressing, so I'll ignore it. Bex, you can stay and listen. I assume I can have your complete discretion, both on the matter of Jud's real identity and of what we are discussing now?'

'Of course, Professor,' Bex said obediently. She tried to hide her surprise at even being asked such a question.

The professor continued, 'Your father says he had no knowledge of this at all until DCI Khan raised it this morning. He was as surprised as I was.'

'Can I talk to him?' said Jud.

'I don't know just now,' Bonati's eyes showed a flicker of concern, and it did not go unnoticed by the agents.

'What's happened?' said Jud quickly. 'He is upstairs, isn't he? I thought he got back last night. You were just with him, weren't you?'

'He did, and yes I was. But . . .' Bonati hesitated. Should he tell Jud the truth, or should he simply say Goode was out on business for the day? He knew the power of these agents' senses; they could detect a person's emotions within seconds. It was almost impossible to lie to them and get away with it.

'He's gone with Khan to help him with his enquiries.'

'He's been *arrested?*' said Jud, in shock.

'No. Not at all. I think we need to remember the assumption of innocence until proven guilty, Jud. Slow down a minute. Of course he has not been arrested. But he was adamant that he wanted to know more – to know everything that the police know. He's as anxious to discover the truth as you and I are. And besides, he has nothing to hide. So he went willingly with Khan to Scotland Yard to help with their investigation.'

Jud wasn't convinced that this was wise. Why would anyone walk into a police station unless they were forced to? He sensed only bad things would come from this, though he knew he was biased, given his own experience at the hands of what was laughably called 'justice'. He could be forgiven for losing all faith in the legal system after what he'd been through – being wrongfully accused and charged with the murder of his mother. How could he ever believe in the criminal justice system after that?

'But why?' he said. 'Why would anyone volunteer to talk to the police like that?'

'I've told you, J. Your father is innocent and wants to help with their enquiries. That is not some kind of code for saying he's been arrested. Now, can we talk about the investigation please? Can I remind you we have a serious case at the moment and a lot of pressure on us to solve it. People are dying out there and there's a real panic spreading. So, what have you found out?'

'Well, sir,' said Bex, before Jud had a chance to answer back and continue the argument, 'I've noticed something on the map. I mean, where all the incidents are happening.'

'Yes? Go on.'

'Well, the dragons that are coming to life are all located in the financial district – where all the banks are.'

'Okay, good. And what does that mean?'

'She means there's a possible link between the incidents involving dragons and the banking crisis,' said Jud.

Now the professor was really interested. 'I'm listening.'

'While you were upstairs, sir,' said Bex, 'we researched the history of these dragon statues, why they were built and so on.'

'And we discovered that in ancient mythology, dragons had a certain purpose,' said Jud. 'In Chinese and Asian mythology they were thought to be the guardians of treasure. That is why you see them bordering the financial district, sir. There is a six-mile boundary that runs around the original city of London, and this is where much of the banking operates from.'

'So the dragon statues are there as symbols of protection?'

'Yes, exactly. That's why they were built in the banking district particularly,' said Bex.

'So are you saying that there is a link between the serious frauds going on in the banks at the moment and the dragons that protect that area?

'Yes, that's exactly what we're saying, sir,' said Bex. 'It can't just be coincidence. Dragons protect treasure. Money is treasure and it's going missing in vast sums at the moment, from under their very feet.'

'Claws,' said Jud.

'Talons,' said Bonati.

'Whatever!'

There was a buzz at the door to Bonati's study. The professor reached across his desk and pressed the button to release the door. It slid across and they saw Dr Vorzek standing there.

'May I come in, Giles?' she said.

'Of course, what's new? How's Grace?'

Vorzek moved into the room and took an available chair near Bonati's desk. 'Grace will be okay, I think. The doctors say the lacerations on her face are nasty and they'll leave scars, but there is no permanent damage to her eye, thank God. She's gonna be alright.'

'That's a huge relief, Kim. Thank you for that. We needed some good news.'

'But there's something else, Professor. While you were with Mr Goode we received two more reports from the police. Firstly, there was another dragon incident last night. Over at Moorgate.'

'But I thought the police had surrounded each statue? We had agents out there too. Didn't you guys see the one at Moorgate?' Bonati said to Jud and Bex.

'We did, but we couldn't watch all of them at the same time,' said Jud. 'We'd moved on to the next one, but when we left there was a police officer guarding it.'

'Apparently it was the police officer who was injured,' said Vorzek. 'He was taken to hospital with serious wounds to his chest and neck. Puncture wounds caused by clawing, is what they're saying.'

'And now the Moorgate dragon has gone too, yes?' asked Bonati.

Vorzek nodded.

'And the other report, Kim?' said the professor. 'You said you had received two reports.'

'Yes, well the other one is even stranger. I don't suppose it's linked at all, I don't know. It wasn't a dragon statue. This was the ghost of an elderly man seen at the Counting House in Cornhill. Eyewitnesses say the ghost was wearing the usual clothes you'd find any banker wearing, but – this is really intriguing, sir – they say it was holding a newspaper, the *Financial Times*, dated February 1876.'

'Really?' said Bonati, now gripped. 'The ghost of a banker, I assume?'

Vorzek nodded slowly. 'It's reasonable to assume so, yes, sir. The pub was itself a bank once, hence its name.'

The professor rose from his chair and approached the giant screen again, looking closely at the ring of red lights that bordered the city of London. You could see it now. It seemed obvious.

There was a brief silence in the room, as those within it contemplated the city above them, its beloved dragons swooping around, defending in the only way they knew how.

'Well done everyone,' he said. 'So there is a great deal more to this banking situation than we, and Scotland Yard, first thought. If the reason why these guardians are coming to life is because their treasure is being robbed, then stop the illegal trading and we will end the dragon incidents. It kind of makes sense. But it's a huge leap of faith here. Thank God we're used to fighting ghosts, otherwise we'd never believe it could happen.'

'Anything's possible,' said Jud.

'But it follows then that if we don't stop the money from being lost in the banks, sir,' said Bex, 'we won't prevent these dragon statues from attacking. And I'm assuming they don't know who's taken the money – how could they? They just sense danger and react to it. But Khan's already said, hasn't he, that his orders are to leave the statues where they are and not remove them altogether, which would be the obvious answer.'

'Yeah, why is that?' said Jud. 'I mean, who ordered them to stay in position?'

'Well,' said Bonati, 'there's a feeling that we'll be admitting defeat and confirming to the public that they are a danger. That would fuel the panic even further and make everyone suspicious of any statue they passed. It's harder to keep this thing under wraps if we go out and remove every dragon statue. It'll spread fear across the whole bloody city.'

'Too late for that,' said Jud. 'It's been all over the news already.'

'Okay. Time for drastic action. If we're not allowed to move the dragon statues – the ones that haven't already vanished, that is – then we send as many agents as we can to all the sites that border the financial district and we arm them with as many EM neutralisers as possible. If we detect any radiation, we neutralise it. I'll disarm those dragons. They won't wreak havoc. Not in this city.' He turned to Vorzek. 'Kim, get me all the EM neutralisers we currently hold in store. I know some agents will have them on other cases at the moment, but we still have a good stock, yes?'

'Of course. And the new versions arrived recently too. They

are more powerful, to be used with extreme caution. I've not yet had a chance to train up the agents.'

'Well, we don't want them to neutralise themselves with the bloody things, do we. I suggest an immediate call of all agents currently not on investigation so you can brief them on the new equipment. Then send them out as soon as possible. These dragons may be protecting the City's money, but they're attacking anyone and everybody who goes near them, whoever they may be.'

'Like guard dogs, they don't stop to ask if you're a burglar, sir, they just attack,' said Bex. 'It's a basic instinct, I guess.'

'I fear you may be right, Rebecca. Tell the agents to be careful, Kim. If there's any doubting, tell them what happened to Grace. That'll make them sit up, I'm sure.'

CHAPTER 15

SATURDAY, 3.14 P.M.

PENTHOUSE SUITE, GOODE TOWER, LONDON

'We'll never get away with this, Jud. It's stupid. I'm telling you, we'll be kicked out of the CRYPT if they find us here.'

Jud had gone too far this time, thought Bex. Maybe he wanted to be kicked out of the place. He seemed hell bent on self-destruction, and this was his most suicidal mission yet.

'Relax,' he said calmly. 'Don't worry about it. No one will know. As long as you don't get an attack of honesty and 'fess up.'

She glared at him across the elevator. 'Don't be ridiculous. You know I'd never do that. I just think it's too risky. If we get caught—'

'We won't,' said Jud. 'Life is about taking risks, you know that as well as anyone.' He watched the LED display above the lift doors continue its rapid ascent through the floors: 16, 17, 18, 19. On and on it rose, smoothly without a sound. The ascending numbers were the only indication that they were moving upwards. Otherwise it felt like the elevator had not even left the ground. It was so hi-tech, so smooth, like everything else in Goode's empire.

The digits reached 38 and the lift stopped without so much as a thud or judder. Within seconds the doors slid open to reveal Jason Goode's marble-floored lobby and the great glass corridor that ran down to his apartment.

'If we're seen up here we'll—'

'Oh, just relax,' Jud interrupted. 'Chill out, will you.'

She rolled her eyes as Jud typed in the secret code on the key panel to release the doors that led into his father's penthouse.

She couldn't deny it was thrilling to be up here with Jud. Alone. And on such a risky mission. She admired his confidence, his absolute belief that they'd be okay and nothing would happen to them. Just like he always said.

They'd been on so many missions together now, and though Jud was moody at times and prone to outbursts of anger, often directed at Bex simply because hers was the first face he saw, she found his sheer, raw courage magnetic. And he'd been right up to now too. Yes, there had been times when they'd found themselves in scrapes that appeared impossible to escape, but somehow they'd always found a way out, just like he said they would. He was quick-witted, stealthy and lethal when he needed to be, like a black panther.

But she feared this panther really had bitten off more than he could chew this time. Of course, the threats wouldn't come from ghosts on this brief mission. This time they faced a much more unpredictable and explosive foe: they were about to enter the private quarters of Jason Goode. Uninvited. It didn't bear thinking about what might happen if they were caught.

Jud had lived inside the Goode Tower so long there was nowhere he couldn't get into. He knew its corridors and rooms, its hidden cupboards and store rooms, even its ventilation shafts, like some resident mouse. This was his building. He'd been in it from the start and belonged there. He was a master at watching people key in codes and memorising the number sequences over shoulders and in his peripheral vision. His was a photographic memory.

The flat was quiet and empty when they entered. The polished, wooden double doors opened to reveal Goode's giant office area in the open-plan apartment, with polished marble flooring and the most sophisticated lighting Bex had ever seen. This wasn't the first time she'd been up there, but it would certainly be the last if they were found out.

Jud went over and sat in his father's black executive chair and immediately switched the computer on. He could see Bex shaking her head disapprovingly and glancing about her like an opportunistic burglar, looking for hidden cameras or recording equipment. She was certain Goode would have rigged the place against intruders, with so much technology at his fingertips. This was crazy.

But Jud knew there was no point in worrying about such things. His father may have had access to the very latest security devices and alarms, but he'd never installed any of it in his own place – he saw such things as an intrusion and completely unnecessary, especially here, thirty-eight floors up. After all, how could a burglar break into the building downstairs and get past the security officers in the lobby of Goode Technology to access the elevator? Plus you had to know the private code to type into the elevator buttons in order to rise beyond the thirty-seventh floor. Not even his employees knew that, or the CRYPT agents. Only Bonati and Jud and Jason Goode himself knew that code. On the rare occasions he had a visitor, he issued them with a temporary code, which perished as soon as they'd left the apartment and returned in the elevator.

'I still don't see what you're hoping to find,' said Bex, watching his fingers click swiftly across the keyboard. 'You heard the professor, your father's not hiding anything, J. He says Mr Goode seemed as surprised by all this as we were.'

Jud shook his head. 'Didn't you see Bonati's face? His eyes? I could tell he wasn't convinced. There was a look of fear – I could detect it. There was a niggling doubt in his mind. I tell you, this news from Khan has rattled him and he doesn't know what to do next. All we're doing is helping him by making sure my father's clean and that there's nothing on his system to suggest otherwise. If I find anything I'll obliterate it, I promise. I just have to know. The professor would never come up here uninvited, you know that. And while my father's at Scotland Yard it's the ideal time to do some fishing around.'

'You don't seriously think your father knows more than he's letting on, do you?' said Bex, coming round to Jud's side of the desk so she could view the computer screen. There was no doubt her curiosity was getting the better of her now; she was less concerned about the possibility of hidden cameras and more interested in viewing Goode's private computer. How could she resist a peek inside his personal files?

'No, of course I don't. My father is completely innocent. But I do think someone is trying to frame him. There is no way he would have employed computer hackers in his company – knowingly or not. His staff are too good. He does his research. The interview process for this place is incredible, I'm telling you. His staff are vetted so carefully, it's like working for the royal family, and they're monitored constantly. Their files are checked and double-checked regularly. My father demands absolute loyalty, always has.'

'You mean they're spied on?'

'What? No, Dad likes to call it "monitored". Believe me, Bex, some of the computer programs and hardware these guys at Goode Technology are working on are top secret. If the plans got into the hands of a rival computer company we'd be in real trouble. Secrecy is everything in this business, when you're at the sharp end of technological innovation. You don't know who is spying from other places.'

'What, like we are, you mean?'

Jud smiled as he continued to stare at the screen, eyes flicking down email after email, lists of senders' names and subjects displayed.

'So what you're saying is if there really were hackers posing as employees for your dad's company, he would know about it?' said Bex.

'Yes,' said Jud. 'That's why I know it's bullshit. There's no way the claims could be true. If a hacker can break into all these banking systems around the world, I'm sure he can then hack into our systems and make it look like we'd done it. We're being framed, Bex. Trust me, it won't have been started by an employee inside Goode Technology. There's no chance of that. This happened from the outside.'

'So what are we looking for? Why are we here, J?'

'Because I want to see if there's anything my father has missed. He's so rarely at this computer, so he might have overlooked something that came in. I don't know, maybe there's evidence of someone he's upset. An angry client with a grudge or someone else he's crossed. Let's face it, he has a temper, my father. He could've upset someone. You don't make the kind of money my dad made without upsetting people. So there might be an email trail that gives us some kind of lead.'

'But won't the police be here to do all that searching eventually? If they do believe your father's company is behind it, they'll seize all this stuff anyway.'

'Exactly. That's why we've got to look first. I won't know what I'm looking for until I find it.'

They read so much correspondence it made their eyes ache. But there was nothing to suggest anyone was out to get Goode. No angry messages or exchanges of bitter words. Just formal emails from suppliers and researchers and associates confirming arrangements for meetings or putting forward proposals. The usual stuff any boss has to plough through. Lots of people wanting his attention.

Two hours passed and still they found nothing of any use. No leads. Jud was about to switch off the computer when there was a 'ting' signalling an email had arrived.

Jud went back into the application and saw a new message, clicked on it and read:

Never believe you can bury the past, Jason. All crimes will come back to haunt you like ghosts. Prison beckons.
Yours,
An old friend

'This is it,' Jud said. 'I told you someone was out to get my father.'

'But who?' said Bex. 'What's all this about? It's a weird message.'

'I don't know. But I know a man who will. Bonati'll tell us. He has to see this.'

Bex was shaking her head and moving away from the desk guiltily. 'Uh, uh. No way. You're saying we should print this off and take it to the professor? Are you out of your mind, J? What are we going to say, we were just passing and happened to stumble into his flat and happened to notice the computer and just happened to accidentally boot it up and read through all his emails? You're mad. He'll know where we've been. This is a serious breach, J, even for you. Bonati will be just as angry. Maybe more so, because he'll blame himself for allowing it to happen while your father was out. We're dead meat, I tell you.'

'Chill. It'll be worth it. Don't you see? This is exactly why I broke into here. I'm protecting my father and there's no way he can punish us for that. Once he reads this I reckon he'll forget how we got it. I'm telling you, he *has* to see it. Come on, let's go.'

He flicked on the state-of-the art printer across the desk and waited for its many lights to finish their sequence, then pressed 'print' on the email and waited for the paper to be spat out.

'Right, let's get out of here. Come on.'

They were just making their way across the giant apartment towards the exit when they heard footsteps. They were coming from the corridor outside the flat. They froze.

The doors began to slide open. There was no point hiding. There wasn't even time to get behind the sofas or dash into another room. They were caught, red-handed.

Jason Goode appeared in the doorway.

Bex's eyes were wide with fear. Jud tried to remain cool, even though his heart was thumping inside his rib cage and he was breathing heavily.

'Good afternoon,' said Goode, smiling wryly. 'So the young lovers have been caught, eh?'

'What?' said Jud, surreptitiously slipping the sheet of paper on which the email was printed into his back pocket.

'Looking for a private place to play, were we? Well, J, you know, I gotta hand it to you. They don't come more private than here. But in your father's own bed, huh? That's pretty cheeky, even for you.'

Bex was studying Goode's face. Was he amused or angry or what? Was he just playing with them as a wild animal toys with its prey before planting a fatal claw? Was he about to wipe the smile from his face and explode at them any second? To be found in the apartment was bad enough, but for the reason he was saying – oh my God, the embarrassment. Bex could feel her cheeks turning crimson and her legs going weak. She wanted to grab hold of something, anything, to steady her. This was excruciating.

'You know, I'd love to admit it, sir. It's kinda cool.' Jud was edging even closer to his father now, as defiant as any teenager caught out, but refusing to show weakness. 'But I think you've got the wrong idea. We weren't here to find some privacy. Although you have given me an idea for the future.'

'Jud!' Bex whispered. 'Shut up. Don't make this any worse. Are you insane?'

Goode smiled. He found Bex's embarrassment quite endearing. She was a beautiful girl, and so intelligent too. She was usually such a confident, self-assured thing. To see her reduced to red-faced whispering like a naughty school kid was charming. Truth be told, the rumours he'd heard from Bonati that these two were becoming close had not angered him. Quite the reverse. She was a great girl. And if anyone could calm his son down and bring him some much-needed companionship, then who better? Someone had to. It was about time his son Jamie learned to love again. Or maybe just lust. Anything was better than the stone wall of emotion he usually showed to those close to him.

But this was a flagrant breach of security and they all knew it. Goode stared at them both – Bex's remorseful face and his son's defiant stare. Just as they would have looked at school. Suddenly they seemed young. Too young to be getting up to this kind of mischief.

Goode found himself wondering what Jamie's mother might have said in a situation like this. He shuddered to think. He could feel anger rising rapidly inside him. But it faded just as quickly when the memories of Tara made him see Jamie in a different light: alone, orphaned, at least by his mother, and, if he was honest, by him too. He was rarely around for him when he needed it. How could he shout at him now, really? The kid had found love and companionship and all the things Tara would have wanted, eventually – if not quite so soon.

'What we were really doing was—'

'I tell you what guys,' Goode interrupted, ready to end this. 'You should consider yourself lucky, you know.'

'Lucky?' said Jud.

'Sure, lucky it was me who walked in on you and not the professor. My God, you'd have been dismissed immediately.

Even you,' he said to Jud. 'Bonati would never have tolerated this. How could he? What would he have said to me, huh?' Bex noticed a slight smile at his lips.

'Oh yeah, I can just see me being kicked out,' said Jud cheekily. 'Bring it on.'

His father stared at him in silence again, his wry smile gone. 'Okay, that's enough. Don't push your luck, son. Now get out.'

Jud shrugged but stayed put. 'So you don't want to know the real reason we're here?'

'Oh, spare me the sordid details, J, *please*,' said Goode. 'I'm a man of the world but I don't need to know everything that went on in here. Just get the hell out and find some other place to . . . er, get to know each other. I've got work to do. A lot of work, believe me.' He turned from them and walked over towards his desk.

Bex made straight for the corridor but Jud grabbed her arm and turned to face his father again. 'No, wait!' he said. 'You've got it all wrong. Believe me. Why won't you listen? I think we can help you.' He retrieved the printout from his pocket and waved it at his father.

Goode noticed the small print that was written across the top.

'Go on.'

'This is an email . . .' began Jud.

'A what?' Goode quickly turned and saw the green light on the printer was on. 'Tell me you haven't just printed that off here? *Seriously?* You've broken into my computer?' His voice was raised now and Bex felt like kicking Jud for pulling her back into the flat when they'd been so close to escaping. 'You really have some courage, you guys. I mean, breaking into the computer of the owner and founder of the entire goddam company? Jesus. You got some balls, I'll give you that.'

His face was hard to read again, yet this was hardly the explosion Bex had been expecting when the real truth came out.

She felt sure, from the moment he had appeared in the doorway, that Goode would dismiss them there and then. She'd imagined the security officers marching them off the premises, pictured herself telling her parents the reasons why she'd been struck off the team. That would be just as unbearable as the last five minutes. Maybe worse.

But Goode remained calm, at least on the outside. Perhaps the interviews at Scotland Yard had unsettled him and robbed him of his usual temper. Maybe he was just too exhausted with it all.

Jud tried to explain. 'Please, sir, can I tell you—'

'And what's with the "sir" business, huh? Come on, J. How stupid do you think I am? Bonati's told me everything about you two. Quit the bullshit, will you? I'm your *father*. Bex knows that. So stop the pretence and tell me what's in your hand. Now! The day did not begin as I had hoped. And believe me, it's getting stranger and stranger by the minute. I've just returned from Scotland Yard and I'm in no mood for playing games. Tell me what you've got to say and then leave me in peace, *please*.'

He brushed past his visitors and made for the kitchen area. He was thirsty and in need of another boost of caffeine.

He turned to them. 'Now sit down. And talk to me.'

CHAPTER 16

SATURDAY, 4.15 P.M.

A PRIVATE BANK, FLEET STREET, LONDON

Annika Premvas knew she should go home soon. She shouldn't even be working on a Saturday, but there was just too much to do. She was still only three months into the job – a post she'd been dreaming of for years, all the way through her time at the London School of Economics. This was her opportunity to make the big time. Impress the bosses upstairs and one day she could be a partner just like them, lunching on lobster with wealthy clients and developing a taste for fine wine.

She was well on the way. Already she'd been noticed by the partners as someone with serious potential. Annika was a fast learner, quick-witted and sharp, and more than capable of dealing with the boyish antics and bullishness of the colleagues who resented her. She was tough and not afraid to take anyone on. And she was not about to waste the opportunity she'd been given by striving for some crappy 'work to life balance' as her soppier friends kept advising. Time off was for softies and Annika certainly wasn't one of those. This was the third weekend she'd worked in a row. Right through. Twenty-one days on the trot. But she'd got the energy and the drive to keep going. The partners at the bank were impressed.

She closed down one of three screens on her desk and picked up her empty coffee cup. She needed a refill. There was still work to be done, and the only thing she had to get home for was her cat, who seldom showed her any affection anyway, so she decided she'd carry on until the guard locked up. The cat could wait. She ran a hand through her long, auburn hair, raised her spectacles from her nose onto her forehead like a hair band and walked out of the room.

The kitchen was down a long, dimly lit corridor, lined with ornate cabinets of dark mahogany and glass, all designed to impress clients and anyone else who passed them. Each cabinet housed volumes of classic books, some non-fiction, written by famous London figures, on banking and the City's glorious history, others leather-bound volumes of ancient law books and case precedents. All were displayed for their aesthetic quality and seldom read.

The floor was white marble with gold beading down each side, in keeping with the grandeur of this solid, square, Georgian mansion – home to the bank for more than three centuries. Three hundred years of managing the multi-million pound portfolios of the country's elite. From titled landowners with vast estates in the North, to wealthy London-based businessmen, the bank's list of clients was like a *Who's Who*. But no one would ever know the identity of any of its clients (or at least they wouldn't hear it from the bank's staff – if identities were ever revealed it was usually by the clients themselves, proudly announcing at dinner parties their meetings with their portfolio managers at this famous and historic bank for the rich, where you needed several million just to open an account).

She left the long corridor and entered the modest kitchen, a third of the size of the partners' kitchen above, of course, which adjoined the partners' dining room and was frequented by a resident chef. Here, on Annika's floor, staff had to serve themselves from the fridge and plain-looking kitchen cupboards. Whenever Annika was invited up to have lunch with the partners she always marvelled at the giant, polished mahogany table, the crystal glasses and the delicious smells that wafted from the kitchen. One day she'd earn herself a permanent seat around the giant table.

For now, though, another cup of instant coffee and a boil-in-the-pot noodle snack would suffice. She wasn't fussy. Years as a student had developed in her a liking – or was it just a tolerance? – for instant snacks and fast food. She waited for the kettle to boil, its explosive rumbling sounding like a jet aeroplane taking off. Eventually the blessed click came and the room fell silent again, other than the ping of a spoon in a cup and the trickle of hot water.

Flicking the light off in one hand and balancing the noodle snack and the hot coffee cup in the other, Annika left the kitchen and made her way down the long corridor back to her office.

A few seconds later she stopped.

'Hello there, can I help you?' she asked, unable to hide her surprise.

There was a man walking towards her from the other end of the corridor, where it disappeared around a corner. As he emerged into view she didn't recognise him as a colleague, but that wasn't to say he didn't work there. There were plenty of people whom she'd not met yet, especially the old, part-time partners and consultants who clung on to the bank long after their official retirement had come. This man certainly resembled one of those, but it was unlikely such a semi-retired colleague would be in at the weekend. They liked to come in when it was busy and bustling and there was the chance of a free lunch and a glass of Chablis with a senior partner.

'Have we met?' she asked politely as the man approached. But he remained silent.

'Excuse me?' she said again as he passed her by. Still no response.

Annika has seen something menacing in his face – a fixed stare in her direction, but somehow looking right though her.

'Deaf as a post,' she whispered to herself.

She stopped walking and watched him shuffle off. He was a tall, heavily built man, in his late sixties at least. His face had looked pale and his hazel eyes had seemed lifeless. It was almost as if he was in a trance, though she'd only seen him for a second as they'd passed each other. Now he trudged on, reaching the end of the corridor and disappearing into the same kitchen she had just left.

Odd, she thought. Rude guy. She considered following him into the kitchen, but there was something remote and unwelcoming about his face that prevented her. 'Miserable sod,' she whispered, far too quietly to be heard.

She returned to her desk and set the coffee cup and snack pot neatly on two coasters. She was about to tuck into the noodles when she paused. The old man's face seemed strangely familiar, now she thought about it. Maybe she had seen him before at the bank at some event or other. He must've been one of the old partners, retired but not gone completely. But sitting there, by herself, knowing there was a guy just along the corridor made her feel suddenly vulnerable.

She decided she'd phone reception. The place was manned every day, even at weekends, so if anyone had come in, the security guard would surely know who they were. Curiosity was getting the better of her and she had to know. She waited through several rings before the security guard picked up. How long did it take to answer a phone that's on your desk? she thought to herself. He was obviously outside on the step, as usual, having a crafty fag.

'Hello?' came the voice.

'Neil, is that you? It's Annika Premvas.'

'Yeah?'

The security guards at the bank were never ones for idle chatter, and Neil Blanchard was the worst.

'Neil, I was wondering who's visited this afternoon? Who else is in besides me?'

'Erm . . .' Blanchard was flicking through the signing-in book. 'Just Toby Manvers. You know, that young guy who started here just before you—'

'Yes, I know him,' said Annika hurriedly. 'Who else?'

'There's no one else. Just you and me.'

She disliked the way he said it so suggestively, and at any other time she'd have had him for that, but not today.

'Why do you wanna know?' said Blanchard.

'Well, you've obviously missed someone else,' she snapped. 'You must've been having one of your smoke breaks outside, I suppose?'

'Sorry, no way, love.' Blanchard resented the suggestion that he might have left his post – even though he did regularly. And besides, there was no way anyone could come through the internal doors into the bank proper unless he released the button. 'Firstly, I haven't had a break since lunchtime, and secondly, no one can get through the security door down here, you know that. Even if the main doors were open, you can only enter the shop floor where the counters are. No one can get into the bank properly unless I say so.' He liked the power this gave him and she could tell.

'In that case, I suggest you get up here bloody quick!' she shouted back. 'Because I've just seen an elderly gent, suited and booted. I passed him in the corridor. Obviously deaf as a post because he just ignored me when I said hello.'

'Impossible. You're dreaming, love.'

'Now look here,' Annika was getting riled now. Who the hell did these security guards think they were? 'We'll deal with this, and your attitude, on Monday morning, okay, but for now, get yourself up here. Third floor, office 315. Now!' She slammed the receiver down. 'Bloody cheek,' she said to herself. 'I'll have him for that.'

Blanchard decided he would finish his tea and reignite the last half of his cigarette outside, which this woman had so rudely interrupted, before he went up to see what she was going on about. They made a right fuss these arrogant bankers, treating his kind like bloody slaves, having to answer their every beck and call. It was like being a servant downstairs while the lords and ladies lived upstairs. Who did she think she was, the Queen? She could wait for a while. He stepped out onto the pavement, lit up and took another long drag from the half-smoked cigarette. The street was bustling with late-afternoon shoppers, all hurriedly trying to get to the shops before closing time. He knew he had just half an hour before he was allowed to close up – she'd have to be out by then, for sure, or she'd be locked in for the weekend. Serve her right.

Five minutes later he stamped on the fag end, glanced up and down the street once again and reentered the building. He made straight for the security door, swiping the monitor with the plastic card that hung on a ribbon around his neck. He entered the lift and pressed '3'.

A few seconds later, Blanchard was walking down the same corridor that led to Annika's office: a large room which she shared with three colleagues.

Blanchard always found it amusing how these bankers would say, 'Come to my office', as if it were theirs exclusively. Jumped-up nobodies.

He found the room with 315 on the door and opened it without knocking. She didn't deserve that much.

'Jesus Christ,' he said, drawing in breath deeply and grabbing the wall to steady himself.

There were three large desks, each one with several monitors on them. The desk nearest to him was empty, and the one to his right. But at the other side of the room, where the third desk was situated, Blanchard's eyes had met with a sight that would haunt him forever.

Annika Premvas was slumped in her chair, eyes bulging, head back, exposing a single red slash across her throat, from which blood spurted uncontrollably.

CHAPTER 17

SATURDAY, 5.01 P.M.

CRYPT HEADQUARTERS, LONDON

'Drink?' Jason Goode made for the elaborate drinks cabinet across the giant living room space in his penthouse.

'Please,' said Bonati, placing the printed email onto a glass coffee table and starting his usual pacing.

When Goode had read the email handed to him from Jud, his first reaction had been to send for the professor. He'd not said anything else, just stared at the piece of paper in his hand. From the tone of his voice, Bonati had realised something was seriously wrong, and had shot up to the thirty-eighth floor, so preoccupied with what could have happened that he'd almost forgotten about his crippling vertigo. Moments later Bonati had walked into the giant apartment to find Goode midway through his second large bourbon and staring out of the glass walls at the world below.

But he'd wondered why Jud and Bex were in the flat.

Now he knew. It had been them who'd found the email meant for Jason – though God knows how, or why; he would deal with their breach of security later. Right now they had the more serious question to answer of who the hell had sent the email, and why?

Jud was getting impatient. 'Will someone please tell us what's going on?' He looked at Bex, who returned his stare with the same puzzlement and concern.

'Jason,' Bonati said quietly. 'Do they need to be here?'

'What?' Goode looked around blankly. His mind had been turning somersaults and he'd not even realised the agents were still in the room.

'Well?' Jud said again, directly to his father. 'Please, Dad. Talk to us.'

'Shut up, J. For Christ's sake! I need to *think*.' He was silent for a moment, staring out of the window at the city below. Then, without warning, he made for the bedroom, slamming the door so hard it rocked the room. The noise of the bang unsettled Bonati and brought back his vertigo in an instant, the violent slamming reminding him acutely that they were perched precariously on top of the world. He stopped pacing and found the nearest chair, his knees feeling weak.

'Listen to me,' he began, his voice shaking slightly. 'We don't know for definite who sent the email. It's probably just a hoax. Some guy who's read about what's happened and wants to rattle your father.'

'Well, it seems to have worked,' said Jud, looking in the direction in which Goode had abruptly exited. 'Tell me what this is about. Please.'

'You father's stressed, you can see that. And you don't need to ask why. It's not this email, it's the case that's building against him. Just drop it, will you.'

'No, I won't,' said Jud. 'I want to know what's going on. Talk to me.'

Bonati shook his head. 'I can't, J. Because I don't know much more than you. A man as successful as your father makes enemies along the way, you know that. It's inevitable that people get jealous or others get angry when decisions don't go their way; staff don't get promotions, or companies don't get orders they were expecting from him. Business can be cruel. But you have to keep battling on. You have to toughen up and carry on.'

'You're not telling us anything we didn't already know, sir,' said Jud, his anxiety rising. 'But who sent the email, huh?'

'I said I don't know, Jud . . . not for sure.'

'Not for sure? So you've got an idea then?'

The professor remained silent, just shaking his head. The room was filled with an awkward silence which Bex felt acutely. Things were happening at such a rate, the world was so different today.

'No,' Bonati finally snapped, 'I don't.' And with that he rose from the chair. 'I think it's time we left Mr Goode in peace, don't you? It's a difficult time for him and he doesn't need us interfering. You have been very lucky that he didn't discipline you for breaking and entering. I would have. Now, let's go.'

Jud and Bex looked at one another before rising. They both knew the professor wouldn't budge on this, at least not now. And he was right, they were lucky not to have been punished for going up there uninvited. Bex was keen to get the hell out of there as quickly as possible, and she was praying Jud wouldn't push his luck any further.

'You heard the professor,' she said. 'Come on.'

'But . . .'

'Come on!' Bex pulled Jud towards the door. 'We'll revisit this another time,' she whispered. 'Let's just get out.'

The three of them made for the door, but stopped suddenly when Bonati's phone rang.

'Yes?'

It was DCI Khan. 'There's been another fatal attack. A banker again. In Fleet Street. Throat cut. I'm on my way there now. There's been no ghost sightings reported, but apparently there was an intruder in the building who got past the guard somehow, and now he's disappeared. I think you should check it out.'

'I'll send someone over now. Let's talk later.'

Bonati turned to the two agents. 'Right, I have the perfect distraction for you two.'

CHAPTER 18

SATURDAY, 5.41 P.M.

CENTRAL LONDON

It was Bex's turn to use her bike and Jud clutched onto her as she wove in and out of the traffic, bound for Fleet Street.

'I'm going to find out who sent it,' Jud said through his headset.

'The email?'

'Yes. There's something they're not telling us, Bex. The message talked about crimes in the past haunting my father. I've got to know what he's done.'

'Jud, I don't think you should push it. Anyway, it might be nothing. Just some jealous ex-employee or rival businessman. It doesn't mean—'

'It said "old friend", Bex.'

'So? That could be anyone. Just because they signed off like that doesn't mean it's genuine. In any case, there's plenty to do here in London. It's not as though we've solved the case, is it. And God knows what we'll find in Fleet Street.'

'No, there's something wrong. I can feel it.'

The Fireblade halted at traffic lights. Bex turned back to glance at Jud through her visor.

'Just be careful, yeah?' Bex engaged the gears and roared away from the junction so fast, Jud had to hold on tight around her waist. She enjoyed the thrill of having him so close. She loved it when he rode pillion. He was in her hands now. At least for a while. She was in control.

The Fireblade roared down the Strand and approached Temple Bar, at the end of Fleet Street.

'What the hell is that?' she said through her headset.

'I don't believe it!' said Jud. 'Are they insane? I mean, what kind of message does that send to the public?'

They were looking at the giant dragon at Temple Bar, outside the Royal Courts. The statue was still in place, as ordered by Khan's superiors, but now there were builders erecting scaffolding over the top of it. The latticework of horizontal and vertical poles resembled a cage. A crowd of onlookers had gathered across the giant intersection, anxiously watching to see if the dragon would move again. Rumours had already spread across the city, fuelled by some thrilling tabloid headlines, their editors eager to sell more copies, as ever.

'I'm gonna ask them what the hell they're playing at,' said Bex. 'It's like a circus round here. They might as well put neon lights above it and start selling tickets.'

'Just leave it,' said Jud. 'We've gotta get to the bank. It's just up ahead. Look, you can see the blue flashing lights down there. Come on, keep going.' Jud hated riding pillion, handing over control to Bex.

He was right, there were lights flashing further up the street, where there appeared to be some kind of road block. The police had obviously closed the section of road outside the bank and erected the usual white tent, the familiar, ominous sign of a murder investigation.

'No, J. This is important. Khan can wait. I wanna know who told them to do this. It's madness. A cage? Seriously? That'll really stop the public worrying about dragons coming to life, won't it? Look at the crowds!'

Without waiting for an answer she pulled the Fireblade into the kerbside and quickly dismounted, Jud in pursuit.

'Excuse me,' she shouted up at the first man she saw. 'Can you tell me what you're doing, please?'

The man turned to see Bex, dressed in black biking leathers, flicking her hair around as she removed the bike helmet, and quickly climbed down the ladder he was on. His smile was lustful. Another guy came straight over to join him.

'Hey, babe. Can I help?'

Jud watched the two lecherous men drool over her. Good luck, he thought. Keep going like that and you'll get a sharp kick in the crotch any minute.

But Bex was restrained.

'Sorry to disturb you, guys.' She flicked her hair again and smiled. 'I just wondered what this is about. It looks like a cage!'

'You look like you should be dancing in a cage, love. I'd pay to see that,' said one of the men, grinning inanely at his mate.

Oh dear, thought Jud. Bad move.

'Agh, Jesus!' The man bent double after the thwack to his groin.

'In your dreams, mate.' Now it was Bex's turn to grin.

Jud rushed closer. 'Sorry, guys, my girlfriend's got a bit of a thing about being called a prostitute. Dunno why. She's just funny like that. Huh, girls, eh?' His sarcasm was not lost on the two men, and neither was the stare he gave them, as if to say, 'Wanna make something of it?'

A man in a shirt and tie and a yellow hard hat appeared from nowhere.

'I don't know what just happened here, but you need to get back to work,' he shouted at the two builders. 'Excuse me,' he said to Jud and Bex, and pulled the men away, sharply. With so many people watching, this was the last thing he needed.

'Can you tell us what you're doing?' said Jud, as politely as he could.

The man shook his head as he walked off. 'Sorry, mate. Classified.'

'Classified?' said Bex. 'What are you, spies or something?'

'That's enough, Bex. You've just assaulted someone. Let's not push our luck.'

He tried to usher her back towards the bike. 'Wait,' she said. 'What're they doing?'

They watched as a giant white canvas was strapped over the top of the scaffolding cage.

'Thank God for that,' said Jud. 'They're making it look like a building site. It's like they're doing renovations or something. You restoring it?' he shouted back to the group.

The man in the hard hat nodded his head this time and then waved his hand for them to back away.

Relieved to see that whoever had planned this sideshow had at least had the good sense to put a cover over it, the agents returned to the bike and set off again. 'So the dragons are being mysteriously restored,' said Bex. 'Not sure how many people that will convince, but it's better than a bloody cage!'

DCI Khan was the first to come out onto the street to meet them. He'd already heard the roar of the Fireblade as it approached, even from inside the foyer. CRYPT agents always arrived in style. Two riders, dressed in black leathers, on a high-powered motorbike. Yeah, thought Khan, very discreet.

A crowd of onlookers had pitched up in Fleet Street too, perhaps attracted by the blue lights visible from the Temple Bar dragon. Jud did his usual trick of keeping his helmet on until inside the building – he was always careful to hide his identity. Even with the change of appearance, one could never be too sure; God knows there had been enough incidents since his release to make him worry. He shunned the limelight and wanted to get inside as quickly as possible.

'Can you tell us what's happened?' a shout came from the crowd. Another reporter, no doubt.

And another, 'Are there ghosts inside? Is it haunted?'

DCI Khan said, 'No comment at this stage. There will be a briefing later in the day. That's all. Please move on.'

The agents entered the building quickly and Khan took them straight into a private room on the first floor. He explained the circumstances which had led to the death, as far as he had discovered: the woman working at the weekend, the security guard, and the strange intruder who had, apparently, entered without the guard's knowledge.

'Is this possible?' said Jud. 'I mean, can someone get into the main part of the bank without the guard releasing the doors? I wouldn't have thought anyone could do that.'

DCI Khan agreed. 'But the guard is certain that the woman reported an intruder in the building just moments before he found her dead.'

'And we're sure it's not the guard himself?' said Bex in a hushed tone.

'No. We're not sure. And believe me, he'll be helping us with our inquiries.'

'Where is he?' said Jud.

'He's upstairs, having a cup of tea and trying to calm down.'

'Okay, we'll see him later. Anyone else in the building at the time?'

'Just one other. Guy called Toby Manvers, a young intern. Came in at the weekend to impress his bosses, no doubt.'

'I bet he wishes he hadn't now,' said Bex. 'Didn't he hear anything?'

'Apparently not,' said Khan. 'Always works with his iPhone plugged in. A jet could've passed over and he wouldn't have heard it over his headphones. So he says, anyway. But don't you worry. He's not going anywhere either. He's in the staff kitchen with the guard. And a couple of our officers. They'll both be coming with us to the station for a little chat.'

'Take us to the body,' said Jud.

They moved towards the lift and within a few moments were walking along the same corridor where the figure had been seen, according to the guard. As the lift doors had opened, both Jud and Bex had felt a distinctly cold chill. The building was well heated and insulated, flanked as it was by similar Georgian buildings either side. There was no reason for the place to feel so cold.

'Feel that?' said Jud as they approached office 315.

'Definitely,' said Bex. 'It's very cold. And ominous. My God, there's anger here. You can feel it.'

Khan pushed open the door to the office and the agents were immediately met by the sight that had shocked the guard earlier.

'Annika Premvas. Twenty-seven. Single,' said the inspector.

'Christ,' said Bex. 'It's brutal. What on Earth had this girl done wrong?'

'Well, that's what my men and I will try to find out,' said Khan. 'I've got officers all over this already, some with her parents, some with her friends. I've got two men at her apartment too, where she lived alone, just a cat.'

'Jealous boyfriend?' said Jud.

'We'll see,' said the inspector. 'But the reason you're here is because of what Miss Premvas apparently said to the guard on the phone moments before he found her. I'll go and get him. You need to hear what he has to say.'

DCI Khan left the room. Two forensic officers closed up their bags and left the scene. As they exited, Jud saw a bloodied kitchen knife in a transparent plastic bag clutched by one of them.

'Murder weapon?'

The officer nodded. 'Found at the scene. We believe it came from the kitchen right here.'

'So the murderer didn't come armed,' said Bex.

'Looks that way.'

Then they were alone with the body. The room felt even colder than the corridor. There were no windows open, despite the stench of blood. Forensics had not allowed anything to be disturbed.

Jud began to unload his rucksack and set up the usual instruments for detecting traces of paranormal activity. The triple axis EMF meter, the Geiger counter, the ionisation indicator. It was all there, and had seen much use in the last twenty-four hours.

Within moments they watched as the needle soared on the EMF meter.

'There's a heavy presence here, still,' said Bex. She walked tentatively towards the body. A fixed grimace of terror was printed indelibly on Annika Premvas's face, her eyes bulging with fear. The gash around her throat was savage, the result of a vicious slash from the knife. Bex looked closely at the dead woman's face. 'What was she thinking? What final thoughts passed through this woman's head, J? What did she see?'

'She saw a killer coming towards her with a knife, Bex. I would have thought that was obvious.'

'No, there's more to it than that. You can feel it. Something else has visited this room. It's different. Something paranormal's going on.'

Khan re-entered the room followed by a pale-faced man. He looked shattered.

'This is Neil Blanchard,' said Khan. 'He's one of three security guards for the bank. He found Miss Premvas's body. Mr Blanchard, these are crime scene investigation officers helping us. Please answer any questions they may have.' Blanchard nodded miserably at them both, then looked curiously at the equipment Jud had set up. Luckily the man was not in a curious mood. He remained silent, refusing to look again in the direction of the body.

'So what happened?' said Bex directly.

Blanchard went through the story again, from the moment Annika Premvas had telephoned him.

'So there was definitely a fourth person in the building?' said Jud.

'According to Miss Premvas, yes,' said Blanchard. 'But I've not seen anyone else. After I called 999 I made my own search of the place. I found Mr Manvers, of course – Christ, he was shocked. Like I was.' His face became vacant again, as he dared to stare at the corpse.

'But no one else?' said Jud, snapping him out of his morbid thoughts.

'What? Er . . . no. I found no one else in the building. But she was absolutely certain she'd seen someone. I dunno. Maybe he escaped out of a window or somethin'. Miss Premvas would not have been making it up. I mean, why should she?'

'And she described the man to you, did she?' said Bex.

Blanchard nodded. 'Yes. She said he was an elderly man. Suited and booted, she said. Like the people we see everyday, I suppose.'

'But she didn't say she recognised him?'

'No. Oh, wait a minute, she said somethin' else too. What was it? Er . . . she said, oh yeah, that was it. She said she thought he was deaf because he just ignored her when she said hello to him.'

'Thank you,' said Jud. 'And when you found her, she was like this, yeah?'

'Yes. Just like that. I've not touched her. I've not moved anything.'

'How long was it between when she phoned you for help and when you actually went up?' said Bex.

The agents could see the man's gaze drop to the floor now. He looked ashamed.

'What?' said Jud impatiently. 'What is it?'

'Well, she called while I was having a smoke, you see. Only she was bloody rude on the phone, ranting on, you know, like these guys do. So I thought I'd make her wait while I went and finished my fag outside.'

Bex raised her eyebrows. But there was no need to say anything. It was obvious this was something the guy was going to have to live with.

'So how long, Mr Blanchard?'

'I dunno. Only a few minutes. Ten, maybe.'

'Okay. There's nothing you could've done. I'm guessing this woman was attacked straight after she put the phone down.'

'And didn't you hear anything? I mean, you didn't hear any screaming? Surely she would have screamed?' said Jud.

'No. This is a back room, isn't it. And I was out on the front step, on the street, wasn't I. By the time I got up here she was . . . you know . . . dead.'

'Thank you, Mr Blanchard,' said Jud. 'That's all for now.'

They watched him trudge out. They knew the police would have far more questions than that, about the woman's habits, her character, anyone who ever visited her. But that was for them to sort out. Right now, Jud and Bex wanted to get the readings taken and then get the hell out of there. If Bonati wanted to plant CRYPT agents in the bank overnight, that was for him to do, though it was unlikely the ghost would still be around. But it was obvious from the instruments' readings that paranormal activity had indeed occurred. They decided to record everything as quickly as possible, then see Khan and make their excuses. They were keen to get back to the CRYPT as quickly as possible to continue their investigations into Goode's threatening email.

'Shouldn't we look around a bit first?' said Bex, seeing Jud packing up the instruments already.

'No, there's no point. If there was a ghost here, it's probably well gone by now.'

Bex could tell Jud was impatient to get going – he must've been, she thought; usually he would give anything for a chance to go ghost hunting – but she knew it would take some explaining to Bonati if they'd not conducted a sweep of the site.

'Jud, I really think—'

'You really think what, huh? That we should waste our time here, with so much going on back at CRYPT? Seriously? You think my father's company, his reputation – who knows, maybe even the future of the CRYPT – is less important than finding another bloody ghost? Come on! We'll tell Bonati we've investigated. You can tell him we carried out a complete search if you like. There's no way he'll know we haven't.'

And then Khan walked in, and they both knew Jud was wrong. The inspector would have much to say to the professor if the agents legged it now. Sure enough, he asked, 'So, have you searched the place yet? Go and have a look round. Don't worry, my officers are everywhere. You'll be safe.'

Jud thought for a moment, the frustration building inside him. 'The place is full of people, Inspector, we'll never be able to take accurate readings. There'll be no paranormal activity now. Not with all these officers around. There's no point.'

'No point! A woman's been murdered, there's no trace of any human activity, no one saw the figure come in through the door, and you say there's no point?'

'But we can't prove it wasn't a human intruder who did this, you know that, Inspector,' said Jud. He was up for a fight now.

'I realise that, young man. You don't need to tell me my job. I'll have men working on this right through the night, and if we do unearth some evidence then I'll tell you. But let's look at the facts. We have reports of hauntings, and I'm not just talking about these dragons, I'm talking about sightings of ghosts, dressed as bankers, across the city. We have a report just like that here, moments before the woman was killed. Now, I'm not a ghost hunter, but I'd say that's a pretty strong case for you to search the place.' He looked at Jud closely. Saw his flickering eyes and his clenching fists. 'You in a hurry, young man, huh? Want to get off somewhere? Oh, of course, it's Saturday night, isn't it? You wanna take this young lady out, I suppose. Well, in that case, why didn't you say? I'm sure Professor Bonati wouldn't mind if you left a crime scene and went clubbing. No, of course not!'

Jud took a deep breath. Bex was staring at him, trying to say 'calm down', but he refused to look at her. He could feel his heart thumping in his chest. Ordinarily he'd have hit this guy. But he knew from past experience that his temper got him into too much trouble. And what difference would half an hour make?

'Okay, okay,' he said. 'We'll give the place the once-over before we pack up. And no, Inspector, I wasn't planning on going out clubbing. We have important research work back at the labs. You don't know the half of it.' He picked up his rucksack of equipment and left the room before Khan had a chance to respond. The inspector watched him leave, smiling at Bex as she followed him.

The bank was built on five floors – a tall, Georgian terraced building, with high ceilings and elaborate plasterwork. It was an opulent, lavish affair, as befitted the business. The clients who visited this private bank were worth serious money and expected such luxury.

They moved slowly down the corridor, entering any room that was open. There were offices similar to Annika Premvas's down each side. At the end of the corridor, the opposite end to where the lifts were situated, was a large wooden staircase that swept up and down the building, its polished brass rail gleaming. An elaborate crystal chandelier hung from the ceiling above them.

They could hear voices coming from the staff kitchen. They'd leave that until last – there was no point taking readings while there were people in it. They pressed on to the floor above, another floor of offices and meeting rooms, some of which were open, others locked shut. Both agents had removed their hand-held meters and were taking readings as they moved. There were certainly traces of electromagnetic radiation here, though not as high as in the office where the killing took place. But it was still cold and the atmosphere was anything but welcoming. After a sweep of the floor they headed back to the giant staircase and walked slowly up to the fifth and final level: the partners' floor.

Here the lavish fixtures and fittings were even more impressive. There were expensive oil paintings on the walls and beautiful chandeliers everywhere. Each door had a brass plaque with the name of its occupant on it. They tried the handles but all were locked. Further down the corridor, towards the lifts, they found a double door which led into the partners' dining room.

The room was immaculately furnished, with a giant mahogany table which ran its full length, decorated with candelabra, place mats and silverware.

'How these private bankers live,' said Bex. 'It's like royalty.'

'Yeah. We're in the wrong job,' said Jud. There were doors at both ends of the long room, one which led to the partners' kitchens, the other to the drawing room, where they met clients in more comfortable surroundings.

'You try the drawing room,' said Jud, 'I'll check out the kitchens.'

'Okay. Do you feel anything in here?' said Bex.

Jud waited for a while, allowing his senses to extend across the room like antennae. 'Yeah. It's unsettling, isn't it? Like we've just walked in on an argument.'

'Exactly,' said Bex. 'Something's sour in here. Nasty.'

They split up and entered the different rooms.

Bex crept into the lavish drawing room. There were leather Chesterfield sofas and chairs, a large drinks cabinet in the corner opposite the door and small side tables with lamps on them. It was dark in there, the moonlight from the windows casting silvery rays across the furniture. Bex moved towards one of the lamps to switch it on.

She turned to take in the whole room and stopped suddenly. She gasped silently.

There was a figure in the corner, standing there, looking at her. She'd not seen it in the dark.

Across the dining room, Jud was entering the kitchens. It was like being in a proper restaurant or hotel. The place was huge. Stainless steel appliances everywhere, and all polished so clean you could see your face in them. With so many ovens and microwaves, there was little point in paying much attention to the EMF meter readings – radiation was going to be high, although Jud was surprised at how quickly the needle on the hand-held set soared.

There was a scream.

'Bex?'

Jud ran out of the kitchen, sprinted the length of the dining room and entered the drawing room, his heart thumping again.

He stopped just inside the doorway. Bex was standing behind a large sofa, staring at something on the other side of the room, obscured by the open door.

Jud's immediate reaction was to get down to floor level. There was another sofa with its back to the doorway and he slid towards it slowly.

He edged to the end of the sofa, just enough to be able to view what it was Bex was staring at.

He saw the figure. There was something in its hand: a knife. It must've got it from the kitchens he had just left.

He sat back against the sofa and thought hard. It was pointless setting up the EM neutraliser – it would take too long to reduce the ghost's energy enough to disarm it.

He looked again at the figure. It hadn't moved yet, but its

gaze was still fixed on Bex across the room. In all respects it resembled any senior partner in a bank: smart suit, expensive shirt and tie, polished shoes. It was just the eyes that betrayed this image.

They were glowing red. Anger was running through its hollow body, the electromagnetic energy inside it rising, strengthening it again. The ghost opened its mouth and emitted a strange, insect-like clicking sound. The agents had heard this before, many times. The ghost was talking, but, as was so often the case at hauntings, the words were unrecognisable. Taking visible form was possible – a disembodied spirit, when charged with anger, could harness enough electromagnetic energy to become solid – but evidence of recognisable communication was rarely recorded.

Jud waited to see what the ghost would do next. It was clearly trying to rattle out its demands, but neither Bex nor Jud could decipher them. But as long as it was talking, it wouldn't strike. It was stalemate.

Jud surveyed the room and his eyes glanced up to a giant portrait over the fireplace on the opposite wall. It was obviously antique, painted in heavy oils with an ornate golden frame. It was of an ageing man dressed in an old-fashioned 1920s suit, clearly one of the old partners. His face was proud and arrogant and . . .

It was the face of the figure they were looking at, Jud realised.

If they needed further proof that the City was not only being haunted by dragons but by the ghosts of past bankers, this was it.

Jud peered at the figure again. Its feet were standing on a long rug, the same one that extended the length of that side of the room, all the way past the sofa he was hiding behind. It didn't appear to have any furniture on it. Grab the rug, pull it hard and there was a slim chance he could topple the ghost. But he had to do it quickly. Pulling the rug would mean he was in full view and the ghost would see him. There was no doubt this would anger it enough to make a move – either lunging at Bex or at Jud himself.

He had to act fast. He summoned up all his strength.

Without hesitating, Jud rolled over, grabbed the rug with both hands and pulled it as hard and as sharply as he could.

It worked.

The ghost lost balance instantly and crashed to the floor. The shock of being toppled reduced its energy sharply. The brittle bones which had been solid enough to take visible form were clearly nothing but hollow imitations. There was a cracking sound, like sticks being stamped on. The ghost was fragmenting. Energy was leaving it.

Jud and Bex lost no time in seizing their chance to break it further. They flew at the fallen figure, stamping on it heavily, ripping its arms and smashing their fists into its face.

The ghost had no chance. Though the anger that had fuelled it remained momentarily, allowing its eyes to glow red for a while, its body was broken and the constant stamping and punching from the agents meant that it was unable to rise again.

They continued their rain of kicks and punches until soon their feet were passing right through the ghost's body. Breaking up the bonds of ionised plasma that bound it together was what they had been taught to do in the countless SPA training sessions, especially when there was insufficient time available to let the EM neutralisers do their work.

Soon there was nothing but a translucent image sprawled across the floor and Jud and Bex were stamping on shadows.

They sank to the floor, exhausted.

'So, you glad we stayed?' said Bex, panting.

'Well, glad it was us and not one of the police officers, yes,' said Jud. 'Otherwise we might have had another killing.'

'But what was angering this ghost?' said Bex. 'I mean, what the hell brought it here?'

'My guess is this is the disembodied spirit of a partner who worked at the bank. I know this is a private bank, not like the giant investment banks we've seen before, where the big losses have been recorded, and my guess is money is being taken from here too.'

Bex agreed. 'And just like the dragons coming to life to protect the treasure, the ghosts of bankers are doing it too.'

'Kind of makes sense,' said Jud. 'Why it killed that woman, I guess we'll find out. Either she was robbing clients of their money or—'

'Someone was making it look like she had,' said Bex. 'And we know who that is.'

Jud got to his feet and grabbed Bex's hand to haul her up.

'Let's go find the bastard.'

CHAPTER 19

SATURDAY, 7.48 P.M. (8.48 P.M. LOCAL TIME)

CLICHY-SOUS-BOIS, PARIS

In a dark corner of a shabby bar, the man sipped his coffee and read his newspaper. He was smiling. He couldn't help it. The headline in *Les Echos* had pleased him.

LA CRISE BANCAIRE APPORTE LE CHAOS
À LONDRES

It was working. Just what he'd hoped for. In fact, as he read on, it was even better than he'd planned. There was talk of ghosts in the City now, even dragons coming to life. No one knew if there was any link between the banking disasters and the hauntings, but it was obviously combining to make serious trouble for London's residents – and especially for those charged with protecting them.

'Rot in hell,' he mumbled as he took another slurp from the frothy coffee.

He rarely ventured outside of his apartment, but today he felt less cautious. After all, what was there to fear? He'd set the ball in motion and now nothing could stop it. And he knew there was one company, one man, for whom this would have the most devastating consequences of all.

The person he was expecting was late. He hated lateness. It did not inspire confidence – but confidence and trust were essential if the working relationship he was about to embark on stood any chance of being successful. He decided he wouldn't raise the matter. This time, he would let it go.

He finished reading the newspaper, folded it neatly, drained the last drop of coffee from the cup then signalled to the assistant behind the counter, a pretty girl of no more than seventeen, for another. She managed to hide her disappointment, as she, along with most of the people in the place, had been hoping he would leave soon. His dishevelled appearance, combined with his frequent explosive coughing, was unsettling.

The man's eyes were fixed on the glass door at the other side of the room. Every time anyone had entered the crowded little bar during the half hour he had been sitting there, he had wondered if this was his contact.

A thick-set, shaven-headed man of around forty pushed the door open with a jolt. He glanced around the room for a moment, then headed straight for the man in the corner.

'Jacob?' he said to the scruffy-looking man who had not bothered to stand.

'*Oui*,' the man lied without emotion. 'Christophe?'

'Yes.'

'Sit down,' said the man. 'Thank you for meeting me here. I don't think we'll be disturbed. Coffee?'

Christophe was surprised. The man in the corner who called himself Jacob had sounded ancient on the phone, his low, gravelly voice and his frequent coughs suggesting someone considerably older. But this man sitting before him could not have been much older than his mid-fifties, though it was obvious time had not been kind and he was not in good health.

'So,' Jacob began, 'I am grateful for your assistance. You have done this kind of thing before?'

Christophe nodded, glancing around the place furtively.

'Don't worry,' said Jacob. 'We won't be disturbed. Now, listen. I can pay you handsomely, but not until the job is finished.'

His guest shook his head solemnly. 'Sorry, man. I don't work like that. You said on the phone there would be an advance and that's what I've come for. No money. No help.' He went to get up.

Jacob grabbed his arm. 'Sit down,' he said in a low voice.

Christophe could have beaten this man to a pulp if he'd wanted. There was nothing to him. But his story on the phone the night before had pricked his interest. The promise of 'riches' had been appealing. He decided to stay seated and listen to what else this man had to say.

'You've got five minutes, then I'm outta here. Talk.'

Jacob coughed sharply and cleared his throat. The pretty girl from the bar brought over a coffee and placed it in front of him, removing his old cup. '*Qu'est-ce que vous voulez?*' she said to Christophe.

'*Un café,*' he muttered.

'I need protection. Not for long. Two weeks, no more. There will be people out to get me, of that there is no question. Your help would be appreciated – and rewarded handsomely. I can't predict the hours yet, but it will be the usual.'

'Eight hours a day for two weeks, right?'

'Twelve, at least.'

'Ten hours. I gotta eat and sleep, man.'

'Okay. But if something happens outside those hours, you come when I tell you to, right?'

'Advance?' was all Christophe said.

'I said you'd be rewarded. I'm sorry if I gave you the impression I would pay you now. I knew you wouldn't meet me unless I did. But hear me out. If you agree to work for me, you will be rewarded in two weeks' time with a fee bigger than you've ever had before.'

Christophe just shrugged and held out his hand. 'Advance now or I walk.'

Jacob knew he would be a tough nut to crack. That was why he was employing him, after all. He wasn't recruiting him for his bedside manner.

'Let me talk numbers then. How much do you earn a day for a job like this normally, huh? Five hundred euros?'

Christophe just shook his head.

'More? Six hundred? Seven hundred? Clearly I should have trained as a bodyguard.'

Christophe looked him up and down and huffed. There was no need to say anything. It was obvious this man would not last long in such a role.

'Let's say you average seven hundred a day. That's a good wage. Especially if there's no trouble. I need you for a couple of weeks. Fourteen days. That's almost ten thousand euros. I'll double it. Twenty thousand. But you'll have to wait for the payment in full. Nothing now, twenty thousand at the end.'

Now he had the man's attention. The girl returned with the coffee and he picked it up without thanking her. He swallowed slowly then said, 'Okay. But fail to pay and you'll soon see why I'm a bodyguard.'

Jacob smiled. 'Deal.' He extended a bony hand across the table but Christophe ignored it.

'One question,' he said. 'Where's the money coming from? I need to know you've got it.'

'Trust me,' said Jacob. 'I'm good for the money. You do a good job, when this is over I might even consider hiring you permanently.'

Promises, promises, from a total stranger. But truth was, he had precious little else on at the moment. There was no way he would tell Jacob, of course, but he'd no other work planned for the next fortnight.

'Start tomorrow?' said Jacob.

'Tomorrow. Here?'

Jacob shook his head. He took out a pen from his coat pocket, picked up the small paper receipt which the girl had left on the table and scribbled down his address. 'Ten o'clock tomorrow morning. Come prepared, it's going to be a busy day. Don't show that to anybody, and don't tell anyone who you're working for or where. Got it?'

Christophe nodded. That wasn't unusual. Much of his time was spent with people who had something to hide for one reason or another. This guy was no different.

They left separately, Christophe exiting first. Jacob paid the bill and left the bar, bracing himself for the cold night air. He tugged his cap low over his face, and pulled up the collar on his old, filthy coat to meet his neck. The evening breeze was chilly and it rattled around his frail bones. But there was almost a spring in his step tonight. He couldn't wait to get back to his tiny spare room, his headquarters, where he would wreak more havoc. Armed with just a few computers but an intellect unrivalled, he knew he could achieve his dream. And across the Channel, in a luxurious apartment in the clouds, there would soon be a man facing annihilation.

He grinned and disappeared into the darkening backstreets of Paris.

CHAPTER 20

SATURDAY, 8.16 P.M.

CRYPT HEADQUARTERS,

LONDON

'So?' said Bonati, impatiently. 'Talk to me.'

'We believe the banker, Annika Premvas, was killed by a ghost, sir,' said Bex. 'Her throat was slashed.'

'How can you be sure?'

'Because it nearly killed me too.'

'What?' Bonati sat up in his chair.

'It's true,' said Jud. 'After taking readings in the room where the killing happened, and finding very high EM levels, we conducted a search of the whole place.'

'And it was on the top floor, where the partners work,' Bex continued. 'We walked in on it in the partners' meeting room.'

'So what was it like?' said the professor.

'Well, that's easy to tell you because not only did we see it, there was an exact portrait of it hanging over the fireplace.'

'Really?' said the professor. 'So it must have been the ghost of a deceased banker, a senior partner, I suppose.'

'Yes, exactly,' said Jud. Then he and Bex filled him in on

what had happened. The professor listened patiently, as he always did when agents debriefed him.

Finally, he said, 'So this is conclusive proof that the hauntings must be connected to the banking crisis. It's far too much of a coincidence for a ghost to be haunting a bank right now, killing randomly. It's linked.'

'And there's the ghost at that bar too, the Counting House, which was once a bank,' said Bex.

'That's right. We have to stop this, and quickly, before there are more fatalities. But you decided to leave the scene. Did Khan know that you'd gone?'

'Yes,' said Jud. 'We informed him of the incident up on the partners' floor, but we told him we'd dispatched the ghost. It's for his officers now to work with the bank's bosses to establish why this figure should return there.'

'Agreed, but I don't see why you left so quickly. How do we know there aren't going to be more hauntings there tonight? How do we know that was the only ghost on the premises?'

'Well, we don't, sir, and if you want to deploy more agents to carry out a vigil overnight, it's probably worth it.'

'And I'm guessing these agents won't be you, am I right?' Bonati knew exactly where this was leading. He could see that Jud looked uneasy.

'Well, we've got work to do on the case elsewhere. Research. In the labs.' Jud was finding it hard to hide his impatience. Being summoned to Bonati's office as soon as they'd arrived back at the CRYPT was not what they'd needed. They'd been hoping to sneak back and get on with the business of finding out who'd sent the email to his father. Do some digging around. Delve into his father's past in whatever way they could. Exploring people's histories was what CRYPT agents did, looking for reasons why ghosts would want to revisit the world of the living. His father was no different. If he was trying to bury something in his past, they'd find it. If something was coming back to haunt him, then Jud wanted to know about it.

'So you still won't tell us about that email then?' said Jud quietly.

Bex shot him a look that said 'drop it'. It was too soon after the incident up in Goode's apartment, and it was unlikely that the professor would be any more forthcoming. Besides, they'd still not been disciplined for being up there. They'd got away with it, or so it seemed. Why push it now?

The professor looked thoughtfully at Jud across his desk. 'You're not going to let this drop, are you?'

'Of course not. Would you?' said Jud. 'If someone's out to get my father then I want to know, Professor. Someone's trying to frame him, aren't they?'

Bonati could see how much this meant to Jud and he pitied him. God knows, the boy had been through enough already. And here he was, on the brink of losing his father too. If Jason was arrested and taken into custody, he doubted Jud would handle it well.

He knew as well as Goode who'd sent the email. Or had his suspicions. But Jason had insisted Jud should not be told about their past. Not ever.

It was an impossible situation. Tell Jud now and risk betraying the trust of his oldest and closest friend, or shut him out and have to watch the slow decline of a boy who was as dear to him as a son.

'Please,' Jud begged. 'If you know something, tell me. This is my father we're talking about. It's family.'

The morose way Jud said 'family' touched the professor deeply. He knew all too well there was no 'family' as far as Jamie Goode was concerned. It had been blown apart.

He had to give him something. But he also knew that once Jud was on the scent of something he'd never give up. He'd hunt down the facts like a starving predator, and he'd not give up until he found the truth about what, or who, was haunting his father.

He rose from his desk silently and went for the door. He opened it and peered outside. There was no one around. He returned, closed the door and locked it shut. Jud and Bex peered at each other expectantly.

Without saying a word the professor crept slowly back to his chair and sat down, chewing his lip nervously.

'Okay. I'll tell you what I know. But you must give me your word – and I mean this, both of you – that you will not tell your father that I've told you. You will have to make up some story that you found it all out by research. He knows what you're like when you're on an investigation. It's possible you could have found out anyway, in time.'

Jud and Bex waited with bated breath. What on earth was the professor about to tell them? Jud felt sick. What had his father done? What was he hiding? Who would hate him this much, and why?

'We think the message may be from a man called Bonaparte, Guy Bonaparte,' Bonati began, his voice shaking. 'Your father always called him Nap, short for Napoleon. He was French.

'Nap was the third person in our trio at Cambridge. We did everything together. He was a seriously bright guy, no question, but he claimed he was the brains behind our computer research. The truth is we worked together and brought equal talent to the table. But he started accusing Jason of taking his ideas – he was wrong. They were your father's own ideas, his own theories. But Nap couldn't handle the success he was having. He always claimed that your father and I had stolen his designs, his ideas.'

'And did you?' said Jud, transfixed.

Bonati fell silent for a few moments, and each second that passed brought a greater sense of guilt. He looked awkward. Was that shame on his face, thought Bex? They'd never seen him like this. He looked smaller somehow, vulnerable.

'There was an almighty fallout,' said Bonati, ignoring Jud's question. It was just after we'd graduated. Nap and your father

130

had this incredible row. They always used to argue, but this was really serious. All sorts of threats were made. Nap was furious that your father was going to use the new technology to set up a new company. Your father refused to accept Nap's story that the designs had been all his idea in the first place—'

'You didn't answer my question,' Jud interrupted. Bex looked at the floor and tried hard to stop her cheeks from flushing with embarrassment. Had Jud forgotten who he was talking to?

'That's enough,' said the professor. 'You're not the judge and jury. Who are you to pass judgement? If you won't listen, I won't tell you. I thought you wanted to hear what this is about, but I don't think you do.'

'I'm sorry,' Jud said eventually. He kept silent, but Bex could see his fists clenching beneath his chair and the muscles in his jaw flexing. He was clearly using all his might to resist an explosion. She raised a hand to rest on his arm but he quickly brushed her off.

'Nap was a difficult man to get along with. He always said he was the genius and that we were riding on his intellect. But it's not true. He would always have these outbursts. He was clever, there was no denying it, but he had a terrible memory and he was erratic. Violent mood swings, all that. Boy, he could be stubborn. We offered for him to join us, but he refused. We tried to suggest we could do this jointly, that he could share in whatever company we built, but he wouldn't have it. He said we'd stolen his ideas. In the end it was just impossible to reason with him and he fled home to Paris.

'Your father went on to gain patents for his computer ideas – I still believe they were rightfully his, J – and the rest is history. The last thing we heard Nap was a drunk, living on handouts in some backstreet in Paris. We tried to contact him in the early days, after university, but he refused to be found. He couldn't get over the resentment he felt over Jason being more successful than he was.'

'So they were good friends at one time?' said Jud.

Bonati nodded. 'The best. We were a trio. Everyone knew us at Cambridge. The dons said we'd go far, provided we managed to keep our tempers at bay. They were heady days – we worked hard and we played hard. Your father and Nap were always falling out over some scientific theory or other, but we kind of got used to it. I was usually the middle man, the mediator. But when they had this almighty row I could do nothing to get them to speak to each other again. Jason said Nap had questioned his integrity, accused him of stealing his theories and ideas. But I promise you he didn't.'

'So where's this Nap guy now?' said Jud.

The professor shrugged. 'We don't know. We heard all sorts of rumours, mostly from other people we were at university with. Someone said he'd been killed in an accident. Others said he'd taken his own life. We assumed he was dead because we've never been able to find him.'

'Find him?' said Jud. 'You mean you've been trying to find him all this time?'

Bonati nodded slowly. 'Your father has often tried, yes. He's employed private investigators over the years.'

'Because he feels guilty?' said Jud.

'No. Because he feels pity. You've got to understand, they were so close back then. We all were. Like brothers. It hurts when one just disappears. You can't forget. You just have to move on. I often told Jason to let it go, but he never really did . . . and now this.'

'How do you know it's this Bonaparte for sure?' said Bex, softly.

'The truth is, we don't,' said Bonati. 'And in a way, that's the hardest part. We eventually started to believe the rumours that he was indeed dead. But the email said "old friend" and we both knew there was only one person who would describe themselves in that way. Besides, look at the sentences again.'

He picked up the paper which he'd brought down to the office with him.

Jud looked again at the message.

Never believe you can bury the past, Jason. All crimes will come back to haunt you like ghosts. Prison beckons.

Yours,

An old friend

'Oh my God,' he said. 'I can see it.'

'See what?' said Bex, taking the paper from him.

'It's not the hardest code to break, but it's just the kind of silly game Nap used to play,' said Bonati.

And then Bex saw it too. Just three simple sentences, but the first letter of each spelt a name when combined. It was obvious.

'So this guy is trying to frame Goode Technology,' said Bex.

'By hacking into the banks' computers, faking these dodgy deals and then placing blame on the people who made the technology,' said Jud. 'But why should they be blamed just for making the computers? It doesn't add up.'

'We believe he's infiltrated the company,' said the professor. 'He's got spies working for him on the inside. He must have. He's been planning this for years. You can bet, when the police investigate this fully, they'll find that the computer hackers were people on your father's payroll, inside the company. So we didn't just make the technology, it'll look like we hacked into the banks too. I don't know whether they're operating out of our offices in Paris, New York, Beijing, or right here below us, but somewhere we have a mole. Working for Nap Bonaparte.'

They stared at one another, their brains racing ahead to try to guess where this would lead. The expressions on their faces showed only bad things could come of it.

'This guy's got to be stopped,' said Jud defiantly.

'Of course, but how?' said Bonati. 'He's been invisible all

these years. And your father can't go after him. The police won't let him out of the country now. This case is building all the time, and if the company really is involved, they're hardly likely to let the owner abscond, are they? They'll think he's jumped ship and fled.'

Jud stood up. 'I'm going to Paris.'

'That's *not* what I meant,' Bonati snapped. 'Sit down and don't be ridiculous. You're needed here anyway. You're a ghost hunter, not a private detective, for God's sake. And in any case, you'll never find Bonaparte. He's a master.'

'Oh, I'll find him,' said Jud, still standing.

Bex felt uncomfortable. There was a game of brinkmanship going on here which she didn't want to be party to. She was no stranger to trouble, usually caused by Jud, but this was one mission she was genuinely nervous about. If Jason Goode found out where they were heading, they would both be dropped from the team in an instant. Besides, tracking someone like Bonaparte would be dangerous and difficult and like trying to find a needle in a haystack; you never know when it's about to stab you.

But Goode's entire career was at stake. Not to mention his liberty. She knew Jud would never sit back and watch that happen to his father, just as it had to him. And if he was going to France, she was going with him, there was no question about that.

'I've already told you,' said Bonati, 'your father and I have been trying to locate him for years. We've had private investigators in France, all over Europe, working on this. No one's ever found him. The closest we came was a couple of years back when one of our men believed they sighted him in Paris, but they lost the trail. The guy's invisible. You don't know what you're dealing with here. He's got all the skills we have, but he chooses to use them for evil. That's the difference. The man's mad. I don't want you near him. Your father would never allow that, and you know it. I'm not discussing it any more. We have much to do.'

The professor sat upright in a brusque and businesslike way and shuffled some papers on his desk. After a few moments of awkward silence, he finally said, 'Well then, agents, I suggest you get back to your rooms and recuperate for a while. It's been a difficult twenty-four hours and you need to rest. I'll put two other agents in the bank on Fleet Street for the night. It's important we have a presence there, in case there are still some clues we can pick up, and to steady the nerves of the partners, who'll no doubt be pulling strings as we speak and talking to our friends at the Met or at MI6 to find out what the hell is going on. I'm sure the place will be buzzing with senior people from the bank this evening and tomorrow, so there's little recording we can do now, but God forbid someone else gets injured or killed when you've left the place unguarded.'

Bonati rose and walked slowly to the door. He knew he should never have told them about Nap and now he wanted to sweep it away as quickly as possible. But it was out there. Pandora's box had been well and truly opened and he had no idea what would happen next. It was the first time the agents had seen him so rattled. They could tell he was losing control of the situation, and his poor attempts to get back to the case in hand had not convinced them otherwise.

'You stay in your rooms, you hear? You recuperate,' he said, trying to regain his authority. 'That's an order, okay? As far as you're concerned, this matter is off-limits.'

But as he watched Jud trudge out, he felt certain it would only be a matter of time before he disappeared.

And there was nothing the professor could do to stop him.

CHAPTER 21

SATURDAY, 8.49 P.M.

(3.49 P.M. LOCAL TIME)

GOODE TECHNOLOGY PLC, NEW

YORK OFFICES

Jason Goode's face filled the giant screen at the end of the long boardroom. He was able to see each of his ten executives, five on each side of the glass-topped table that swept down the centre of the room. He could also see the worry on their faces. They all knew why he'd called this emergency meeting. How could they not know? The news that Goode Technology had somehow been implicated in the London banking crisis was the biggest thing they'd ever faced. The news had sent shockwaves around the global offices, manufacturing plants and distribution warehouses on every continent. The fact that their CEO and founder had been 'helping the police with their enquiries' sent a chill down everyone's spine. Where the hell was this going to end?

News that there was a saboteur, maybe several, at work on the inside meant that suspicion was rife in every office. Employees were looking at one another nervously every day. Who was it? Where were they? Working relationships were taking a pounding as trust was slowly corroding. Jason Goode wanted to steady the ship. He was holding executive meetings in every one of his main offices, from Beijing to New York. The technology meant that he could get face to face with anyone he wanted, at anytime. Luckily it was mid-afternoon in New York; the Beijing staff would not be so lucky, and they were next. Employees had been warned to get to their offices for 5 a.m.

Goode's voice boomed out over the speakers fitted neatly into the ceiling, between the halogen spots. 'Thank you everyone for coming. I know you're busy people. And I know too that you're worried people. But don't be. This'll pass. And when it does, we'll be stronger. This company is bigger and better than anyone out there realises. We're a tight group. We pull together. We survive.'

His words were welcome. Staff smiled encouragingly at each other across the table, safe in the knowledge that they were being watched. Positive reactions were expected. No one wanted to be on the sharp end of Goode's tongue. He was dynamic and effusive, but could snap at any point if he didn't like someone's attitude. He 'only did positivity', that was his mantra, so they dutifully nodded and smiled back at the screen when he'd finished.

'How's things over there, Jay?' asked Mitch Deverel, Chief Operating Officer for the US. 'You okay?'

'Yeah, Mitch. Thanks. It's a storm, I can't deny it, but we'll ride it out.'

'So what do you want us to do, boss? We're ready and waiting.'

'As far as anyone else is concerned, you keep goin', business as usual. Any talk of this issue among the regular guys must be stamped on, y'understand? I don't want this to become a distraction. We've all got work to do.'

Everyone nodded their agreement.

'But as for you guys at the top,' Goode continued, 'you gotta get to the bottom of it for me. Hell, I don't know if it's even true that we've got a mole on the inside, working from within our corporation. It may not be. But just in case it is, you gotta start investigating for me. I sure wish I was there with you guys, but I can't be.'

Straight away his executives feared the worst. Was he being prevented from travelling? Had Scotland Yard taken his passport? Told him to report to the station every day? Hell, was he under surveillance?

Goode caught the mood. He could see his staff needed further reassurance. 'I've not been arrested, you know! I'm a free man, for God's sake! But my place is here, where it's all kickin' off. If I desert the ship now, it'll send out the wrong message to my guys here. Besides, I've got my own investigations going on. God help the mole if he's working for me here in London. In my building.'

'So we start interviewing, yeah? See what we can unearth?' asked Monica Hernandez, Head of Human Resources.

'Sure,' said Goode, smiling at Monica. 'You go for it, girl, but for God's sake do it gently. We don't wanna give everyone the impression there's a witch hunt on. You can invite people to come see you if they have worries or concerns. Get 'em talkin'. You know, let them tell you everything. Just don't go in there and interrogate everyone. Build an open dialogue. People can come see you with their questions – or suspicions. But, Mitch . . . ?'

'Yeah, Jay?'

'I want you to start a programme of monitoring phone calls and emails. Elijah, you can help.'

Elijah Moore, Head of Communications, looked up. 'Of course, boss. Right away. Everyone knows phone calls are monitored periodically anyway, it's what we do. But I'll step it up across the campus. And in Baltimore too. You spoken to Baltimore yet, boss?'

They watched Goode shake his head. 'Nope, not yet. Mitch,

you make the call first, then get Elijah to speak to his people down there and get it set up. Be subtle, yeah? Remember, no witch hunts, just routine monitoring. Same with Atlanta too. You contact them.'

'Sure, I've had Don Anderson from Atlanta on the phone already. He's worried, Jay.'

'Yeah, well I've told you before what I think about people who worry. We only do positivity. You know that. Keep the ship steady, Mitch. Like you always do.

'And Jonathan, you got the biggest job of all. You all set?'

Jonathan Fisher, Head of Infrastructure, nodded. 'Yes, boss.' Goode had already been on the phone to Jonathan several times that day. They'd agreed the plan, together with Mitch, as to how they were going to monitor all computer use across the site, and in the Baltimore and Atlanta sites too. It was a huge operation to 'go fishing', as Goode called it, to track what his technical staff had been up to and highlight any activity that looked even vaguely suspicious.

'My team's on it,' Jonathan continued. 'I've got people working round the clock, sir.'

'Okay. Good man. Remember, guys, I'm always at the end of a phone. You call me, or Mitch, if you dig up something you're not happy about. It may be a throwaway comment from someone, it may be an email or a phone call that's out of the ordinary, or maybe some suspicious-looking research. But by God we'll find it.'

'Okay, guys,' Mitch clapped his hands together. His energy was infectious. 'You heard the boss. Let's get on top of this.'

'Thanks, Mitch. Oh, and by the way, people, I nearly forgot. There's a ten thousand dollar bonus, cash, for the guy who provides the information which leads me to the mole. You got that?'

Everyone smiled again and nodded their appreciation.

'I thought you'd like that. But keep it to yourselves, you hear?

Just you guys in that room. Some people would shop their own granny for that kinda cash. Now go to it. And take care.'

They watched Goode move to the monitor and turn it off. The screen went dead.

'Okay, meeting over,' said Mitch. 'I want you all back in here, nine o'clock tomorrow morning. Now go find me some good news.'

CHAPTER 22

SATURDAY, 10.03 P.M.

ENGLISH CHANNEL

Jud sipped his hot chocolate and stared at the night sky and the dark, ominous seas that swept past their window. The alluring smells of chips, fried fish and cheap lasagne wafted over to them from the canteen a few feet from where they were sitting. The ship's dining room was surprisingly quiet for a Saturday night, though the previous two crossings had been busier.

The staff were beginning to look weary as they collected empty plates from tables, wiped and stacked trays, or served up twice-fried chips from behind the counter. It was a strange life to be on the waves every day, working their shifts, but never venturing any further than the twenty-five-mile stretch of water between the two countries. The same views, the same land masses and the same kinds of people, day in, day out; only the weather changed, though their sea legs had become so accustomed to the shifting motions of the ship, it was rare for them to notice the dramatic rising and falling that the less-experienced passengers found so unsettling. Cups slid from one end of a table to another, passengers swayed and giggled and pretended to be caught up in some tempestuous storm, but the listing and lurching rarely caused so much as a raised eyebrow from the staff in the canteen.

The giant car ferry swayed to the right and then again to the left. It was turning into a rough crossing and they both clung onto their mugs, preventing them from sliding across their own plastic table.

The crossing was no more than an hour and a half in length, and Bex was grateful for that. She had always suffered with sea sickness and the weather had rapidly deteriorated since they'd departed from Dover. The white cliffs, lit up by the orange glow of streetlamps from the giant port beneath, had slowly shrunk in the distance as she and Jud had stood on the top deck braving the wind and rain.

Bex had been keen to put the bike on the Eurostar train instead; it was quicker and smoother and involved no sea sickness. But Jud had insisted on taking the ferry. He loved the sea air and hadn't expected a crossing as rough as this. Once the cliffs had faded into the darkness, they'd come inside for a much-needed warm drink.

'How's your stomach?' said Jud, half smiling.

'Don't ask.'

'You want some more fresh air?'

'You're joking,' said Bex. 'It's freezing out there. The wind will blow you overboard.'

'Come on, you softie. It's bracing. I love it. It blows the cobwebs away. It'll wake us up for the long night ahead.'

'You mean we're not checking into a hotel?'

'Yeah, in Paris, of course,' said Jud, 'but we've got a long ride ahead of us before we get there, and then there's work to be done. I want to set up the laptops as soon as we check in and start scouring the city maps.'

'For what exactly?'

'Bonati said the last they heard this Bonaparte guy was spotted in some poorer district on the outskirts of Paris.'

'But it'll be like looking for a needle in a haystack.' Bex voiced her earlier concern.

Jud shook his head. He fished around in his rucksack on the seat next to him. Eventually he retrieved his phone. He opened up an email and showed it to Bex. It was from Bonati, and it contained the scanned image of an old photograph.

Bex could see younger versions of Goode and Bonati with a man in between them.

'Bonati sent you this? It's your father in his student days at Cambridge, isn't it? That's Bonaparte in the centre, I presume.'

'Yep.'

'Jud, this was years ago. How the hell are we going to recognise him now?'

'It's a start, Bex. And we have his name too.'

'He'll probably be using a different one by now.'

'Maybe so. But look.' Jud pointed lower down in the email. Bonati had given them the name of a café in which their private investigators had once seen the man. 'I've already Googled it and it still exists. It's in a district called Clichy-sous-Bois. We can't guarantee that's where he lives, but it's a start. It'll be the first district we try.'

Bex was shaking her head, but smiling. 'I admire your confidence,' she said. 'You just don't give up, do you?'

'Give up?' said Jud. 'I've not even started yet. Now come on, finish your drink. Let's get some more of that fresh air in your lungs.'

They opened the heavy door that led out onto the upper deck and braced themselves against the wind. It was blowing a gale, but at least the rain had abated. They held firmly onto the railings as they edged down the walkway to get a clearer view of the sea. The lights of Dover had disappeared and the sky was too dark and misty to reveal any signs of Calais yet.

Bex watched Jud close his eyes and take in deep breaths. Though he could be infuriating, secretive and so, so hard to love, she couldn't imagine being with anyone else now. He was right too, the fresh air was settling her stomach. She did feel better out here, albeit freezing.

'It's so *cold*,' she said.

He moved behind her and wrapped his arms around her waist as they both stared out to sea. She could feel his warm body leaning into hers. They were alone, on the ocean, bound for Paris, the most romantic city in the world. Okay, so they were on a mission, which would be anything but romantic to most people, but that's how their relationship thrived. Danger brought them closer. They were at their best when working together on a mission. It was when they had nothing to do, kicking around at the CRYPT, that Jud was at his most difficult. But here, right now, she could pretend. And dream.

What would they do when their time at the CRYPT was at an end? She knew they couldn't stay there forever. The agency had a policy of moving agents on every three years – with luck, into jobs in the security forces, perhaps MI5 or MI6, if they were good enough. But would Jud be able to do that? From what he'd told her, Bex believed that he was effectively under house arrest, the responsibility of Bonati and Goode. It was a better alternative to prison, but it wasn't freedom. And would those parole terms ever change? If not, Jud would be the only agent to remain at the CRYPT forever. She supposed he would eventually join Vorzek and the others on the staff.

And what would happen to them then? Jud's secret history would mean an ordinary life together was out of the question for them, but saying goodbye would be impossible.

She quickly brushed all thoughts away and held his arms tight around her. She would only live for the present, as she had done since arriving at the CRYPT. Nothing else mattered except today.

'I've got something to tell you, Bex,' said Jud.

She turned around to face him. 'What?'

'Well, I don't know how to say this, but we won't be alone in

Paris. There's someone else who'll be helping us. And luckily he speaks French.'

'Who are you talking about?' said Bex, puzzled. 'The only French-speaking agent was Luc. So what are you saying . . .' She hesitated.

'You said the only agent who spoke French was Luc, right?' Jud whispered. 'So?'

'Talk to me,' was all she could say.

'I've made contact. I've spoken to him.'

'You've *what*?'

Jud nodded. 'It's true, Bex. I've reached him. At last.'

'When?'

'A couple of weeks ago. In the SPA room. Why do you think I've been spending so much time in there?' He was smiling now.

'We all know why you've been in there, but none of us knew you'd managed it. How? Why didn't you tell us? Tell me, at least? I can't believe it, J. I mean, I just—'

'Slow down. Listen to me.'

'But Jud, this is massive. I mean, I can't believe you've done it! So, what did he say? What's it like? When did he—'

'Wait, wait!' Jud found Bex's excitement cute, though he didn't want to get her hopes up too much. 'It was only brief contact, but I did break through. We can all sense ghosts, Bex, this is nothing new, when you think about it.'

'No, J. We can sense ghosts when they come to us, but we've never been able to summon one from the afterlife at our choosing. They've never come when we've asked, you know that. It's only when they come back to haunt that we can see them, talk to them. It's their anger that fuels their energy, you know how it works as well as I do. This is different, J. It's massive. Please tell me.' She stared at him, her eyes wide with curiosity. Her lips were trembling.

Whether it was the cold, or the fact that they were so close, alone together, or something else entirely, she didn't know, but

Jud held her face and gave her the longest kiss they'd ever had. His lips were warm and soothing. He felt her cold nose press against his own and it made him wrap his arms around her even tighter.

When they parted she looked at him. 'Jud Lester, you're a complex animal, you really are.'

'Maybe. It's what makes it fun, though.'

She rolled her eyes, but he caught a trace of disappointment in her face, like she was waiting for something more, anything, to show he cared.

'Look, all I know is I couldn't do any of this without you, okay?' he said quickly, before the flush of embarrassment came.

They locked in a tight embrace, gazing over each other's shoulders rather than into each other's eyes. Jud's words, though blurted out quickly, had felt real enough. They hugged to shut out the cold wind and the uncertainty of what lay ahead.

'So?' Bex eventually said. 'You can't distract me that easily, Jud Lester. You were about to tell me more about Luc.'

'Was I?' He smiled, and they both leant over the railing, staring down at the violent sea, wondering how deep it ran and how cold and dark were its depths. Their nostrils filled with the now familiar smell of salt water.

'I was in the SPA room when it first happened. Bonati was there.'

'The professor was with you?' said Bex, surprised. 'He never told me.'

'Well, it was early days. It was just after we'd lost Luc. It was too soon to go telling everyone.'

'I'm not "everyone", Jud.'

'I know, and I'm sorry we kept it from you at the time. But in any case, it was only a voice back then.'

'You heard Luc's voice? But how? What did you do to make contact? How did it work? Did you summon him or did he just come to you?'

Jud saw her eagerness to know more.

'Well, you see, my father and the professor had been working on something just before Luc died. An electromagnetic tracking device – an EM tracer. It identifies the unique energy pattern that a person's spirit emits and then tracks it. We know energy never dies with us when our physical body dies, so it kind of makes sense to try to follow where it goes. And just as everyone has a unique DNA makeup, we have a unique energy radiation too. It's as individual as our fingerprints, Bex. And it *can* be tracked.'

'But Luc died before you had a chance to use the EM tracer, surely? His spirit was gone.'

'No,' said Jud. 'Don't you remember? He didn't die right there, on the train, when Grace was with him. He died days later in hospital. And though we didn't know it at the time, Bonati flew straight to the hospital to operate the tracer before we lost him. Luc was no longer conscious, of course, but they did it.'

'Did *what* exactly?' said Bex. She wanted desperately to understand, but it was beginning to sound like some sci-fi movie. It just didn't seem real. 'What was it, a chip inside his head or something?'

'No, not at all. Remember we're not dealing with solid forms here. We're not talking about *mass*, we're talking about *energy*. Everything in the universe is made up of either mass or energy. And both can be traced and monitored. Bonati used the EM tracer to scan Luc's energy pattern and lock onto it, which he managed. Then they were able to monitor what happened to him once he died. What happened to his spirit, I mean.'

'This is incredible, J. It's huge. And you're saying it actually *worked*?'

'No, not at first. Nothing happened. We just thought that was it, we'd lost him forever. But then one night the professor brought me down to the SPA rooms and showed me something.'

'What?' Bex was getting impatient.

'Well, not *showed* me exactly, because there was nothing to see, other than the energy patterns which were registering on the EM tracer. But after we'd monitored the energy levels that we'd picked up, we heard it. Luc's voice. It was unmistakably him, Bex. It really was.'

'And you'd summoned him, I mean, like on demand? You reached him first before he contacted you?'

'Well, yes, I suppose so,' said Jud. 'Only that was all we managed. Nothing else. We couldn't see him. I thought I'd never see him again. All we heard was a faint whisper of his voice. At first it actually made it worse for me. Imagine hearing him but not being able to see him. It was too painful. Why do you think I was so withdrawn? I just couldn't handle it. I didn't want to see anyone. I just needed to process it. I couldn't get on with grieving for Luc because in one way he'd not really left, but I couldn't see him, or reach him either. It was like a memory, a faint echo of the past that was haunting me, but it wasn't really him.'

'So what's changed? Why do you think you can reach him properly now?'

'Well, I kept going down to the SPA to see if I could reach him again. I used the EM tracer. Most of the time it registered nothing. And then I started to pick up a trace again. It was Luc's pattern. And it grew stronger. It was like I was summoning him to the SPA, closer and closer. The EMF meters showed the radiation was growing stronger each time, and the EM tracer proved it was him – the readings matched the ones Bonati took in the hospital. Then I began to hear him again. And eventually, after a while, I could see him.'

Bex's face was incredulous. '*See* him?'

'Yes. I told you, energy doesn't die. His spirit didn't die with his body, we always knew that – or hoped it was true. And soon I could see that it was, and how Luc did it.'

'Did what?'

'How he attracted the plasma to become visible. I watched it happen, Bex. Right there. It was incredible.'

'Wait a minute,' said Bex. 'Are you sure this isn't basically a hologram you're talking about. It was in the SPA after all. We know we can do that in the SPA. We've done it before. We've made the ghosts ourselves.'

'No, holograms are different. We use them all the time in the SPA. We know the difference between a hologram and a real ghost. One is made by us using light projections and digital images, and the other comes to us in the form of plasma. Real plasma, that hardens with intensity. It's not a light projection,' said Jud. 'But the difference here is we *both* did it. Luc and me. It was like me being there, tracing his energy pattern and locking onto it, somehow made it easier for him. I watched to see if the radiation – his radiation – was increasing. And when it did, I was there to see what happened.'

'So do you have to be in the SPA for it to happen every time then?'

'No. You've got to stop thinking it was the SPA equipment that conjured him up. It wasn't, Bex. You know that real ghosts don't appear in the SPA, they're only simulations that we make. The only reason Bonati and I used the SPA, and the reason I kept going back there, was because—'

'It was private?' said Bex.

'Exactly,' said Jud. 'Think about it. Where else could I go? My room? One of the labs? People can enter those, you know they can, and they always do. The only place that's really secure are the SPA rooms. No one goes in there when a simulation's in progress, do they? I just needed to get into there whenever I could and lock the doors, with the data panel outside saying there was a SPA session going on. No one disturbed me.'

'So, let me get this straight,' said Bex, her hair still blowing across her face in the strong sea breeze. 'You're saying you can contact him on demand, yes?'

'Well, not exactly. But I can tell you he is watching us.'

'How do you know?'

'He proved it to me. Last time we were in contact, he told me what I'd been doing, the cases we'd been working on. He can see us, Bex, honestly. He's watching us.'

'Guardian angel?'

'If you like. Call him what you want, but the disembodied spirits of those close to us are free to be with us, especially when we need them. And the energy they draw on allows them to attract the plasma in the usual way. And we can see them.'

'But I thought a ghost always needed to be highly charged to return? You know, charged with enough emotion to raise the frequency which then causes the plasma to become opaque.'

'That's true, Bex. But you see, with the EM tracer, we can help it along. Locking onto a spirit's individual electromagnetic radiation – its unique energy pattern, if you like – gives it a kick-start. It's like we're opening the door for it. And it comes through, eventually. But believe me, Luc was angry enough, don't worry about that. He was charged up. Wouldn't you be?'

'Of course I would. No one wants to be shot. But it still doesn't explain why some ghosts break through and others don't. Why does it seem to be the dangerous spirits who come through more?'

'It stands to reason, doesn't it? They're the strongest – they can break through. They're fuelled with enough emotion – usually revenge for something – that they're able to break through into our mortal world. Revenge is powerful, you know that. Look at all the cases we've seen.'

Bex looked only half-convinced.

'Remember we're talking about dark matter, Bex. Nobody knows what it really is or how it behaves. But what our experiments proved was that if you can identify a person's energy pattern *before* they die, or at the moment they die, you can trace them and make it easier for them to return.'

'So, the big question is, what's it like?' said Bex.

'What's what like?'

'The other side, stupid. What did Luc tell you? This is massive, J. I can't believe it. What did he say to you? What can he see?'

Jud was locked in thought. He gazed out over the dark sky. The waves continued their rolling and surging as the giant ferry, lit up with life, ploughed on through the nothingness. With no horizon to orientate them, it felt like they too were journeying through the cosmos.

'He said it's peaceful, Bex. You reach a higher plane.'

He could see that wasn't going to satisfy her, not by a long way. Talk of a calm, peaceful heaven wasn't going to be enough for Bex.

'Look, you know we live inside our heads, don't we?' he said. 'I mean, that's where we *exist*. We see our hands, our feet, we feel things, we touch everything around us. But our thoughts are just as real too. Maybe they're the *only* things that are real. And though they're invisible, and you can't touch them, they're what make us who we are. Our mind or spirit or soul, call it what you like. It's no different in death. It lives on.'

'Consciousness?'

'Yeah, I guess so. Scientists have tried for ever to understand where consciousness is located. We believe it's in the brain. When parts of the brain are injured, we know people think differently. Sometimes they even have personality changes. But no one has ever linked the stuff that makes up the brain to consciousness itself. *What is it?* The thing that makes us *us*? Our spirit. Where is that? Think about it. If our conscious being is *not* mass, then it must be energy. And energy doesn't die. Luc said he's still *him*. He can think and remember and dream still. But he's free.'

'And can he see?'

Jud was thinking again, trying so hard to put the revelations

Luc had passed to him into words. Bex was the sharpest person he knew, cleverer than he was, maybe. And he so wanted her to understand it all, but how could she until she'd seen it herself? Soon she would, he knew that. 'I tell you what,' he continued, 'when you close your eyes, can you still see?'

'No,' said Bex simply. It was a straightforward question after all.

'Are you sure about that?' said Jud, smiling and flicking her hair behind her ear. 'Close them again. Go on.'

She rolled her eyes at him and shook her head playfully, then slowly closed them as he'd asked. Jud leant in closer and kissed her mouth. He felt her lips quickly break into a smile.

'Okay. So I understand,' she said, pulling away slightly. 'Of course I can see. I can see your eyes looking at me. I can see the sky and the water behind you. I can see everything.'

'There you are,' said Jud. 'You can "see" everything, and more. There's no limit to what you can "see". You don't need eyes to see the things in your mind, do you? You don't need the physical senses to exist. What you're really doing is escaping from them.'

'Yeah, it's called imagination, Jud. I'm not stupid.'

'Sure, call it that. It's the bit inside. The bit that scientists can't find when we're alive. But it survives death, Bex. It really does. In fact it's much freer. Luc said if I closed my eyes, remained still, blocked out all the things my usual senses were telling me – my touch, hearing, taste, everything – did I still exist? Of course I did. And we feel more free when we do that than when we retune back into our normal senses again and are trapped by the physical reality that comes to us through those senses. Understand?'

'Yeah, of course. It's our imagination, I said that.'

'But it doesn't mean that's what the universe is *really* like, Bex. What we see and what we hear around us. That's only the universe we inhabit at the moment.'

'So the physical world we know is defined by the physical

senses we have,' said Bex. 'Anyone knows that. We can't prove there's anything beyond that, because if there was, we couldn't sense it.'

'Exactly. But now we can. That's what I'm saying. We *can* prove there is another dimension, because Luc tells us there is.'

'And when our senses come to an end and our physical body dies, *we* still live on, through our spirit. Is that what you're telling me?' said Bex.

Jud's face lit up with a smile – a beaming grin of relief, like a huge weight had been lifted from him. And it thrilled Bex. She'd never seen him like this.

'It's what Luc is telling us. It's a never ending story, you see. Never ending. Death is a new chapter, that's all.'

Bex fell silent again, staring out to sea. Taking it all in. A new kind of peace was coming, comforting her, as the regular rhythm of the ship rocked them up and down, as a mother rocks a pram.

'You planned to tell me here, didn't you? That's why you dragged me outside in the cold? Everyone must think we're mad standing out here.'

'Maybe we are.' Jud smiled.

'Jud Lester. Jamie . . . I think . . .'

'What?'

'Nothing.'

'What were you going to say?' Jud asked gently.

'I'm . . .' She took a deep breath and averted her gaze for a moment. She knew it was now or never. There wouldn't be a better time to say it. 'I think I'm . . . falling in love with you,' she murmured.

He kissed her.

'Falling?' he whispered. 'I've already fallen.'

CHAPTER 23

SATURDAY, 10.23 P.M.

PENTHOUSE SUITE, GOODE
TOWER, LONDON

Jason Goode was alone. He preferred it that way. Bonati had offered to come and have dinner with him, to talk things over and hatch out some kind of plan, but he'd declined the offer, saying they would catch up in the morning. Right now, Goode wanted space to breathe and think. The conference calls to his various headquarters across the globe, in which he'd tried to appear positive and upbeat for all his top executives, steadying the ship and restoring confidence, had been tiring. Especially when he felt anything but positive inside.

He sat slouched on the black sofa, staring out at the glass wall ahead of him. The lights of London stretched before him.

For the first time in a while, Jason Goode felt depressed. The communication from Nap had rattled him, he couldn't deny it. But it had done more than that. It had allowed so many memories to come flooding back, like a tidal wave washing over a beach, raking up the sand, displacing the stones and bringing all manner of flotsam and debris with it. His spirit was disturbed, his mind confused. He knew he should be sharing these memories with his closest friend, who had been there through it all with him, but the nostalgia had quickly led to grief when, inevitably, after thinking about his time at Cambridge, he had throttled forwards through the years and his graduation from student to businessman to husband.

And father. A happy family. Or so it seemed looking back, though he knew deep down it had never been so.

But now it was gone.

Images of his wife, Tara, flickered through his mind, prompting a tear to fall gently down his cheek. She'd been so young when death had claimed her. He had relived that fateful night at his castle home in Buckinghamshire so many times in the miserable years that followed; how things might have been different if he'd got home sooner that evening. He could've prevented her fatal fall from the top of the tower, could've got there first and scared away the ghosts, whatever they were, before they'd had a chance to rob him of his wife and force him into a life of mourning. If he'd never even bought the damn castle in the first place, then things would be different.

He remembered Jamie's pitiful pleading in the dock: 'The ghosts did it. It was the ghosts, I swear!' And he remembered the cold, cynical views of just about everybody in the courtroom, as the prosecution rounded on his son like a pack of wolves. There had been nothing he could do but watch the terrible scene. How could people ever have believed his son was telling the truth? Ghosts, *really*? He remembered the tears he'd shed when they took Jamie down the dark stairs that led from the dock to the cells beneath.

But he'd never doubted him. Not for one second. Not least because he could never have believed the alternative, what the Crown Prosecution had argued: that Jamie had killed his own mother. It was absurd and cruel and the stuff of nightmares.

He recalled the prosecution's barrister being savage to Jamie as he stood there, silently, in the dock. The allegations were unbearable to hear. That he, his only son, had got into a fight with his mother, lost his temper and pushed her over the edge of the tower himself, with his bare hands.

It was a chapter in their lives that seemed unreal now. But it had been real enough at the time. And it had launched Goode headfirst into serious depression and an all-consuming obsession with proving the existence of ghosts. It was the only way to get people to believe his son could have been telling the truth. The rest, of course, was history. The CRYPT was established and now there was irrefutable proof that ghosts really did exist, so they *could* have taken his wife as Jamie had argued all along. He wanted everyone to believe his son, as he did. And Bonati, thank God. At least his friend had never doubted Jamie.

But what if he had got home sooner? he thought to himself again. Regret – deep, powerful remorse – was such a familiar feeling, and it ate away at his body and mind in quieter moments, like rust on an old car. It was corrosive. If only he could go back in time, he kept wishing. Change things. What if he had put his family first instead of his work all those years? It had been just another meeting, as always, that had prevented him from getting home to the castle earlier that night. What if he'd finished sooner?

What if?

But there were too many 'what ifs'. He knew there was little point in thinking such things. Tara was gone and that was that. He'd tried so many times to make contact, to raise her spirit. If only they'd had the EM tracer in those days. There was a chance, even a slim one, that they could have tracked her as he knew Jud and Bonati had been trying to do with Luc. All the experiments and research he'd done over the years to find a way. And now it was too late.

Friends had called him obsessed, and maybe he was. What was wrong with that? Why shouldn't he be? Tara had been his world. What was he supposed to do after she had gone – forget about her and move on? Marry again? Forget it. He knew that was impossible. Tara featured in his thoughts and dreams every day. And time spent with Jamie now, though rare, of course, served as a painful reminder of Tara because he looked so much like her, even with the thin veil of disguise. He *was* her.

He recalled the day Jamie was born. The excitement of seeing him, holding him, for the first time. The smell of him, the sound. The strange bluish tinge of his slippery body when they first scooped him from his mother and laid him in her arms. Tara's tired but happy face, the sweat on her brow, the tears that smudged her mascara. Then cradling him himself and feeling the tiny but determined beat of his little heart.

And then the first time he spoke, and the first time he tottered across the living room floor, pushing his blue and yellow truck. How he wished he could rewind the clock. Go back. Do it again. Why did time have to march on so mercilessly, never turning back, never looking round? Never pausing for just one second so he could appreciate the things he had before they shrank to memories in a winding wake behind him.

He would do things differently if he could.

But he'd missed it all and it was too late now. Work had always played such an important role in his life – more important than anything else, even his own family. As soon as Jamie had been old enough, they'd shipped him off to boarding school in England, allowing him and Tara to get on with their busy schedules undisturbed, travelling across the world, seeing Goode Technology grow and grow.

And for what?

The return to England to buy the family home had come too late in Jamie's childhood, and Jason knew it. By then the gulf between them had grown so wide, it was impossible to bridge it with fake interest in how he was doing at school, or what friends he'd made, or what football matches he'd played in, or what songs he was listening to with his mates. Jason should have been there to share each moment as it happened, not to receive match reports after the event. *He should have been there*, and so should Tara. Parenting, for anyone, was a long, protracted process of grief, watching their little ones vanish as older people emerged, and for Jason the grief was doubled.

Tara had always been his travelling companion. Business trips abroad meant the two of them could be together. And with Jamie safely tucked up in boarding school they could go anywhere.

And now she was gone, Goode had nothing. Nobody. He was a single, middle-aged man with effectively no family. His son rarely spoke to him, though if anyone deserved to be a troubled teenager, Goode knew it was Jamie.

Shrugging himself out of his morbid thoughts, he got up from the couch and walked towards the drinks cabinet. It was late and he'd already had too many drinks, but just one more wouldn't hurt. He poured himself a large bourbon on the rocks and returned to his seat. He picked up the TV remote, switched it on, and the large screen set into the opposite wall blinked into life.

It was a news channel, as ever; it was all he seemed to watch these days. But the headline running at the bottom of the screen, and repeated in large letters behind the newsreader, caught his attention: 'BANKING CRISIS DEEPENS'.

The newsreader was flanked by two men in suits. They were being asked for their opinions on the imminent collapse of several banks in the City. They postulated their 'intelligent' views on how these rogue traders had been allowed to get away with it for so long. Evidence pointed to debts being amassed over a longer period of time than Goode had first thought. But they amounted to millions of pounds. According to the newsreader, traders were being exposed and sacked in many of the City's largest and most famous banks.

Theories were offered as to why so many banks were involved, and why at the same time. The guy on the left of the newsreader suggested that the bankers were working together, perhaps as part of some pre-meditated plan to bring down the banks. Or maybe they were working together to disguise the fact that the money was being shipped elsewhere.

Conspiracy theories abounded and Goode was getting fed up. But at least no one had yet mentioned the suggestion that the illegal trades and resulting losses had been caused by computer hackers outside the banks. As yet, none of the facts given to him during his interview with Khan had reached the public domain, thank God. So far, no one outside Scotland Yard and the CRYPT had any inkling that a third party could be involved, let alone Goode Technology.

He swigged his drink and changed channel. Another news programme. This time there were several people lounging on sofas, with one presenter sitting on a chair between them. Newspapers were strewn across a large coffee table in the centre of the studio. Goode recognised it as one of those late-night chat programmes, where arrogant people with no jobs but large personalities dissected the newspapers and debated the issues of the day as if they had the answers to everything.

Bullshit. Goode was about to go channel-hopping again when a comment from a man to the far left of the screen made him stop.

'I think it's computer hackers, Julian.'

The presenter replied, 'Evidence, Clive?'

The man called Clive sat up from his slouching position and delivered a face that meant business. His fellow guests in the studio rolled their eyes, suggesting that this guy was no stranger to wild conspiracy theories. Of course, that was probably why he'd been invited onto the programme in the first place. This stuff made good telly, so the producers thought.

'You see,' he continued, 'all these banks think their computer systems are secure. But I tell you they're not. If some amateur geek in his bedroom can break into the Pentagon, then believe me, anyone can hack into a bank's files. Robberies, heists, call them what you will, but they rarely involve guns and stockings over your head any more. These days it's all done over the internet.'

'This is all interesting stuff, Clive,' interrupted the presenter, 'but are you saying that this is what's happening here in London? I mean do you have proof you can share with us?'

Clive shrugged. He'd nothing but his wild, exciting theories.

A woman opposite Julian said, 'Clive may well be right, of course. And the banks would certainly rather it was an imposter doing all this than one of their own employees. It's an easier thing to sell to the public. They become the victim rather than the villain then, don't they? It's not their fault exactly, it's the fault of some stranger, some saboteur.'

The presenter, together with everyone else in the studio, nodded in agreement.

Clive continued, 'Janine's right. And all it takes is—'

'Yes,' interrupted the presenter, in his usual way, 'but do we have *proof*? Without that, it's just speculation.'

'It's all God damn speculation!' Goode shouted at the screen. 'That's what your programme's about, you damn fool.'

'Well, I can't reveal who,' said Clive, 'but one source I spoke to earlier today suggested that he could prove that the squillions of pounds of losses recorded in recent weeks was definitely the work of saboteurs hacking into the banks' files.'

'Really?' said some other guy to Clive's right, half-smirking. 'So, was this some guy in the pub, or on a bus, or someone you met in a bus queue?' The rest of the panel of nobodies chuckled.

'You may laugh,' said Clive, 'but I can tell you, this was a reliable witness. Very reliable. Naturally I can't reveal my sources, but it was someone important enough to make me believe it.'

'Okay,' said Julian, keen to move the conversation on, 'let's say the banking crisis has been caused by undesirables hacking into the banks' computer systems and making the losses for them. *Why*? Why would anyone do that? What would they gain from it? Or is it just wanton sabotage? A protest against capitalism, maybe?'

'Never mind why,' said another guest, 'we haven't established *how* yet.'

'The how bit is easy,' said Clive. 'I've told you, anyone can hack into anything these days, if you're the kind of person with the know-how and the technology to do it.'

'You sound like you have a person in mind,' said Janine.

'Careful,' said the presenter. 'No names, please. We don't want to be sued for naming someone on air!' he chuckled inanely.

Clive was laughing. 'No, we certainly don't, but I'm reliably informed that the people behind this may work for a large company that would have the latest technology at their fingertips. They built most of it.'

Goode sat up. What the hell did this guy know? Who was he?

Julian heard the producer's whispered voice in his earpiece, 'Move on, *now*!' He knew if this continued any further there'd be recriminations and expensive lawsuits. 'Well, I think we're going to have to leave it there, and perhaps it's just as well. We have lots of other issues to discuss tonight, and we've spent long enough on the banking situation already. We'll wait and see how it plays out tomorrow, shall we? Let's talk about something else.' He picked up one of the newspapers from the table. 'We move onto dragons, ladies and gentlemen. If eyewitness reports are to be believed, not only does the city of London have the banking crisis to contend with, but it also has the small matter of stone dragons coming to life and flying around the place. Whatever next!'

The guests around the table couldn't hide their cynical smiles. It sounded far-fetched after all.

'Well,' continued the presenter, turning towards the camera

ahead of him, 'we decided to send out our very own St George onto the streets of London earlier tonight to find out more. Intrepid reporter, George Brennan, has been investigating . . .'

The screen switched to a man standing on a rain-soaked street, with a couple of shoppers, eagerly awaiting to get on the telly and tell their story.

'Oh, great,' said Goode. 'So now we're spreading fear too. Thanks, George. The end of a perfect day.' The shrinking ice cubes in his glass of bourbon rattled as he drained the glass and the phone on his desk sprung to life. He picked it up. It was Bonati, and from the tone of his voice, Goode could tell he was bringing more bad news.

CHAPTER 24

SATURDAY, 11.35 P.M.

THAMES RIVERSIDE
APARTMENTS, LONDON

Harry Parkin leant against the chrome-plated rail that ran the length of his balcony on the seventh floor of the giant block of steel and tinted glass that overlooked the River Thames. He sipped his Martini and gazed at the twinkling lights that ran along the riverbank below. The bars and restaurants were shutting up for the night and a few casual drinkers were finishing their conversations and parting company. The faded white canvas roof of the smoking shelter outside the riverside pub below Harry's apartment block welcomed three pigeons, who waited anxiously for the drinkers to leave so they could move in and hoover up any crumbs beneath the picnic benches. It was cold, but the hardy smokers preferred to eat and drink and laugh loudly outside, punctuating their meals with necessary cigarettes.

There was the noise of shrieked laughter and the sound of stiletto heels clicking on the hard pavement as Harry watched a group of scantily clad girls leave the building in the direction of the taxi waiting for them up on the bridge. Taking them on to nightclubs, no doubt, he thought. Harry watched them stagger towards the steps, giggling and splaying out their wrists like little children learning to walk. Tottering on high heels and exposing bare legs to the wintry air was a ritual for many on a Saturday night.

Harry shook his head and chuckled. There was a time when he would have been down there in two minutes flat to join them, with a witty chat-up line or a joke. But that was before he met Cecilia. Now he was content to stand on his private balcony and watch others pursue their weekly quest for the perfect partner. He'd already found his.

He could hear the clink of glass behind him and Cecilia returned to the balcony with the Martini bottle. 'Another?' she said, the effects of the last one already evident in her slurred words and tipsy smile.

'Stirred not shaken,' said Harry. 'Or should that be shaken not stirred?'

'Whatever,' Cecilia said inelegantly, attempting to bring the open bottle neck to his glass for a refill and failing. Wasted drops of the expensive liquor fell onto the ungrateful potted plants on the metal balcony floor.

He took the bottle from her, filled up his glass again and set it safely down on the iron-effect table behind them, far away from her unstable body. He grabbed her and held her upright and together they gazed at the opposite riverbank and the streetlights and the high-rise buildings beyond.

'It's beautiful,' she said.

'It's bloody cold,' said Harry. 'But you're beautiful, so that'll do.'

'Cheesy, but I like you,' laughed Cecilia. 'What's that?' she said, pointing her wobbly hand to the other side of the river, straight ahead of them.

'What?'

'That, over there. Look. Is it a bird? It's a big one if it is.'

Harry couldn't see what his girlfriend was pointing at. It was dark and the streetlights served little purpose up on the seventh floor. 'Where do you mean?' he said.

'Over there! Coming towards us. It's a bloody great pigeon, I think. Huge!'

He suddenly caught sight of what she meant. There was a large gull of some kind flapping towards them from the other side of the river. 'It's not a pigeon!' he scoffed. 'It's a sea gull. You're right, though, it's a big one.'

'It's enormous!' she giggled. 'You could ride on it. Imagine that!'

There was the sound of a car horn peeping as another taxi drew alongside the kerb down on the bridge to their left, summoned to collect more drinkers. Harry watched as yet more girls left the bar below and made their way to the steps that led up to the bridge, tottering on the usual high heels.

'Hey, just you keep your eyes off 'em,' Cecilia said. 'You don't need— Aagh!' she shrieked.

'What? What?' said Harry.

Without saying anything, she ran to the open door, pulling Harry with her.

'Ouch!' She'd pinched his arm tight. 'What're you doing, you silly cow?'

He didn't have time to turn around to see what had startled her. She continued to pull him into the small living room and fumbled at the handle to close the door quickly.

Harry went to help her. And as he approached the glass his eyes opened wide with horror. His jaw dropped and all he could say was, 'What the . . .'

The giant bird she'd seen flapping towards them was approaching.

Only it wasn't a bird.

It was a grey dragon. And it was alive.

The glass sliding door was little defence against something so hard, so heavy, moving so fast. It smashed its way into the tiny apartment and caught Harry head on. He lay spread-eagled on the floor, his face pulverised, his eyes ominously closed.

Cecilia screamed and fell backwards against the sofa. The dragon flapped its wings, crashing into the three walls in turn, disturbing lamps and pictures and ornaments, like a panic-stricken bird. Its frantic movements were terrifying, especially inside such a cramped space. It opened its giant jaws and let out a deafening screech, somewhere between a squawk and a roar, before finding its way back through the smashed glass door and out into the night sky again.

Cecilia fell to the carpet. 'Harry!' she cried, holding his chin and shaking it vigorously. '*Harry!*'

Chapter 25

SATURDAY, 11.03 P.M.

(12.03 A.M. LOCAL TIME)

A16 AUTOROUTE, PARIS

The sleek, black Fireblade hurtled down the autoroute. Bex leant in close to Jud's body as they both bent over against the harsh wind that was pounding them from ahead. The traffic was very light at that time of night, so the journey from Calais to Paris was quicker then they'd expected. Even so, it was going to be the small hours of the morning before they checked in to their Parisian hotel, and Jud hoped there would be someone still manning the place.

The wide, flat countryside seemed to stretch on for miles, with nothing but the odd lights of village houses, that flanked the stretch of road from time to time, to provide any interest to the eye. They met the occasional heavy goods lorry rattling along the wet road, but Jud gave each a wide berth, avoiding the spray that the juggernauts coughed up.

They relieved the monotony of the journey by chatting over the headsets, mostly focusing on the images they had in their minds of what Guy Bonaparte would be like when they finally caught up with him. And what they would do when they did.

'So you're going to hit him I suppose, J?'

'Of course not. You know me.'

Bex huffed.

'Seriously. Remember this guy will have no idea who we are. So we can be anybody at first. We don't need to get into a fight or anything.'

'What're you thinking?' asked Bex. 'Pizza delivery man?'

'If we can find him in the cafés and bars, we'll follow him home. Find out where he lives and then let the police know.'

'The gendarmerie?'

'Hell, no. Khan and his men. They can come and get him. But they'll need proof first – a reason for them to bother coming over. We have to get into his house or flat, or wherever he is. See what he's up to.'

'Yeah, like that's going to be easy.'

'That's what makes life fun, Bex. You know that. And I've told you before, we're not alone.'

Bex recalled the conversation they'd had on the ferry crossing, how Luc had made contact with J. It had seemed plausible then, on the wide ocean, with the infinite stars overhead – anything had seemed possible. Now, in the harsh reality of the autoroute, with the ordinary, mundane cars and trucks they passed, the idea seemed unreal once again. A fantasy.

'I'll believe it when I see it,' said Bex.

They continued in thoughtful silence for a while, until they saw the outskirts of the capital and the infinite number of intersections and junctions that served to baffle any motorist daring to enter the labyrinth of Paris.

'I hope you know where you're going, J.'

'There's enough signs saying "*Centre Ville*", Bex. We'll get closer to the centre and then stop somewhere and use the GPS on the phone. I've already put in the postcode for the hotel.'

'Is it a nice one?' said Bex, hopefully.

'Yeah, it's a pretty postcode if you like that sort of thing. The letters go well together.'

'The hotel, you idiot!'

'It'll do,' said Jud. 'We won't be spending much time in there anyway.'

Pity, Bex thought to herself. Alone with Jud in a Parisian hotel, she could think of plenty of ways to occupy their time without having to set foot outside. But she decided not to rush things. Though she'd leapt at the chance to come, she knew there was a job to be done, and she also knew that the longer they were away from London, the more trouble they'd be in on their return. They had to work quickly. Goode would know of their escape by the morning – Bonati would never be able to keep it from him. And then he'd begin worrying. She half expected him to pitch up there with Bonati himself, except she knew he probably wouldn't be allowed to leave the country, what with the investigation going on.

Half an hour later, and not before Jud had taken several wrong turnings and dangerous, screaming U-turns, they reached Belleville, the district of Paris in which the hotel was located. Jud pulled into the kerbside as soon as he could and checked the GPS on his phone. The Hotel des Anges was not far away. He looked at the route, memorised it and set off again.

A few minutes later they drew up outside the hotel and were soon assisted with their bags by the concierge. He instructed Jud, in a begrudging attempt at English, where to park the Fireblade, at the rear of the hotel, while Bex went inside and checked in.

When the assistant behind the counter asked if it was one or two rooms they had reserved, Bex was so close to saying, 'Just the one, please,' but decided against it. The joke would not have been so well received by Jud, especially after their long journey from London through lashing rain and winds. All he would want was a hot bath and a sleep. For now.

Jud returned and they quickly went up to their rooms,

adjacent to one another, just as Bex had requested. She had asked the assistant if the rooms had interconnecting doors. 'No,' had been the stern reply. And the look the assistant had given her had made Bex flush with embarrassment. Luckily Jud had arrived after the conversation had finished.

'Meet you in the lobby at, shall we say, eight a.m.?' said Jud, turning to Bex down the corridor.

She smiled and nodded to him. 'I can be up whenever you want. I can bring you breakfast in bed, if you like.'

Jud smiled but said nothing and slid the plastic pass key into the slot above the door knob. The little red light blinked green and he entered. Shutting the door behind him, he stood against it and caught his breath. The idea of Bex sleeping just the other side of the wall was enticing, and it took all his effort to resist going straight back out again and asking if she wanted to share rooms instead. They were alone in a hotel in Paris, no Bonati, no Goode, no other agents. Strangers in the city with a whole night ahead of them.

'No,' he whispered to himself. His body was tired and he needed a warm shower after the freezing journey on the bike.

He unpacked his bag and took his phone from his pocket. The sound of running water from the bathroom in Bex's room made him pause. It was weird having her so close by. His cool disinterest in her had worked for a while. But he couldn't deny his feelings now. Her long, dark hair, her exotic eyes, her slim, sexy figure. And the way she carried herself around the place; she lit up the dimly lit corridors of the CRYPT for every guy. There had been times, of course, when others had tried to chat her up. Why wouldn't they? She was the best-looking agent in the place. But she always turned them down, politely and coolly, which usually made them want her more.

But it wasn't just Bex's looks that drew her to Jud, or the touch of her gorgeous body; it was her courage, her sassy, self-confidence. He admired the way she greeted every new challenge with such self-belief and determination. She always wanted to do the right thing and she wasn't afraid to take on anything thrown at her.

Luckily the phone provided a much-needed distraction, as he noticed the tiny light in the corner of its screen was flashing, indicating he'd received a text. It must have come in as he was parking the Fireblade.

It was from his father. Had he discovered they were gone? Had Bonati told him already?

He clicked on the text and braced himself.

Hey J. I knew you'd go, whatever Bonati said. You'll get a call from Anatol Stokowski in the morning. He works in my Paris office and I've just called him. He'll give you whatever help you need. He's a good guy. Stay safe. x

CHAPTER 26

SUNDAY, 7.29 A.M.

(8.29 A.M. LOCAL TIME)

BELLEVILLE, PARIS

'I thought you said we were meeting at eight a.m.?' said Bex, half smiling at the dishevelled figure approaching her table.

Jud nodded wearily. 'Sorry. Have you eaten yet?'

'No, I was waiting for you.'

They quickly ordered coffee and croissants and freshly squeezed orange juice.

'Sleep well?' asked Bex, looking radiant and fresh.

'Yeah, went out like a light. Had some weird dreams though. We were on a bike together, on a giant motorway. I dreamt I was riding to Paris. Bizarre.'

'Yeah, very weird,' she said, smiling at him. 'So what's the plan?'

'We head straight over to Clichy-sous-Bois, see what's there. Check out the cafés and bars. See who's heard of this guy. Someone will have done, I'm sure.'

'Good job I like the taste of coffee, I reckon we're going to be drinking a lot of the stuff,' said Bex, as the waitress brought the tray. Their espressos were rich and warming. The fresh croissants exploded as they cut into them, showering their inadequate plates with shards of pastry.

'I heard from my father,' said Jud.

'What, already?'

'Yeah. He texted late last night. Bonati must've told him soon after we'd gone. Maybe he had an attack of guilt or something. I don't blame him. He didn't have a choice, I suppose. He couldn't exactly make up an assignment, say we'd gone away on some other case and expect to get away with it. My father would never have bought it. And if he'd waited until they both found out we'd slipped away today, he'd have been in trouble for not keeping control of his agents, I guess.'

'So what did he say? You in trouble?'

'Strangely not,' said Jud. 'I think he's worried about us though. I tell you, I don't know what this Nap guy is like, but I've rarely seen my father concerned like he was yesterday when we showed him the email. He's not reacted like that for a long time. Now he's told me to get in touch with one of his men in Paris. He'll help us all we need, apparently.'

'It's nice of the guy to offer to help.'

'Not really. If my father tells you to help someone, you do it. I don't suppose he gave him much choice. But my father says he's a good man.'

'So what can he do for us?'

'He's a techie guy, so I'll get him to start making searches online for us – hospitals, doctors, council records, that sort of thing. Bonaparte may not be using his real name, but my guess is he would have done so at some stage, even way back. He's been here years, I think. And maybe he's arrogant enough to believe no one will ever come after him, so why hide his name?'

'Besides,' said Bex, 'we don't actually know for sure he's done anything wrong yet, do we? He might be living a peaceful life as a hermit for all we know.'

'No,' said Jud. 'The email proves he's out to get my father, and his company, and all of us. Why else would he write it?'

'*If* he wrote it.'

'Well there is that, I suppose, but few people would know about him and his history with my father. It's unlikely someone else would have pretended to be him. It's Bonaparte, alright. Look at what the first letters spelt. You saw it, Bex.'

'Well, if it is from him, it still doesn't mean he's responsible for everything. It's in the news everywhere. Maybe he just read it and thought it was a good opportunity to wind your father up. It doesn't mean to say—'

'No, it's him, Bex. I can feel it.'

'Okay,' she said. There was no point in pushing it any further. 'So what're we going to do if we actually find him?'

'I've already told you,' said Jud. 'We'll tip off Khan and his men. They can come and get him. I'm not here to arrest the guy myself. But I wanna see if it's really him. I need to watch his pattern. What he does. He won't know who we are, so he won't suspect anything. But I wanna see the whites of his eyes.'

Bex was unconvinced. 'You're going to attack him, aren't you? I know you are.'

'I'm not that stupid, Bex,' said Jud. 'Believe me, if he really is behind this entire thing, then he's going to have a lot of friends. Not even I'm crazy enough to take on someone like that. I just want to be sure it's him. And then we can tell my father and let him decide what to do next. I just want to find Bonaparte for him. I owe him that much.'

Bex decided not to debate this one any longer. She could tell from Jud's face that he was determined to do it. It was the first time he'd really been able to help his father and nothing was going to stop him. And given the threatening nature of the message they'd intercepted from Bonaparte, it wasn't surprising Jud was so determined to catch him. Bex knew very well that if Goode Technology was sabotaged, it could mean the end of the

CRYPT, and while the other agents could find jobs elsewhere, what would Jud do? The conditions of his parole dictated clearly that he was being released into the custody of the CRYPT. With that gone, it would mean a one-way ticket back to prison.

'Everyone can be traced somehow, can't they?' she said, more encouraging now. 'The electoral register's our best bet. I'm guessing he's a proud Frenchman, so he wouldn't want to miss out on the vote. We could trace him that way.'

'Good idea. I'm sure my father's contact over here will have associates. People he knows and trusts. He'll know someone who can help us. I'll call him as soon as we've finished. Ask him to get a lead for us.'

'Seen the newspapers?' said Bex.

'Not yet, why?'

'It's in the French papers too – not only the banking crisis, but the ghosts in London. The journalists are having a field day.'

'Oh, great,' said Jud, sarcastically. 'Well, there's nothing we can do about it here. I'm glad to be out of London.'

'Yeah, but all the publicity is going to make the investigations over there so much harder. You know how it's always difficult to take accurate readings when there are crowds at a scene. You can forget trying to use the EM neutralisers.'

'Well, the agents will handle it. Have you spoken to Grace yet?'

'Nope,' said Bex. 'But I will. I caught up with Raheed before I left and he said she might be coming out of hospital today. She's on the mend but she's going to be badly scarred. I only wish I could have seen her before we left.'

'Don't worry, you'll see her soon,' said Jud. 'Let's get going. It's gonna be a big day.' He rose from the table. 'I'll go and phone this Stokowski guy. Maybe we'll meet up with him first and work out a plan. See you down here in ten?'

'I need to come up anyway,' said Bex, joining him.

As they left the restaurant together, a man who had been

watching them since they'd entered from the other side of the room, picked up his mobile phone and called someone.

'Get out, quick,' he whispered into the phone. 'They're coming back up.'

'Relax,' replied the voice at the end of the line. 'It's done. I've already planted the bug in the guy's jacket. He's a messy son of a bitch. Teenagers never tidy their rooms these days, do they?'

CHAPTER 27

SUNDAY, 7.56 A.M.
(8.56 A.M. LOCAL TIME)

ALLÉE CHÊNE POINTU,
CLICHY-SOUS-BOIS, PARIS

A deep, throaty rasp echoed around the giant tower blocks of Allée Chêne Pointu as the ugly, dark grey Yamaha XJR1300 entered the car park. It was not a subtle bike. Fashioned in an old school design, it was more muscular and thuggish than sleek and racy. Its rider enjoyed the dominant presence it gave him in traffic, though, especially when he was behind some puny moped or, even better, a cyclist. He enjoyed revving its colossal engine to give unsuspecting cyclists and pedestrians a fright. Here, in the half-empty car park, surrounded by vast concrete walls, its echoing roar was particularly pleasing to Christophe.

He got off and heaved the giant beast onto its heavy stand, released beneath the engine. He removed his helmet and carried it under his arm as he strolled confidently towards the third of the huge apartment blocks that stretched up into the cloudy grey skies above. His thinning black hair was cut short and his black stubble, deep-set eyes and prominent jaw gave him the appearance of a man you'd not stop to ask directions from in the street. Like his Yamaha, his presence was bullish and unwelcoming.

A few minutes later, Bonaparte opened his door, pushing the debris of cardboard boxes and bin bags out of the way. One day he'd take it all to the local recycling site. One day.

Christophe entered the flat, trying hard to hide his reaction to the appalling smell that assaulted his senses. His large frame filled the hallway and he seemed oversized for the poky apartment. Bonaparte was small and slender and he beavered about the place like a mole underground, but Christophe was wide and tall and his boots clomped on the tiled floor.

'You're late,' said Bonaparte, showing no emotion.

'By five minutes. Relax, man.'

His unimpressed host ignored him and shuffled off into the tiny kitchen at the back of the flat, where he began rifling through the cupboards to find a couple of clean cups. Failing, he washed some that had been discarded on the sticky, mouldy worktop beside the sink. Christophe wondered how old the instant coffee would be that stuck to the jar missing its top. But it would suffice for now. If he was going to be spending some time in this place, he'd remember to bring his own coffee next time.

A few minutes later they were in Bonaparte's living room.

'So what's the plan today?' asked Christophe.

'Same as everyday from now on. Like I said, protection. Nothing else. You're here in case trouble comes knocking, not to go looking for it.' He sipped from his coffee cup and Christophe could see his hands were shaking slightly, just as they had been when he was making the coffee in the kitchen.

'So you have enemies, *oui?*'

'Perhaps. I don't know. But that's what makes life interesting, isn't it?' said Bonaparte, without fear. 'Are you armed as I asked?'

Christophe nodded silently.

'Good. I have some errands to run today, people to see. The

next two weeks will be dangerous and difficult for you. There will be people looking for me. You don't need to know why.'

'The police?'

'I said you don't need to know why. You understand? You keep silent, you earn your money. Just do as I say. Nothing more.'

'Suits me,' said Christophe. Who the hell did this guy think he was? He could break him in two with his bare hands if he wanted.

Christophe took out his revolver from the holster inside his jacket and began checking it was in good order. He always enjoyed admiring it; it gave him a confidence and a sense of power over others.

'Put the shooter away, you damn fool!' Bonaparte snapped savagely. 'I don't want to see that again unless absolutely necessary. You got that?' The effort of shouting so loudly shook him into a coughing fit.

Christophe was taken aback by the venomous anger that seemed to come from deep inside this pathetic weakling. Though the man was slender, pasty faced and far from healthy, Christophe was beginning to feel uncomfortable as he seemed so hot-tempered and, after all, you didn't need to be the world's strongest man to pull a trigger behind someone's back. What was he doing here? Why had he agreed to work for this weirdo? Why would his host live in this way, like some feral animal? He stank, and all this coughing was unpleasant to witness. Still, he thought, it wasn't as though he had to marry the guy. A couple of weeks and he'd never see him again, provided he paid the money in full – otherwise he'd soon put him out of his misery with a clean bullet to the temple. Until then, it wasn't a difficult job to sit on his butt and wait for this crank to give him his next orders.

'I'll be in my study,' said Bonaparte. 'Where I don't wish to be disturbed. Make yourself at home. We'll be going out later.

Until then, the place is yours.' He walked out of the living room and slammed the door.

'Gee, thanks,' Christophe shouted after him, then picked up one of the many old newspapers from the floor and reclined into the saggy sofa for a long read.

CHAPTER 28

SUNDAY, 8.16 A.M.
(9.16. A.M. LOCAL TIME)

BOULEVARD DIDEROT, PARIS

The Honda Fireblade moved swiftly through the Parisian streets.

They were heading back towards the centre of the city. Stokowski had suggested they meet him first, before embarking on their search of Clichy-sous-Bois. The Paris branch of Goode Technology was vast, even bigger than the Goode Tower in London. It was Goode's first European headquarters, before the new London premises had been built.

'He said we'll recognise the building,' said Jud. 'Apparently you can't miss it.'

'Why's that?' said Bex.

A giant block of concrete appeared at the other side of the intersection up ahead of them. The size of a hangar, it dominated the area. It wasn't the design of the building that impressed – it was a straightforward rectangular block – but its sheer size. Rarely had the agents seen one continuous building on this scale. It seemed a mile wide and was ten, maybe twelve storeys high.

'Is that it?' said Bex.

'Yep. Must be. He said it was big. Like a giant grey shoe box, he said.'

Stokowski's description had been spot on. It resembled a vast nuclear bunker, just plain grey walls of featureless concrete, punctuated at regular intervals by little square windows that seemed disproportionately small. It would not have been surprising to see bars on each one, given how the building resembled some futuristic prison.

'How the hell did they get planning permission for that?' said Bex. 'It's hideous.'

'I think it's what they call Brutalist style. Like some of the buildings in Britain built in the fifties and sixties. It's all about concrete boxes.'

'Listen to you! How do you know that?' said Bex.

'Wanted to be an architect when I was kid. Still do, really. But things didn't exactly work out as planned.'

'The only buildings I've seen like this in Britain are multi-storey car parks,' said Bex.

'Exactly. Same style,' said Jud.

'And your dad built this for his company?'

'No, no. He moved into it well after it was built. I don't know what it was before then. Maybe a factory? I remember him opening this branch, though. I never saw it, I was locked up in boarding school at the time, but I remember him saying it was massive. He ran the Europe arm of the company from here until he built the place in London.'

'And we're meeting your contact in there?'

'Yep.'

Ten minutes later they were signing in at reception and moving towards the lifts. The interior was about as inspiring as the outside, just plain walls and strip-lights and devoid of any character whatsoever. Everything was functional, no need for decor – that was the style. Goode liked it because its simple, warehouse-like design contrasted so well with the hi-tech brand of his company that now operated inside its walls. Of course, when it came to his new building in London, he had decided to have a change and had gone for the very latest in fixtures and fittings, more like the giant glass and steel banks that rose to the sky in Canary Wharf, with marble floors, ultra-modern lighting and designer furniture from Scandinavia. But this place was austere. Unwelcoming.

The lift pinged as they reached the seventh floor, and there was a man to greet them as soon as the doors swung open. In his late thirties, he had a friendly face and a shock of chestnut brown hair, combed back with a floppy fringe that he kept running his hands through. He wore expensive-looking spectacles with dark frames, behind which piercing blue eyes were revealed. By the look of his athletic build, he was obviously no stranger to exercise.

'Mr Lester and Miss De Verre, *oui?*' he said. 'It's good to meet you both.' His English was good, though his accent didn't sound French.

'You're Anatol Stokowski, I presume?' said Jud.

'I am. But please call me Ant. My name's a bit of a mouthful, I realise. My father moved to France from Poland when I was young. Anyway, welcome to Paris. Mr Goode has told me all about you.'

I doubt that, Jud thought to himself, and responded with a smile.

Stokowski managed to hide his surprise at the age of his visitors. He'd been told they were private investigators, but they didn't look old enough to be out of school, he thought. But then he wasn't getting any younger, so anyone under twenty-five looked young to him. Stokowski had seen many new recruits come and go through the Paris offices, and every year they seemed to get younger and younger.

'Please, come this way,' he said warmly. 'We can chat in my office. It's quiet today, of course. Nobody here. We can talk in peace.'

They followed him down the long corridor to a room at the end: Stokowski's office.

'So?' he said, sitting behind his desk and waving a hand for them to take the seats opposite him. 'I understand you need my help finding someone over here, *oui?*'

'Uh huh,' said Jud. 'Has Mr Goode explained who, and why?'

Stokowski nodded. 'He has, yeah. I can't believe this banking thing. We're all worried about it here, I can tell you. It's incredible. I mean, how can Goode Technology be involved, huh? It's madness. And this guy, the one Mr Goode mentioned. Is he for real?'

'Oh yeah,' said Jud. 'As real as you and I. And he's out to get Mr Goode. To get all of us.'

'So you're private investigators, right?'

'Yeah,' said Jud, relieved that his father had had the good sense to make up roles for them. He could hardly tell the man they were ghost hunters. The presence of the CRYPT was a secret to most employees outside London. 'We're based in London, but we work all over the place. Whenever a client wants someone found, or discreetly watched, we're called in.'

'Okay. Sounds good. You been to France before?'

'Oh yeah, many times,' said Bex, keen to show Jud that she could lie with the best of them. 'We've done a few undercover operations over here. Usually husbands playing away, if you know what I mean. Suspicious wives in London with a lot of money to spare. Their husbands tell them they're away on a business trip, the usual story. Then we follow them and find them in some seedy hotel with their secretary. You get the picture.'

'*Ah, la cité de l'amour,*' said Stokowski, smiling. 'It's a very different case this time then?'

They nodded.

'So what's your brief? You find him and then tip off the police or something?'

'No, we find him and then tell Mr Goode. It's up to him what he does next. So you'll help us, yeah?' Jud was keen to get the meeting done so they could get back out onto the Parisian streets and find Bonaparte.

Stokowski nodded. 'Of course. I've lived in Paris for twenty-five years. I know this city as well as anyone. And if this guy is out to harm this company, then I'm as keen to find him as you are. So how can I help?'

Jud explained that they needed access to council records, hospitals, you name it. Wherever this guy's name appeared. Any address or contact would do.

'Well, I've already been doing some research for you. Mr Goode gave me the details last night, he even emailed me a picture of him. Ugly guy. Anyway, I think I've traced him to the Clichy-sous-Bois area.'

'That makes sense,' said Jud. 'It's the place we've been advised to begin the search. Any address yet?'

Stokowski shook his head. 'Not yet, but there was a man by that name on the electoral register once. And he's visited a hospital in that area too, a few times. He's disappeared off the radar now, but my guess is he's still in that district.' He pushed a piece of paper across the desk towards them. 'I've found a more recent picture too.'

They looked at the scanned image of an old man. He appeared much older than Jason Goode. A thin, gaunt figure, with grey eyes and a lined face. Though he was years older now, Jud still recognised his aquiline face from the photograph Bonati had sent him of the three of them in their student days at Cambridge. It was definitely Bonaparte.

'Where did you get this?' he said.

'Easy. From the *Pôle-emploi*. It's like your job centre, or whatever you guys call it. This guy must've been claiming benefits at some stage.'

'How did you get it from them?' asked Bex.

'Easy when you know a few people,' said Stokowski, smiling. 'I've been here a long time and this company has a big presence in the city, as you can imagine. A lot of people know us. I just called in a few favours and managed to get it from their online records. You just need to know where to look.'

'Well, thank you, Ant,' said Jud ̄ ̄this is really helpful.'

'No problems, you can take it with you,' said Stokowski. 'You might be able to find someone who's seen his ugly face before. I'd start with the bars and cafés over in Clichy, if I were you. You never know.'

'Thanks.'

'Meanwhile, I'll see if I can locate a more recent address for you. The one I've found online is not his any more. There's a different person living there now.'

'Oh?' said Bex. 'So you did find an old address for him then?'

'Yeah, sure. From the local *Mairie* – I think you call it a town hall. But I checked and someone else is registered there now. If you think it's worth a try, then by all means take it. Perhaps the guy there can tell you more.' He scribbled an address on a slip of paper and handed it to them.

'So it's in Clichy-sous-Bois then,' said Jud. 'That's a good start.'

'Yeah, go and see it if you want to. You never know your luck,' said Stokowski. 'Well, *bonne chance*, guys, and let me know how you get on. Anything else you want, just call me, okay? Are you staying somewhere nice?'

'Yeah, it's not bad,' said Bex.

'You need a car? I can get you a taxi and a driver if you want. We have plenty here. I can arrange for one if you need it.'

'No, no, we're fine,' said Jud. 'I prefer the bike.'

'Easier to get around our mad streets, huh?' said Stokowski. 'Have you got used to the French way of driving, yet? No rules; whenever you see a gap, just jump in and pray.'

'Don't worry about him,' said Bex. 'He was already a mad driver before we came. He'll fit in nicely.'

Stokowski smiled again and rose from his desk. 'Well listen, you guys. Anything else, you just shout, yeah. You have my number, don't you? Paris is a big city, but I'm sure you'll succeed. Good luck.'

Jud and Bex got up and left the room. Stokowski accompanied them to the lift and pressed the button. Within a few seconds the doors swung open and Stokowski wished them well.

'Nice guy,' said Bex as the doors closed.

'Bit old for you, isn't he?' said Jud, a trace of jealousy detectable in his voice as he leant in for a kiss.

CHAPTER 29

SUNDAY, 11.30 A.M.

VICTORIA EMBANKMENT, LONDON

It was a cold but bright, blustery morning in London. The trees that lined Victoria Embankment shook as their leaves rustled in the fresh air. There were few cars on the road, just the regular taxis and coaches of tourists, en route to the famous landmarks, where they would merrily click their cameras and record their trip to one of the world's most famous cities.

The boats on the Thames passed slowly – grimy, worn passenger ferries, cargo ships and barges, and the odd luxury yacht freed from its overnight moorings, its owners nursing hangovers from a raucous Saturday night in the city's high-class restaurants.

It was a rare moment to be thankful for living in London. A time when the city paused for breath, when newspapers were read and cappuccinos were sipped in its many bars and hotels. A steady trickle of optimistic joggers lined the Embankment, marked out by their brightly coloured running tops, mittens and head gear. Sunday was a day when the city and its inhabitants recovered from the past week, reflected on the week ahead, and took a brief moment to 'live' in contrast to the 'survival' that occupied the days between weekends.

It was a day Grace needed. It had been a terrible ordeal up in Farringdon; an experience that would leave scars on her face forever. The surgery had been successful and she had felt an overwhelming relief that she would not lose the sight of her left eye, but the scars that ran down her cheek had been hard to come to terms with. Her parents' anguish had been unbearable. Her father had said that was it, she was never going back to the CRYPT again. They wanted her home and in a normal job. But Bonati had managed to persuade Mr and Mrs Cavendish, not for the first time, that this was what Grace had chosen to do and she was finding much success. She was a valued member of the team and her years at the CRYPT would doubtless be rewarded with a fine job afterwards, perhaps at MI5 or MI6, or in one of the many research or communications departments of the security forces. Grace would never forgive them if they forced her, in a weaker moment, to close the door on the opportunities that awaited her.

Raheed had come to meet her too, and accompany her back to the CRYPT. But against the advice of her parents, she had refused to take a few days off. She wanted to be back on the case again, straight away, taking her mind off what had happened and helping to protect the public and avoid further incidents like hers. Bonati was proud of her determination and resilience. And Raheed had been pleased to get his new partner back.

And now here they were, walking down Victoria Embankment towards the dragon statues. Originally positioned under the entrance to the London Coal Exchange in Lower Street, these were the original statues on which all others had been modelled in London: the gateway to the city's financial heartland.

Raheed noticed Grace slow her pace as the dragons came into view, or at least the scaffolding and canvas wraps which had been placed around them. It was obvious what lay lurking beneath.

'You okay?' he said.

'Yeah, I think so.'

A heavy goods van thundered past and the sound of it made Grace shiver momentarily. She felt prickles run up her spine and a tingling sensation across her skull.

This was not going to be easy, but she knew the best way to recover from her ordeal was to get face to face with a statue once again. Lying in a bed feeling sorry for herself was not an option, no matter how much her parents had pleaded with her to do so. She knew she needed to be out on the street again, working with Raheed. But memories of the incident at Blackfriars came flooding back as she drew closer to the plinths on which the giant silver statues stood.

There was a group of people at each statue on both sides of the street, some taking shots with phones and cameras, others just looking at the ominous shapes in their canvas shrouds. There was fencing around each one so it was impossible for anyone to get too close. Beneath the canvas was the latticework of thick metal scaffolding surrounding the dragons.

The agents noticed a police officer standing nearby, ensuring no one was foolhardy enough to get any closer than was permitted. They could see the officer was getting tired of the many questions and comments from onlookers. Neither Raheed nor Grace had been at Temple Bar when Bex and Jud had spoken to the builders there, but they had already been briefed by Bonati about the official word being given to the public: that the statues were being covered in preparation for restoration work. Like their fellow agents, they'd found it unlikely such a story would be believed. And given the number of people crowding around the sites, it was clear that word was still spreading about the infamous dragons that were coming to life across the city. No one wanted to be on the receiving end of an attack, but no one could hide their excitement at seeing one for real. The covers and the scaffolding only added to the suspense.

'With so many people around, how are we going to take readings and find out the EM radiation levels of these?' said Raheed. 'We need to know if they're active, or about to be. But the number of people here, especially with all their phones and cameras, will make any recording impossible.'

'Then we move them on,' said Grace. 'We'll speak to the officer first.'

Raheed had been impressed by his partner's courage and determination. She wasn't afraid to wade into a scene and take control. He watched her walk boldly up to the police officer and speak to him quietly. Within seconds they were moving the bystanders on, and Raheed quickly joined them.

'What did you tell him?' whispered Raheed.

'Pretty much the truth. Just flashed my official identity card and explained we were taking some important readings as part of an on-going investigation. He didn't dare question me, given everything that's been happening. I said we're crime scene special investigators, and that's what we are. There was no need to talk about ghosts.'

'Okay,' said Raheed, 'I'll start setting up the equipment.'

Across the road, where the other statue was located, the crowd of people was dispersing, as the police officer had told them to. From where they were standing, Grace, Raheed and the officer could see that someone had refused to move on and had hidden himself beneath the canvas wrap. They saw his body disappear underneath the canvas; only his legs were poking out.

It was a young student. He'd been too curious to just disperse like that. He wanted to get a closer look – much closer. He'd whispered to his friends, 'You go on ahead, I'll catch you up. I just want to sneak another photograph.'

His friends had known exactly what he was doing. He'd been boasting all morning that he was going to get a 'dragon selfie'.

Since the news of the ghost dragons had come to light in the city, there was a mad, suicidal craze spreading on social media sites. Everyone was tweeting about it. The challenge was to get close to a statue and take a photograph of yourself with a dragon whilst it was still lifeless. A 'dragon selfie'. It was just the kind of daredevil stunt that you found on the internet, and one that could quickly earn its maker thousands of hits. People would do anything for a moment of fame and celebrity.

And this student was determined to get the best selfie ever. He reached up inside the thick, white material that covered the entire statue. He squeezed his body between the scaffolding poles, around to the front of the dragon, where he could get the best photo of all. The great jaws were fixed open and they revealed a giant, red tongue, fashioned into the shape of an arrow head which thrust forward from the mouth.

Awesome, he thought.

He turned his back on the dragon and held up his iPhone, set to camera. He pressed the reverse button and immediately saw himself next to the dragon's face. He angled the camera better, to include as much of his own face as possible.

And then he noticed something.

At the moment when his thumb pressed the little circle with a camera on it to take the shot, the great red tongue that was now close to his ear twitched slightly. He saw a tiny trickle of what looked like smoke or steam descend from the dragon's giant nostrils through the screen in his now trembling hand.

He daren't turn round, but instead pushed frantically at the scaffolding poles and the heavy material. There was so little room inside there, he was squeezed tight against the body of the dragon, with the thick material up against his face. He tried desperately to sink to his knees, to get underneath the poles and the canvas wrap to escape, but it was tied shut. He'd entered from the other side, where the canvas was looser and had flapped against the scaffolding. Here it was tightly wrapped.

He screamed.

Grace and Raheed were already running across the road and they heard his pitiful screams.

Raheed took out a penknife from his kit bag and slashed the canvas on the opposite side to where the student was now held. Quickly, with the help of the police officer who'd joined them, they pulled hard and ripped the material away from the statue.

Released from its tight shroud, the body of the student slumped to the pavement. The dragon had sunk its teeth deep into the student's neck. He was haemorrhaging blood, quickly soaking the white canvas around him, but he was alive. There was still time. Raheed ordered the dazed-looking officer to call for an ambulance.

'Now!' he yelled.

The dragon was moving slowly now, free from the white wrap but still fenced in by the scaffolding poles. But its sheer bulk and weight, and the fact that it was made of stone, gave no guarantees at all that it would remain imprisoned for long. It began slashing at the scaffolding, the poles buckling as it stabbed and kicked at them. Its strength seemed immense. The agents were just the other side of the poles, standing back to avoid the sharp jabs from the dragon's claws.

Up ahead, the last few onlookers who'd refused to disperse when the officer had told them to, watched in horror as the dragon flexed its limbs and thrashed inside its cage. Steam was now pouring continuously from its giant nostrils, and whirling up into the cold, morning air as smoke rises from a coal fire.

Without a second to spare, the two agents threw their back-packs down and quickly rummaged for their EM neutralisers, stored securely in the inside pockets. They knew the handheld devices were unlikely to incapacitate the ghost statue entirely, but there was a chance they would be able to reduce enough of its energy levels to prevent it from breaking free from the scaffolding cage that enveloped it. If the cage could hold it in place, the neutralisers would have a chance.

The new models, issued by Dr Vorzek only a few days earlier, were the fastest and most powerful neutralisers yet. They pointed them straight at the statue, held steady and prayed.

But would the devices work in time? The dragon showed no sign of losing its power, as it raised its giant claws from the plinth and thrashed out at the pole nearest to it, which buckled and bent.

'It's not going to work, Bex,' shouted Raheed, unable to hide his nerves. 'We're going to have to run for it.'

'No,' said Grace, calmly. 'We stay. Keep trying.'

'But it'll kill us any second!'

'And anyone else nearby,' said Grace. 'Don't you understand? That's why we do this job, to protect the public. We're the first line of defence. No! Don't move. Keep it on. If the dragon goes for us, at least that'll give the others time to flee. It's our *job*.'

Raheed couldn't believe what she was saying. Stay there and be killed? Was she serious? He raised his other hand to steady the one holding the neutraliser.

'Keep going. We'll do it. It can't get at us yet,' said Grace.

They were just feet away from the dragon, so close they could smell the stench that emitted from its gaping mouth, and see the hot breath that continued to burst from its flaring nostrils. Raheed watched, wide-eyed, as the statue raised up on its hind legs for another powerful stab at the pole.

Its punch was not as savage as the previous ones and the pole remained intact. The dragon brought its front legs back down to the plinth. Its head began to lower slowly and they could see the cloudy stream coming from its nostrils was beginning to lessen.

'It's working!' said Grace. 'Keep the neutraliser on full setting. Hold it steady. It's reducing the radiation levels which the dragon's drawing on in order to move. It's getting weaker. Look, you can see it. I don't think it's going to break through the cage now.'

'You hope,' said Raheed, still far from convinced.

They watched as the dragon made a couple more weak attempts to lash out at the poles that imprisoned it, but it was no use – it was becoming too weak to break free. They could see its movements slowing.

The distant sound of a siren was heard and soon an ambulance hurtled down Victoria Embankment. The student was still lying on the floor but the officer was able to stem the flow of blood and the victim was showing signs of consciousness. He'd be alright.

Grace turned to an exhausted Raheed. 'Welcome to CRYPT,' she said.

CHAPTER 30

SUNDAY, 12.00 P.M.
(1.00 P.M. LOCAL TIME)

ALLÉE CHÊNE POINTU,
CLICHY-SOUS-BOIS, PARIS

Christophe had been sat in the same dingy room for several hours and was getting restless. He'd read every old newspaper available and was pacing the floor like a caged animal. He'd asked Bonaparte if he needed any provisions from the local shop, just to have an excuse to get out for a while, but he'd said he didn't need anything. Christophe wondered what this guy lived on. He had no food in his cupboards and no drink.

He was just about to grab his helmet and go out for a baguette and some cheese when Bonaparte entered the room unexpectedly. His face was unusually animated. Since they'd met the day before, he'd never shown anything other than morbidity and misery across his wrinkled face, but now there was a look in his eyes, a spark, that suggested something was about to happen.

'It's begun,' he said.

'What has?'

'The reason why you're here. The reason why I've employed you.'

Christophe continued to look unimpressed.

'They're coming,' said Bonaparte excitedly. 'They've travelled a long way to see me and at last they're on my patch now. Let the game begin.'

Christophe just shrugged. He was becoming accustomed to his host's cryptic riddles. He had no idea what he was talking about, but if it meant that he would get the chance to do some protecting, and use the skills he'd been employed for, then it was fine with him.

'Who's coming?' he said casually, staring out of the faded lace curtain at the car park below. His bike was still there.

'Like I said, you're on a need-to-know basis and you don't need to know who is after me, just that they're on their way. Get ready. Action stations, my friend.'

Action stations? thought Christophe. What the hell was this guy like? It wasn't a submarine they were in, though it was poky and dingy and smelly enough to be one.

'You want me to go and patrol outside?' he said.

Bonaparte shook his head.

'How do you know someone's coming after you, Jacob? How do you know they're on their way? You've not been out of the flat.'

Bonaparte hesitated for a moment. He was finding it hard getting used to his codename Jacob. He knew it was unwise to start bandying his real name about – no one needed to know that – but answering to Jacob felt weird. 'I have eyes and ears everywhere. I have friends,' he said.

The last remark surprised Christophe, though he tried not to show it. Friends were something he'd never needed personally, and from the looks of his new employer, neither did he. He couldn't imagine anyone wanting to be a friend of his.

'So, what do you want me to do if they get here?' he asked.

'Nothing. Yet. Let's take our time with this. It's a game of cat and mouse and it would be very dull if we killed the mice straight away. I want to play with them for a bit.'

'So?'

'I want them to find us. In fact, I've helped them along a bit. They'll be on their way to us soon enough. And when they do, let them come up and knock on the door. We won't open it. If they break in, you can let them have it, but I don't think they will yet. They'll just watch the place for a while and then clear off. When they do, that's when you follow them. Give them something to worry about. You know, shadow them. Let them know you're following them. That'll make their tiny hearts race.'

'And then?'

'Then just let them go. We'll have some more fun tomorrow, and the next day. What fun we'll have. And then, when the plan is complete and we have no need to distract them, you can kill them in any way you like. I'll let you choose.'

Christophe turned to face Bonaparte. 'Woah, wait a minute,' he whispered gravely. 'You said protection, yes? You never said anything about taking someone out.'

'You scared?' said Bonaparte.

Christophe just stared at him and laughed. 'Scared? I don't think so. But my fee's just gone up. You want a hired killer, you pay killer rates. You're paying me protection rates, that's all.'

'I'm paying you double your normal rate, man!'

'Yeah, you're paying double my protection rate, not my killer rate. You can double it again if you want the shooter involved.'

'Whatever,' said Bonaparte as he trudged towards the door. Christophe's pathetic fees meant little to him, compared with what he was going to earn once his plan was complete.

'Deal?' shouted Christophe from the living room.

'Deal. Just be ready when I say. And keep watch at the window.'

It was another two hours before anything happened. Christophe had been staring out of the window at regular intervals for all that time, waiting to see if anyone would arrive and approach their particular apartment block. It was still only mid-afternoon and there was nobody about. No one had returned home from work yet, if anyone had a job that is. The estate was one of the most deprived and dilapidated he'd seen, and he hardly expected a flurry of workers returning home at rush hour, but at least he would have someone to watch.

Finally he saw a black motorcycle sweep into the car park. It was a Honda Fireblade, one of the new breed of pretty bikes which he loathed. Why did so many people choose to opt for imitation race bikes, the kind modelled on machines built for the race track but modified to suit the roads? What was the point? They were girls' bikes. His own machine was a proper bike, a man's bike.

He opened the window to hear the sound of the engine. It was barely audible compared to the thunderous roar of his Yamaha. He strained to see where the bike had gone, but it must have vanished behind a wall or vehicle somewhere. Soon the sound of the engine stopped. He leaned further out of the window and caught a glimpse of the bike again, parked up close to a wall across the car park. He could make out the back wheel and the riders as they dismounted. They had matching black leathers, just like the bike.

'Pretty boys,' he muttered to himself. He hoped to God these were the people his host was expecting. He would love nothing more than to shake them up, thunder after them and hassle them at every traffic light from here to the Champs-Élysées.

He could just make out the two riders removing their helmets. He was surprised to see one of them was a girl with long, flowing dark hair. Quite a looker. The other was some grubby-faced teenage guy who clearly thought he was the business. If that was his girlfriend, she could do better, he thought. 'Play your cards right, *chérie*,' he muttered at the window. 'You could ride with a real man.'

Though he was pleased to watch a sexy girl like this step off a motorbike, he was disappointed as there was no way this young couple could be the people Jacob was talking about. They obviously lived in the area and were returning home or to visit a friend maybe.

He looked across the car park and on towards the street to see if anyone else was coming. No one. And then a car swept into the estate. Maybe this was it?

He watched it park up quickly outside the block opposite and a man got out, but he quickly disappeared inside the door of the building. He looked as though he knew where he was going, so perhaps he was just a resident too.

Christophe glanced back to where the bike had pitched up. He could see the riders still there, talking and glancing up at the tower blocks that surrounded them. They were still behind the wall of a set of garages, but Christophe could just see them. They were looking in his direction now.

No, seriously? thought Christophe. Is it going to be this easy? Is it really them?

Sure enough, the guy in leathers took out a small scrap of paper, showed it to his partner and together they looked over in Christophe's direction again. Were they working out which flat to search first? Did they have this actual address? If so, how the hell did they get it? It seemed to Christophe that Jacob was some kind of recluse, with no friends and no reason to see anyone. So how could they have found his address so easily? Who would have given it to them?

He watched the two people in the car park moving towards his building, darting between cars and vehicles, never walking into open space. Christophe shouted to Bonaparte.

'Jacob? I think we've got guests.'

'Yes, I know,' came a voice in reply. 'I can see them.'

Bonaparte had been watching exactly the same scene from his office window down the hall. He'd been excited to see the young kids pitch up, especially the guy. Eavesdropping on the agents all morning had been interesting to say the least. It had been quite a revelation to hear the male voice refer to Jason Goode as his 'father'. What a bonus this would be. Not only would he put his old rival in prison, to rot for the rest of his life, but he would be able to take out his son too. Bonus.

Bonaparte had traced the life of Jason Goode for years. He knew everything about him – not only his business enterprises, but his obsession with ghosts too. He knew all about the CRYPT, and Goode and Bonati's first attempts before that. The PIT, as it was called back then, had been an amusing project to watch from a distance. All those failed attempts, the accusations of spreading fear wherever they went, the chaos and the eventual order from the police to close it down. It had all been so entertaining to watch.

But despite watching his old enemy's success in building the new ghost-hunting agency, CRYPT, Bonaparte had known nothing about him having a second son. He knew the first son, the lad they called Jamie, was still in prison. But how old would he be now? About the same age as this kid. And he knew Goode had not had twins.

But this kid looked nothing like Jamie, from the photographs he'd seen of him in the years spent stalking Goode after university. He'd never lost touch with him, though Goode never knew it, of course. And he'd thought he'd known everything about him – but another mysterious son appearing from nowhere? Someone referring to Goode as 'Dad'?

Unless. Unless . . . It seemed too good to be true. Unless this guy in the car park, just moments away from his grasp, *was* Jamie Goode? If he had been released from prison, it stood to reason that he would stick closely to his father. His mother was long gone and he had no one else. The kid's murder trial had made fascinating reading in the papers. Bonaparte had enjoyed every minute of it, watching Goode crumple as his life fell apart around him.

Could this really be the same kid? If so, he'd had a serious identity change. But that wasn't surprising. Any kid accused of killing his mother was never going to be a popular figure after being released. People had long memories. No wonder he'd changed his appearance.

He watched the two agents approach the main doors to his building. He could feel the unfamiliar tinge of excitement as adrenalin flowed through his veins. This was a bonus beyond his wildest dreams. Send Goode to prison, drive his company into the ground by implicating it in the world's biggest bank heist, then, at last, build up his own empire using the same technology that had been rightfully his in the first place. And, on top of all this, take out his only son too.

No wonder the adrenalin was pumping. He felt alive, at last. He clenched his fists, looked down at his weak body and felt a surge of energy running through him. But the excitement brought on a fit of coughing so bad it made him double up and fall against the desk.

Christophe heard the commotion and shouted from the living room. 'You okay in there?'

'Yes,' choked Bonaparte, still coughing but grinning now. 'I'm fine. The best I've felt in a long time.'

'Sounds it,' said Christophe sarcastically.

'Trust me,' Bonaparte shouted. 'It's gonna be a good day. *Très bon.*'

CHAPTER 31

SUNDAY, 12.20 P.M.

BANGROVE CASTLE,

BUCKINGHAMSHIRE

It was nearly lunchtime and Pauline was running late. She'd already spent the last few hours prepping the vegetables and getting everything ready in saucepans. Timing was everything when cooking a roast lunch. Provided you had done the preparation properly, it was just a matter of getting it all ready for the same time. Pauline had been cooking roasts for decades, for her husband, for her children and now for her grandchildren. But today was extra special. Her second son, Mark, was coming over with his new bride, Katie. It had seemed at one stage that he would never get married, but finally he found the girl of his dreams and on a cold but sunny morning in late November he had become an honest man at last.

Today was going to be special. Mark and his wife had returned from their honeymoon just a couple of days before, and this was the first time they had visited Pauline as a married couple. Her husband, Greg, had been busy ploughing through the list of DIY jobs he'd been given for the weekend, mostly in readiness for the 'royal' couple's arrival, as he called it.

Everything was going to plan until Pauline discovered the problem. During the week, Pauline worked as a housekeeper to a wealthy businessman. She remembered asking her employer if she could bring home the fancy dinner service, just for the weekend. The expensive plates and dishes and cutlery would look wonderful on their dining table at home – like a banquet – and she'd been delighted when her boss had granted her the favour. She remembered packing up the crockery so very carefully into two separate boxes – one would have been too heavy for her – and placing them by the front door ready for her departure. But it was only when Greg had come into the kitchen and enquired if she wanted him to lay the table that Pauline realised she'd forgotten to bring the boxes home.

'Oh, Greg!' she'd cried. 'I knew there was something!'

She'd told her husband to turn the potatoes down on the stove and keep a close eye on the beef in the oven whilst she whizzed up to the big house to retrieve the boxes of china. Luckily, since getting the jobs of housekeeper and gardener, she and Greg had been given the lodge house to live in. It was important that they were on site 24/7. Their employer was so rarely at home, but someone needed to be present to look after the place and provide some security. Bangrove Castle was one of the largest private residences in the county, and one of the few castles in the UK which was not open to the public at all.

Its owner was a private man, seldom seen, even by Pauline and Greg. They communicated over the telephone mostly, from his apartment in London. He'd had no problems at all when she'd asked to borrow the dinner service. 'Yeah, sure,' he'd said generously, 'take whatever you need.'

But how stupid she'd been for forgetting to bring it all home! She cursed herself as she sped up the long drive to the castle up ahead. It was only a ten-minute walk, but she knew she could never manage the boxes by herself and so it was better to drive the short distance.

As her car approached the main drive and the tyres crunched on gravel, she gazed up at the great façade and the impressive towers. The crenellations ran right across the top of the main house, forming an impressive set of battlements that stretched from one tower across to the other. It was, some said, more a fortified mansion than a real castle. There wasn't a moat or drawbridge or portcullis. This was no Warwick or Windsor. But as a private home it was surely the most impressive in Buckinghamshire.

Pauline drew up to the main door and then reversed up to the steps to make it easier for her to load the car. Just before she stopped and turned the engine off, her eyes noticed something in the rear view mirror. She could see the large windows of the drawing room to her left and she felt sure she'd seen something, someone, pass quickly between the curtains.

The place was empty, as it always was on a Sunday. The other staff on the estate had gone home, and there was just she and Greg left. There couldn't have been anyone in there.

Was it a burglar? she thought. Her heart was beginning to speed up as she glanced down at the pocket in the glove box where she usually put her mobile phone. She wanted to ring Greg just in case, but it wasn't there. She'd only popped up for the boxes. She hadn't needed it.

She told herself to stop being silly. Of course it wasn't a person. There was no way anyone could break into the house. It was virtually impregnable. The alarm system was top of the range, and she and Greg always set it religiously whenever they left. And it was a castle after all.

It must have been a trick of the light, or maybe the reflection of the car as she'd reversed past the window. She'd ask Greg to pop up this afternoon, after lunch, just in case. The boxes were just inside the hall, right by the door, so she could easily retrieve them and be gone in seconds.

She unlocked the great oak door with the double set of keys, one for the main lock and another for the deadlock at the top. It opened and she braced herself for the loud beeps that emitted every morning when she arrived at work, but there was silence. The alarm had not been set. She quickly thought back to who was the last to leave on Friday.

It was Greg! She remembered she'd asked him to bring the boxes home and he must've forgotten! It was typical of him not to own up to this just now, but it was unlike him not to set the alarm for the place.

The boxes were lying just next to the door and she quickly picked one up and carried it down the steps to the car boot which she'd already opened. As she returned up the steps and into the house for the second box, a thought suddenly struck her. Perhaps the thing she'd seen through the window in the drawing room wasn't a reflection, or a burglar, but a ghost?

She felt a shiver run up her spine. It was well known that Bangrove was haunted. That was why her employer loved it so much. But it was easy for him – he didn't have to live in the place all year round and experience what it was like in deepest winter when it was dark by four o'clock.

Could it have been a ghost? Pauline had always been slightly spooked by the place, but Greg had often said she was being silly, and of course there was no such thing as ghosts. She'd been watching too many movies, he usually said.

Without daring to open the door to the drawing room and find out, she picked up the second box and carried it straight out to the car. She shut the boot with a thud and ran back up the steps to close the door. She decided not to investigate why the alarm had not sounded. Greg could do that after they'd eaten. Time was ticking on. Mark and Katie would be here in less than an hour and she'd not even set the table yet, or got changed into something smarter. She smelled of beef and boiled cabbage. And she still had her pinny on.

The giant door thudded and she ran down the steps to the car.

Moments later, from a shadowy corner of the drawing room, the man in the dark hood watched the car tear across the gravel and disappear down the long drive. If he had been seen by the woman, he knew it wouldn't be long before someone would come back to investigate. He didn't have much time. He moved swiftly down the great hall.

Towards Jason Goode's study.

CHAPTER 32

SUNDAY, 12.41 P.M.
(1.41 P.M. LOCAL TIME)

ALLÉE CHÊNE POINTU,
CLICHY-SOUS-BOIS, PARIS

Jud peered through the windows of the apartment. If someone was inside, they weren't in the mood for visitors. They'd rung the bell and knocked on the door several times but no one had answered.

They'd rehearsed their lines and were ready for Bonaparte. All they wanted to do at first was establish if this was where he lived and if he was who they thought he was. Jud had been certain that he wouldn't have a clue who they were, and so it was possible for them to be discreet. Find out if this really was the man who'd written the email, and then quickly report back to Goode and Bonati in London. They'd take it from there.

Jud was disappointed not to be able to see the man face to face, but at the same time he was relieved. He just didn't know if he could trust himself not to attack the man there and then.

'Let's go and see if any of the neighbours recognise his picture,' said Jud. 'At least we have that.'

They trudged to the next apartment, along the open concrete

balcony that ran the length of the building. Similar balconies ran along every floor in the building, increasing its resemblance to a multi-storey car park. The ground beneath them was hard concrete and there were stains of various kinds everywhere.

The red paint on the neighbouring front door was peeling badly and a window to the right of it was cracked and taped up. Jud saw a bell to the left of the door and he pressed it. To their surprise it worked. But no one came. Bex pressed it again and waited. Still no one.

The apartment further down the balcony looked much the same. It was sad to see people living in such soulless, harsh surroundings. No answer again.

Up ahead they could see someone had tied a short washing line from an open window to a rail on the balcony wall opposite the apartment. A few shabby clothes had been pegged to it: some large underpants, a bra and a couple of faded T-shirts.

'Let's try there,' said Jud.

There was no bell this time, so Jud rattled the letterbox. Nothing. He knocked sharply on the glass window pane set into the top half of the door.

They were just about to move on when there was a rattle of keys and the sliding of a bolt from inside the apartment. The wizened face of an old lady peered through the gap in the door. Jud could see a small chain was still attached to the door, preventing anyone from pushing it right open.

'*Oui?*' said the woman.

'*Excusez-moi, madame,*' said Bex, quickly turning to Jud and taking the photo of Bonaparte from his hand. '*Avez-vous vu cet homme?*' She flashed the photograph in front of the woman's face.

'*Pourquoi?*' she said suspiciously. '*Qui êtes-vous?*' Her voice was unusually deep and gravelly and her eyes were a faded hazel colour.

'*Je suis sa nièce et lui c'est mon petit ami.*'

'*Oui*,' the old woman said. '*Il vit là-bas.*' She pointed a skinny finger in the direction of Bonaparte's apartment. '*Au revoir.*'

The old lady shut the door before Bex had a chance to ask her when she'd last seen Bonaparte.

'So I'm guessing the "*oui*" meant he lives here, yes?' said Jud, impressed not only by her French but by the sexy accent she used.

Bex nodded.

'I must ask you to speak French to me sometime.'

She smiled. '*Tout ce que vous voulez que je fasse.*'

Jud didn't know what that meant, but from her face he guessed it was something good.

They walked back towards the elevator shaft.

'Who did you say you were?' he asked.

'His niece.'

'And me?'

'What?'

'You looked like you were introducing me,' said Jud.

'Oh, just a friend,' she lied. She decided not to confess that she'd introduced him as her boyfriend. He didn't need to know that. She handed the photograph back to Jud, which he quickly pocketed inside his leather jacket. 'I can't believe we found him so quickly,' she said. 'It doesn't seem right.'

'Why?' said Jud. 'What do you mean?'

'Well, think about it. Your father said he's spent years trying to find him and now we find the guy on the first day. Something doesn't add up.'

'Maybe we're just lucky.'

'No, there's something else going on. I mean, how come Stokowski managed to find his old address but never gave it to Goode all these years?'

'Why should my father have ever asked him?' said Jud. 'Bonaparte's got nothing to do with Goode Technology. It would never have come up in conversation, I guess. I doubt anyone would have known my father was looking for him until now.'

'I suppose so,' said Bex.

'And anyway, my father obviously trusts this guy Stokowski. And he doesn't trust many people, believe me. If he says he's okay, then we've gotta trust him.'

'So, what now?'

'We get back to the hotel and I put in a call to Bonati. He's going to be pleased,' said Jud.

'Hang on,' said Bex. 'We've discovered where he lives, but that doesn't mean we've found him, does it? I mean, he could have left the place ages ago.'

'She would have said,' replied Jud. 'The old woman would have mentioned it, surely.'

'Not necessarily. Did she strike you as someone who was regularly out and about, talking to neighbours? Knowing what everyone's doing? For all she knows he might have left months ago.'

'Okay. Let's come back again later. We'll find somewhere to hide the bike and watch the apartment for a while, see if we can see anything. I don't want to spend too much time here; people will get suspicious if we're seen too much. I wanna get back to the hotel first anyway, and report in.'

They returned to the Fireblade which, much to Jud's relief, was still there, parked behind a garage wall. They put on their helmets, climbed on the bike and set off. As they sped out of the car park, they didn't notice the man walking to his own motorbike behind them. He'd slipped out of the fire exit long before they'd entered the lift and raced down the long staircase, jumping the steps three at a time.

The Yamaha roared into life and he quickly raced across the car park and out onto the main road. He could see the Fireblade up ahead. This was going to be fun.

Up in his apartment, Bonaparte smiled to himself and sipped another coffee. Their conversation had been interesting to hear.

His niece indeed! He was surprised the old lady had fallen for that, but it didn't matter. The plan was working beautifully.

In the meantime, he was going to have some fun for himself. The newspaper reports on the banking crisis had been entertaining enough, but news of these so-called 'phantom dragons' had been another bonus. He'd read with excitement of the panic that these ghostly statues were wreaking on London's streets. He'd no idea why this was occurring; unlike his old Cambridge associates, he'd never had any interest in ghosts or paranormal activity. He'd always said it was bullshit, a figment of an underdeveloped, childish imagination. Like being scared of anything that went 'bump' in the night. Even if the dragon statues weren't part of some great hoax and really were coming to life, it didn't bother him. But what it did mean was that the CRYPT was being stretched to full capacity and he was thankful for that. Any extra inconvenience he could cause Jason Goode and Giles Bonati right now was welcome.

But he'd come up with a plan that would bring him even more joy. And quickly too. It wouldn't take long, given his knowledge and extraordinary insight into IT systems, and with his men in place too, it would be easy to ramp it up and cause maximum effect to millions.

First he was going to try it himself and then, if it worked, he would employ his secret contacts to repeat the process across the whole of London, maybe throughout the country. What he had in mind would cash in on the dragon hysteria. Ramp it up a bit.

He was grinning when he sat down at his desk, facing the bank of monitors and rows of different keyboards. He rubbed his bony hands together, took a swig of cold coffee and set to work. He liked to operate several machines at once, each one talking to the other and opening up many screens simultaneously on the monitors in front of him. If he could do this quickly and efficiently, it would be easy to train up his contacts in the UK so that they could do it the same night. Oh, what fun Monday morning would be. Chaos.

He typed quickly, burrowing deeper and deeper, like a mole, into online places which anyone else would think were impossible to access. To Bonaparte, the internet was a labyrinthine maze of tunnels and dark shadowy corners, all just waiting to be explored. How little ordinary people really knew and how laughable it was how they hid behind their 'online security systems'. The phrase always made him laugh. Nothing was secure, not from Bonaparte. If files existed online, no matter where in the world they'd been inputted or where they were stored, he could find them. And with a quick piece of effective, incisive coding, he could send shockwaves across the world like a tsunami.

About an hour later he'd done it. The first wave. He sat back and smiled.

'Let the fun begin,' he said.

CHAPTER 33

SUNDAY, 1.03 P.M.

SCOTLAND YARD, LONDON

Khan walked into his office and quickly shut the door. This was going to be a difficult phone call and he didn't need people eavesdropping. He rang the number which had become so familiar to him now.

'Bonati,' said a voice after just two rings.

'Professor, it's Khan. May I talk with you?'

'Ah, Detective Chief Inspector Khan. What a pleasure.' He glanced across his study at Goode and rolled his eyes. They'd both hoped it was Jud calling.

They'd been discussing the case all morning. Since hearing the news from the professor the night before that Jud and Bex had escaped to France in search of Bonaparte, Goode had spent most of the night thinking about his Cambridge days and how and why their friendship with Nap had gone so sour. Though he had many phone calls and matters to attend to, he'd spent most of the morning in Bonati's company. He was clearly agitated – he couldn't believe the professor had allowed the agents to go to France and put themselves in so much danger. The phone call the night before had been a fraught one, to say the least. Relations between the two had never been so strained.

'I have two reasons for calling,' said the inspector. 'Firstly, it's about the killing of Annika Premvas.'

'Go on,' said Bonati. Goode had returned to the chair he had leapt from when the phone had first rung.

'Well, I received a phone call from one of the partners at the bank in which she worked. It seems she had incurred serious losses.'

'What? So she was losing their clients' money?'

'Yes, and some considerable sums allegedly. The bosses at the bank have been conducting a search of Miss Premvas's computer this morning. They have found evidence of serious losses in the last forty-eight hours. It's a private bank, of course, so it's their clients' portfolios she was messing around with. Still, it's big money. I don't know what the partners will say to their clients. There's evidence of real fraud here.'

'This is significant, isn't it, Inspector? Another banker who's been losing money, allegedly, acting fraudulently. And then another ghost appears on the scene. It's more than coincidence. She was killed because of the losses made, I'm sure of it.'

'It would seem so,' said Khan.

'And it is reasonable to assume that the ghost seen at the premises yesterday could have been a former partner at the bank. If the fraud is as big as you say, then any number of deceased bankers could feel angry about it – enough to harness the energy needed to return.'

'It's possible, Professor. But there's more, I'm afraid.'

'Go on.'

'Well, it seems the partners found evidence of something else. Emails. I'm informed that they found emails on her system from someone we both know well.'

'Who?' Bonati hated the way Khan built up the tension when he knew something the professor didn't.

'A Mr Jason Goode.'

Bonati fell silent for a moment. The inspector didn't know

that he was currently sharing the room with Jason. It would be impossible to have a conversation now. He decided it was best to tell him and hand the phone over.

'Before you go on, Inspector, I can tell you that Mr Goode is here with me now. You can speak to him direct.' Without waiting for an answer, Bonati handed the receiver to Goode.

'Hello, Khan. Yes?' he said abruptly.

'Hello, Mr Goode. I'm afraid it's bad news.' He explained about the emails.

'Well, that's ridiculous, I've never even heard of the woman. What was the bank again? No, never had any dealings with them in my life. The emails are fake, clearly. I've told you, Inspector, someone is trying to frame me.'

'Well, that's for us to find out, sir.'

Goode noticed it was the first time Khan had called him 'sir' for a long while and it unsettled him. He knew the inspector would have used the word deliberately to remind him that he was a police officer and Goode was a civilian. There was no trace of friendship now.

'Are you seriously saying you don't believe me, Khan?' said Goode. Bonati flashed him a look from across his desk, as if to say 'take it easy'.

'Look, I've told you it's my job to conduct an investigation. If I receive evidence, I have to act on it. And that includes these emails.'

'What did they say?' said Goode.

'Now, you know I don't have to tell you that at this stage,' said Khan.

'Oh, for God's sake. Don't be a fool. I wanna help you guys get the guy who's behind this. I wanna help. How the hell can I help you if you're going to role-play like this? I'm not a God damn criminal, Khan. You know that.'

Bonati made a sign with his hands to say 'calm down'. He knew this was going to help no one, least of all his old friend. 'Take it easy, Jason,' he whispered.

Khan declined to enter into an argument with Goode. Instead, he spoke calmly and professionally, devoid of any emotion.

'I'm sorry, sir, but I'm afraid I have more to tell you, so if you'll hold your temper and let me finish. We have gained a search warrant for your home in Buckinghamshire.'

'You what?' Goode stood up and started pacing the floor. He ran his hand through his short hair and glanced at Bonati. 'They wanna search my home now,' he whispered.

The professor looked aghast but then shook his head. 'You've got to let them do it. You have no choice.'

'Hello? Mr Goode?' Khan was saying.

'Just a minute,' Goode snapped, and placed a hand over the receiver. 'Are you saying they can do this and there's nothing I can do to stop them, huh?'

'Yes, that's exactly what I'm saying, Jason. You have no choice, so you're better off being seen to cooperate. I don't know what they think they'll find there, but you have to let them look.'

'You can search all you like, Inspector,' said Goode. 'Do you have something in mind? Are you looking for something in particular? Is it about this Premvas girl now?'

'No, sir. Not at all. The reasons we have for searching your home, and the equipment you hold there, have nothing to do with that part of the investigation. But my orders are to conduct a proper search. We will start with your place in Buckinghamshire and then, if necessary, we will come to your office too.'

'Jesus,' said Goode. The thought of police officers crawling over his castle was bad enough, but the idea of them waltzing straight into Goode Technology and searching the place in full view of his staff was too much to bear.

'Why the castle, for God's sake? I've not visited it in ages. I'm never there.'

'Are you saying you would rather we searched your offices first, sir?'

'Hell, no. I mean, whatever. Christ, I don't want to say any more.'

'Then I suggest you don't say anything,' said Khan calmly. 'It is quite customary in any investigation for my officers to conduct searches of a suspect's property.' His voice was a whisper now, as he glanced towards his office door and prayed no one would intrude. 'Look, before you jump down my throat again, you already know you're a suspect, but you should also know that I'm doing all I can this end to help you. Okay? My superiors wanted me to start searching both your home *and* your office two days ago, but I managed to stall them. Said we didn't have enough reason to search yet. They want me to come straight to your office now, but I've managed to stall them again by saying we'll start with your home and then come to the office only once we've done there. Understand? Hopefully, by the time my men have finished in Buckinghamshire your guys will have unearthed something and the next search will be called off.'

Goode took a deep breath. 'Okay, thank you, Inspector.'

Bonati nodded at him across the room and smiled.

'So do you wish to be present?' said Khan.

'What? Oh, no. You can help yourself. I'm tellin' you you'll find nothing there. No incriminating evidence, as you guys say. If you're not going to tell me what you're looking for then there's no point in me being there to help you. My staff will be there first thing in the morning.' He suddenly thought of Pauline and Greg and the others all worrying like mad as Khan and his men searched the place. 'No, wait a minute,' he said. 'When do you want to search the place? Do you wanna go today?'

'At the earliest opportunity. We can go later today if you like?'

'Okay, I'll come. I don't want my staff wondering what the hell's going on. I've tried to keep them out of this so far. Whenever they've asked, I've just told them it's a smear campaign – which it is, I might add – and they shouldn't worry. You turn up in your police cars and they'll think you're coming for them.'

'Is there a reason they should worry?' said Khan.

'No. I mean . . . Look, wait a minute, will you? You're twisting my words,' shouted Goode. 'Of course there isn't any God damn reason why they should be worried. They've got nothing to hide, Khan. Look, just meet me at the castle tonight. Say, seven o'clock.' Goode hesitated. 'No. In fact, hell, let's go now. You come to the office and I'll drive you there myself. No police cars. How many are you planning on bringing with you, huh? A whole army?'

'No, no. Just me and one of my DCs. Thank you, we'll see you there shortly.' Khan hung up.

Goode stared at Bonati.

'Well?' said the professor.

'They wanna search the castle, Giles. What the hell is going on?'

The professor remained calm. 'Nothing, Jason. Don't worry. I'm sure it's standard procedure. You have computers there, you have files and records. It's perfectly understandable they'd want to pay a visit. What surprises me is how they haven't come barging in here yet with their magnifying glasses.'

'That was the plan but Khan managed to stall them, or so he says. They're going to the castle first to buy me some time, apparently.' Goode's tone sounded like he was neither convinced nor grateful.

'Well, there you are then,' said Bonati. 'You should be grateful for that.'

'Oh, sure,' said Goode. 'I'm all smiles.'

CHAPTER 34

SUNDAY, 1.30 P.M.
(2.30 P.M. LOCAL TIME)

ALLÉE CHÊNE POINTU,
CLICHY-SOUS-BOIS, PARIS

Jud wound back the throttle and let the Fireblade glide down the main road, cutting through the slow traffic like a knife through butter. Driving on the right in France had little meaning for Jud, as he usually spent most of his time in the centre of the lanes wherever he was riding, overtaking cars. His patience was running thin and he wanted to get back to the hotel to call Bonati with the good news. He could have called on the mobile from the apartment block in Clichy, but they felt conspicuous in the car park and were keen to get out of there as soon as possible. Besides, he had poor reception on his phone and the landline at the hotel would be better. They were both gagging for another coffee too.

The bike slowed as they hit yet another traffic jam caused by yet another set of traffic lights. The traffic lights were fixed to giant metal bars that stretched right across the road above them. You could never use the excuse of not seeing the lights if you ever jumped a red, and Jud was not about to make that mistake.

He glanced around him and felt surprised to see so many cars made in France. It wasn't the same in London, but then the UK seldom made any cars now anyway, compared with the giants of Peugeot and Renault in France, and BMW and VW in Germany. Maybe the French were just more patriotic too. There were Peugeot 205s and Renault Clios everywhere, their drivers treating them like dodgem cars, driving virtually anywhere they wanted. Intersections in Paris were notoriously carefree affairs, where you didn't wait to be let in by passing traffic, but just bullied your way in as soon as you saw the slightest gap. You needed courage to drive in Paris; it was no place for shrinking violets. They were surrounded by Vespas too – tiny motorbikes with engines no bigger than a lawnmower that whined and screeched as they passed, their teenage riders winding the throttle as far back as it would go and leaning close to the bike to try and inch the little machine beyond 40km per hour.

But there was one motorbike that was anything but a little Vespa. It was a bulky and muscular Yamaha and it had been following them for some time now. That in itself was no surprise – they were on the main route into *centre ville*, and there would be plenty of people heading into the city, whatever day of the week. But it was curious that its rider hadn't tried to overtake them yet, or take on the Fireblade in a race like a lot of big bikes did in London. The guy sat on the bike was bulky too, making even the Yamaha look small, which it wasn't. Jud recognised it as an XJR1300, a serious bike for the traditionalist, one of the old school. Its classic design attracted men of a certain age, who needed something to get them through their mid-life crises and help them feel young and reckless again. Jud looked forward to the time when he too would exchange his smooth, sleek racing machine for something more rock 'n' roll.

As the lights overhead blinked to green, he set off again at a sharp pace. The Yamaha behind them had drawn up unusually close, as it had done on the previous set of lights, but it still didn't try to overtake Jud at the junction. It just stayed behind them.

'Do you think he's following us?' said Jud through his headset.

'Who?' said Bex.

'Look behind.'

She turned around quickly and saw the gun-metal grey Yamaha weaving through the traffic as Jud was doing.

'Dunno. Probably just heading into town. Why?'

'Because he's been on our tail since Clichy. But he's not made any attempt to overtake us,' said Jud.

'Well, it's not easy overtaking you, Jud Lester. You always seem to go everywhere and do everything at full speed!'

They thought nothing more of it and watched the buildings and gardens that gradually became more and more ornate as they approached the centre of the city again. Belleville wasn't far now. Soon they'd be in the warmth of their rooms, sipping cappuccinos.

And then Jud noticed something in his wing mirror. The giant Yamaha was drawing so close it was nearly touching his rear wheel.

'What the hell?' said Jud, as he accelerated even faster, being careful not to clip the wing mirrors of the cars he thundered past.

'What're you doing?' Bex shouted over the din.

'The guy behind is a maniac,' said Jud. 'He seems to want to stick to my rear wheel. Is he blind or something? Let's boot it.' They both leant down towards the bike as Jud floored it.

It was no use, the Yamaha was still hassling them. It was impossible to have a straight race in the traffic, otherwise the Fireblade would have won on acceleration; it was lighter and more nimble than the Yamaha. But here, in the busy streets of Paris, there was no escaping the reckless idiot behind them.

There was another junction up ahead and Jud was forced to

slow down quickly as the lights were changing to red. As they reached the line, the Yamaha pulled up alongside them. The guy was huge and he flicked open his visor to stare at them. Jud was just about to give him a two-fingered salute when he stopped himself. The man raised his right hand and pointed it towards them in the shape of a gun. He simulated shooting it.

'Saddo,' said Jud.

'Yeah, loser,' said Bex, though there was something about the guy's eyes through his open visor that looked frightening. Why he was pretending to shoot them was anyone's guess – presumably it was his own way of causing offence. Either way he was weird.

As they waited for the lights to change, he raised one of his heavy boots away from the body of the bike and slammed it into Bex's leg.

'Ow! God! What's he doing, J?' cried Bex.

Before Jud had a chance to get off the bike and pull him to the floor, the lights changed and the Yamaha roared away. Jud hurtled after it.

The road ahead was more open now and he was able to come parallel with the biker rider again. They saw him winking at them and waving his pretend gun in their direction once more.

'What is this guy on?' said Jud.

'Let's ignore him, J. He's clearly mental. Just pull over somewhere and let him clear off.'

'No way,' said Jud. 'If he wants a race, I'll give him one.'

'Don't be stupid,' said Bex. 'We've got work to do. You said you wanted to call Bonati. We're going to miss the turning. It's coming up now. Just forget about him.'

'Bex, the guy assaulted you!'

'Yes, and my guess is he'll do it again if we give him the chance. Just let him go.'

Jud knew she was right. There was something in this guy's

eyes that looked deranged. Like he was high on some kind of drug or just drunk. Either way it was not safe to get any more involved. But the guy had assaulted Bex! How could Jud let him get away with that?

They were still racing parallel, but there was another junction up ahead. The main roads into Paris were punctuated with so many lights, they'd lost count. There was clearly not enough space for them to remain parallel; one of them was going to have to fall behind to make way for the cars all around them. But every time Jud sped up or slowed down, the Yamaha matched his speed, making it impossible either to get ahead of him or drop behind. They reached the lights and drew to a halt, forcing the car that was about to draw alongside them to brake suddenly and allow them to stay in front.

Bex looked straight ahead and refused to give the guy the satisfaction of glaring at them again or making some weird sign. But Jud stared at him and shook his head. He raised a finger to his helmet and pointed at his skull as if to say the guy was insane. The rider just smiled at him. He looked ahead at the lights. Just as the red changed to green, he raised his heavy boot again and slammed it into the petrol tank of the Fireblade. The blow was so heavy, Jud lost control of the bike and it toppled to the ground, trapping Bex's leg.

'Oh, God, get it off!' she cried.

The car behind stopped and the driver got out to assist them. But the Yamaha just sped on, leaving the scene. The weight of the bike was crushing Bex's right leg. Her left leg still ached from the guy's sharp kick, and now her other leg was agony. Her ankle was bent awkwardly and it wasn't until Jud and the driver had lifted the bike vertical again that she was able to move it.

'Ow!' she shouted. 'It's my ankle. The exhaust pipe crushed it. Ow!'

'Don't move,' said Jud, staring briefly down the road to see if he could see the Yamaha. He'd rip the guy limb from limb if he had the chance. Jud didn't care how big he was; he was pumped up and ready to kill him. But he knew he couldn't leave Bex. He helped her slowly to her feet.

'Do you think it's broken?' he said.

Bex shook her head. 'No, I'd know if it was. It's just bruised. I think I can walk on it.' She winced as she put pressure on the ankle, but she was able to stand. 'I don't wanna see what it looks like,' she said. 'But I'll be okay. What the hell was that guy doing? I mean, who was he?'

'I don't know,' said Jud. 'But I tell you, if I see him again he's a dead man.'

The driver shook hands with Jud and said something very quickly in French that he didn't understand.

'He's saying he saw what happened and would be a witness if you wanted,' said Bex.

'What? Oh, no, don't worry,' said Jud. The last thing they needed was the investigation being slowed up by a visit to the gendarmerie, where they'd have to explain how a local Frenchman assaulted two British tourists. Jud thought it was doubtful somehow their story would be believed, or acted upon, even with a French witness to help them. Besides, it would take ages for the gendarmes to find the guy. There was no point. Jud wanted to act out his own form of justice, if he ever had the chance, but in a city of two million people, it was unlikely he would.

They got back onto the bike, which luckily seemed to have survived its fall, its most vulnerable parts having landed on Bex's ankle and leg rather than meeting with the tarmac and concrete curb, and set off again towards the hotel in Belleville.

A few moments later Jud manoeuvred the Fireblade through the archway that ran through the middle of the building and led into the small car park at the rear. As they found a small space at the far corner they saw the familiar sight of the grey Yamaha riding slowly past the archway, back on the road. The rider waved to them.

'Great, so he knows where we're staying,' said Bex. 'Who is that guy?'

'I don't know,' said Jud, 'but something tells me he knows us. And I reckon it won't be the last time we'll see him.'

CHAPTER 35

SUNDAY, 3.18 P.M.

THE STRAND, CENTRAL LONDON

Maxi was running late. She was due to meet her friend Daya at a bar in Leicester Square before going on to the Odeon for a movie. Sunday afternoons and evenings were her favourite time of the week. It had become something of a ritual for Jayne and her. Sometimes others tagged along – Yasmin, Tia, sometimes Lenka and her boyfriend Mariusz – though they preferred it to be just girls, if they were honest. Lenka was more fun when she was on her own anyway.

But Maxi and Daya were the two die-hard movie goers. They never missed a week. She ran on, down the Strand. She was about to turn and run up Bedford Street when she paused and decided to use the cash machine on the corner. She knew she needed cash and could have used the many cashpoints in Leicester Square, but they were almost always busy with queues. It was such a tourist hotspot, and Sundays were no exception. Better to get it now, even if it meant it would make her late.

There was no one waiting so she took out her purse and removed the bank card before she'd even reached the machine. She inserted it into the slot and drummed her fingers on the square metal panel.

'Come on, come on!' she said impatiently. Why was it everything in London seemed to go slower on a Sunday? Even the machines.

She was asked for her PIN code and she dutifully keyed it in. She pressed the 'cash only' option and requested £80. That would be enough for the cinema ticket, a meal and some drinks. She was very particular about using cash these days, ever since a bad experience she'd had the month before when someone had clocked up over £300 on her card in a scam. It was traced to a dodgy little newsagent's across town. She vaguely remembered the man there saying the card was 'playing up' and him disappearing out the back to speak to his colleague who knew how to 'fix it'. He'd taken the card with him and she'd not even thought to stop him. Would she ever learn?

The message on the screen now read 'Please take your card and wait for your cash'. She waited for it to reappear in the slot like a tongue out of a mouth but it didn't.

'Come on!' she said again.

Still nothing. And no cash too. Had the bloody thing eaten her card? The message was still on the screen, suggesting that the card was coming and that £80 had been debited from her account. She banged the key panel in frustration and placed her hand expectantly at the slot.

And then she suddenly stepped back.

'Jesus!' she said aloud, staring wide eyed at the screen. 'What the hell?'

Her card had still not appeared and neither had her cash, but the message on the screen had gone and in its place was a gruesome picture that shocked her to the core. It was the face of a dragon, two jets streaming from its nostrils, mouth open, and two large red eyes that emitted a light so bright it temporarily blinded Maxi, like a camera flash.

The image made her shiver. not least because she and Daya had talked about nothing else but dragons on their way home together on the tube on Friday night – reports in the *Evening Standard* that night had meant dragons were a topic of conversation throughout the train. And it had been on the news too.

And now she was staring at this unexpected and ferocious image. Convinced the card was lost forever and startled by the picture on the screen, Maxi turned and fled up Bedford Street towards Leicester Square. Thank God she was meeting Daya. She suddenly felt alone, very alone, in a city which, if the rumours and reports were to be believed, was rife with real-life dragons attacking you at every turn. And she'd no money on her and no way of getting home. She ran quickly, not stopping to look over her shoulder or glance at her reflection in the windows she passed.

Little did Maxi know that up in Leicester Square there were dozens of people with the same concerns: no money, no cards, and what the hell was that dragon thing?

It was like pouring petrol on a fire. The fear which had already started spreading across the city was reaching new heights.

Just as Bonaparte knew it would.

CHAPTER 36

SUNDAY, 3.18 P.M.

BANGROVE CASTLE, BUCKINGHAMSHIRE

Bonati's sleek Maserati swept into the drive and they waited for the electronic gates. The lodge house was just to their left, but Goode decided not to bother Pauline and Greg. It looked like they had visitors, and besides, there was no need. Though his visits to the castle were rare, they were never planned and his staff had got used to him pitching up at any time. From the passenger seat of Bonati's car, Goode waved to Greg, who was standing in the window of the Lodge House. He must have heard the car and wondered who it was. It looked like he was trying to signal to Goode that he wanted to have a quick word, but Goode thought it wise to keep going, especially seeing as who else was in the car with them. He'd catch up with him later.

The Maserati cruised up the long drive and crunched over the gravel.

'Nice place,' said Khan.

'Gee, thanks,' said Goode. 'Now let's get this over with and get back to London, okay? I don't want it to take too long.'

'It will take as long as it takes,' Khan said coldly.

They'd said little on the journey over. Khan had chosen not to talk any more about the Annika Premvas case or other aspects of the ongoing investigation. It was unlike Khan to be so closed, though Goode and Bonati both knew that it was because Jason was a suspect now and their relationship had suddenly changed.

They got out of the car and Goode approached the oak doors at the top of the steps. He unlocked them and entered. The alarm sounded as it always did – Greg had headed straight up to the castle as soon as his wife, Pauline, had returned with the boxes. It had made him miss the arrival of his son and new daughter-in-law, but he was keen to check the place out. He'd found nothing, though he felt sure he had set the alarm on Friday night after work. He'd resolved to contact the security company on Monday to get them to come and investigate why it had not gone off when Pauline had entered earlier. But he'd set it properly on leaving and returning for lunch.

Goode pressed in the coordinates in the usual way and the loud beeping ceased, bringing a welcome silence to the great entrance hall in which they found themselves.

'So this is home?' said Khan.

'Well, it was,' said Goode, gazing around the place with sad eyes. 'I already told you I hardly ever come back these days. But my staff keep it ticking over. It's a big place to manage.'

'It certainly is,' said the Detective Constable who was accompanying them. DC James Craven had just joined the Met from a force over in Cambridgeshire, where he had worked for six years. He had always wanted a transfer to the Metropolitan Police and his chance had finally come. Being assigned to DCI Khan had been a dream come true – homicide was always the most interesting detective work, and Khan's reputation at Scotland Yard was well known.

'Make yourselves at home,' said Goode sarcastically. 'Go anywhere you like.'

'Thank you, sir,' said DC Craven.

'We'll start with your study, please,' said Khan. 'If you can direct us there?'

Goode pointed a finger towards the far left corner of the entrance hall. 'Down there. First on the left. Enjoy your search, But I'm telling you, you won't find anything. I'm assuming you don't want me to join you, huh?'

'That's correct,' said DC Craven. 'But thank you all the same.' And they shuffled off.

'Well?' Goode said to Bonati. 'What do we do now?'

'We sit and drink coffee and try to get a handle on what the hell's going on,' said the professor. He waited until the police officers were completely out of sight. 'I had a phone call from Jud while I was waiting for you in the car back in London.'

'What? Why the hell didn't you tell me?' said Goode.

'You arrived with Khan and his stooge, I didn't want to discuss it in front of them.'

'So what did he say?' asked Goode anxiously, as they walked towards the kitchen. He switched on the large, black coffee machine and filled the metal scoop with fresh coffee from a jar. 'I wanna know. Are they safe?'

'Yes, of course. Don't worry. They're okay, although Jud said they were followed today.'

'Followed? By whom?'

'We don't know. Some maniac on a motorbike who pushed them off, apparently.'

'Pushed them off?' Goode turned to Bonati. 'What do you mean, pushed them off? Are they okay?'

'Yeah. It was at some traffic lights. They weren't moving at the time, but Bex was hurt. I've spoken to her and she's alright though.'

'So?' said Goode impatiently. 'Have they any news for us?'

The professor nodded. 'They certainly have.' He was smiling

now. 'They've found Bonaparte. At least they know where he lives.'

Goode looked startled. 'You're kiddin' me, Giles. They've found him? Honestly? I've been looking for the little weasel for years. How the hell did they find him so fast?'

'Well, apparently, your guy in Paris – Stokochi?'

'Ant Stokowski, yeah. Did he help them?'

'Apparently so,' said the professor. 'He managed to get an old address for him from some council records somewhere. Anyway, he didn't think it was a current address, but Jud thinks he's still there.'

'Have they seen him?'

'No, not yet.'

'Then how the hell do they know he's still living there?'

Bonati filled him in about the elderly neighbour.

'At last, we've got some good news!' said Goode.

'Jud said he and Bex are going to keep returning to the apartment block, see if they can see him.'

Goode looked worried now. 'But they're not going to approach him, are they? I mean, that's where I draw the line, do you understand? I do not want them going near the guy. He's a dangerous son of a bitch and if he knew who Jud really was he'd take him without hesitating. Do you hear me? I do not want them approaching Nap. I mean it, Giles.'

'Okay, okay. I've already warned them.'

'And they listened?'

'Yes. I said it was serious now.'

'So? We go to Paris, yeah?' said Goode, handing the professor his coffee and sipping from his own glass espresso cup.

'Well, I'm afraid that depends on what the detective chief inspector says, doesn't it, Jason.' Bonati spoke gently, knowing that this would only anger Goode even more. But it had to be said. They were standing in his home whilst police officers searched the place. He was hardly a free man right now, able to take off whenever he liked.

'If Jud's there and in danger, I'm going, Giles,' said Jason defiantly. 'You seem to forget I've not been arrested.'

'I'm sorry, Jason, of course you haven't.'

They took their coffees and moved out across the hall into the large drawing room. Goode was clearly agitated. Having someone rifling through his things, especially in his precious castle, home to so many difficult memories, was excruciating. He was beginning to wish he'd not volunteered to drive them there. Now he was stuck. He wanted to turn right round and head back to London, but he knew he couldn't. Khan's eager new assistant had made it clear they didn't require him to help them in their search for incriminating evidence, and so he had no choice but to sit and wait with the professor.

'I've been thinking about Nap a great deal,' said Goode, as he sat in one of the luxury leather armchairs near the large and ornate fireplace and drummed his fingers anxiously against the rim of the coffee cup. A mahogany grandfather clock in the corner of the room continued its steady tick-tock, a sound that would normally soothe and calm anyone who heard it; today it was yet another source of irritation for Goode. He was fidgeting in the chair, unable to get comfortable.

'I know, me too,' said Bonati reassuringly. 'We're bound to, Jason. This thing has stirred up so many memories for us both.'

'We were the famous trio, weren't we?' said Goode. 'The whole of Cambridge knew about us. We were going to set the world on fire. What a team we were.'

'And you did change the world. Look at what you've achieved.'

'Yeah, but we were going to do it together, all three of us. Where did it go wrong, Giles? How on earth did one of us end up living like a poor man in some backstreet of Paris, huh? The guy has a lot to be angry about. He's gonna be bitter, you can be sure of that. Real sore.'

'You've done nothing wrong,' said Bonati. 'So don't you dare start doubting yourself. All those theories and designs and drawings – they were yours, Jason. Rightfully yours. You had the ideas all along. Nap and I developed them, sure, that's true. We researched and pushed the boundaries to test what you were coming up with, but you were the dynamo, Jason. You were the generator, churning out the new ideas. If Nap believes otherwise he's deluding himself. You've got to believe that, and stay strong. The technology behind your hardware and gadgets started in *your* head, no one else's.'

'Sure. The same technology that's being blamed for the mess we're in.'

'Rubbish. It's not the technology, Jay. It's people, one person – I don't know how many. But we'll root them out, don't you worry. We'll expose the moles and bring them to justice. Trust in the system. You've got to.'

'You're right, Giles,' said Goode, getting up to light a fire in the huge space beneath the stone fire surround. He grabbed a couple of firelighters from a small box on the mantelpiece and placed them in the iron grate. He carefully placed several bits of kindling over them and put a match to the miniature pyramid. Within a short time, flames began licking up the chimney and Jason could place larger logs on the fire.

Bonati watched the flames rise as the clock chimed four o'clock, each ring a reminder of the passing of time, the years that had marched on. The decades.

'Remember the day we all met?' said the professor.

'Yeah, of course. You sure looked like an academic, even in those days, with your tweed jacket and your floppy hair.'

'It's what we wore,' said the professor.

'It's what you wore. Not me.' He managed a smile.

'True. You always were the scruffy one.' He looked him up and down now and smiled. Nothing much had changed.

Goode's smile faded. 'I knew he'd be back, you know. I had a feeling about it. Always have had. That's why I've been trying to find him all these years.'

'It's easy to say that now. Neither of us really knew what he'd do. He was volatile even back then. Unpredictable. You know he was. There were many times when he'd just stay up in his room at college, never coming out with us. God knows what he did in there. We were his only friends, Jason. And he hated it when we went out with other people. He just couldn't handle it. No one else would talk to him. We tried our best. We weren't to blame. He was always pretty mixed up.'

'But all these years that have passed. So much time gone, Giles. Why now? Why's he coming after me *now*? Do you think he's been planning this all that time?'

'Who knows? You can't spend your life worrying about what someone else thinks of you or what they're planning, Jay. You have to get on with life. You know that as well as I do. It's every man for himself in this life. You work hard, you stay focused and you find success. You earn it. Okay, maybe to him your success meant his failure, but that's not your fault. It's his problem.'

'Yeah, but now it's mine.' He glanced anxiously towards the door, pictured the policemen rifling through his things.

'I'm worried, Giles. I don't know where this is leading, but I know I can't stop it any more. It's my fault. I should've done more to help him. Shouldn't have just let him disappear. Alone. With no prospects. He didn't deserve that. He needed help.'

'Stop it,' said Giles with his usual authority. 'Nap was a grown man. He could look after himself. You had to get on with your own life. God knows, Jay, there were times when he sulked for days, when he just disappeared inside his head and wouldn't talk to any of us. But we just carried on, we had to.'

'And now?' said Goode. 'Where's this leading, huh? I've got two guys next door going through my files, for God's sake. He's gonna win, isn't he? He's been planning it and he's gonna finish me. This is the end.'

This was so unlike Goode and Bonati knew it. Maybe it was being back at the castle that had made things worse for him. It had been a long time since the professor had set foot in the place, and he never really knew what his old friend was like whenever he was back here, though God knows it must've held bad memories for him. It was a damn nuisance having to sit through this search. He knew he should have tried to talk Goode out of accompanying the officers here, should have persuaded him to let them come alone. It was too painful for him, maybe for them both.

Bonati remembered the day Goode had telephoned him with the news of the accident: Tara's shocking death. He remembered his friend whimpering down the phone like a tiny child, alone, lost. He didn't know what to say then and he was finding it difficult to think of anything helpful now.

And then Tara's funeral. What an agonising day it had been for everyone who knew them, and made so much worse because of the arrest of his only son. It was unimaginable. More like fiction.

But they'd got through it, together, he reminded himself. And they'd get through this too. There was no way he was going to let his closest friend fall to pieces now. Not again.

'Drink?' said Bonati, standing up decisively and warming himself against the rejuvenating flames. 'I must say, you're not the host you once were, Jay. You're slipping, boy. We've been sitting by the fire for ten minutes now and you still haven't offered me a whiskey to warm the cockles!'

Goode smiled and shrugged. He rose slowly from the chair. 'You're right. Where are my manners, Professor?' He placed another log on the fire, which sent tiny sparks drifting out of the hearth and into the room, burning out like miniature comets. He went to the glass drinks cabinet across the room. 'We can have a quick one, can't we?'

They sat back with their drinks and let the soothing smell of wood smoke wash over them as the clock kept ticking.

Meanwhile, over in the oak-panelled study, DC Craven had found something. And it was just the kind of evidence Khan had feared they might find.

Not even he could protect Goode now.

CHAPTER 37

SUNDAY, 6.25 P.M.
(7.25 P.M. LOCAL TIME)

ALLÉE CHÊNE POINTU,
CLICHY-SOUS-BOIS, PARIS

Jud felt a vibration deep inside his leather jacket pocket and he quickly fumbled for his phone. His hands were cold from waiting outside in the shadows with Bex for more than an hour now. It was dark already and the open sky above them brought a wintry chill. From their vantage point in the far corner of the car park they could see up to Bonaparte's apartment. They knew they couldn't move until something happened.

Jud looked down and saw it was Bonati on the phone.

'Hello, sir,' he said quickly. 'We're here at the apartment as planned. Nothing to report yet but he has to come out sometime. We'll stay all night if we have to. I want to see if it's really—'

'Jamie, listen to me,' the professor interrupted. His voice was sombre.

'What? What's happened?'

There was a short silence and then, 'I'm afraid your father's been arrested.'

'*What?* When? Why?' He flicked a glance to Bex and she could tell something was seriously wrong.

'Late this afternoon. Look, I don't have many details, J. Khan isn't saying much, but they found some evidence at the castle.'

'Evidence? At the castle?' said Jud. 'What the hell are they doing there?'

Bex looked anxiously at him. '*What?*' she mouthed.

'It's standard procedure, J,' Bonati continued. 'Khan wanted to make a search of your father's things – look through his files and all that. He's saying they've found something that links not just Goode Technology to the banking crisis, but your father himself.'

'Sir, we know someone's been trying to frame my father. There's supposed to be a mole inside the company. Khan knows that. So what's changed? What could they possibly have found that would make them really think he's actually involved? It's ridiculous.'

'I don't know, J. And there's nothing we can do about it at the moment. But I wanted you to know in case you were trying to call him.'

'How is he?'

'He's okay,' Bonati lied. 'You know your father. He's tough and he's smart, but he was as surprised as you are that they found evidence at the castle. I'm guessing it's on his home computers. I don't know, maybe some communication or something. Or some files. But whatever it was, it was enough to make Khan take him in. He's there now.'

'Overnight?'

'Probably. They'll want plenty of time to question him. We're as much in the dark about this as you are, but I tell you, Jamie, you've got to nail that bastard over there.'

It was the first time Jud had heard the professor swear in a long time. And use his real name too. Jud knew things had to be serious for Bonati to lose his cool like this.

'You want us to go in and get him?' said Jud. He could feel the adrenalin beginning to pump around his body and he clenched his fist. He wanted to go straight up to Bonaparte's flat and smash his face to a pulp.

'No, wait,' said the professor, sensing exactly where this was heading. He'd deliberated for a while before calling Jud, knowing exactly what his reaction would be. But Jud had to know how serious this was and how important he was to the investigation now. 'Wait!' he said again. 'Listen to me. I want you to get into his apartment when he goes out. I don't care if you have to wait there all night and all day. He has to go out sometime, and when he does, you've got to get yourselves in there and find some proof of what he's up to. Something we can take to Khan and his team. Something that'll get him off your father's back.'

'Okay, sir. We'll do it. But if I meet this guy, I swear—'

'No!' shouted the professor. 'You keep your cool. You get in there and you find whatever you can. He'll go down for this, don't you worry. The guy will never see freedom again when the courts have finished with him. But you have to trust in the system. You cannot go meting out your own justice, J. You understand?'

'Okay, okay. We'll get in there,' said Jud, trying to calm his nerves. 'But we think he's got protection.'

'Of course he will have. He's going to need it.'

'Someone was on to us today. Some guy on a bike was following us.'

'I'm not surprised. But at least that means the guy's guilty. He wouldn't put a trace on you unless he was worried about what you might find. And he wouldn't do that unless he'd got something to hide. He's obviously worried about you. But you're smart. And you're quick. You'll do it, J. You both will. Is Bex there? She okay?'

Jud looked across at her. She was staring at him impatiently, wanting to know what the professor was saying. Wanting to get on with it. 'Of course,' he said. 'She's fine. You know Bex.'

'Good,' said Bonati. 'I would say, you look after her, but we all know it's she who looks after you. Now report to me when you have something . . . And stay safe, both of you.'

Jud was about to tell the professor not to worry – they wouldn't be the only CRYPT agents in Paris. That Luc would be on their side. But the phone went dead and Bonati was gone before he had the chance. Maybe it was just as well, he thought. The professor would have had strong feelings about that. Although it was Bonati who'd first told Jud that Luc had been in contact after his death, he had also said that this was still early days in their research into forging regular contact with the spirit world, and no one really knew what might happen if they went chasing after spirits voluntarily, even ones like Luc who they assumed meant no harm. Jud had always protested, of course, that Luc would never hurt anyone or obstruct their work in any way – why should he? – but the professor had quite rightly asked, How did he know that for sure? How could anyone know what went on in the disembodied minds of the dead? Where was the precedent for such things? They both knew the only ghosts they'd experienced so far had been ones fuelled by revenge and anger and a deep longing for justice. Few had ever come peacefully. It was their anger, after all, that had enabled them to harness enough energy to reappear in their mortal world. Jud knew the science, of course, but he also knew Luc, better than anyone. He could sense that he was there as a force for good. Watching him.

He resolved to try and make contact again tonight. He and Bex had been thinking about little else since the ferry crossing over and the long ride to Paris. They'd both said they felt they were not alone.

'Well?' said Bex anxiously. 'Talk to me, J!'

Jud relayed the conversation as quickly as he could. He was

never one for detail, much to Bex's constant irritation, and his summary of the discussion with the professor lasted a few seconds.

'*Arrested?*' she said incredulously. 'What could they possibly have found at your home that would give them grounds to arrest him?'

Jud shook his head. 'Dunno. But I think that bastard is capable of anything, especially where computers are concerned. He'll have hacked into my father's files and emails and planted something incriminating, no doubt. If he can break into the IT systems at work – and we know how secure they're supposed to be – then he can sure get into the ones at home. Or maybe he just sent someone over to break in.' He pushed his phone back into his leather jacket and his hand caught something sharp as he brought it out again.

'Ow,' he said. 'What was that?'

'What?'

He showed his hand to Bex. A scratch had appeared right across the back of it.

'I dunno. A zip? Oh, you poor thing. Bex kiss it better for you?'

Jud tried to fish his hand back into his pocket to feel what it was that had caught him. He pulled the phone out and handed it to Bex. He rummaged around in the pocket again and his fingers touched on something sharp and thin.

Quickly he removed the jacket and pulled the pocket inside out, revealing a small pin and a wire buried inside the lining.

'I don't believe it,' he said. 'It's a bug. I'm wired, Bex.'

'You're joking. Who's done that? And when?'

Jud shook his head. 'Your guess is as good as mine. But I'm bloody glad I've found it.'

'Yeah, but how long's it been there?'

'Who knows.' He ripped it from the lining, threw it to the ground and stamped heavily on it until it was mashed up. 'At least we now know why the guy on the motorbike was following us. And how he knew where we were.'

'You shouldn't have destroyed it,' said Bex. 'Knowing it was there was all we needed. We could've used it to our advantage, J. We could've had fun with that, making up some shit about where we were going. It could have backfired nicely for whoever planted it.'

'Sorry, you're right,' said Jud. 'But at least it proves that someone's interested in our movements. And that means someone's got something to hide. It's all the proof I need that we're in the right place, Bex. If we were wired, we were onto something.'

'So how're we going to get inside the apartment?' said Bex. 'The guy never comes out. He's probably some kind of recluse.'

Jud was deep in thought. A plan was forming in his mind. 'We need to get him to want to leave. We need to flush him out of his own accord.'

'You've got something in mind?' said Bex. She knew his face. She could always tell when an idea was about to hatch.

'What's the one thing that makes everyone run?' he said coolly. 'The one thing everyone is scared of?'

'Don't tell me, ghosts,' said Bex.

'Uh huh.'

Bex's eyes grew wide, reflecting the moonlight, just as they'd done on the Channel crossing the night before.

'Luc,' she gasped.

'Uh huh.'

'And we're in France, of course! He'd probably rather come back here than anywhere else – he was French, after all.'

Jud nodded.

'Oh, but wait a minute,' she said. 'Do you have the EM tracer here?'

'Of course,' said Jud, removing a metal box from one of the Fireblade's panniers. It resembled a large camera case, the kind that houses a serious piece of equipment – shiny aluminium with chrome-coloured edging and a handle. He set it down on the seat of the bike and flipped the catches. As it opened, Bex saw a black hand-held device set into plush grey cushioning, with various smaller devices and cables.

Jud removed the tracer and switched it on. It wasn't too dissimilar to the EMF meters they took everywhere with them, only larger and with not one but two LED display screens. Jud waited for one of the screens to light up and then inputted a sequence of digits. There was a tuning dial which he fiddled with for a while, until eventually they could see hundreds of different numbers flickering on the screen. It took ages for them to settle. The second screen blinked into life and soon showed more numbers, rapidly changing.

'I suppose it's like the old analogue radios or TVs,' said Bex. 'Are you tuning into Luc? Finding his energy pattern.'

'You could say that,' said Jud, eyes fixed on the little screens as more numbers flickered across at speed.

This went on for some time and Jud began to worry that they would not find Luc at all that night. It was Sunday evening and the apartment blocks around them were lit up with living-room lights and the cool, bluish flicker of television screens. 'It's not going to be easy here, Bex, we're surrounded by electrical equipment. EMF meters don't operate well when they're surrounded by so much radiation, and this is no different, really.'

'But I thought you used it in the SPA?' said Bex.

'Yeah, but you know the equipment's different down there, isn't it? It's geared up to emit low radiation, and in any case most of it was switched off. I only went in there for privacy, don't forget. I wasn't using most of the stuff in there, only this device. We're going to have to find somewhere quieter.'

'And what will you do if you make contact tonight?' said Bex.

'We'll see if Luc can do some work for us. He might enjoy being the one doing the haunting for a change. But we're getting ahead of ourselves here, it's still early days, Bex. I can't guarantee we'll see him, or even hear him.' Jud was desperate not to get Bex's hopes up, just like he had done himself every time he went back to the SPA. All those nights of disappointment, those hours spent locked away, alone.

He switched the tracer off and placed it back inside the case, which he then returned to the bike pannier. 'Right, let's go and find somewhere quieter where we won't be disturbed. We've got to make contact tonight. We have to get this guy out of his apartment and get in there ourselves, before his honcho arrives again, the one who followed us.'

'Yeah, don't remind me. I've still got the bruises.'

They placed their helmets on, straddled the bike and soon swept out of the car park into night traffic. In a bustling city like Paris, it wasn't going to be easy finding somewhere quiet and without the risk of being disturbed, but Jud already had somewhere in mind – and if they could find a way to sneak in, it would be perfect.

Luc used to say it was his favourite place in Paris.

CHAPTER 38

SUNDAY, 10.20 P.M.
(11.20 P.M. LOCAL TIME)

MONTMARTRE, PARIS

'You are joking?' said Bex through the headset. They'd been riding for some time now, Jud weaving the bike in and out of the evening traffic, clearly heading somewhere, though he'd refused to say where exactly. The last quarter they'd travelled through had been Montmartre, a beautiful, bohemian kind of place, all restaurants and art shops and late-night artists huddled next to easels with lamps, making sketches of gullible honeymooners in search of keepsakes. It was a village oasis of leafy, cobbled streets and fashionable townhouses with shutters and iron balconies, more like a stage set than a suburb of Paris. Even on a Sunday evening the artisans' village was popular, with late-night tourists out for a stroll and the obligatory holiday snapshots. Bex had recognised some of the picturesque scenes from French textbooks at school. Montmartre was, after all, one of the most famous districts of Paris, a necessary chapter in every school book and a favourite haunt of language teachers, perched as it was at the highest point in the city, with views of every landmark across the capital.

And just when Bex thought they couldn't climb any higher, Jud kept on pushing the Fireblade up the winding cobbled streets to the base of the great Basilica.

If this was the place he was intending on using to make proper contact with Luc, then he was either losing his marbles or had just been watching too many movies, thought Bex. 'You're winding me up,' she said. 'This is all part of some practical joke. You're not going to make contact here?'

'Chill out,' Jud whispered through the helmet. 'It's perfect.'

'Perfect?' said Bex. 'You serious? When you said you wanted to find somewhere secluded, where we could be sure we wouldn't be disturbed and would get a clear signal on the tracer, I thought you meant a backstreet somewhere, or a disused building or—'

'A church?' interrupted Jud.

'Well, yeah, I guess so.'

'And isn't this a church?' he said coolly.

'Yeah, but it's—'

'Luc's favourite place in Paris. In France. He loved it. He always used to talk about it. And we even used it on an Xbox game once. We used to explore it sometimes, usually hunting for bad guys, of course. I feel like I know it as well as he does. And like I say, it's the place he would most want to come back to.'

'But it's the Sacré Coeur!' she protested. 'You couldn't get a more famous place than this in the whole of Paris!'

'Eiffel Tower?' said Jud, half amused by her reaction.

'Yeah, but not even you would have chosen that. It's just as busy at night time as it is in the day, I should think. It doesn't close 'til midnight or something. I went there on a school trip, like everyone does.'

'Well, this place isn't busy now. Not at this time of night. Everyone will have gone home. Luc used to say it was busy in the evenings, but it mostly on a Saturday night, he said. He used to love coming up here and sitting on the steps with his family, looking out over the city. He loved it, Bex. It's the perfect place to entice him to come back. He won't be able to resist.'

They parked the bike at the foot of the steps to the Basilica and gazed up at it; the floodlighting was stunning and gave it an eerie, fantasy feel. Like Saint Mark's Basilica in Venice, which they'd seen together on a previous investigation, this place looked too perfect to be real. The subtle lighting helped the building to retain its pearly white colour, which was even more impressive with the dark night sky behind it. The three white domes, with their ornate turrets and arches, soared into the sky, the middle one of which was so vast it could have rivalled St Paul's.

They gathered their equipment, including the metal case containing the EM tracer, and started on the long climb up the three hundred steps to the top. The night was quiet, few people were still around – it was a Sunday after all, and the Saturday night revellers and tourists were long gone. After a while – about halfway up – they paused and turned around to admire the views of Paris.

'Stunning, isn't it?' said Bex.

'Yeah. It's impressive,' said Jud. 'Although if you've seen one city you've seen them all.'

'Oh, come on!' said Bex. 'It's unmistakably Paris.'

'Don't tell me, la cité de l'amour?' said Jud, cynically.

'Well it is!' said Bex, refusing to budge, as Jud started to climb again.

'Come on,' he said. 'We've got to get up to the top quickly. I want to get back to Clichy as soon as possible and see if we can flush this guy out of his apartment. Time's running out for my father.'

'I know, I'm sorry.' The place had seemed so enchanting, so other worldly, it was easy to forget why they were in the city in the first place. And yet, up here, climbing the steps that led to such a religious landmark, it seemed appropriate to be doing what they were doing. With each step it felt like they were leaving the mortal world behind them and climbing closer to heaven. Maybe Jud had chosen the right place after all. It had attracted millions of pilgrims over the years, perhaps many of them coming for similar reasons, to be nearer to loved ones who had passed over, or to be closer to God. Somehow their mission to contact Luc didn't seem so fantastical the closer they came to the magical building.

It seemed like they'd been climbing forever, but there was still some way to go. The three arches of the stone-built balcony and viewing platform at the foot of the Basilica towered over them like some elaborate viaduct. It was hard to appreciate the sheer scale of the place until you were closer. An unsettling feeling of agoraphobia was creeping into Bex, though she was never going to admit it. It wasn't just the height and the huge expanse of city that stretched out behind them, it was the overwhelming thought of what they were about to do.

Both she and Jud were hardly strangers to the supernatural. They'd been experiencing hauntings ever since joining the CRYPT, perhaps even before that. They knew better than anyone how close the afterlife was – how it wasn't just some distant fantasy depicted in oil paintings and stained-glass windows in churches. It was here, all round them. And glimpses of it could appear at any time. But it was all on such a grand scale here. Bex could feel her legs becoming weaker and she knew it wasn't just fatigue.

As she ascended further and further, she gazed upwards at the Basilica, now looming even larger, and looked beyond it, past the domes and towers to the sky above. It was easy to think – because every child is taught it at school – that heaven is skywards, a long way up. Now she felt like a tiny ant crawling up a vast tree trunk, or a desert rat in the Sahara, the overwhelming scale of it all weighing heavy. How far up did the sky go? How far down did the earth go? And beyond that, how far did the great black drop of space extend beneath them all? She felt an overwhelming need to kneel down and touch the stone step beneath her. To sit and take stock of it all, to centre herself for just a few precious seconds and get a grasp on reality again. But she knew Jud would interpret any request to pause as a sign of weakness, and weak was one thing she certainly wasn't.

Finally they reached the top and stood out on the vast viewing platform below the great white Basilica. The giant arc of sky stretched east to west and, below it, the metropolis lay before them.

Bex turned round to face the huge white façade. 'You weren't hoping to get inside it, were you? At this time of night?'

'No, of course not. It was out here that Luc always said he loved, just sitting and watching the city. You can't do this in London, unless you're on top of some skyscraper. There's no natural hill in the city like there is here. You can see everything. Look at the Eiffel Tower, all lit up like a Christmas tree. It's amazing, don't you think? I can see why Luc loved it so much. Peaceful, isn't it? Bex? You okay?'

She'd found a bench and slumped onto it. Jud couldn't tell whether it was sheer exhaustion or something else, but she wasn't herself.

'What's wrong?'

'I don't know,' she said, her voice choking slightly. 'I guess . . . well, I dunno, maybe Luc's death has only just really hit me. I mean really sunk in.'

Jud knew what that felt like. He'd always been surprised how little she'd talked of Luc. It was easy to forget that he was her friend too, and Grace's. Jud had been so bound up in his own grief and misery and despair these last few weeks that he'd never given a second thought to how Bex might be feeling, or Grace for that matter. And he'd assumed that she would be able to handle the news that he was making contact again. After weeks of desperate searching and experimenting, it didn't seem so shocking to Jud. He'd longed for it so much it wasn't a surprise any more.

But until only a few days ago, Bex had assumed he was gone forever. She'd been so determined to rescue Jud from the depths of depression that she'd never given any thought to how she felt about the great loss. And no sooner had Jud opened up and reassured her that he was okay, so that she could start to deal with her own grief, than here they were, about to contact Luc again. It was so much to take in. No wonder she was feeling unsettled.

'Talk to me,' he said, sitting next to her and holding her hand. 'How do you feel? I'm so sorry I've never asked you properly until now. I was just so consumed with it all, I never stopped to see how you were. You're always a . . . well, you know, a rock. Always there for me. I'm sorry.'

Bex gulped in the night air and stiffened herself. There wasn't time for this, she knew that. It was hardly the time or the place to lose it and drown in a tide of grief and loss. They had to get on and sort this. 'I'm okay,' she said. 'It's just a lot to take in. I dunno, I've been dealing with ghosts for ages now – we all have – but somehow it's different when it's someone you know. When it's not some spirit intent on harm; when we're not defending the public from some evil haunting. It's more personal this time. More real.'

'You're right,' said Jud. 'Of course it's different. It means more. And maybe it's harder to take in. There's no adrenalin rush like there usually is when we're fighting. We're not in battle mode and so it hits us more deeply. But it's got to be a good thing, Bex. Hasn't it?'

'Yeah, of course,' she said. 'If what you say is true and we really can see and talk to Luc, then of course it's a good thing. I'll be fine. I'm just, well, I dunno . . . nervous, I guess.'

Jud smiled and placed an arm around her. It was the first time he'd seen her like this. She was the bravest of them all and, my God, they'd been through some scrapes together. They'd faced the kind of ghosts that would make anyone else scream and run – and probably never be the same again. But she'd taken it all in her stride. She was Bex de Verre, the toughest girl at the CRYPT and the one most likely to survive in any encounter with evil spirits.

Jud began to realise that he'd been so close to this research, so close to the whole business of EM tracers and making contact with the other side, that he'd never really stopped to appreciate the significance of what he and Bonati were doing. It was good news, yes, but it was undeniably shocking. And here, in the vast open air, with the colossal city below them and the Goliath-sized Basilica rising to the sky behind them, no wonder Bex was feeling daunted.

'Come on,' he said, squeezing her hand. 'Shall we do this? It'll be fun.'

His attempt to make light of it was well meant, and Bex allowed a wry smile to leak from her lips at the word 'fun'.

'Life's never dull with you, Jud Lester. Never dull at all.' With that she stood up, placed her hands on her hips and said, 'Right. You pick the spot and let's get started, shall we? I'm ready, bring it on.'

Jud grinned and reached for the metal case containing the EM tracer. 'It's too exposed out here, even at this time of night, so let's go just inside the arches over there, in the porch, or whatever it's called, of the Basilica. No one will see us there.'

They looked around and saw a couple of other late-night walkers and lovers on benches nearby, but there was no one else around.

'Come on, it's darker over there, more private.' He held her hand and led her towards the three giant arches that formed the portico entrance to the vast building.

'There's railings all the way across. The gates are closed so you can't get near it,' said Bex.

'What does a railing matter? Here, hold this for a second,' said Jud, already leaping onto the metal fence and vaulting his way over the top. He landed with a loud thud which attracted the attention of the few onlookers further down the slope, who just shook their heads. It wasn't the first time kids had tried to get inside the place out of hours and it wouldn't be the last. They knew the giant doors to the Basilica's actual interior would be closed, so there was precious little damage these intruders could do. And it wasn't their business anyway. Who cared?

Bex passed the metal carry case over the top of the railings and vaulted them herself, quicker and far more elegantly than Jud. Hers was an almost silent, controlled landing, like a gymnast from a vaulting horse.

Quickly they disappeared behind one of the great pillars that formed part of the central arch of the portico. Jud took out the EM tracer from its case, switched it on. The two screens began processing their numbers again, just as before. The agents watched, hoping they would settle at a sequence.

'You sure it's going to work?' said Bex.

'Yeah, definitely. It was harder back at the apartments – we were surrounded by television sets and cookers and microwaves. There's no one here. Be patient. Can you get the EMF meter and the Geiger counter? We'll need those.'

Bex took out the devices and set them up on the floor beneath them. It seemed like forever, but eventually they saw the numbers on the EM tracer settle and several lights come on at the base of the device.

'Can you feel him coming?' said Jud, smiling.

'No.'

'Close your eyes.'

'Not that again,' said Bex. 'You want me to imagine him, I suppose?'

'Of course not. It's not in your mind this time. But we're

ghost hunters, aren't we? We'll sense him coming. Just need to concentrate.'

They stood in silence for a while, catching the night air and letting the atmosphere flow through them. They played the usual game of trying to beat the EMF meters to register something paranormal. Their ESP was so finely tuned now, and out here, in these surroundings, high on top of the city, they felt something stirring.

'Anything?' said Jud.

'Yeah. Images of Luc's face keep flashing into my mind. I suppose it's because we're concentrating on him, but it's like I'm not imagining him myself.'

'It's working,' Jud smiled. 'Keep concentrating.'

They stood, still as statues, concentrating hard, letting their ESP flow like radio waves from their minds. It was like an invisible radar sweeping the air, reaching up to the skies in a giant arc and flowing around them.

The agents had often tried, back at the CRYPT, to explain to each other how it felt. It was like listening very hard, or screwing up your eyes to focus on something in the distance – only on a bigger scale, much bigger. The air was always full of energy and they just needed to tune into it. Sometimes they'd pick up emotions – anger or jealousy or revenge of some kind – other times it would be deep sorrow that found its way into their consciousness, flowing from the disembodied spirits that floated through the ether, undetected by most of us.

At other times it was vivid pictures of the deceased which drifted into their mind's eye, as it was now. Both of them could see flickering images of Luc flashing past the backs of their eyelids, like slides on an old-fashioned projector. Yet they weren't memories. These were images of Luc which they knew they couldn't possibly have seen before. He was younger, with his family, laughing, playing, running around some street somewhere, jumping up steps. They could see him, no more than ten years old, ascending a great staircase, the city rolling behind him. Then they could picture him at home, in the garden, then at school. Then with friends, out on the town. Laughing and joking and singing. Their emotions were doing somersaults, one moment elated at such a happy childhood, the next moment grief-stricken and angry.

In each image, in every scene, Luc was looking at them. It was like watching a movie where the hero was always looking at the camera.

'I can see everything,' said Bex. 'It's Luc, isn't it? It's him.'

Jud was leaning against a stone pillar beside her, his eyes closed just the same. 'Yes, me too. I know it's him. I recognise his family from his photos. He's coming, Bex. He's close now.'

Jud opened his eyes and looked down at the EMF meter and EM tracer set on the floor beside him. The needle on the meter was soaring through the levels; it was clear paranormal activity was happening. The EM tracer had settled on a sequence – and Jud recognised it as the same series of numbers he'd seen in the SPA when contact had been successful.

'Can you hear anything?' he whispered to Bex.

She shook her head. 'Not yet, can you?'

They stood in silence, sifting through the mortal sounds around them, the distant traffic, the birds, the footsteps of people leaving the scene and walking down the steps, the wind rushing through the great portico and out over the city again.

And then Jud heard something. It was low and faint at first. Somewhere in the space between reality and imagination, an almost inaudible whisper. But it was there. He'd heard it. Someone was repeating his name.

'J . . . u . . . d . . . J . . . u . . . d.'

He opened his eyes wide and looked around the dark shadows between the pillars.

'Hear that?' he whispered to Bex.

She shook her head but said nothing, fixed intently on her

hearing, extending beyond it, using senses so few of us ever use, connecting with the air and the highly charged atmosphere.

'J . . . u . . . d. I'm here.'

This time they both heard it and it made Bex jump slightly. She felt a prickly sensation run down her spine. She encountered more ghosts than most agents at the CRYPT, and she was rarely surprised by anything, but this was different. It seemed so . . . personal. So intimate. So *real*.

Their eyes scanned the scene and moved deeper into the portico entrance, closer to the giant doors that barred their way into the Basilica itself.

'B . . . e . . . x. It's . . . me. I can see you, Bex.'

She felt her heart thump loudly in her chest and the blood rush from her head. She steadied herself against the stone pillar for a moment and took some deep breaths. This was incredible. She glanced at Jud, who was smiling at her and raising his eyebrows as if to say 'told you so'.

But still they couldn't see anything. No trace of a figure. The EMF meter was going crazy, giving readings higher than they'd ever seen. Their bodies were tingling, and a prickly sensation ran across their skulls and down their spines. They were connecting. Hypersensing.

'What was that?' Bex said quickly, pointing a finger towards a dark corner of the portico to her left.

'Where?' said Jud.

'Over there. I saw something. Didn't you see it?'

They edged closer, breathing calmly and glancing all around them as they went, allowing their senses to remain on full alert.

'I'm here . . .' a familiar voice whispered.

They stopped and stared excitedly at one another.

Then, out of the shadows, they saw him.

'Luc!' Bex said, wide eyed.

'Hi there,' said Jud gently. 'It's so good to see you.'

The shadowy figure in front of them moved closer, and

though it was dark inside the portico, there was enough light spilling in from the lamps outside to see the outline of his body. He was wearing his usual clothes – jeans and a dark sports top. But there was something different about his body. It wasn't transparent, but neither was it solid. It was like seeing yourself in a shop window, its interior still visible through your own body. It resembled a holographic image, but one so real, so sharp, you felt you could touch it. The agents had grown accustomed to encountering ghosts that were even more solid than this, as an apparition's anger fuelled the energy which attracted the ionised plasma, bringing a form as hard and as strong as themselves. But Luc's figure was different. Less intense, less threatening.

But it was definitely him. His face was so familiar and they felt comforted to see him. In many ways, Bex had been dreading this moment. Battling with frightening, dangerous ghosts was something she took in her stride, but coming up so close to a friend, a deceased friend, she had thought that would play havoc with her emotions and burst the bubble of grief she had been hiding for so long. She expected to be consumed by emotion. But this was different to what she had feared. Though the edges of his face and body were hazy, they could see it was him. He was smiling, that infamous, charming smile that used to light up the room back at the CRYPT. His eyes were just the same too, though they lacked the pearly white gleam of before. They seemed more hazy, like a person gazing at nothing in particular but locked in thought.

'It's just so good to see you,' Jud said again. 'We've . . . missed you. I can't believe it's finally happened.'

'Believe it,' whispered Luc. 'But you never needed convincing, did you Jud? You knew it was possible. We both knew it.'

Luc raised a hand towards them. Bex, who'd been silent so far, just staring incredulously at the figure, now embraced it, but she'd not been prepared for the temperature that met her skin.

It was freezing cold, and though she cold feel it moving in her hand, it felt lifeless and icy. It was like touching a slab of meat in a deep freeze.

Luc was dead. Realisation dawned and she felt an uncontrollable sob welling up inside her. Tears rolled down her cheeks and Jud quickly held her before she collapsed. She felt his warmth and strength seeping into her, such a contrast to Luc's cold, frail hand. She let it go and quickly buried herself inside Jud's embrace.

'I'm so sorry,' she said. 'I just can't—'

'Shh,' Jud whispered. 'It's okay.' He stroked her head and drew her in close.

'It's a big deal. For all of us.'

Together they stared at Luc's face. His expression hadn't changed. He was still smiling, but more gently now; a brave, sympathetic smile that showed such understanding. He knew it would be like this. How could it have been different? These were his closest friends and they'd been grieving all this time. He knew it was going to be shocking for them, but he also knew if anyone could handle it, they could. And he so wanted to be with them, just like before. He needed to be with them, to show them it wasn't over. It had only begun.

Jud quickly explained what they needed Luc to do. He was to enter Bonaparte's apartment and spook him out so that he fled the place.

Luc was silent for a while, and they watched his shadowy face contemplating what they were saying. Eventually they saw his smile return and a glint in his eye which wasn't there before.

'We have much to catch up on,' he whispered. 'There's so much to say. So much to tell you. But we have time for that. We have eternity. For now, I'll help you. Gladly,' he whispered. 'I can spook like the rest of them. I'll enjoy that.'

As he said this, his face became translucent, more holographic now. They braced themselves, worried he was about to do something terrifying.

Was he about to change his face? Dislocate his jaw? Make his eyes grow or something?

'No!' said Jud sharply. 'Don't.' Now it was his turn to falter. Bex could feel his hands trembling. Ghosts were one thing, but when it was his friend, it was different. Unbearable.

They held their breath and through the murky gloom saw his face become more solid again. A cheerful expression returned and they breathed a sigh of relief.

'Don't worry,' he said, 'I'll not show you what I can do. But trust me, I can be scary when I need to be. You know that better than anyone. Leave it to me.'

'Do you need to know where to find him?' said Bex quietly.

'Set up your device outside his apartment and I'll know where to come. We'll connect again. Call me. I'll be there.'

It seemed as casual as a friend saying 'phone me', and it brought a much-needed comfort to the agents. They watched him fade into the darkness, just as he'd arrived.

'You've done it,' said Bex, holding Jud tight. 'You've actually done it.'

'Come on,' he said, taking her by the hand and leaving the portico, heading for the steps down to the city and the Fireblade below. 'Let's do this.'

CHAPTER 39

SUNDAY, 12.43 A.M.
(1.43 A.M. LOCAL TIME)

ALLÉE CHÊNE POINTU,
CLICHY-SOUS-BOIS, PARIS

'What do you mean you can't come?' Bonaparte demanded. He was drumming his fingers on the desktop nervously and glancing across at the window where he'd just been standing for too long. The dirty lace curtain, stained with cigarette smoke, was pulled to one side, revealing a clear view of the car park and the two agents standing in the shadows on the other side. He'd watched them exit hours earlier and had assumed they'd got bored and cleared off to their hotel for a better time. So he'd been surprised to see the bike's headlights sweep across his window again. But they'd chosen a different place to pitch up this time, on the opposite side to where they'd hidden the bike before; another set of garages, away from the streetlamps. No one else would have noticed them, but Bonaparte had spent a lifetime staring out of this window. He knew every car and recognised every person who visited the apartment block, though he rarely spoke to anyone, of course. The slightest movement alerted him and there was no way they could hide the sound of the bike.

But their return was making him nervous now, not least because he was no longer able to listen in on their conversations, ever since the young guy had found the listening device planted in his jacket and ripped the damn thing out.

'I said, I can't come over now,' Christophe shouted down the phone. 'You don't seem to understand, Jacob, so let me say it again. I work for you ten hours a day. You can make those hours in the evening if you wish, but that means I start later. I was with you this morning, sat in that room of yours for hours, doing nothing. I'm not coming over again at two a.m., for God's sake. Are you mad? I'll see you in the morning.'

'If you don't come now, you needn't bother coming in the morning.'

'Whatever. Suits me.' Christophe cared little if it meant he didn't have to spend another minute in that filthy, stinking apartment with the cantankerous old fool. Jacob clearly wasn't stable and Christophe disliked the way he seemed so unpredictable, his behaviour so erratic. He was about to tell him so when his employer ended the phone call.

'Scum,' Bonaparte said aloud. 'Lazy, useless scum.' He decided he'd call his other contacts in the morning and get another hired thug. They were easy to come by. The contacts who'd planted the bug in Jud's jacket would find him another one. And, if he paid them enough, they'd do away with Christophe too. No point in having people like that knowing too much. It was easier to get rid of him, less messy. He had to call them anyway, since Jud had found the bug.

It had been a frustrating day from the start and he was quite happy to rid himself of another employee. The men who'd wired Jud had done their job but had demanded twice the payment they'd agreed. When Bonaparte had refused, they'd threatened to cut transmission to his computer, disabling the line and plunging him into radio silence. So he'd paid their demands. And now, just a few hours later, the kid goes and finds the bug and breaks the transmission anyway. What a waste of money! And why hadn't the men he'd recruited told him yet that the transmission had stopped? Probably weren't even monitoring his movements anyway. Probably propping up some bar somewhere, drinking their profits. He'd have serious words in the morning.

But then he wasn't exactly working with people known for their reliability or for playing things by the book. Hired thugs, burglars, hackers – they were all he seemed to deal with these days. It was a far cry from his Cambridge days, or from the world his arch rival inhabited in London. Life had dealt him so many cruel blows, leaving him to live in squalor.

But it would soon be over. And at least he had his contacts in London and New York. They weren't hired thugs – anything but. Of course they were going to cost him serious money, but it would be worth it.

He moved to the window again. The light was off so no one could see into the room, but he could see out and he had a clear view across the car park to the agents. He watched them from the shadows of his room for another few minutes and then decided to let them stew. If they wanted to come back and stand in the cold all night, glancing up at his room, why stop them? His plan to get Christophe back to scare them away had failed, but it didn't matter. He knew he wasn't strong enough to go out there and face them down himself, but why should he bother? It was obvious they were waiting to see with their own eyes that he was living there, so why should he grant them what they wanted yet? He'd let them freeze outside all night. Dumb kids. They'd soon get bored and clear off again, just like they had before. They meant nothing to him, other than as a source of mild amusement. He'd got lots more planned for them tomorrow, and he was sure Christophe would come sloping back in the morning – people like him could never refuse great wads of cash. It was all they lived for. He'd keep him better occupied this time, doing what he did best, hurting people.

He trudged back towards the kitchen for a refill of coffee. It had been a long day, but an entertaining one. The cash machine gag had worked a treat. Not only had it fuelled the panic on the streets, and ramped up the hysteria about dragons even further, it had had an added bonus too – he knew very well that much of the IT programming that was behind many of the city's cash machines was developed by Goode Technology. Perfect. Yet another nail in Jason Goode's coffin.

But there was still a long night ahead of him. Dealing with people in countries on the other side of the world meant he rarely slept these days. He had several people who would be reporting in soon, just as they'd been told to, from London, New York, and here in Paris too. The plan was spreading and he was at the centre of it all. The hub. The conductor. Power was an addiction and he was hooked. He knew his contacts felt no particular loyalty to him, that they were only in it for the promise of big cash at the end of it, but he could pretend they were his team, his followers. It was about time he had people working for him, just like Jason Goode had had all these years. It was his turn now. And very soon he'd be employing thousands. Vast sums were being wired into his private accounts across the globe. His fortune was growing. And when Goode Technology was nothing but a broken empire, its founder banged up in prison, he would acquire it – come to its rescue as an angel investor. Pump money back into it and reap the glory.

But it was never about the money for him. Just revenge. The chance to own what was rightfully his anyway: an empire built on his genius, not Goode's. Years of injustice would finally be brought to an end and Goode would be punished for the crime he'd always denied. The computer hardware on which Goode Technology had made its name had been designed by Bonaparte, he was sure of it, back in their student days. Of course his two student friends had never accepted it – why would they? – but Bonaparte knew otherwise. They had been his drawings, his programming, his work. But he'd watched his two so-called friends sweep the awards and accolades ever since.

Goode's company, and the patents he'd gained, had been built on a lie, and now, like a house of cards, it would all come toppling down. Bonaparte knew he'd never be able to prove he was right in the courts – it was his word against theirs, and the other two would close ranks on him, just like they always did. So he knew the only way was to kill off the company with a scandal first and then breeze in there and pick up the pieces. Watch the share prices plummet as a result of the hacking scandal and then acquire the company for himself at a rock-bottom price. Then, with the real brains behind the business in the driving seat, where he belonged, he'd build the company to newer heights, create newer technologies, change the world. It was his destiny – it had been all along.

Revenge would be sweet. Goode and the professor would learn never to steal someone else's idea again. Their arrogance made him feel sick. He despised them for what they'd done to him. Robbed him of everything. Enjoyed the glory while he rotted in poverty.

The kettle finished its gurgling and rumbling with a definitive click that shook Bonaparte out of his vengeful thoughts, and soon the little room was awash with steam that whirled and spun like silver candyfloss. He poured the boiling water into the stained cup and stirred. He placed the spoon back onto the sticky worktop and returned down the hall to his office.

As he passed the open door that led into the poky living room, he saw something out of the corner of his eye and it made him stop abruptly. Coffee spilt over the edge of the cup and plopped onto his bare feet, causing them to sting with the heat.

What the hell was that?

He was sure he'd seen a dark shadow sweep across the room, just in front of the window. He slowly poked his head through the open door.

Nothing. A faint glow of orange streetlamps spilled into the cluttered room through the net curtains, but there was nothing in there out of the ordinary, just the usual mess. The newspapers Christophe had left behind were strewn over the sofas, along with all the other crap on the floor and cabinets.

He turned around and made for the study, but as he left the room there was a dull thud from the corner, by the lamp.

He quickly doubled back and re-entered.

Nothing.

He waited a few more seconds, standing in the doorway, his heart beginning to beat faster now. He coughed heavily, causing his weak frame to tremble and the coffee cup, still in his hand, to spew up yet more coffee, which fell onto the newspapers on the carpet.

He suddenly felt something brush past his face. It was like a freezing cold wind from an open window, but he saw they were shut fast, as they had been for years. Sealed shut with paint and grime.

He rubbed his face and it felt deathly cold.

'Sleep,' he mumbled to himself. 'You've gotta sleep.' It was hardly the first time his mind had played tricks on him due to a lack of sleep. Too many days and nights glued to his computer screen fighting away tiredness and pumping himself full of caffeine had begun to take their toll, and it was little wonder he was beginning to imagine things. The dark shadow, the noise, the cold wind on his face – these were nothing but symptoms of a tired mind that was slowly losing its grip on reality. It was all bullshit. He just needed some shut-eye.

He left the room and returned to the tiny box he called an office. He closed the door, walked to the old familiar chair, now moulded to his frame, and collapsed into it. He so wanted to walk into the bedroom opposite and fall into a deep sleep, but he knew now wasn't the time. Just another couple of days and he'd be able to sleep for as long as he liked – a long, soothing sleep beneath a warming sun on a tropical beach for a while. Just what he needed.

He drained what was left in his coffee cup and began working again.

His eyelids felt heavy. Drowsiness was calling, the heavy hand of sleep trying to wrestle him into unconsciousness, but he fought it away. He stared, eyes forced wide open, at the screen in front of him.

There was a face looking at him through the screen. He saw the reflection of two large eyes and the faint outline of a jaw.

He spun his chair around. There was no one behind him.

'Stop it!' he shouted. 'Get a grip, man.'

He looked back at the screen. There it was again: black pupils, pale eyes, and the faint trace of white teeth forming a smile on a dark face. Looking straight at him.

He felt freezing cold again. A shiver ran up his legs and rattled through his bones. His neck felt prickly.

He shook his head violently and rubbed his eyes.

It was gone.

'Jesus,' he said. 'Keep control.' He knew it was only a matter of minutes now before the first of his contacts would be calling. He *had* to keep awake. Then another couple of hours and the next contact would report in. And the next. Updates on the plan would be coming in thick and fast.

He was about to close a file down and open up another when he felt something touch his hand as it lay on the mouse. He flicked his arm quickly, the jolt causing his chest to rattle and explode again. He descended into a coughing fit that lasted several minutes and caused a fountain of dribbly phlegm mixed with blood to burst from his mouth. As he wiped it away and ran a mucousy hand down his thigh and over the chair, he saw something in his peripheral vision.

Over by the bookcase to his left. Next to the filing cabinet. The outline of a body.

CHAPTER 40

SUNDAY, 12.50 A.M.

ISLE OF DOGS POLICE STATION, LONDON

Jason Goode perched on the edge of the hard, metal bed in the corner of the cold brick cell, lost in thought. He'd not moved from his position for an hour and a half. His hands were still tightly clasped beneath his chin and his gaze remained fixed on the brick wall opposite.

He was trying to get a handle on the situation.

He replayed, over and over again, the brief, cryptic conversation he'd had with Detective Chief Inspector Khan back at the castle. It had all happened so quickly. One minute he'd been drinking whiskey by the fireside with Bonati, and the next he'd been bundled into the back of a police car which had pulled up at the castle and carted off back to London, to the cell where he now sat. Bonati had promised he would drive Goode's precious Maserati back to the CRYPT, where he'd said he 'would not rest until he got him out of custody and put an end to this nonsense'.

Goode recalled the professor's fury – he was angrier than he'd ever seen him – as he'd watched his closest friend being arrested and bundled into the back of the police car. He remembered his shouts and protests as Goode himself had remained still and surprisingly calm – though it was obvious to Bonati at the time that Goode's silence was due to a defeatist, resigned attitude that it was over; the professor had seen that face before.

Now, staring at the empty cell in front of him, the bare room seemed a metaphor for his life: devoid of love or ambition or any reason for going on.

Khan's speech had been brief and brutal. He'd read him his rights, telling him he did not have to say anything, but that it may harm his defence if he did not mention when questioned something which he would later rely on in court. It was all bullshit. What the hell could he have said? Suddenly Khan held all the cards and Goode had been reduced to a suspect, nothing more. There was nothing either he or Bonati could have done. So he'd said nothing at all and had just lowered his head and allowed the officer to push him into the back seat of the car as if he were a common thief.

Khan had said he had found evidence which gave him reason to arrest Goode on a string of charges of serious theft, fraud in connection with computer activity, unauthorised computer accessing, hacking, deception and obstructing a police investigation. The list went on. If found guilty, Goode knew he would never see the light of day again.

Khan had given no indication of what he and DC Craven had actually found in his office, only that it was incriminating enough to arrest him. His mood had changed as soon as he'd come back into the drawing room to find Goode. He had been unwilling to enter into any kind of conversation, but had played it by the book – impersonal, official, and with a staggering lack of emotion. It was almost as though he'd switched into robotic mode if only to be able to get through his speech. Goode remembered seeing the man's hands trembling slightly as he spoke, until Khan had noticed him looking and quickly folded them behind his back. DC Craven on the other hand had almost seemed to be enjoying it. It was a huge, huge case, and everyone back at the Met knew it. Goode knew this would send any young and ambitious police officer's career soaring.

In stark contrast, Goode's career was finished. Over. He had nothing but the suit he came in with and the shoes on his feet, the laces of which had been removed by the custody sergeant in order to 'prevent him from harming himself'.

Goode had resented the suggestion that he would end it all here, in a police cell, several feet below ground, like some kind of murderer destined for the gallows. Though sitting here now, with the cell door firmly locked shut and nothing but his haunting memories to occupy his thoughts, it was going to be a long, long haul to stave off the depression that he knew he was so prone to.

Bonati had been seriously worried about him, Goode had seen it in his eyes as he'd glanced backwards out of the rear window of the police car, the professor's figure framed by the giant castle behind him, floodlit in the night sky. Then the car had swept down the drive and away. So quickly. Like a nightmare.

The last time he'd seen blue flashing lights at the castle had been just as bad, worse.

He stood up, finally, all too aware of the destructive power that such memories could wreak on him. Blue flashing lights in the courtyard was something he'd vowed he would never picture again. That way was self-destruction, for sure.

He paced the tiny cell, up and down, up and down. There was little light in there, only the silvery rays of moonlight that pushed their way through the bars at the tiny window up on the far wall. It was the middle of the night and he had no control over the lights in the cell; those were directed by the custody sergeant and they wouldn't be back on until the morning.

After pacing up and down for too long, he knelt on the floor and positioned his body ready for press-ups. It was the only way he could prevent his mind from wandering again. It would be a race to the pain barrier until it consumed his thoughts. He would pump his body harder and harder, until tiredness would, eventually, bring its blessed relief from the ghoulish reality that was enveloping him. He needed to sleep, and he prayed it would be inevitable once he'd pushed his body to the limits of exhaustion.

He placed his hands across the floor and splayed out his fingers to steady himself. Then he stretched his legs back, dipped his head and started counting, his nose touching the dirty stone floor on each descent: 'One . . . two . . . three . . .'

CHAPTER 41

SUNDAY, 1.16 A.M.
(2.16 A.M. LOCAL TIME)
ALLÉE CHÊNE POINTU,
CLICHY-SOUS-BOIS, PARIS

For the first time in his life, the first time he could remember at least, Guy Bonaparte felt the unsettling pangs of fear somewhere deep inside him.

Seeing the outline of a dark figure in the corner of his little office, he'd run through to the kitchen and quickly shut the door. He'd poured himself another strong coffee and smoked his way through half a pack of cigarettes, bringing his trembling hand to his mouth quickly before his chest had had a chance to cough up the smoke and descend into spasms.

The coffee would work. It usually did. It would shake him out of this crazy nightmare which had engulfed him, caused, he was sure, by a severe lack of sleep.

It wasn't the first time he'd caught himself hallucinating, he thought to himself, in search of comfort, some rational explanation for what he had just seen. No, he'd seen things before, many times, when he'd pushed his mind to the limit and sleep deprivation had caused its usual landslide from sanity to loss of reason, loss of logic. He just needed to wake up the reason inside him. There wasn't actually anything in his office – just him and his computers. He hadn't really seen a figure – it had all been in his mind. No one had a more vivid imagination than his, he knew that. Years and years of withdrawing into it, conjuring up adventures and imaginary friends, were perhaps now taking their toll, and the lines between what was real and what was dreamed were becoming blurred.

He'd finish his second cup, take one last suck on the cigarette and go back in there to carry on. There was no way he was going to sleep now – he'd gone past it, as usual. Fatigue often came calling late evening, but he pushed on through it, like a runner surging beyond a stitch that could cripple a man's chest. Push beyond the pain barrier and you find a new reserve of energy. That's all he needed to do.

He stabbed the cigarette end into the pile of stubs that cascaded up and over the edge of the glass ashtray on the kitchen work top. A cloud of ash rose into the air, forcing the coughing fit he'd been trying to avoid. After his chest had finished heaving and wheezing, he downed the last gulps of coffee and slammed the cup down with a definitive strike. He took a deep, crackly breath and opened the door of the kitchen. He was going back in there. He would blot out all thoughts of ghosts and strangers and mysterious bodies and just get back to the computer screen. Stop being a soppy kid. There was still much to be done. And then, when he was ready and not before, he would permit his brain to enter the world of sleep and dreams and conjured images. He was in control, nothing else. He was master of his own body and mind. If sleep tried again to invade his conscious thoughts with images and hallucinations and that unsettling feeling of being caught between reality and fiction, then he would bury himself in a bottle of vodka and put a stop to it.

He shuffled down the corridor, refusing to glance again into.

the living room, where he had first seen – or thought he had seen – a figure.

He opened the door to his study slowly, with a controlled and deliberate movement. This was his mind, his body and his apartment. He entered the room.

'Ah! Christ!' he shrieked, and the shock of what he saw took his legs from under him and he went down onto the carpet like a marionette with its strings cut. He put a hand to his face and peered through the gaps in his fingers.

There, motionless, but as real as his own hand, stood the figure again, at the far wall of the office. And it was looking straight at him. Its face was dark, and its body was in shadow, save for the stripes of orange light that seeped through the gaps in the venetian blinds and illuminated it in segments. It was grinning at him, a huge mouth that seemed too large and wide to be human, out of proportion with the rest of its face. And its eyes seemed to emit a reddish glow. It was tall, far taller than he was. It raised its arms in his direction and began to walk, slowly but purposefully towards where he lay frozen on the cluttered carpet. The ghost's mouth widened still further and suddenly it emitted a deafening screech, half human, half animal. Bonaparte put his hands to his ears and bent his head. The noise was ear-splitting and it seemed to come from deep within the ghost, like a never-ending tornado, a continuous scream.

Bonaparte tried desperately to get to his feet. The ghost lunged at him, bringing a sharp kick to the backs of his legs. He was coughing uncontrollably now and trying to propel himself along on his back, across the carpet, pushing himself by his feet towards the open door of the office.

The ghost closed its cavernous mouth and the screeching stopped, but what happened next made Bonaparte himself emit a deathly scream. The figure began shifting shape and size. It seemed to shrink, like a balloon deflating, its head narrowing and reducing in dimensions as its now wispy body slunk towards him. It was becoming more animal-like than human, its hands shrinking to the size of small claws, its legs nothing but short stumps. It was hideous and Bonaparte put a hand to his eyes as he got to his feet, left the room and slammed the door quickly. He ran to the front door and fumbled desperately for the door knob. He turned it sharply to the left and pulled.

Nothing. The latch was still on, and the dead lock down by his knees. The key! Where was the key?

And wait a minute . . . Where was his phone? And his passport? My God, he'd nearly forgotten them. Without them, he might as well stay and end it all right now.

He turned ominously towards the hall and the closed door. The sight in the hallway made his heart pound and he thought it was going to give out altogether. Somehow, the ghost had come right through the closed door and was now in the hall. But it was shifting shape again, growing taller now and floating, the outline of its body resembling an oil slick on the sea, black and liquid and constantly altering in form. All the time he could see the ghost's eyes remained intact, staring at him.

The key for the door was in the top drawer of a small side cabinet in the hall, between him and the ghost. Mercifully, he knew his mobile phone and passport were in the same drawer, where he always kept them. Though every fibre of his being was telling him to stay as far from the ghost as possible, he knew he had to get closer to the cabinet, so he edged nearer. The ghost's eyes glowed redder now, an intensity that was almost blinding. Bonaparte shielded his eyes with one hand and scrambled around with the other, running it over the cabinet and quickly finding the drawer. He opened it, fished around inside and grabbed the key. He felt the mobile phone but no passport.

The ghost was getting closer. It rose up towards him, increasing in size by the second, filling the hall. But Bonaparte wouldn't budge. He *had* to find the passport. Desperately, his hand continued to rummage around in the darkness, while he looked away from the ghost, back down the hall towards the door to freedom.

'Come on!' he whispered. At last his hand struck something at the very back of the drawer and he grabbed it, together with the phone and the key. He dashed for the door, still refusing to look at the ghost that was now just inches away from him. Why it had not yet held him or attacked him, he couldn't say. He'd expected to feel its clutches any moment, but he was still free and he made a last dash for the door.

As the ghost emitted another deathly screech, so audible it could be heard outside, Bonaparte fumbled frantically with the locks, his trembling hands missing the key holes but eventually finding them in turn and releasing the door.

And then he was gone.

Down in the dark car park, Jud and Bex looked up in the direction of the screeching they'd heard, to see a small figure flee from an open door and scurry along the balcony towards the elevator. The man had moved so fast he'd not seen the small metal devices positioned at the side of the front door. Their little lights were fading now, and the sequence of numbers that had remained fixed for a while were flickering again.

Luc was leaving the apartment.

CHAPTER 42

SUNDAY, 1.40 A.M.
(2.40 A.M. LOCAL TIME)

ALLÉE DE GAGNY,
CLICHY-SOUS-BOIS, PARIS

Bonaparte had only been running for a short while – maybe ten minutes – but it had been enough to almost kill him. He stopped at a bench on the pavement, a few hundred yards down the deserted main road. He'd run from the estate out of a little-known back entrance, a safe distance from where the agents had been waiting, and obscured from view, devoid of any streetlamps. He'd made it this far down the long main road but could go no further.

He checked his pocket for his mobile phone. It was there. He felt relieved. That was one thing he knew he'd need.

There was little doubt that the kids watching him from across the car park would have noticed his dramatic exit from the building, heralded by the unearthly screeching and his own human screaming. And there was little doubt too that any moment now, if not already, they would be entering the place, nosing about, rifling through his papers and files, finding out everything they could about him.

He knew, of course, that this would have happened eventually, but he couldn't deny it had come slightly sooner than he'd planned. But no matter. They couldn't prevent anything now. They were much too late for that.

Dumb kids.

He sat back against the hard, cold frame of the bench. It was sodden and soon he could feel the damp seeping through his shirt and into his bony spine. The rain increased and he was quickly getting saturated. In such frail health already, he knew it was likely that much longer spent outside and he'd end up in hospital with pneumonia. It was so rare for him to be outside that the cold air bit into his frame and brought a rattle to his bones and a trembling to his hands.

He removed the phone from his pocket, checking his passport was still there too. He'd call a taxi soon, and find a place to stay, maybe a nice hotel across the city – somewhere he could take a hot bath, order room service and then drink the mini-bar dry. Then he'd put the rest of his plan into effect – get to the Gare du Nord and catch a train that would lead him through the Channel Tunnel to Britain. He'd be making the trip earlier than expected but it didn't matter.

But first he had two important tasks to complete. And they both involved his phone – thank God he'd remembered to pick that up before fleeing.

The first job was to call his contact in England. He would have been expecting a call from him in the morning anyway, but he'd call him now, get him out of bed and find out the state of play.

The number was already programmed in. He pressed 'call' and waited.

'Come on!' he said aloud. 'Pick up, God damn you.'

Just as he braced himself to hear the wretched voicemail, a familiar voice answered.

'Yes, sir?' It was the middle of the night, but the man on the end of the line knew there was no point in complaining. He tried his best to remain as positive and helpful as he could, quickly trying to wake up and sound alert. He knew Bonaparte would expect nothing less. 'Is everything okay, sir?'

'*Oui, bien sûr.* I just couldn't sleep, you know. Didn't want to wait until our scheduled call in the morning. Any progress yet? All proceeding to plan, *oui?*' Bonaparte's voice was low and gravely but deadly serious. He knew there was no acceptable answer to his question other than 'yes, sir'.

'Yes, sir,' came the reply. 'Just as you asked. We arrested Mr Goode this evening.'

'You've charged him, yes?'

'Of course. Every crime you can think of.'

'And the evidence. You planted it at the castle, *oui?*'

'Yes, sir. I accompanied my superior myself, just as we planned. It was textbook, sir. I got into the study and found the evidence my guy had planted there earlier, just where we agreed. It couldn't have been easier.'

'Good. Well done. You'll both get your reward, don't you worry.' Bonaparte couldn't hide his pleasure at the news. 'And Goode. He's in a cell somewhere?'

'Yes, sir. In London. Once I'd found the files, DCI Khan had no choice but to arrest him and take him with us there and then. He couldn't believe what I'd found. There was no going back. The guy was guilty. We took him to a central station and locked him up. In the circumstances bail is out of the question. He'll be there until the preliminary hearing and then he'll be carted off to prison to await trial.'

'Well done. Pass on my thanks to your contact who broke in for us. He's done well too. Right, I'm coming over.'

There was a brief silence at the end of the line. This was not the plan they'd agreed. Not yet.

'So soon?' said DC Craven. 'What's happened? Are you—'

'I'll call you when I'm in London. That's all.' Bonaparte

ended the call before DC Craven had a chance to ask anything else. It was not his place to ask questions like that. He was an employee, just one of a long line of servants. Nothing more. Bonaparte hated the way he sounded so familiar whenever they spoke, as though they were friends or something. Minion, that's all he was. A tiny link in the chain. But he'd done a good job, there was no denying that.

Relieved that the plan was reaching its conclusion, and Goode was now safely behind bars, Bonaparte knew he could go ahead with the second task. It was another call, of sorts. He keyed a code into his phone and placed it next to his ear. He listened intently, raising his other hand to his other ear to block out the sound of the rain and the wind and the rare passing car on the road.

A few seconds passed and then he heard a beeping sound. This was the signal for him to press in a second code, which he did quickly. Soon the sound changed to a higher pitched, rapid beeping.

Job done. The timers on three incendiary devices in his apartment had been set remotely. Thirty minutes would be more than enough time for him to get in a taxi and be gone, well before the blast.

CHAPTER 43

SUNDAY, 2.02 A.M.
(3.02 A.M. LOCAL TIME)
ALLÉE CHÊNE POINTU,
CLICHY-SOUS-BOIS, PARIS

They found the front door wide open, the way Bonaparte had left it. They were surprised, but relieved, at how little interest the neighbours had taken in the screams and shouts that had come from the apartment a few moments earlier. Looking up from the safety of the car park, they'd seen a few lights come on in neighbouring apartments, but no one had come out to see what the commotion was. Perhaps they were used to the sound of arguments and fights. Bex imagined them rising out of bed, shuffling to their own front doors to check they were locked and double locked before sloping off to bed again.

They had passed no one on the way up to the apartment, no one in the elevator, and there was no sign of anyone on the balcony as they crept along it, taking care to stay out of the light as much as possible, so as to arouse no more suspicion.

Light from Bonaparte's hall was spilling onto the walkway outside and, once they'd entered, they shut the door quickly and switched the light off. Stumbling through the darkness, they soon found another open door at the end of the hall and Jud's hand quickly found a light switch on the wall.

'Yuck!' said Bex. 'It's disgusting. I can't believe someone lives like this.' The stench had hit their nostrils pretty much as soon as they'd entered the place, and here, in the kitchen, it was intense. Stale food, rotting coffee and a strange, rancid liquid in the old washing up bowl combined to make a heady cocktail that would have made even the hardiest of cleaners retch.

'Believe it,' said Jud. 'The guy's a worm. Subhuman. He deserves to be imprisoned in a place like this. We should wait til he comes back and lock him inside it forever. Put bars on the windows. It's worse than prison, believe me, I know. He'd rot from the inside, just like the place itself, decaying. I'm surprised he's lasted this long; some of this rubbish has obviously been here for ages and the germs must be rife. For God's sake wash your hands when we get back to the hotel. You could catch anything in here.'

Convinced they would find nothing but shit in the poky little kitchen, they quickly retreated and moved into what they soon discovered was the living room. More discarded rubbish.

'I can't believe this is someone's home. Someone actually lives here. It's sad when you think about it,' said Bex.

'Sad? Think about what this guy has done, is still doing, to my father. To all of us.'

'I know, I'm sorry.'

'Come on,' said Jud, 'there's nothing in here but old newspapers and rotten food.'

'Hang on,' said Bex. 'There's books here, a lot of them. Shouldn't we go through them, see if there's any clues here?'

'Maybe,' said Jud. 'But let's check over the whole place first, see what else there is. Then we'll come back to each room and start searching properly. I don't know how long we've got until he comes back, but I'm guessing he won't return until it's light again. He'll be too spooked.'

They left the room and moved further down the hall, in the direction of the front door. There were two more doors, one on either side. They tried the left-hand one first.

'My God,' said Jud as they entered. They'd never seen anything like it. There were clothes strewn across the floor, more abandoned coffee cups and glasses and ashtrays everywhere. The stale smell of stubbed-out cigarettes was rank. Everything was covered in a layer of grey ash. The duvet on the bed was screwed up and dirty and littered with more cigarettes and the stains of drink or urine – the smells suggested either, or both.

'And you thought my bedroom was bad,' said Jud.

'Keep going the way you are and it'll end up like this,' said Bex, smiling. 'But can you imagine sleeping in here? This guy must be seriously deranged. He's living more like an animal than a person.'

'Some people do this, I suppose. When they've got nothing else to live for. No one comes round.'

'Yeah, I guess so. If he doesn't mind the mess, no one's going to clear it up.'

'But do you see anything?' said Jud. 'I can't. There's still no evidence that helps us. And we can't get the guy locked up for not tidying his house, can we?'

'Let's try the other room, come on,' said Bex.

They crept across the hall to the other door which was closed. Bex opened it slowly and felt around the wall for the light switch.

'Bingo.'

'It's the jackpot,' said Jud. 'I knew it. I absolutely knew it. This is where he does it all from. It's HQ. It's gotta be.'

They scanned the room and its computers, monitors and all manner of other electrical equipment, all designed for one purpose – online sabotage.

'We'll need to look closely though,' said Bex. 'You can't get arrested for having too many computers. Wait a minute, this one's still on.' She grabbed the nearest mouse on the desk and they were surprised to see three monitors blink into life. 'It's too easy,' she said.

'No, it makes sense,' said Jud. 'The guy was scared out of his wits and just abandoned what he was doing, I suppose. It's all going to be on. We don't need any passwords. Just get fishing for clues.'

Bex sat at the desk and started flicking through files and emails, while Jud rifled through the filing cabinet and shelves. It was an Aladdin's cave of evidence – hard evidence that would put the guy away for the rest of his life.

It was obvious their suspicions were correct. Communications to various names – they presumed they were codenames – revealed the extent of Bonaparte's plans. It was true, he'd planned this from the start, and he'd amassed a team around him who would help him bury Jason Goode forever. It was incredible. Records of offshore bank accounts, emails from associates saying 'job done' and 'mission complete', and a long history of monitoring and tracking Goode himself was all evident. They'd got their man.

'Can you see a printer?' said Bex. 'We can't carry the computers out with us. We can hardly take them on the back of the bike. We need to get printing, and fast. There's enough evidence here to bury him for good.'

Jud looked around the place and saw a large, old printer in the corner of the room. He switched it on.

'Working?'

'Yep,' said Bex, as she saw the little icon appear in the corner of the screen. She worked quickly, opening and printing off as many incriminating emails and documents as she could, while Jud continued to search the place for any other evidence that would help to bury the guy once and for all.

He continued to search through drawers and cabinets, while Bex was at the computer, pausing occasionally to say, 'Oh my

God' and 'I can't believe this guy.' The old printer continued its whirring, spewing out paper at a fast rate.

Jud was rifling through the drawers like a man possessed, looking for anything else that could connect Bonaparte to crimes in London: letters, documents, plans, drawings – anything. 'The guy must have been here for years, there's so much rubbish in here. It's like a nest.'

He continued his searching, and then something made him stop suddenly.

'Bex.'

'Yeah?'

'Erm . . .'

'What?'

'You better look at this.'

She rose from the chair and came over to a small chest of drawers in the corner. Jud had pulled the lowest drawer open.

'What the hell is that?'

They stared at a small black metal box, which had tiny wires leading from it to the rear of the drawer system and out the back of it to the wall. They traced them around the back of the desk. There was an LED screen strapped to the top of it. And on it there were numbers.

The little red digits read: 49 . . . 48 . . . 47 . . . 46 . . .

They stared at one another in total shock.

'Are you thinking what I'm thinking?' said Bex.

'He's wired the place,' said Jud. 'The bastard's not stupid. He's wired it. It's going to blow.'

42 . . . 41 . . . 40 . . .

'Run!'

They grabbed the wad of paper now sitting on the printer and fled the room. They hurtled to the front door and made for the elevator.

'Come on, come on!' yelled Jud as he pressed the button by the elevator doors.'

'What about everyone else?' cried Bex, her voice choking with emotion.

'We can't do anything now,' said Jud. 'There's no time.'

'But . . .'

'Get in!' he yelled, as the doors swung open. 'Bex!' He pulled her in just as the doors were closing.

'Oh my God. Oh no. Jud!' She grabbed him and squeezed hard. 'How long? How big will the bomb be? It could blow the whole estate.'

'Shh,' he said, holding her close. 'There's nothing we can do now. We're in the safest place we can be – it's a metal box. It'll protect us.'

'Not if the bomb's huge. Oh my God, J. It'll blow the lift shaft and the cables and we'll—'

'Stop it. Do you hear me?' He held her face. She was crying now. 'Stop it. We'll get out in time. Trust me.'

Mercifully the lift reached the ground floor quicker than they'd expected and as soon as the doors swung open they ran. There was no time for the Fireblade, they had to get out into the street. Away from the buildings. As far from the place as they could.

They reached the road and buried themselves under the nearest metal bench on the opposite side. They covered their ears and pressed their bodies close to the pavement.

They held their breath and waited for the blast.

When it came it was not as deafening as they'd expected. The place had clearly been wired, but with enough explosives to take out its contents without bringing the whole building down.

Bonaparte's disregard for human life was sickening. As they knelt to the ground, they pictured the people sleeping in the apartments either side of Bonaparte's own.

'They'll not have survived that. He's killed them, J. He's killed them all.'

Jud didn't answer at first. He was reaching for his mobile phone inside his jacket pocket.

'Bex, what the hell is the number for 999 over here?' he said. 'Quick.'

CHAPTER 44

MONDAY, 9.00 A.M.

SCOTLAND YARD, LONDON

The room was packed with noisy, inquisitive journalists, all out to get the best headline for their tabloids. The table at which DCI Khan sat, flanked by DC Craven and several other important-looking officers, was crowded with microphones. There wasn't a major newspaper or television news channel that wasn't represented.

The developments over the weekend, which had seen huge numbers of the city's residents and visitors unable to withdraw money at cash machines, and shocking images of dragons confronting them on the little screens, had added to the hysteria that had already been mounting over the fatal dragon attacks on the city's streets. The police knew that the new working week would bring further chaos, and they were right.

Breakfast news programmes were full of the stuff. Experts were being hauled in from anywhere they could be found – security advisers, financial experts, IT wizards, everyone. Television and radio channels were debating the matter constantly, whipping up yet more fear and spreading panic across homes and on the streets of the capital. Companies were already seeing record absences that morning, many of their employees either unable to get to work due to the loss of their credit and debit cards, or because they were too scared to come into London for fear of yet more dragon attacks.

DCI Khan knew that he had to find some carefully chosen words to steady the ship, bring some much-needed comfort to the journalists, and restore the confidence of the millions of viewers at home. He'd had virtually no sleep since returning from Goode's castle in Buckinghamshire and had not eaten for twenty-four hours, but none of this mattered. His superiors had given him the task of delivering the press conference first thing Monday morning and there was no going back – it was down to him now.

'Quiet, ladies and gentlemen, please. Settle down. If I can begin.'

The noise began to subside. A few pushier hacks still shouted questions at the inspector before he had even started. They in turn were shouted down by other journalists sitting near them, and eventually a fragile sense of calm descended, for the moment.

'Thank you for coming this morning. I won't detain you for long since I know you will all want to return to your places of work and get reporting on what is a source of grave concern for us all.

'But I want to tell you what we have achieved so far in this investigation, which is changing rapidly, as you will appreciate. There have been many unfortunate developments over the weekend, and may I assure you that we have all officers available on this case.'

'What about the cash machines?' someone shouted from the back.

'Do you know who's behind it yet?'

'Is there a connection between the fraudulent banking deals and the cash machine crisis? Or the fatal attacks from these dragons?'

Khan waited for the questions and cries to die down before

he spoke. He was not going to shout over their heads in order to provide answers. They were on his turf now, his conference. He remained silent until others in the room hushed up their impatient colleagues.

'I will be answering as many of your questions as I can in a moment. Please listen first to what I have to say. This is of supreme importance to the people at home, and you must give me the chance to address them as well as you here in the room.'

Everyone waited with bated breath.

'We have made an arrest.'

They weren't expecting that, and his sentence gave rise to yet more comments and questions.

'*Please*, ladies and gentlemen.' Khan waited again for silence. The officers either side of him were agitated now and they shook their heads in disapproval at the rabble in front of them.

'As I was saying. We have made a significant arrest of the person we believe is behind the chaos and crimes that have been committed. We are able to confirm that our investigations so far lead us to the conclusion that the banks themselves, and their employees, may not – and I stress *may* not – be responsible for the significant losses we have seen in recent days.

'We have good reason to believe that this is being master-minded by one person, one company, and we have the prime suspect in custody.'

'What are the charges?' a man yelled from the centre of the room.

Khan ignored him and continued, 'We will be giving you updates on the suspect in question in due course. But we must follow legal protocol. Please be assured that this is very significant progress in our ongoing investigation. My officers are, as we speak, working closely with the Police Central ecrime Unit and representatives from the National Fraud Authority to ensure our banks' computer systems are made safe as quickly as possible. There are many, many people working on this.'

'But have you fixed the cash machines?' shouted a journalist.

'We are working with our partners across all sections of the National Cyber Security Strategy to make sure normal service is resumed as quickly as possible.'

'So have you fixed it?' a woman shouted from the back.

'We are making good progress in this regard and I hope to have more updates to give you later today. Until then, all cash machines in the city are closed. Many banks across the capital opened especially early this morning, and members of the public are advised to go into their nearest branch, provide identification, and they will be able to withdraw funds immediately.

'Where cards have been retained by cash dispensers, the card holders are advised to visit the branch where it happened today and their cards will be returned safely to them.'

'But what about the dragons?' someone yelled. 'What about the killings? Are the streets safe, Inspector?'

'I am coming to that,' snapped Khan. He was trying so hard to keep his cool, but sleep deprivation and lack of food were playing havoc with his recurring stomach ulcers. He'd rattled some pills down just before entering the conference and he was still waiting for the acid that was welling up inside him to be dissolved. He paused and took a deep breath, managing to hide the pain and stress he was harbouring from showing in his face.

'As to the other part of our investigation, the situation with the dragon statues is stabilising. We have that under control. Every statue across the city has been fenced off from the public and scaffolding placed around it. We do not yet know how or why these inanimate objects appear to be coming to life. It is a first for all of us.'

This was a significant shift in the police's strategy, and it had not gone unnoticed. Up until that point, Scotland Yard had not made any comment on the rumours and speculation surrounding dragons coming to life across the capital. The reasons given for placing scaffolding and wraps across the statues were building and renovation work. Now this had changed, and it whipped the journalists into a frenzy.

'So the rumours are true, Inspector?'

'The city is under siege?'

'Is it ghosts? Supernatural forces?'

'Quiet, please everybody. You must remain calm. Hysteria like that serves no one. I repeat, we have this situation fully under control. We are looking into the hows and whys behind this. I cannot offer you an explanation at this time, but I can say that the situation is under control. These dragon statues pose no danger to the public now.'

Khan knew, as soon as the words left his lips, that he shouldn't have said them. He hoped and prayed that those words would not come back to haunt him in the next twenty-four hours. If there was another incident, perhaps even a fatal injury, he would lose his job.

'Now,' he said, 'I have said all I can at this particular time. Your questions please.'

The conference descended into chaos as the journalists all shouted questions at the panel, like an angry mob at a witch hunt.

CHAPTER 45

MONDAY, 9.48 A.M.

MI5 SECURITY SERVICE
HEADQUARTERS, THAMES
HOUSE, LONDON

Commander Andrew Drummond-Moray was not a man prone to angry outbursts. His was a cool, reserved character; it needed to be for his job and his rank. His gentle, refined Edinburgh accent, his discreet manner and his forgettable, expressionless face made him ideal for a senior ranking officer with the British Intelligence Service.

But he could feel his patience ebbing away. He switched off the television set in the corner of his room and turned to his guest.

'Look, what *is* going on?' he demanded. 'Do you have any idea what this means? Not just for you, but for us? Hmm?'

Drummond-Moray was not the only person acting out of character. The man seated opposite him in the large, oak-panelled office was feeling nervous and unable to find any words of explanation. He was not in control here, not by a mile. This was Drummond-Moray's domain, his territory, and his nerves had kicked in as soon as the phone call had come in with the order for him to come immediately to Thames House. On the journey over there he had wondered what the hell he was going to say, since the events of the last twenty-four hours had left him baffled and speechless. Very out of character.

'Well?' Drummond-Moray was tapping his well-manicured hands on the mahogany desk. 'Hmm?'

Professor Bonati shook his head. 'I don't know, Andrew. I've already told you what I do know and it isn't much.'

'But I'm sorry, Giles, that's just not good enough. I fail to understand how this has come about. If what you say is true, and I'm not prepared to even countenance the idea that it's not, then why the hell would Goode have been arrested? And what the hell did DCI Khan find at his home? You say you have no idea. But you must have. I mean, you've known the guy for all these years. You must have some idea what he could have found there?'

Bonati shook his head again. 'I'm telling you, Andrew, we're all in the dark here.'

'But how could this Bonaparte guy have got access to Goode's files? He's supposed to lead the number one global company in IT and communications, for God's sake, and yet you're telling me not even his own computer systems are secure. It's beyond me.'

'Me too.'

Drummond-Moray rose from his chair and paced the floor, just as the professor was prone to doing in his own office back at the CRYPT. He felt the urge to do the same, but realised he was a guest now and should remain seated until told otherwise. Two grown men pacing the same floor was ridiculous, after all.

'So. You say your agents have at least found this Bonaparte, yes?' said the commander.

'Indeed.' The professor gulped nervously. He knew where this was leading and he'd been dreading this particular line of questioning. When Jud and Bex had reported in earlier that morning, with the good news that they'd found Bonaparte's secret hideout, only to then say it had all gone up in smoke, he knew their investigation was going to be hard. But at least they had the emails which they'd had the good sense to print off before leaving.

'So,' continued Drummond-Moray, 'We can get our tech guys over there and bring the hardware back, yes? We can trace his moves, transactions, everything. Yes? Something to show he's the damn mastermind behind it all. Hmm?'

Bonati took a deep breath and began. He filled him in on the latest developments as relayed to him from Jud in Paris. Although Bonaparte's equipment was destroyed, at least they had the printed evidence. That would be enough, surely.

The commander didn't say anything at first, just listened, but Bonati could see from his rigid stare that a volcano was about to erupt any moment.

'So he's torched the lot? Then we're all sunk. You understand? Mr Goode, the bloody CRYPT, you, us because of our wretched association with you guys. We should never have struck the damned deal in the first place. Never. I knew it back then and I know it now. Ghosts indeed. This isn't something we should have dragged MI5 into.'

'Now wait a minute, Andrew,' said the professor. He had listened intently to the commander's ranting for too long now and he had heard enough. More than enough. He'd resented the 'order' to report immediately to him and he hated the fact that he had felt nervous about coming here. Who the hell did this guy think he was to start questioning the very existence of CRYPT and their alliance, when everyone knew – at least those who were aware of the Covert Response Youth Paranormal Team – that its agents had done an incredible job since the team's conception. It was preposterous to start questioning its work, or its purpose, now. Besides, none of the allegations made against his colleague, Jason Goode, were true. The professor thought the commander was at risk of forgetting that, especially in his rush to save his own skin. And finally get rid of the CRYPT. That was what this was really about, and the professor knew it. Drummond-Moray was worried about his own job being on the line. But Bonati would not descend into a slanging match, no matter how much the commander wanted one.

'Your concerns are understandable,' he said coolly. 'I appreciate why you are frustrated. But like I said, we have the printed emails – proof of what Bonaparte was doing. You know as well as I do that's enough.'

'It may be but we don't know. If your bloody agents hadn't gone in then we might have been able to save the lot. Avoid it being blown up.' said Drummond-Moray.

'Of course you wouldn't,' said Bonati. 'He'd rigged the whole place for God's sake. He was prepared for this.'

'I still think you could have handled it better, Giles. This is not CRYPT's job. You're out of your depth. Your agents have brought us nothing but trouble. And as for Goode. Well, he's let us both down. I mean, he's—'

'Now wait a minute,' Bonati said firmly. If you're suggesting either that what has happened brings into question the purpose of the CRYPT and our alliance with you, or, even worse, that Jason is somehow guilty of something, then you are very mistaken. And I am disappointed in you. I expected better than that, Andrew.'

The professor's tone made it seem like the commander, a younger man by several years, was being admonished by an uncle. For a moment Drummond-Moray looked at him and was about to jump down his throat, but he checked himself and paused.

'Whether your friend is or is not guilty of anything remains to be seen, Professor. We shall trust in her Majesty's legal system and let the courts decide, shall we?'

The commander walked to the door and held it open. 'This meeting is closed. Good day, Professor.'

CHAPTER 46

MONDAY, 10.35 A.M.
(11.35 A.M. LOCAL TIME)
RUE LOUIS-BLANC, PARIS

Jud rattled through the gears of the Fireblade and pushed it as hard as it would go. Bex clung on tight to his waist and kept her head down, allowing herself to move with the motion of the bike. Riding pillion was never her preferred option as it seemed counterintuitive to lean with the bike when all you wanted to do was lean the opposite way to prevent it from toppling over. Such thoughts never entered her head when she was in control of her own bike. But then Jud was pushing it within an inch of its life, it seemed.

The blast at Clichy had rocked them both. It hadn't just been the noise itself, though it had still been shocking to hear, it was the callous disregard for human life. They'd called the emergency services, just as others in the neighbourhood had done, and then returned to the scene of the explosion. Bonaparte had achieved his objective. There was precious little left of his apartment. But there was little left of the apartments either side either, or of the flats directly above and below. It was a miracle that the blast had not ripped right through the building, bringing supporting walls and girders down with it. But most of the apartment block had remained intact.

Fatalities were inevitable, however. The agents had watched as rescue teams climbed the fire exit staircases up to the wreckage. The entire building had been evacuated and terrified residents had anxiously looked around to see who was still missing. A glance up at the building was enough to tell them who would not be coming out alive.

The place had been lit up with the blue flashing lights of ambulances and police cars and fire engines. Luckily Jud's Fireblade had been sufficiently far enough away on the other side of the car park to dodge any of the flying debris that had ricocheted around the concrete walls like balls in a pinball machine. It had been a mercy that no one had been around at that time of night. Other vehicles in the place had not been so fortunate and there were shattered windscreens and dented cars everywhere.

Jud and Bex had found the Fireblade and exited quickly, just as everyone else was trying to leave. It had been a chaotic and distressing morning.

Back at the hotel, Jud had put in the call to Bonati and given him the bad news. Predictably, he had told them to get themselves out of France as quickly as possible. They couldn't take any chances and, in any case, there was no reason to be there now. Bonaparte was long gone. It was anybody's guess where he might have gone – though Jud suggested London would probably be his first choice. He would want a ringside seat to watch his father's downfall.

And now here they were, dashing across Paris, en route to Calais. The Monday traffic was as wild as anything they'd seen before, and it had not been helped by the road blocks that were eventually put in place in the region around Clichy.

Jud pulled up at yet another set of traffic lights and waited impatiently.

'Come on!' he kept saying through his earpiece. 'Come on, change!'

'Don't worry,' said Bex. 'We'll get out of here.'

Just as the lights changed to green, Jud noticed something in his wing mirror. It was a Yamaha XJR, the same dark grey, ugly machine that had plagued them the day before.

'I knew it,' he said. 'I knew we'd not get away without our friend giving us a send off.'

'Floor it,' said Bex decisively. 'You can beat him. Push it.'

Jud didn't need to be told. He wound back the throttle and let the Fireblade roar.

The Yamaha disappeared behind them for a while; its acceleration from standing still was no match for the Honda's. But Jud knew it wouldn't be long before it drew nearer again – there were two of them on the Fireblade, after all. He wove the bike in and out of cars, desperate to keep as much distance between them as possible. But the Yamaha wasn't giving up. They just needed to get to the open road – on the autoroute there would be no contest. The Fireblade was lighter and far more streamlined, and even with Bex on the back, their top speed would still eclipse the Yamaha's.

More traffic lights, but Jud ignored them, almost causing a pile up of angry motorists, all keen to show what they thought of him with hand gestures and loud, French swearing. The rider of the Yamaha tried to do the same but had to wait for a large lorry to move across the junction.

'Keep going,' shouted Bex, 'we're losing him.'

They passed a junction on their left and saw two more motorbikes jump the red lights and screech to within kicking distance of them.

'What the hell?' said Jud. 'There's more of them.'

It seemed the man on the Yamaha had friends. And it was clear their mission was to prevent the two agents from making it out of the city unscathed. Or even alive.

One of the new riders pulled up alongside them. Bex glanced quickly across at him and saw through his tinted visor. She recognised him instantly. How could she not? She'd studied Stokowski's face intently when they'd first met, finding his features attractive: his square jaw, his fashionable stubble and his piercing eyes. It had to be him.

'It's Stokowski!' she shouted. 'Oh my God. He must be working for Bonaparte.'

'No way,' said Jud, still focusing on the road ahead and continuing to weave in and out of slower vehicles, gaining ground all the time. 'It can't be him.'

'It is, I'm telling you!'

The bike reached them again and its rider signalled for them to follow him. It was a large, gun-metal grey BMW tourer. Jud was able to get a fleeting glimpse and he knew Bex was right. It was Stokowski.

'Maybe he's trying to help us,' he said. 'We have to believe him.'

'Your call.'

Jud decelerated slightly and followed the path of the BMW. The other two bikes, one a dark red Ducati and the other the grey Yamaha, were gaining on them now.

'I hope this guy knows where he's going,' said Jud.

'Yeah, and let's hope it's to safety and not straight into a trap,' said Bex. 'We don't know this guy any better than the others.'

'My dad trusts him, so that's enough for me,' said Jud. 'It has to be. We might shake off the Yamaha on the autoroute, but not the Ducati. And in any case, there may be more of them coming. Trust me.'

For a large tourer, the BMW was fast, and it helped that Stokowski knew the roads better than anyone. Jud had to keep his right hand wound back and lean in low to the fairing in order to maximise his speed. They were gaining ground all the time and the two bikes behind them were losing pace. Stokowski shot into a small side street to their right with almost no warning, and Jud had to battle quickly to follow him.

The backstreet was much quieter, just a few parked cars and office blocks. Jud looked in his wing mirror. Had they done it? Had they lost their pursuers? It looked that way.

And then they heard a gun shot.

'Jesus Christ!' said Jud. 'What was that?'

Bex looked frantically around her and saw to her horror that the red Ducati was in pursuit, its suicidal rider holding the handlebars with one hand and pointing a revolver at them with the other.

'Oh, God, J. I'm gonna get it. I'm gonna get it in the back!' She started to cry.

They were so close to the BMW their wheels were almost touching, and when Stokowski locked the brakes and swerved unexpectedly in front of a large lorry, Jud nearly ran into the back of him. He screeched his own brakes and managed to manoeuvre the Fireblade just in time to avoid him. They now had the lorry between them and the Ducati. Stokowski slammed his brakes on again and swerved violently to the right, disappearing within a second into a small archway. With lightning speed reactions, Jud followed. They were entering a small, private car park, hidden from the road. Bex glanced behind her and held her breath. The red Ducati went hurtling past, soon followed by the Yamaha. They'd lost them.

They moved the bikes into an open garage to the side of the car park, well hidden from the entrance and the backstreet beyond it. Stokowski removed his helmet.

The agents held their breath and Jud refused to turn the engine off. He was ready to turn and slam the bike right into Stokowski if he was about to pull a gun on them.

'It's okay, it's okay,' said Stokowski, his palms raised in the air in a sign of surrender. 'It's me, for God's sake. Get off the bike, quick.'

Jud turned the engine off and they quickly dismounted.

'Come with me,' said Stokowski. 'Now!' He pulled the roll-up garage door down with a slam and made for a small door in the corner of the space.

Without stopping to question what the hell was happening and how on earth he'd known where they were, they followed him, discarding their helmets.

Stokowski led them up a small, dirty staircase to the fourth floor of the building. He rattled some keys and opened a door at the far end of the landing.

'What the hell is happening?' said Jud, following him into the apartment. It was a barely furnished one-bedroom flat, dark and gloomy and clearly abandoned. 'Are these Bonaparte's men? How many more does he have, huh?' He ran to the window, then to a second one, looking around, his muscles braced and ready, his eyes darting out into the street below them and then back across the room, scanning for exits.

'Take it easy,' said Stokowski. 'Slow down. I'll explain everything.'

'Go on then,' said Jud. 'Start talking.' They sat on the floor.

'First of all, this is the apartment of a friend of mine. He doesn't use it any more. We'll be safe for a while. No one will think of looking here.'

His guests looked relieved but there were still so many questions to ask.

'How did you find us?' said Jud.

'It's a long story and you won't like what you hear, but let me finish before you jump down my neck, okay.'

Jud and Bex remained silent and stared at him expectantly.

'I know more than you think. Much more. You see, I worked for Bonaparte for a while.'

'You what?' Jud looked like he was about to get up from the floor.

'Wait!' shouted Bex. 'Let him finish.'

'You don't know him like I do. You don't understand. The guy is deranged. If he asks you to do something you don't question him. You don't say, "thanks but no thanks". If he decides he wants you on his team, you have no choice. If you say "no", he kills you. That's it. I had two colleagues right here in Paris. They were both killed in road accidents, one four years ago and the other last year. Bonaparte told me they'd declined his offer to work for him. And so he had them killed. I had no choice. If I'd told Jason Goode, Bonaparte would have killed me too. He tapped my phone. He bugged my house. He knew everything and anything about me before I'd even started working for him. So there was no way I could say no.'

Jud couldn't hide his disgust and he turned away from Stokowski, clenching his fists and trying with all his might to resist punching the guy there and then. How much of this was true, after all?

'So why the change?' Jud said flatly.

'I'm coming to that. Bonaparte has a network of associates – hired hit men and computer hackers – across the globe. I don't think you realise what you're dealing with here. I was just one dispensable body in his army. The only way to stay alive was to do what he said.'

'Which was?' Bex asked.

'I think you know the answer to that. To help him bring down your father. And then to follow you.'

'My *father*?' said Jud, surprised. How did he know Goode was his father? And then he realised. Of course. 'The bug in the jacket?'

'Yes. That was me and another of his men. We heard everything.'

'But wait a minute,' said Jud. 'My father asked you to help *us*. That's how you knew about it.'

Stokowski shook his head. 'He obviously didn't tell you the whole story. I called him first. I got him talking about what was happening and asked if I could help. That's when he told me. It seemed the sensible thing to do. But I approached him first.'

'But how did you know to call? I mean, how did you know we would need your help? How did you know we were coming?' said Bex.

Stokowski looked at her. His eyes were sadder than when they'd first met. There was an expression of defeat across his face. He looked broken. Ashamed. 'We know everything, Bex. There is nothing Bonaparte doesn't know. About any of you.'

They sat in silence for a while, staring at the dark, empty walls, trying to take in what Stokowski was saying. They felt violated. Dirty. Like animals in a cage, gawped at with nowhere to hide. How much did Bonaparte know? For how long had he been following the CRYPT? Who was being bugged? Who was being watched?

And who could they trust any more?

The world as they knew it was unravelling and it was hard to keep a handle on this.

'So what's changed?' said Jud. 'Why are you helping us?'

'It was the bombs at Clichy,' said Stokowski, shaking his head pitifully. 'He went too far. You were supposed to be in there. It wasn't just to kill his evidence, it was to kill you too. I couldn't do that to Jason.'

'You've got a funny way of showing it,' said Jud. 'Jesus, you could've warned us. You could've told us not to go in.'

'Yes, and I was planning to. I'd decided I was going to come to your hotel today. How was I supposed to know Bonaparte was going to leave so soon? We'd planned for him to go eventually, but not yet. I don't know what the hell happened in there last night but something made him run. And once he'd fled, of course, he had to blow the place up.'

'And so he was banking on us finding him and entering the apartment all along?' said Bex.

Stokowski nodded. 'Why do you think I gave you the address? Didn't you think it was all too easy, huh?'

She nodded. Of course it had been. She felt stupid now. It seemed so obvious when she thought about it – how could Stokowski have found his address so quickly? He had to have been in on it from the start.

'So how did you manage to break free?' said Jud. 'How do we know you're not being bugged right now. You could have brought us in here as a trap. Bonaparte could walk through that door any minute now. If we'd not followed you we could've been halfway to Calais by now.'

'No, you'd have been dead. You'd never have made it,' said Stokowski. 'You think those guys on the bikes were his only men, huh? The guy knows everyone. I know for a fact there were more waiting for you on the autoroute. And if they didn't get you, there are more at Calais. You'd never have made it out of France alive. Believe me.'

'And now you think we will?' Jud replied. 'Just how are we going to do that exactly?'

'With my help. The helicopter is already on its way.'

'What?' said Jud. 'Whose helicopter?'

'CRYPT's. Whose do you think?'

The agents stayed silent again. This was happening so fast it was difficult to keep up. Jud knew that his father had been arrested and was sitting in a police cell somewhere in London. So had Bonati deployed the 'copter? But how would Stokowski know him? And then he realised: if Bonaparte knew everything and everyone at the CRYPT, then so too did Stokowski.

'Bonati?' Jud said.

Stokowski nodded. 'I called him before I set off on the bike. He doesn't know I was working for Bonaparte. I didn't tell him that, not yet. He'd never have believed I'd defected. I just told him you were in trouble and I knew Jason would want you home now. I told him you were being chased and that was enough. He sanctioned the 'copter straight away. Trust me.'

'But you still haven't told us how you found us,' said Bex. 'Jud destroyed the bug so you've not been able to listen in.'

'Didn't need to. We've had men watching you. They were outside the hotel. They saw you leave and radioed me. It was easy.'

'So Bonaparte still thinks you're working for him, yeah?'

'No. We're all wired, you see. He keeps tabs on all of us. I ripped mine out when I got on the bike. It's the first time I've disappeared off the radar since the start. And it feels good.'

'So when is the helicopter arriving? And where the hell is it going to land in the middle of Paris, huh?'

'Goode Technology, of course. We have our own landing pad. You should know that. It's how your father travels here usually.'

'And just how are we going to get there?' said Jud.

'I have a car coming for us.' He glanced at his watch. 'It should be here in about twenty minutes. As soon as I receive a text we'll go down. You'll need to hide in the boot. It's not far. Trust me.'

'In the boot?' said Bex.

'Sure. Or you can ride in the car with me if you don't mind being seen. And shot at. I mean, it's up to you. It depends if you want to survive or not.'

Jud looked at Bex. Should they trust this guy? Once they were inside, would the boot ever be opened again?

It was a chance they were going to have to take.

CHAPTER 47

MONDAY, 11.10 A.M.

CRYPT HEADQUARTERS, LONDON

Bonati was in a furious mood, the most agitated Dr Vorzek had ever seen him. She tried to think of some words of comfort, but there were none. The situation was slipping out of all control, and if there was one thing she knew the professor hated, it was not being in control.

Bonati wasn't a control freak – at least he didn't act like one. He was polite and charming and always measured and calm when in the company of others. He rarely raised his voice and he was an extremely good listener. But he liked to know what was happening and he liked to be in the driving seat, not for the rush of power like some egomaniac, but because he felt wholly responsible for the CRYPT agents, like a headmaster or a principal. These were his 'students' and he cared for them very much. Just as he cared deeply for his closest friend, Jason Goode.

And now, here he was, completely unable to do anything to help anyone. Bonaparte had ripped through the CRYPT and the Goode Technology empire like a destructive tornado, and things would never be the same again.

Vorzek tried to cheer him up with the fresh coffee she had just made and now brought to his desk. She was always such a support to the professor. He knew she was much more than his technical advisor. She'd worked with him long enough to know how he operated, and how he cared deeply for his agents, and for his oldest friend.

'At least Jud and Bex survived,' she said. 'That was a close one, from what you said. Things could have been much, much worse. We could have lost them both. At least no one has died, Giles.'

'That much is true,' he said quietly, 'But Jason might as well have died. And I know he'll feel the same. Can you imagine? Sitting in that police cell, knowing that your world, everything you've built – everything we've built together – is unravelling, Kim.

'And it's down to one man. One person.'

'We'll get him out,' said Vorzek. 'He'll be released soon, you'll see.'

'What, with a set of a ladders and metal cutters, d'you mean?'

Vorzek smiled. 'We've got the evidence from his apartment. It's not much but it'll be enough. It's proof of who he was communicating with and why. Okay, so he destroyed everything else, but there'll be more evidence we can find across the globe. The people he was in communication with. It's impossible for him to cover all his tracks. With so many people working for him there will be leaks, cracks appearing. Someone will defect. And when they do, we'll have him.'

The telephone on Bonati's desk sprung into life and he quickly answered it.

'Yes?'

'It's a call for you, sir,' his assistant announced, 'a Pauline Donaldson?'

'Pauline Donaldson?' said Bonati quizzically. 'Who the hell is she?'

'Would you like to take the call, sir?'

'Put her through.' Bonati waited a moment and said, 'Hello, Professor Bonati speaking.' The name was beginning to ring a bell in the back of his mind, but he couldn't place it.

It was a soft, warm voice which spoke, hesitant but kind. Bonati did not recognise it at first. 'Oh, yes, hello Professor. Erm . . . yes, well, I'm sorry to disturb you. Erm . . . my name is Pauline Donaldson.'

'Yes, how can I help?'

'Well, you see, I'm Mr Goode's housekeeper.'

'Of course you are!' said Bonati warmly. 'I'm sorry, Mrs Donaldson, I couldn't place the name at first. You'll have to forgive me, it's been very busy of late.'

'Well, of course it has, dear. I mean, my goodness, what a mess. Greg and I have been reading about it all in the papers. You must be very anxious.'

'Indeed.'

'Well, I won't keep you long,' said Pauline. 'It's just that I can't seem to raise Mr Goode, you see. I have something I want to tell him. But he's not answering his phone, I'm afraid. And what with the police at the castle and everything . . . Greg and I saw them leave.'

'Yes, don't worry about that. They were just there to advise us on security systems. Mr Goode is ramping up his security at the moment, nothing to worry about, and he asked the local officers to attend and give him some advice.'

Bonati decided it was best not to inform Pauline of the real reason why the police were there, and why Goode was out of contact now. She had obviously not seen him sitting in the back of the police car as it sped off. And it would certainly worry her if she knew the truth. She'd worked for him for so long she was practically family.

'He's very busy, Mrs Donaldson. I suspect he's in a meeting. May I help?'

'Oh, well, yes indeed. Thank you. You see, it happened when you came to the castle the other day.'

'What did?' Bonati liked the Donaldsons very much, but he was in no mood for a long and protracted story. Why couldn't she get to the point?

'Well, I was there earlier in the morning, you see. I'd gone to get some things which I needed for the lunch party I was giving. My son and his new bride were coming over, you see – it was the first time we'd seen them since–'

'I'm sorry, Mrs Donaldson, I'm about to dash off to a meeting. Might I ask you to come to the point? I don't mean to be rude, I just don't have much time.'

'Oh, yes, of course. Silly me! Well, you see, I'm sure that I saw someone. In the castle. Actually inside it, I mean. Before you arrived, Professor. I wanted to come and tell you, but when I saw the police cars I naturally assumed you already knew and that's why you were there. I half expected you to come down and ask us about it, but then you all left quite suddenly, so I didn't have a chance to explain. I've been trying to call Mr Goode ever since to tell him but have had no luck. I don't know if this helps at all?'

'Yes, Mrs Donaldson, it helps a great deal. Can you describe the person you saw?'

'No, I'm afraid not. It was too dark in there. I'd turned the lights off, you see. I didn't need them on, I was only fetching something and then nipping home again. But I know what I saw, Professor – it was definitely a person. Someone had broken in.'

'Okay, well thank you for informing us, Mrs Donaldson. We really appreciate this.' He raised his eyebrows hopefully in the direction of Vorzek, who was clearly anxious to know what this was about. 'We'll be in touch again if we need anything. Until then, you stay safe, okay? Mr Donaldson is well?'

'Oh yes, he's fine. He says he's coming with me every time I need to go into the castle now. I tell you, he's so protective these days. I mean, the other day I went—'

'Thank you, Mrs Donaldson. I must dash. Thank you again. Goodbye. Goodbye.'

CHAPTER 48

MONDAY, 11.30 A.M.
(12.30 P.M. LOCAL TIME)

RUE LOUIS-BLANC, PARIS

They followed Stokowski down the stairs to the garage at the bottom. It was dark and dingy in there and the agents were relieved to see the Fireblade was still there when Stokowski put the light on. He walked to the end of the space and slid up the roll-top garage door. There was a large Renault saloon with its engine running waiting for them on the other side. A man got out and spoke quietly to Stokowski.

'What about the bike?' said Jud.

They didn't hear him so he shouted louder. 'I said, what about the bike? Who's going to bring that home for me, huh?'

Stokowski turned and came over to where Jud was locking away the helmets into the side panniers.

'Don't worry about that. I'll send someone over with it later. You'll get it back. It's more important to get you and Bex home safe than worrying about the motorbike. Trust me, you'll see it again.'

They'd heard the words 'trust me' too many times already from this guy whom they barely knew. And any minute now they were going to have to 'trust' him again and climb into the boot. Jud and Bex walked towards the large, black saloon.

'Why can't we just hide in the back seat?' said Bex. 'We can always duck down. No one will see us.'

'I wouldn't bet on that,' said Stokowski, exchanging looks with the driver of the car. He walked even closer to Bex. Too close for Jud's liking. He braced himself and clenched his fists by his side. Say one bad word to Bex and I'll floor you, he thought. But there was something about Stokowski that seemed believable. His confession up in the apartment had sounded genuine enough.

Stokowski spoke quietly now, glancing around the small car park and the backs of the old buildings that surrounded them. 'Look, Bonaparte has men all over this city, d'ya understand? Those guys on the bikes? They're just the start of it. He's got far more than that, and if I know Bonaparte, he'll have deployed them everywhere to find you. I said trust me. Yes?' He was staring at Bex and Jud now, a deadly serious expression on his face. 'We're not messing about here. I told Bonati I would get you back in one piece and I'm going to.' He walked back to the car and opened up the boot. 'Now get in, before someone sees us. Now!'

They approached the car. Stokowski could see they were still hesitant. 'Look, if there was space in the bloody thing I'd climb in there with you! Now get in! It'll be fifteen minutes max. Before you know it we'll be in the helicopter and away. Come on!'

A quick glance at each other and the agents climbed in. The boot was slammed shut. They heard two car doors slam and the car moved away. The motion of the car caused Bex to roll further towards Jud and he embraced her. In any other circumstances, being so close like this, in a private, snug place, might have been welcomed by both of them. But the solid thud of the boot closing and the darkness they'd been plunged into was frightening. Would it be opened again? Or were they locked in for good. Or perhaps they were being driven to some place of Bonaparte's choosing, somewhere quiet and secluded where they'd receive a fast and efficient bullet to the head.

'I'm scared, J. This is madness.'

'What choice did we have?' said Jud gently. 'If Stokowski is lying then he'd have pulled a gun on us as soon as we'd tried to escape. If we'd got away, it wouldn't have been long before Bonaparte's guys got us. We're still alive. That means we still have a chance.'

'Yeah, some chance,' whispered Bex. 'Trapped in a boot being driven to God knows where.'

'It's better than being shot.'

'Which we're about to be, I'd say.'

'No, I believe Stokowski,' said Jud. 'I think he's genuine. I'd never have got in this car if I didn't. Trust me.'

'Not you now. I'm getting sick of those words,' said Bex.

Ten minutes passed, though they felt like hours. The car was being thrown about the streets, lurching left and right, screeching to a halt and then speeding away at what they guessed were traffic lights. Soon they could feel the motion of the car slowing once more and it came to a halt. The engine stopped. They heard doors slamming and footsteps coming around to the rear of the car.

'This is it,' said Bex. 'We'll see if you were right.'

CHAPTER 49

MONDAY, 11.51 A.M.

FOLKESTONE, ENGLAND

The train hurtled through the deep tunnel cut into the English hillside as the bright, midday sunshine vanished quickly into darkness. A few moments later Bonaparte's carriage was lit up again and he watched as the patchwork countryside swept past: field, hedgerow, sign, roof top, field again. The landscape was so different to the giant arable farms that spanned the route from Paris to Calais. What was it about the English with their fascination for clipped hedgerows and fences and fields so small it was hardly worth ploughing them? The giant combine harvesters of France were replaced by quaint tractors pulling all manner of rusted machinery. But the sunshine was welcome and it was in stark contrast to the dark chaos he'd left behind.

Though it was the first time he'd ventured abroad for several years, and it had been unsettling at first, being so far from home, he felt rejuvenated, and the motion of the train, plunging forward, brought a sense of momentum to his plan. It was working. Soon, soon he'd reach his goal.

There was no going back now. His apartment was gone. All evidence burned to a cinder. He'd not given much thought to the possibility of casualties. It was a necessary risk – collateral damage.

Now, in the comfort of his quiet, first-class carriage, with no one around him but the occasional hostess to refill his coffee cup, he felt a growing sense of excitement. It was fortunate that his carriage was empty because he stank. He'd decided to wait until London before he bought a change of clothes and checked into a top hotel to freshen up. He knew that he had to become respectable now. It was his turn. He would go straight to Jermyn Street, buy some smart clothes and then check in somewhere fancy to shower and shave. He had phone calls to make, people to catch up with. He hoped progress was being made. It had better be.

The train continued its high-speed journey to St Pancras International. Bonaparte sat back in his oversized chair, dwarfing his slight frame, and read the entertaining headlines of broken banks, missing credit cards, and dragons, dragons everywhere you turned.

This would be fun.

CHAPTER 50

MONDAY, 12.50 P.M.

ENGLISH CHANNEL

The black HT1 Squirrel helicopter raced over the grey seas, heading for the long sweep of white cliffs that rose up in the distance. It was always thrilling to approach Britain this way, seeing the cliffs rise from the waters and the rolling green carpet of the fields above them.

Jud peered down at the giant ferries that seemed almost stationary compared to the speed of the Squirrel.

It was good to be free. Good to be alive.

Stokowski had been as good as his word and had delivered them safely to the giant shoe box that housed the European headquarters of Goode Technology, and then up to the helicopter pad on its vast roof. The Squirrel had set off as soon as they were inside. They'd watched as the sprawling metropolis had shrunk beneath them, replaced by the open plains of wheat farms and autoroutes.

Soon they would be arriving at Battersea helicopter pad, where a car would be waiting to whisk them straight to the CRYPT, and a reunion with Bonati. Jud wished desperately that his father could have been there too, but he was too painfully aware that he was still cooped up in some grimy cell in the bowels of a city police station. Seeing the mainland from the air highlighted the fact that his father was somewhere down there, alone, imprisoned.

He would get him out. Or he'd die trying.

He turned to Bex who was gazing out of the opposite window.

'You okay?' he said.

'Yeah. Relieved.'

'Me too.' He took her hand. 'We'll go back to Paris. I promise.'

'I've gone off the *cité de l'amour*. Venice is better.'

Jud smiled at her and recalled their assignment to the island city and the terrifying expedition to Poveglia.

'I don't know,' he said. 'That was pretty scary too. There's something to be said for staying at home.'

Jud removed his phone from his pocket and checked the bars again, seeing if the reception had improved. It had. 'I'll call Bonati,' he said.

He dialled the number and waited.

'Hello, Jud,' came the familiar voice. 'You in the air?'

'Yes, Professor. We're with Stokowski. He's here.'

'Good. Tell him I'm very grateful and so will your father be. He's a loyal friend.'

'Yes, he is,' said Jud. With Stokowski sitting up ahead with the pilot, Jud decided now was hardly the time to explain how this 'loyal friend' had once worked for the enemy. But he too had been grateful for his assistance. And he couldn't deny he'd been relieved to climb out of the car in Paris and not find Bonaparte pointing a gun at his head.

'I have a job for you when you get back,' said the professor.

'Already?' said Jud.

'Of course. We're in chaos here, J. I've already told you your father has been arrested. But there's been a development.'

'Oh?'

'Your housekeeper from the castle has been in touch.' Bonati filled Jud in on the conversation he'd had with her and the news that she'd seen an intruder in the house the day he and Goode had visited with the police.

'You want me to go there?'

'Yes. You can take Bex. Whoever was there will come back, I'm sure of it.'

'But what about the situation in London?' said Jud. 'Don't you need us at the CRYPT? Any more fatalities? More dragon sightings?'

'Don't worry about that. I have agents everywhere. We're doing all we can. We must focus on getting your father freed. With Bonaparte's apartment up in smoke, we have no real evidence to take to Khan yet. We have to look elsewhere and my guess is it'll be at the castle. I've got this place covered. If anyone tries to infiltrate the building, including the offices upstairs, he won't last long, believe me.'

'So we're not coming back at all?'

'No. You can tell the pilot I've told you now. He already has his instructions. He'll drop you in the grounds of the castle and then come back here with Stokowski. I've got some questions for him.'

'OK, Professor. I'll call you when I get to the castle.'

Bex heard Jud's words and she looked across at him. Her face said it all.

So they were going to the castle, at last.

CHAPTER 51

MONDAY, 1.40 P.M.

TEMPLE BAR, FLEET STREET, LONDON

A large delegation of photographers wrestled for position outside the Royal Courts of Justice, there to capture a front-page photo of some warring celebrity couple, going through an acrimonious and very public divorce. Just the kind of gossip-ridden, real-life soap opera the tabloid papers loved – because their readers loved it too.

Someone in the line of photographers had heard from someone inside the building that either the celebrity husband or his catwalk-model wife would be exiting the building via the main entrance sometime soon, and the assembled group were noisy with anticipation, notepads and cameras and recording machines at the ready.

Behind them, the busy intersection of Temple Bar was as crowded as ever, even at this pre-rush hour time. In the centre of the junction was the giant dragon statue, still wrapped in its thick, white sheeting, inside of which was the metal scaffolding. In addition to this, the police had now put in extra security measures consisting of a cordoned-off area of cones and police ticker tape. Two officers were patrolling the intersection, where they had been since taking over from their colleagues at nine o'clock that morning. The rattle of passing traffic and the cold of the wind that blew down Fleet Street had combined to assault their senses and bring unwelcoming grimaces to their faces. Few people bothered to stop, and when they did they were soon moved on. A stare and a gesture of the hand was enough from the policemen, though occasionally they also opened their mouths to grunt, 'Move on, please.'

Over at the Courts, something was stirring. A door had opened and a forgettable-looking man in a suit with a large file under his arm had exited with his personal assistant. The photographers emitted a collective sigh of disappointment. False alarm.

At the intersection, a trio of two photographers and a reporter were attempting to negotiate the traffic and get themselves to the Royal Courts as quickly as possible, before anything juicy happened. It would be just their luck for the star singer or his estranged wife, or even both at the same time, to exit the building before they got there, then every other reporter would get the best shots while they would have to settle for the backs of their heads walking down Fleet Street or their legs getting into a taxi.

'Come on!' shouted one of them at the passing traffic that snailed its way past.

'Don't panic, we'll get there in time. There's no sign of 'em yet.'

'Yeah, chill out. We'll do it.'

'If you tell me to chill out once more I swear I'll bloody—'

He stopped. Stared to his left.

'Jesus, Gary!' shouted his colleague, as he grabbed his arm and wrenched him out of the path of a passing bus. With inches to spare, he pulled him to the kerb as the great vehicle swished past and its driver rolled his eyes and shook his head disapprovingly.

'What the hell are you doing, huh? Do you wanna get yourself killed? You nearly bought it then. What're you doin'?'

'Did you see that?' said Gary.

'What?' his two colleagues replied.

'There! The statue. Where I was just looking. Didn't you see it?'

'It's a bloody great statue wrapped up in a bright white wrap, of course we can see it, Gaz.'

'Yeah. What're you on about? Come on, we gotta get there. They'll be out any minute now and we'll miss the scoop.'

'No, seriously,' said Gary. 'Watch. Follow my finger – just there, halfway up the statue. Watch.'

The three men stood on the edge of the kerb, their backs to the Royal Courts, staring up at the square scaffolding, covered in sheeting like some badly wrapped gift box. A few members of the press behind them noticed and wondered what they were looking at.

'Wait. Don't move. Just watch.

'But we've got to get to—'

'Shut up! I'm tellin' you. Get the camera out, now!'

Nothing happened at first. And then they saw something quickly jab against the inside of the sheeting, as though something was poking it.

'There. See it?' said Gary.

'Yeah. I'm gonna film it.'

There it was again. And again. Something was jabbing at the sheeting. And then it burst through and the three men gasped.

'Holy shit!'

It was a large, black claw with talons like giant razor blades. It slashed through the cover again and again, leaving the white wrap in tatters halfway up the statue on the same side as the men were standing. The two police officers, realising what had caused such attention, ran over to the kerb and held them back.

'Move away! Clear the area!' they yelled. But more

photographers ran over from where they'd been camped outside the Royal Courts. The dragon statues had been on everyone's minds for days and it was obvious to anyone wise enough to be looking what was happening. Desperate for a story and high on the idea of being the first to capture it, they jostled and shoved for a better view. The police officers were being pushed into the road now. There was a screech of brakes as a car turned into the road, narrowly missing one of the policemen.

The dragon moved again, from deep inside the wrap, imprisoned by the scaffolding but clearly gaining strength and thrashing around like a wild bird in a cage.

'It's got scaffolding around it, right?' one of the men shouted to the police officers.

'Yeah. But get back! Now!' He turned to his colleague. 'Call for backup, for God's sake!'

'Don't worry,' said Gary, 'it can't get out. But it'll make one hell of a front page. Keep it rolling.'

Yet more photographers arrived and pushed again to get the best vantage point. No one wanted to get too close, and with the giant zoom lenses it wasn't necessary anyway, but the momentum of so many people flooding through the gates and onto the pavement meant that the police officers' attempts to hold them back were useless.

There was a deafening sound as the dragon's limbs clattered against the metal poles that held it in place. Much of the frame was exposed now, with the canvas ripped and flapping in the breeze. With each rip they gained a better view of the beast inside. Cameras were clicking furiously, people were shouting. Pedestrians on both sides of the intersection were gathering now too.

'Look at this!'

'Oi, come 'ere. Watch this.'

'It's alive!'

'Wow!'

'Get back!' the policemen yelled, daunted by the situation

and terrified that it was about to get very serious indeed. Though they could clearly see the thick, metal poles held rigidly together with the large bolts and clips, no one really knew what strength the dragon had in store.

And soon their fears were realised. With a sound like a half screech, half roar, the great beast rose onto its hind legs and stabbed both its claws at one of the poles. It buckled and snapped like a twig. One pole gone. And another. And another.

Screams were heard on all sides of the junction. People started running now, fleeing into nearby shops and bars. Traffic had ground to a halt on both sides of the junction but no one got out. They stared with terrified faces as the statue broke free from its cage. Its wings expanded to a colossal width that almost spanned the entire traffic island on which it stood.

The photographers had been watching it through their giant lenses and now they turned and ran too. Cameras crashed to the floor, lenses shattered, tripods and bags were kicked in the stampede.

Behind them, the doors of the Royal Courts opened and the singer appeared, flanked by his QC and his solicitor. There were no cameras to capture his victorious, smug smile. No one to see his cool and rebellious nod of defiance. He turned towards the great crowd that was quickly dispersing outside the gates and his mouth fell open.

The dragon had freed itself from the plinth and now swooped down over the fleeing people. It grabbed one of them in its claws – one of the first photographers to see it. He screamed a deafening, blood-curdling screech as the dragon lifted him up and took off in the direction of Fleet Street.

Onlookers looked in horror as the man thrashed and writhed about helplessly, still screaming. 'Help me! Agh! Help! Get it off! Agh!'

And then he fell silent and his body hung limply from the beast's claws, like a dead rat.

His corpse dropped from a vast height and landed on a car with such force that it dented the roof and sent the driver, still seated inside, into terrified spasms, screaming and stabbing at the steering wheel in panic.

Stunned pedestrians on the street, drivers in their cars, and workers behind shop windows and in office blocks, all watched as the dragon took off over the rooftops, soaring higher and higher. Then, when everyone thought it was gone, it turned, banked around and swooped straight down again, like a hawk spying its prey. There were more terrified squeals as the dragon indiscriminately lashed out with its razor-sharp claws, lacerating the faces of those who were too slow to dive to the pavement.

Suddenly the roar of engines could be heard, approaching from the other end of Fleet Street. The noise rose to a thunderous din and onlookers saw six black motorbikes screech to a halt a few metres away. The riders, dressed in black leathers, leapt off and removed something from their panniers. They held the devices in their hands and ran into the middle of the road, pointing them at the giant beast overhead.

The dragon was still thrashing around and swooping low to the ground, sending anyone in its path into terrified chaos, fighting over one another to get out of the way and then hit the deck as quickly as they could.

Still the six riders stood firm, their arms raised into the air.

The dragon's wings flapped and its front legs writhed around, as if fighting with some invisible force around it. Soon its thrashing became less erratic and its flapping became slower. It was losing height now. It caught one of the riders with its giant claw and he fell to the ground, clutching his arm. It turned to another rider and stabbed at his helmet, but the figure remained still, the device clutched firmly in his hand.

The beast was just feet from the ground now, twisting and turning like a bird in pain. The riders remained where they were. It was working.

Soon they saw the giant statue flop to the ground. It was over.

The CRYPT agents, still wearing their helmets, encircled the body of the dead beast.

CHAPTER 52

MONDAY, 2.19 P.M.

SAVOY HOTEL, LONDON

The man in the tailored tweed suit, pink checked shirt and brown suede loafers seated at the table was unremarkable in such surroundings. He'd politely requested some tea and a copy of the *Financial Times*. His smile to the waitress had been charming without being unsavoury. And the guests seated on neighbouring tables had nodded politely as they'd exchanged glances with him. No one would have guessed that just hours before he'd been a filthy, unshaven tramp who had blown up his own apartment and killed his neighbours. The transformation was remarkable, and had mostly taken place in the public toilets not far from Jermyn Street where he had bought his new attire. Stopping at a branch of Boots to buy shaving equipment and a much-needed can of deodorant, he'd then caught a taxi to the Savoy and introduced himself as Mr Jeremy Buxton. His chequebook, with the insignia of an elite private bank in London, had been enough to satisfy the receptionist. He was only staying for one night, no questions asked, no need for idle chatter, though he'd rehearsed a speech if it were needed. He was a wealthy hedge fund manager from Singapore, staying in London on business. Just a quick overnight stay and then onto the US.

He knew he wouldn't be staying the whole night, of course. He just needed some proper food and a hot, restorative bath, before embarking on the next stage of his plan. But he resolved to return to the Savoy soon for an extended stay. When money was no object.

For now, Bonaparte enjoyed the illusion and sipped his Earl Grey from the china cup. The *Financial Times* arrived, carried pointlessly on a tray by a waiter who looked to be of Danish extraction, or perhaps Norwegian. His hair was blond, almost white, and his face was square and muscular, like a Viking's.

'Thank you,' said Bonaparte.

A few minutes later, his tea finished, save for a few drops left in the bottom of the cup in which real tea leaves floated, from when he'd missed the strainer whilst pouring the heavy china pot, he rose gently and walked smoothly across the lobby towards the elevator. He had some phone calls to make and preferred to do so in private.

He reached his room and locked the door.

A few moments later an unlikable, nasally voice answered, 'Yes, sir? You made it to England then?'

'My whereabouts are of no concern to you. Have you reached the destination yet?'

'Already here. Safely in position, in the cellar, like we said. We have all we need.'

'So you'll have everything ready by tonight, yes?'

'Of course.'

'The fuel?'

'Yeah.'

'You have enough?'

'Of course. This place is gonna go up like a firework. There won't be a shred left. Just ashes.'

'Ashes indeed,' said Bonaparte smugly. 'Ashes everywhere. A life in tatters. It isn't necessary, of course, just a little indulgence of mine. The icing on the cake, you might say. Are his staff still on site?'

'Yeah. But they're in the Lodge House some distance away. They'll be safe, I think. They should get out in time.'

Bonaparte laughed. 'You misunderstand me. It is a matter of no interest to me if they're caught in the blaze. I merely wanted to be sure you have not been seen.'

'Oh, no, of course not, sir. We entered the same way as before. The alarms were off for some reason. It was as easy as Goldilocks. No one saw us come in. We're in the cellar now but we'll start soaking the place during the night when there's no one around. No one'll see us leave when we've done it. We'll be out quickly.'

'You better be,' said Bonaparte. 'The place will be lit up like a beacon when you've finished. The flames will be seen for miles. A glorious burning of a career and a life. I can't wait to see it.'

'See it?' said the man, a worried tone detectable in his voice. 'You mean you're *coming*?'

'Certainly.'

'But I didn't think—'

'I should be there by about one a.m.,' interrupted Bonaparte. 'Wait for me to arrive before you torch the place. I don't want to miss it.'

The man on the end of the phone fell silent. Bonaparte could hear his breathing had quickened. He realised this was a change of plan, but he didn't care. Why shouldn't he be there? And in any case, he was never completely sure he could trust his men. He couldn't trust anyone. Only himself. And he wanted to be there to throw the first match.

'I'll bring some sausages to barbecue,' he said.

The man emitted a nervous chuckle but soon stopped. He'd learned that his employer could be viciously unpredictable. If he didn't like the way you laughed, or if you laughed at the wrong time, you were as good as dead.

'I'll be at the back entrance to the building. Make sure you're there to let me in. One o'clock. And then we'll have our little bonfire party,' said Bonaparte, and ended the phone call before the man had a chance to decide whether to laugh again or not.

CHAPTER 53

MONDAY, 2.35 P.M.

BANGROVE CASTLE, BUCKINGHAMSHIRE

The castle and its grounds loomed into view as the helicopter began its descent. The estate was much bigger than Bex had imagined. She knew Jud's father was a wealthy man, with a technology empire that spanned the globe, but Jud just didn't seem like the kind of guy to have been brought up with a silver spoon in his mouth, so the sheer scale of his home surprised her.

She saw acres and acres of parkland, an arboretum, miles of drive fringed by neatly clipped lawns, and the roofs of so many outbuildings it looked more like a village than a single dwelling from the air. And at the centre of it all, an ornate fortified house. It was more of a country mansion than a castle, though the crenellated roofs and the huge stone tower made for a real landmark. It was beautiful and Bex couldn't believe she was finally going to be there, with Jud.

The dangers of Paris and the chaos that had swept through London seemed a world away. She felt a twinge of guilt that they had not returned to the CRYPT to join their fellow agents in trying to limit the spread of panic on the streets. She was keen to see Grace again too, to see if she was alright after her ordeal. She'd spent so long wanting to visit this place – but in these circumstances? With Jud's father locked up and the very existence of CRYPT now threatened? It wasn't how she'd always imagined this trip would be.

Jud had remained silent for some time now and she'd been sensitive enough not to say much as they drew closer to his home. Despite the fact that to an outsider this looked idyllic, Bex knew better than anyone that the place held such painful memories for Jud. She decided she'd try hard to stay quiet and treat this like any other assignment. This was a mission more important than any they'd done before, after all. If they could prove there had been an intruder, it would help Jason Goode's defence, and he needed all the help he could get right now.

'Anywhere on that lawn down there will do,' said Jud to the pilot. It was not his usual pilot and so he wasn't sure if he would know where to land. 'Just in that clearing down there, behind the outbuildings. That'll do.'

The trees on the edges of the lawn bent and their branches swayed and swirled as the rotary blades drew closer. Soon the 'copter was down, though the giant blades continued their rotation.

Bex could see two figures approaching down the long drive from the direction of the main gates and the Lodge House.

'Who's that?' she said quickly.

'Don't worry, it's the Donaldsons,' said Jud. 'Staff.'

She nodded and they climbed out of the helicopter.

'Thanks,' Jud said to the pilot.

They ducked under the blades, even though they were several feet above them. Once they were safely away, the helicopter took off again. They looked up and watched it disappear, the pilot waving from the cockpit. Helicopter takeoffs always seemed so immediate, and it wasn't long before it was high in the sky and away.

Jud walked briskly in the direction of the Donaldsons. He introduced Bex, though it was clear he was in no mood for a lengthy catch up.

Mrs Donaldson looked tired and her eyes suggested she'd been crying. She couldn't have known about Goode's arrest, could she? Bonati would never have told her, thought Jud. But then he knew it didn't take much to upset her these days, especially since the tragic death of his mother at the castle. It was a wonder she and her husband had chosen to remain living there after that. Talk of an intruder in the grounds and the sight of police cars the night before would have certainly unsettled her. Besides, she'd always been emotional when seeing Jud – it was so rare these days, and the sight of him always brought back the same painful memories that haunted him too.

She wasted no time in telling them what she had told Bonati about the intruder. Her husband, Greg, seemed less convinced, almost embarrassed by his wife's overactive imagination, but he said nothing to contradict her. Truth told, he was embarrassed they had allowed it to happen, and he still wasn't sure whether he'd set the alarm or not when he left the place on Friday evening.

Jud thanked them and said they'd be fine. It was good of them to come and meet them, but they didn't need to stick around. Jud would look after the place now and lock up that night. He was always keen to be alone whenever he returned. Though the Donaldsons were friendly and always seemed so pleased to see him, deep down he resented having anyone else there – it was his private sanctuary, or had once been. He returned so rarely these days it seemed unfamiliar even to him, but it was the closest thing he had to home.

'Okay then,' said Pauline, sensing they were not needed and that Jud was anxious to get inside. 'Well, we won't disturb you. You know where we are if you need us.' Greg nodded politely, and for a brief second Jud saw a slight smile and a raise of his eyebrows as he glanced at Bex. He felt a twinge of embarrassment as he realised what Greg might have been thinking – that Jud was alone in the castle without his father around. And with a stunning-looking girl.

But Greg knew better than to say anything, and he shuffled after his wife who was already striding down the drive. She'd written him a list of DIY jobs for the day and he was barely halfway through it.

Jud and Bex approached the doors to the main house. Greg had left the place unlocked for them – Bonati had already called ahead to say the agents were coming.

He turned the iron knob and the large oak door opened with a creak. Bex was surprised by the warmth that met them as they entered the hall. She had expected it to be much colder than this, with a feeling of abandonment. She'd not realised that the place was looked after so regularly, with Goode's staff living on-site. She'd had visions of a dark, gloomy castle keep with cold stone walls and draughty floorboards, but the interior was as welcoming as any country house, albeit quiet. It was so very quiet. Her ears detected a comforting tick-tock coming from the drawing room to their right. Jud entered it, saying nothing, and Bex followed. The fireplace showed evidence of a recent fire; ashes had fallen through the grate and the log pile had been disturbed in the great hearth. He saw a whiskey glass on a side table next to one of the fireside armchairs, and another across the room, which still had a measure left in it.

It dawned on him how suddenly his father and the professor must have left, accompanied by the police officers, and it brought a sinking feeling to his stomach. Bex watched him go visibly pale as he picked up one of the glasses and sniffed it, then gazed at the empty chair. The grandfather clock continued its tick-tock and then burst into three loud chimes for three o'clock.

'Come on,' said Bex, coming close to Jud and placing a hand on his arm. 'Shall we make a drink? Where's the kitchen?'

'Okay,' was all Jud said, before moving swiftly from the room towards the kitchen across the entrance hall.

They made themselves some coffee and raided whatever was in the cupboard – just some chocolate biscuits, Pauline's little habit.

'So what're we looking for?' said Bex. She was keen to keep Jud feeling positive and not allow him to sink into a depression. With his mum gone for good and his father locked up in a police cell, it was going to be hard – there were too many reminders all around them of a happier time – but she knew him better than most people and she appealed to his work ethic. This was a job, an assignment, after all.

'Erm . . .' Jud said nonchalantly, gazing around, 'I don't really know. Pauline said she'd seen someone in the drawing room, so we'll go back in there and have a good look. But my father's study is the key place. We're not just here to find clues though. We're here in case someone returns.'

'Do you think they will?' said Bex.

'I'm sure of it. I don't believe my father's company is the only thing Bonaparte wants. I wouldn't be surprised if he pitched up here himself. We know he's got nowhere to live in Paris now. And we know how much he wants to hurt my father. He'll be planting more evidence here, I'm sure. Or one of his cronies will. This place and the offices in London will be their targets, I'd say.'

Bex watched him shake his head and gaze out of a window.

'I'll be ready for him,' he said with steely determination. 'I won't let him win, Bex. I'll kill him first.'

'Okay, J. Let's take one step at a time. Do you wanna show me round?'

'No.'

She knew it was a stupid thing to say and exactly what she'd vowed she wouldn't say on the way here. 'I mean, do you want to show me the study then?'

'Yeah. This way.'

They moved back out into the entrance hall and crossed to the opposite side, down a corridor lined with gothic-style wall lights and little else, to the closed door at the end.

The place had been ransacked: files opened, papers splayed out, desk drawers open.

'What's going on here?' said Bex.

'Well, it's either the police not clearing up after themselves, or someone else has been in here since. Either way it's a bloody mess. This is my father's property. What the hell has he done to deserve this, Bex? Tell me.'

She nodded sympathetically. 'I know. It's hard, J. But we'll sort it. He won't win. We'll clear up.'

'No. I'll do it later. I wanna check out the rest of the place first. See if anything else has been disturbed.'

They left the room and spent the next few minutes touring the ground floor. There were so many reception rooms, most of which were sparsely furnished – the odd fine painting, a cabinet or two, some expensive-looking chairs, but little else. It was obvious to Bex that no one really lived here, or had done for some time.

They finished checking out the downstairs rooms and headed for the grand staircase that led up from the entrance hall. Polished ebony banisters rose up from an elaborate pillar at the bottom, topped with a wooden carving of an eagle. Jud led the way and Bex was about to follow when she noticed a small door set into the side of the staircase.

'What's that?' she said.

Jud was halfway up the first flight by now. 'What?'

'This door. Where does that go?'

He stopped and looked over the rail. 'Just the cellar. There's nothing of value down there. Come on, I'll show you my bedroom.'

She turned and leapt up the stairs after him.

CHAPTER 54

MONDAY, 9.30 P.M.

BANGROVE CASTLE, BUCKINGHAMSHIRE

Jud stoked up the fire and fed it with another large log. The flames rose again, casting shadows on the far wall of the drawing room. They'd pushed their chairs closer to one another and placed a small, wooden table between. The sound of a car crunching on the gravel was heard and they saw the delivery man disappear back down the drive. They'd ordered enough Indian food to feed an army, and the silver foil containers filled the entire table: chicken dansak, prawn masala, lamb madras, saag aloo, samosas, salad, poppadums and pilau rice. A feast.

'So? What do you think's going to happen?' said Bex, breaking a poppadum and thrusting a large piece into the small plastic tub of mango chutney. It broke off and she fished it out with her fingers before licking them clean.

'What, tonight?'

'Yeah. I mean, do you think someone will really try and break in again? What for? They've got what they wanted. Whoever came last time must've planted some evidence in your father's study, which the police then found. Why would they come back?'

'I dunno,' said Jud. 'I just think they've not finished yet. This Bonaparte guy isn't going to stop. It's personal, don't forget. He doesn't just want to send my father to prison, he wants to bury him. If the police have been round once, they'll come again. And when they do, I suppose they'll find something else.'

'What else could they find?'

'More evidence to incriminate my father, I guess. I don't know. More files or communications. Maybe they'll frame him with something worse. I wouldn't put it past Bonaparte to take someone out. You know, have someone killed and plant the evidence here, or in London. It's practically impossible for anyone to get into my dad's penthouse, so this is a more likely place for them to target. And we can't expect the Donaldsons to protect it. She looked frightened when we saw her today. It's been a strain for them too.'

'Yeah, I can imagine. Were they here when . . . you know, that night.' As soon as she'd said it, Bex wished she hadn't. The evening had gone well and Jud was finally beginning to relax. Why had she brought it up now?

But Jud's face was kind. And he was relishing the food. She'd got away with it, she hoped.

After a while, he said, 'Yeah, they were both here. They ran up as soon as they heard the sirens and saw the flashing lights.' His eyes glazed over again and stared into the fire for a few seconds.

'Sorry, forget it,' said Bex, quickly.

'No, it's okay. I don't mind talking to you. I mean, it's good. I've not talked to anybody really. There were therapists and all that bullshit, but they were useless. They couldn't possibly understand what it was like, for all of us.'

He looked across the room at a chair beneath a large window that, in daylight, overlooked the gardens at the side of the castle. Bex had noticed how beautiful the view had been when she'd first entered the room earlier.

'That's where she used to sit. It was her favourite place. She loved to just sit and watch the gardens. I remember she had a row of bird feeders outside that window, near a willow tree out there. It was her favourite tree. It was where . . .'

He trailed off and looked back into the fire in silence.

Bex remained silent. This was his time. They'd go at his pace. He didn't need to say anything.

'Eat up,' she whispered kindly.

Jud took another forkful of food and chewed in silence.

'She loved to watch them all feeding,' he continued. 'My mother loved the wildlife round here. And they loved her. She had this way, you know. Like some people do. The birds and the rabbits and sometimes even the foxes used to come to her. She was gentle. Unlike my dad and me. She was the one that kept us all sane. She had a smile that . . .' He fell silent again and returned his gaze to the flames.

'Come on,' Bex said. 'I'll eat all the samosas if you don't speed up.' They exchanged a knowing glance and Jud smiled at her.

'Her smile was a lot like yours.'

It was the nicest thing he'd said to her, and she felt a warmth flow through her body.

'I'm glad you're here, Bex. It makes it easier somehow. I wasn't ever going to come back, you know. I'd told myself that was it. I was going to ask my father to sell the place. But . . . well, I know we can't.'

'Can't? Why not?'

Jud remained silent for a while, locked in thought. Eventually he said, 'Let's just . . . talk about something else. It's good food, isn't it?'

Bex took the signal to move on, and together they polished off most of the takeaway. The remains were left to congeal in the silver trays for another hour, as the two of them sat back in contemplative silence, watching the mesmerising flames lick up the chimney and listening to the hypnotic rhythm of the grandfather clock.

When Jud saw Bex's eyelids closing and her head drop, only to spring up again in a feeble attempt to show she was awake, he knew it was time for her to go up. He'd watched his mother do the same thing on some nights, shaking herself awake only to let her head plop onto her chest again moments later.

He led Bex by the hand up to the room she'd chosen. and told her he'd see her in the morning, early.

'Are you not going to bed too?' she asked wearily.

'Soon. I'm going to sit up for a while. But you get some sleep now. I don't think anything will happen tonight, so you might as well get some rest. I'll do another quick sweep of the place and we'll make a proper search in the morning, and catch up with the Donaldsons. They can help.'

She watched him move down the hallway and saw him hesitate for a moment. He turned to look at her.

'It's good to have you here,' he said. 'Kinda feels right, you know.'

She smiled at him and gently shut the door.

CHAPTER 55

TUESDAY, 12.36 A.M.

BANGROVE CASTLE, BUCKINGHAMSHIRE

Bonaparte walked carefully along the grass verge that lined the quiet road. Fortunately, the moon was almost full and there were few clouds, so the silvery glow was bright enough for him to make out the dips and holes and verges in front of him. He could make out a large ditch running between him and the hedgerow to his right. He didn't want to stumble into it accidentally, but it was useful when cars passed. He had no intention of being seen out in the middle of nowhere at that time of the morning, especially given what he was about to do. The large and blinding headlights of another vehicle came into view further ahead and he quickly made for the ditch. He lay there, his face touching the soggy earth, until the lorry had thundered past him. He was wearing the same old clothes as usual, having carefully placed his new suit in the wardrobe in his room at the Savoy. He would collect it later in the day.

He'd requested a late checkout and had asked not to be disturbed by the chambermaids until then, so there was plenty of time to get the job done and still be back in London before the two o'clock deadline he'd negotiated with the receptionist.

Sneaking out of the hotel had been easy, via a fire exit in the back staircase. The 'do not disturb' sign he'd placed on the handle of his bedroom door before leaving would ensure no one would know he was gone.

The castle was less than half a mile further down the road. The taxi driver had dropped him close by, at an entrance to a different house about a mile back. He'd told the driver he didn't want him to take him all the way up to the house as he'd probably wake his family, and luckily the man had believed him. He had pretended to walk a little way up the drive to the house until the taxi had disappeared up the road.

Finding a nearby house had been easy. It had all been planned to the finest detail weeks before. Countless times he'd used online maps to zoom in and patrol up and down this road, rehearsing the route and seeing aerial shots of the castle itself. Though it was dark, he'd memorised the lie of the road, its bends and dips, and he knew he was close now.

A few minutes later he saw through the gloom the large metal gates and the pompous stone pillars either side. This was it. He recognised it, even in the darkness. He felt a surge of excitement run through his body and it rejuvenated his weary frame. Not long now. Nearly there. Soon the final nail in Goode's coffin would be driven home. Stripping him not only of his liberty but of his home too was an enticing little trick too good to resist. An added bonus. He knew, of course, that Goode would never visit it again anyway, banged up in prison, but knowing it had burned to ashes would be an extra source of misery for him, and that made Bonaparte feel good.

He checked to see that the road was quiet and there was no chance of a passing car, and then climbed up and over the metal gates. He made sure to land softly and managed to stifle a coughing fit brought on by the exertion of vaulting the gate. He cupped his mouth and spluttered silently through his fingers. The Lodge House was close by and he didn't want to wake the people living in it. He knew from his contacts that Goode employed staff at the place and, though he was quite ready to take them out if necessary, it would be an unwanted distraction and a waste of precious time, not to mention bullets. He checked his inside pocket and felt the heavy bulge of his revolver.

He made straight for the bushes and trees that lined the drive. Soon he could see the silhouette of the giant house up ahead. So this was it. All the years spent viewing it from above on Google Earth. Zooming in to get a closer look. Seeing its vast floor plans online. Touring the roads around it. Finding pictures of it. It felt exhilarating to be here, at last, seeing it for real in all its majesty. He couldn't wait to burn it to the ground. The castle represented everything he hated about his former friend's success: a large, arrogant place, standing proud in its parkland, with its ridiculous tower and battlements. Who the hell did Goode think he was? Lord of the manor? A king surveying his estate? It was loathsome and Bonaparte felt sick to the stomach seeing it. He stood there for a while, hidden from view under the trees, just staring at the place. He thought of the years he'd spent in his own squalid apartment while Goode had been jet-setting between his English country estate, his skyscraper penthouse and his New York apartment. And all made possible because of Bonaparte's genius, not Goode's. It had always been his. His ideas, his theories, his voracious capacity to push the boundaries of computer science and seek out new technologies. The same technologies that Goode had made his own and which had brought him fame and fortune. Soon he'd be ruined and it would all be Bonaparte's, at last. The castle had to be burnt, along with everything it represented. Soon his men would be drenching the place in petrol and igniting a flame so big it would be seen for miles.

Revenge was sweet. And it was already proving to be well worth the wait. He thought of Goode now, sitting in his empty cell, with all luxury gone, just a memory.

Bonaparte approached the castle and crept around the side of the building to the back entrance, passing under the willow tree. He hoped his contact would be at the back entrance. He'd better be.

Fortunately the man was waiting for him, as agreed. Even though he'd been standing out there, in the dark, for twenty minutes, he still looked startled to see Bonaparte. His phone call the day before had left him shocked. He couldn't believe Bonaparte was coming to the castle himself. In person. He was used to communicating by telephone, and never thought for one moment the man would turn up in the flesh. He found him creepy at the best of times and here, looming from the shadows outside the castle, he seemed stranger than ever.

'You didn't need to come, sir,' he whispered.

'I know, Michael. I don't *need* to do anything. I wanted to. And I'm glad I did. I shall enjoy seeing this place destroyed.'

Michael looked nervous. He didn't know how he was going to say his next sentence, and it didn't help being called by his proper name. No one did that other than Bonaparte and it unsettled him. What would his employer's reaction be when he heard the news? How was he going to tell him? He took a deep breath and just went for it.

'We have a problem, sir.'

'Oh?'

'We're not alone.'

'I know, Michael. You've brought Donovan, yes. He's here to help, I presume?'

Michael nodded. 'Of course. We came together. He's in the cellar waiting for us. That's not what I meant.'

Bonaparte's expression turned ominously serious. 'Then what the hell do you mean?' he whispered angrily, glancing up at the castle for signs of life.

'I mean, I think the son's here. You know, Jamie. And he's brought someone else with him. A girl. We could hear them yesterday afternoon.'

'Really?'

'Yeah. It sounded like teenagers, so I guessed it was him. I thought they were going to come down to the bloody cellar.'

'And why didn't you tell me this yesterday?'

'I don't have your number, sir. You always call me, remember. I never call you. That's what you said. I'm sorry.'

But he noticed Bonaparte's face had changed. His grave look had gone and a wry smile was surfacing. Michael saw his eyes glinting in the silver light. There was a look of pure evil in his face.

'And you think this is a *problem*?' he chuckled. 'It's not, Michael. Oh no. It's yet another bonus. I didn't think this could get any better, but it just did.'

'So we're still going through with it?' Suddenly the plan was taking a very different turn. This wasn't what they'd agreed. Torching the place while it was empty was fine. Quite fun, in fact. But burning its residents alive, that would cost Bonaparte more. Much more. Michael stared at him for a while, choosing his words carefully. He had nothing to fear from this guy, so why was he always so nervous around him? He was a pathetic old man whom Michael could break with one sharp blow. But Bonaparte had this effect on him, on everybody who worked for him. 'That's not what we agreed,' he said coolly.

'I beg your pardon?'

'I said, that's not what we agreed. If we're taking out the kids too, that's a different job.' He took a deep breath of the cold air, stood tall and puffed his chest out. He was considerably bigger than Bonaparte and he wasn't going to be pushed around any more. There was no way his employer could do this by himself. He needed him, and Donovan. Even if he was carrying a gun, which Michael assumed he probably was, he knew he wouldn't pull it on him. Not yet, anyway.

Bonaparte looked at him in disgust and shook his head. 'Don't tell me, your rates have just gone up, am I right?'

Michael nodded. 'Double.'

'You people are all the same. Cowards, the lot of you. Okay, listen to me. You do the job, we'll talk, how's that? If it goes to plan I'll consider raising your fee. But I'm not standing out here wasting time negotiating with you, d'you understand me? You're gonna get inside, you're gonna get Donovan, and together we get this place ready. Okay?'

That was good enough for Michael, and he knew he wasn't going to get any further anyway. Besides, he could hardly walk away now. He was in it too deep already, and if he did run, then wherever he went, wherever he chose to hide, he knew Bonaparte would find him, or employ someone else to. He'd be gunned down in a week.

He turned and went through the door.

'Wait!' whispered Bonaparte. 'You've disabled the alarms, yeah?'

'Of course I have!'

Bonaparte followed him down the corridor to the entrance hall, where he saw Donovan waiting by the door which led down to the cellar. He was a smaller, weedier man with a shifty face and deep-set eyes. There were two large cans of petrol at his feet.

'Hello, sir,' he said nervously.

Bonaparte nodded to acknowledge him standing there, but wasted no time exchanging pleasantries. The man meant nothing to him.

It was gloomy inside the castle. Bonaparte looked up the stairs and pictured Jud and Bex sleeping in their beds. Probably together, he thought. Dirty little teenagers, messing around while the father was away. He'd enjoy seeing them burn.

'Torch the whole bloody place,' he said coldly. 'I want to see it burnt to the ground.'

'You coming with us?' said Michael.

'No. I'm paying you to do this, remember? I'm a spectator tonight. I wanna see it done. I'll wait here, make sure I don't hear anything upstairs. Be quick. I'll give you thirty minutes to drench the place. Put some in each room so the fire spreads quickly. Then come back here and we'll get out together. Leave enough fuel for us to pour a trickle down the hall to the back door. Then we throw the match in and run. I'm staying here. Now move!'

He was lying, of course. He had no intention of staying there to wait for them. There was one more trip he couldn't resist. It would be the only time he'd get the chance, the only time anyone would. Once the castle was on fire, that was it, he'd have to evacuate like his men. He'd go out and watch from a distance as the flames rose high into the sky. And he'd enjoy picturing the agents being burned alive.

Thirty minutes would give him enough time, though. It wouldn't take long. There was one place he wanted to see. He knew from the floor plans of the house where the door he wanted was located. He waited for the men to disappear into other rooms, heard the sloshing of petrol onto the floors and furniture, then crept across the entrance hall to the far corner, where a door was set into a curved part of the wall. He opened it silently and edged through. It was dark inside, but he felt his way across the round walls and found the steps with his feet. He started climbing. The round staircase was narrow and the triangular-shaped steps shrunk to nothing at the centre of the spiral. He tried to stay close to the wall at its edges. One slip and he'd be at the bottom and he was in no condition to survive such a drop.

On he climbed. There was a sliver of moonlight visible just up ahead, where a narrow window was set into the tower. It cast silver beams onto the grey stones above him. He reached it and stood on tiptoes to look out. The moon was full and there was an eerie atmosphere outside. The trees swayed in the breeze like giant fingers, and there was a whistle that ran down the staircase from above. He was close now. A few more twists. The little door at the top was unlocked and he could feel the draught on his face as he reached the top, puffing with exhaustion.

He crept out onto the roof of the tower. The wind was strong and he pulled his coat tight around his tired, cold body. He glanced out across the estate, lit up by the moon in the clear sky.

Bex sat up in bed, her heart racing. It had been a dreadful night and she'd been unable to sleep. When she'd finally dropped off, the hot, spicy food inside her and the heat from the fire that evening had combined to bring nightmarish dreams. Now she was sweating and her heat-oppressed brain was bringing a wave of delirium that prevented her from thinking straight. Was she still dreaming? She shook her head and rubbed her eyes, trying to shake off the unsettling images in her mind. She was caught in a dark, frightening place between sleep and consciousness. Her head felt huge, bigger than the room itself. Her hands were trembling. Not since childhood had she felt like this. She knew, deep down, that she needed to cool her body. She remembered her mother placing a cold flannel on her forehead and her father bringing a glass of cold water.

Still half delirious, she got out of bed and tiptoed to the door in her nightie. She crept outside onto the dark landing. A shiver went through her as her body tried to adjust to the cold air after the thick, sweaty heat of the bed sheets.

She snuck past Jud's room and on to the staircase at the end. There was no way she was going to wake him. She knew he needed his sleep as much as she did. Maybe more. She remembered where the kitchen was and would be able to find herself a glass of cold milk. By the time she returned to the bedroom she'd have shaken off the delirious feeling and would be able to sleep again. Jud need never know.

She moved silently down the stairs, treading on the sides to avoid the creaks in the well-worn centre of the wooden steps beneath her bare feet. As she approached the bottom she felt a draught on her face. It was coming from the far corner of the entrance hall, where she noticed a door had been left wide open. A shaft of grey light cascaded onto the stone floor.

Jud? Maybe he couldn't sleep either. What was he doing?

Curiosity getting the better of her, she crept along the flagstones to the open door. Her feet were freezing but the icy cold was helping to cool her body and bring her mind back to reality. If the door was open, Jud must be inside. It was not a room she'd been in yet, but the harsh breeze that was pushing through the opening suggested it led outside, or at least that a window was open. But why? She started to worry. What was Jud up to?

In the darkness her hands splayed across the wall to find a light switch but there was none. Instead, she felt her way across what seemed like a curved wall. And her feet struck the bottom of a step. My God, she thought, it's the tower.

Jud!

Quickly she began the steep climb. Higher and higher, the icy wind pushing against her face as she rose. A steely determination was blocking all thoughts of danger or fear now. She was on a mission to find Jud and discover what the hell he was doing. If he was retracing his steps from that fateful night, then she wanted to be with him. He mustn't be alone. Not here, not now.

She passed the thin window but didn't stop to gaze out. On she climbed, the adrenalin in her body now blocking out the cold.

'Jud?' she said. 'Are you there?'

No reply. She felt her heart thumping. There was a sickness rising inside her as thoughts of him raced through her mind.

'Jud?'

Still silence. She reached the top of the spiral staircase and braced herself against the cold night air.

Out on the roof the wind was whipping up, and it blew her

hair across her face. She quickly flicked it out of the way and then stopped in her tracks.

She screamed.

Bonaparte lunged towards her and held her throat.

There was another deathly scream that rattled down the staircase and on into the house.

His grip was like a vice. His bony hands were locked around her throat as he dragged her across the roof. She kicked violently but he'd moved behind her, away from the violent jabs of her bare feet. She wriggled and stabbed her elbows into his chest. He was coughing and spluttering but clung onto her, his body forcing hers closer to the edge of the tower. She felt him spit on her neck as the coughing continued and he began to wheeze.

He bent her over the battlements. The rough, stone edges cut into her chest. He had a hand at her mouth now to silence her screams. Suddenly she felt something hard in the small of her back. He was pressing a gun to her and its barrel pushed deeper into her spine.

There was a sudden sound of footsteps behind her.

Bonaparte surged backwards as someone grabbed him from behind and ripped him off Bex. He fell straight to the floor. Before he had time to react, his hand was stamped on and his crippled fingers released the gun. He felt a sharp kick to his kidneys. His assailant knelt on his stomach and rained down punches onto his face, bursting his nose instantly and ripping his lips apart. Still the blows came, heavier and heavier. His eyes welled up and he could barely see straight. The face upon him was silhouetted against the bright moon, but he caught a sudden glimpse of Jamie Goode.

Bex tried to pull Jud off but he refused to budge. He raised Bonaparte's head by the throat and smashed his skull against the hard floor.

'No!' cried Bex. 'You mustn't! We need him to talk. Jud! Stop it, *stop it!*' She tried again and eventually managed to prise him off Bonaparte, who lay there, still conscious but barely moving. Bex quickly picked up the gun and hid it from Jud. She knew he'd kill the man if he saw it. He almost had already.

Jud got to his feet, exhausted and dribbling like a wild dog after a vicious attack. She held him tight to her freezing body. They said nothing for a while, each trying to get their breath back and releasing their anger and emotion through the strength of their embrace. Bex could hardly breathe for Jud's tight grip.

'It's okay,' she said, stroking his hair. 'It's okay. I'm fine. Really, I'm fine, J. I'm glad you came when you did.'

They separated and stared down at the crippled figure on the floor.

'Shoot,' said Bonaparte in a husky whisper. 'Shoot, damn you!'

Jud shook his head. 'Don't tempt me.'

'Do it.' He put a hand to his ripped mouth. His face was drenched in blood, his body was in agony, and he just lay there, still, waiting for death. He realised there was no point now. It was over. He'd failed. 'Go ahead and shoot. Please.'

They just watched him, writhing pitifully and staring at them with a death wish on his pummelled face.

'Do it!' He knew there was nothing to live for. Nothing left, except one thing.

What he knew.

If he told them, Jud wouldn't be able to resist putting a gun to his head and ending the misery, for them both, at last. And he could finally escape his broken, mortal body.

Though his face was pulverised and he was choking on the rivers of blood that poured from his lips down his throat, he had to get the words out. He had to watch the reaction on this pathetic kid's face when he told him. He deserved that much. Just one last thrill before the darkness claimed him.

'You can't bring her back,' he muttered.

'What?' said Jud, kneeling next to him.

'I said, you can't bring her back.' A sickly grin formed at his swollen mouth and Jud went to thrash him again.

'No!' said Bex, pulling his arm away. 'Let him speak. We have to hear it, J.'

Jud resisted the temptation and stood away from him.

'You said it was ghosts.' Bonaparte tried to laugh but was cut short by a coughing fit. He took a deep, crackly breath and continued, 'Ghosts, you said. You're a damn fool! It was my men. I did it, you see. I took her from you.'

'What?' Jud couldn't believe what he was hearing. The man was delirious or making it up to hurt him in the only way he could.

'I paid them to do it. I enjoyed it, y'understand?'

Jud stared in disbelief.

'It was a pleasure. I robbed you of her. But it was meant to be your father. She was wearing his coat that night. Don't you remember, Jamie? The night we took her. Took her from you. They came here to take your father. That was the plan. They dressed up. It was easy. They thought I was some kind of pervert, asking them to dress up like that. They were supposed to spook him first. Watch him plead for mercy. Then kill him. But they got her instead.'

'You?' said Jud, his voice choking with emotion. 'It was *you*!' All these years of grieving for his mother, the time spent in a cell, lamenting her death and being wrongly accused of her murder. The nights he'd spent grieving for her, just like his father had. And now the bitter truth – it had been Bonaparte all along. It was too much to take in and Jud felt sick. His head was spinning and his heart was racing, as adrenalin surged through his body.

And now Bonaparte was grinning at him, basking in Jud's despair. Enjoying the power. One last thrill.

Jud looked away from the monster on the ground.

'And now we're all going to burn in hell,' Bonaparte whispered.

'What did you say?'

'You heard me. We're all going to burn. You can't stop it.'

'Get up!' Jud shouted. 'I said, *get up!*' He went for him and brought him to his feet. He weighed almost nothing.

His body was broken and his face hideously misshapen, but there was still glee in his expression. He summoned up what little strength he had left and released himself from Jud's arm. Jud was too dazed to stop him. They watched him stagger to the edge of the battlements. He leant over. Turned towards them and shouted, 'Burn in hell!' Then he leant further over the wall and was gone.

Seconds later the thud they heard was deathly. Like a sack of bones hitting the solid ground. Jud had heard that sound once before and he threw up over the cold stones. He bent double as the vomit dribbled from his open mouth. He gagged again and Bex held him from behind. She squeezed him tight, pushing the bile out of him, the pain and the misery. She would release him from this, from everything that had plagued his soul for so long. He was on his knees now, staring at the cold stones, stained with Bonaparte's blood and his own mess.

Bex said, 'Burn in hell. That's what he said, J. He said we're all going to burn and we can't stop it.'

Jud didn't move.

'Jud! Listen to me. There're others here. There has to be. He wouldn't have come alone. They're going to torch the place. That must be what he meant. Why he kept saying it. Come on!'

Jud remained still, trying to recover. Trying to take it all in.

'Come on!' she pulled him to his feet. 'Wake up!' she shouted angrily. 'There'll be time for all this. We'll talk it through. I'm there for you, J. But if we don't move, we'll be dead. Now move!' She dragged him towards the open door and they climbed down the spiral stairs, bracing themselves for the smell of burning.

They reached the entrance hall.

Silence.

There was no trace of anyone yet, but a different smell greeted them. Petrol.

'My God!' said Bex. 'They *are*. They're going to torch it!'

The pungent smell of fuel had shaken Jud from his grief and he grabbed Bex's arm and pulled her towards the front door. He fumbled with the locks and released it. They ran outside, across the gravel drive, the sharp stones stabbing their bare feet.

Bonaparte's body lay just feet away from them. It was a hideous mess. His neck was broken and his head lay at right angles to his punctured body. Blood poured from the back of his skull. But they could both still see the shocking expression of glee on his face, like he'd embraced his death willingly. Gleefully.

'Sick, sick bastard,' said Jud. 'I didn't know evil really existed in the living.'

'Let's get out of here,' Bex said anxiously. 'It could go up any minute.' She pulled him away again and they ran across the great lawns, around to the side of the house. Jud led her under the giant willow tree.

'We need to get further away,' said Bex. 'What're you doing? Come on!'

'No, look,' said Jud, pointing towards the rear of the house. They saw two figures sprinting across the grass and disappearing into the trees. 'They must've heard us.'

'They must've been waiting for Bonaparte to show, and when he didn't, they gave up,' said Bex, panting. 'Thank God, J. You could've lost it all.'

Jud stared in silence at the castle.

'Come on. Let's get inside. We'll call the police and get this place cleaned up. We'll tell Khan everything. We've still got all the emails and documents from Bonaparte's flat, remember? We have all the evidence we need. They'll have to release your father when they read what we've got. And when we tell them what happened here. *Come on*, let's go,' she said excitedly. 'The banks will get their money back eventually. You know they will. Khan

355

and his officers will see to that. Stokowski will help with locating Bonaparte's accounts; he'll do anything to avoid prison.

'And then, when the money's returned, the dragons should rest easy again. We know that's why they came to life after all – to protect the treasure, the money in the banks. There'll be no reason left for them to react as they did. It's over, J. Let's go back.'

'Not yet.' Jud took her hand and led her deeper under the willow tree, into the shadows beneath.

A few feet from the trunk, there was a gravestone.

They had buried her beneath her favourite tree.

Jud knelt on the wet grass and traced his mother's name with his fingertips. The wind abated for a moment and the rustling of the trees stopped. The moon cast silver rays across the lawn, lighting up the castle in the still, night air.

The willow swished gently and he heard a faint whisper on the wind.